DOWN BY THE RIVER

Books by Randy Rawls

Beth Bowman Series
Best Defense
Hot Rocks

Tom Jeffries Series
The Runaway
Thorns on Roses

Ace Edwards Series
Jeb's Deception
Jasmine's Fate
Jingle's Christmas
Jade's Photos
Joseph's Kidnapping
Jake's Burn

DOWN BY THE RIVER

by

Randy Rawls

DOWN BY THE RIVER

Cover art and design by Michael James Canales,
MJCimageworks.com

Rawls, Randy
Down By The River / Historical Fiction / Randy Rawls

ISBN: 978-0-9899904-0-0

DEDICATION

Especially for Tracy and David, my children, with my love. And for Ronnie, My Honey in every way. For those who tolerate me and critique my writing: Sylvia, Earl, Ann, Gregg, Richard, Stephanie, and Vicki. For Joanne at *Murder on the Beach Mystery Bookstore*, a friend to every author.

DOWN BY THE RIVER

PROLOGUE

February 1956

Screams and curses fractured the air, sounds of hatred not heard on Main Street in Dawson, North Carolina since the Civil War—if then. But it wasn't only those noises that caused lights to pop on in the homes bordering the small downtown. It was the unmistakable sound of flesh on flesh, fists on bodies. The grunts of combatants intent on destroying one another. The screams of whites attacking coloreds, coloreds attacking whites, and a few rational shouts for order.

Henry Flanagan watched in horror as the free-for-all intensified. He saw people he knew swinging and punching, people he'd exchanged pleasantries with on the street that very day.

The police were in the middle of the chaos, shoving, pushing, trying to separate the races, trying to restore order. However, it was obvious they were making little headway. Henry feared they might be overwhelmed and have their weapons taken and used against them and others.

Henry went down with a thud, a large Negro riding his back. He pushed the body off, then rolled away. "Wha . . . who . . ."

"I's sorry, Muster Flan'gin. I didn't know it was you." The man jumped up and ran into the fray, leaving Henry staring wide-eyed at the fighting in front of him.

He scrambled to his feet and retreated, far enough away for safety, but close enough to watch the brawlers. One side of his mind screamed he should take action, do something to stop the fighting. No matter the rights or wrongs of their grievances, fists and feet wouldn't settle it. It had to be stopped—and stopped now. But his journalist training demanded he remain above it and document everything in an objective manner. He was witnessing history. Capturing it for his readers and the generations to follow was the most important contribution he could make.

That's what he did. He wrote furiously, names of those he recognized and descriptions of those he didn't. As best he could, through the filter of mob action, he recorded who assaulted whom and with what. His newspaper would report the facts as they occurred. And if the authorities needed details, he'd share them. The outrage would have to be resolved by the justice system in an equitable manner. There could be no white man's justice this time.

He wasn't surprised to see Judge Jackson in the middle of the crowd, fending off attackers with his open hands, his mouth working, no one listening. Henry worried he'd be hurt. The Judge was such a gentle man and those near him were in anything but a mood for gentleness. Yet he seemed to move as if wearing a protective cloak. No blows came his way—even from those in the white sheets.

Henry wanted to wade into the mob and pull the Judge clear, but knew he'd be wasting his time. Even if he could get to him, the Judge would refuse to leave. His love of law and order would prevent him from doing the only smart thing in this instance—getting out of harm's way. Instead, Henry buried his impulse, jerked his attention away from the Judge, and returned to documenting the event.

Sirens whined in the distance, announcing incoming emergency vehicles. Henry looked toward the sound, urging them to hurry, hoping they carried enough policemen to stop the carnage.

The cars screeched to a halt a half-block away. Deputies poured from them, nightsticks at the ready, and ran toward the brawlers.A shot sounded, freezing everyone in Henry's view. Then the frenzy intensified as if each fighter felt he must end it or die.

..*

Hours later, Henry sat in his small office in the *Dawson Times*, exhausted, his emotions as flat as the terrain of eastern North Carolina. He'd written a front-page article for the paper, but knew it wasn't complete, not the piece he wanted. He'd rewrite it many times before it went to press, perhaps in a special edition out by noon. For now though, events were too close, too raw for him to document them. This had to be done right. He had witnessed an event so despicable, yet so inevitable, he knew it was a moment that would occupy a prominent place in the history of Noland County.

Fragments of an editorial played at the edge of his mind, an editorial that could be the most important he ever wrote. But he was too tired, his emotions too turbulent to do it then. His mind closed out the night and turned to the town and the people he'd adopted and loved, trying to pinpoint the moment when the horrible actions of the evening began—and what had caused them.

He was well aware that Dawson, the county seat of Nolan County, had changed little since the Yankee troops left after the post-Civil War occupation. Henry knew there had been progress, but it was limited to small pockets. Many farmers in the area used a tractor, replacing the mules their ancestors owned. Television sets were in some homes and the telephone had come to stay. But overall, it was the same agriculture-based economy it had always been—carrying the same prejudices that those who came before nurtured.

Then, in 1954, the US Supreme Court announced its decision on *Brown vs Board of Education*, a ruling he expected to change the South and the country forever. As with most things, it took several months for the news to seep into the soul of Nolan County and even then, it was pretty much ignored. Washington, DC and its liberal court were far more distant from Dawson in outlook and attitude than in miles.

Henry needed to isolate, to concentrate on the most important happenings that had led to the brawl. His eyes glazed with the effort, his thoughts drifting.

Judge Jackson, the catalyst. Everything seemed to revolve around Judge Daniel J. Jackson and a young Negro called Scooter.

Harry remembered the town of Dawson as it was on a typical Monday morning when Recorder's Court was in session . . . before it all began.

BOOK ONE

CHAPTER ONE

March 1955

The young Negro turned onto Valdese Street, pushing along until he reached Nolan Supply Store. Leaning his beat-up scooter against the brick front, he sat on the sidewalk. "Hope somebody want a shine today. I needs the money." He took the polish and brushes out of his box and arranged them for use.

He shivered slightly in the chilly morning air, crossed his arms, and hunched his shoulders, pulling into himself. "Be glad when this ol' winter ends. Got to find me a new coat 'fore the next one. This ones 'bout had it."

Scooter's attire today was the same as every other day—worn, faded, and patched dungarees, a cotton jacket with frayed cuffs, collar, and elbows, a battered baseball cap that appeared to be held together by grease, and fabric sneakers with loose threads popping out. Under the jacket was a plaid shirt that also showed the ravages of wear. In spite of their age and lack of fashion, everything except the cap was clean.

The stop in front of the farmers' supplies store was part of Scooter's weekday ritual. Sometimes a customer would come by and have Scooter take care of his shoes. Sometimes it was a wasted hour.

A shadow fell over him. "You that nigger they call Scooter, ain't you?"

Scooter jumped to his feet and spoke in a subservient way, his head tilted downward. "Yas suh. That's what they call me. They calls me that 'cause—"

"I don't give a damn why they call you that. Do Brother Douglas know you embarrassing his customers? Ain't he told you to stay out from in front of his place?" The speaker was a large white man wearing dirty overalls and needing a shave. He'd parked his muddy pickup truck along the curb.

"Sometime, suh, he let me stay," Scooter said. "Do y'all wan' a shine, Muster Burnette?"

The man looked at his brogans that wore the mud and marks of many hard days in the fields. "Don't you call me by my name. You ain't allowed. You just a town nigger what ought to be whupped with a 'bacca stick. My name's for folks worth a shit. And, nah, I don't need no damn shine from you. I know a white boy what shines shoes, and a damn sight better. Now, you best git outta here 'fore I git upset and take you out in the back lot and teach you your place."

"Yas suh, I's leaving," Scooter said. He began to gather his tins of polish, brushes, and rags, and put them in his box.

"Move yo' ass, boy. Leave that shit right where it is. I ain't got no more time to waste on you."

..*

"Anybody got a problem here?"

Scooter looked up while the farmer turned toward the new voice.

Burnette said, "Naw, Chief. Thar ain't no problem. I was just telling this nigger to move on. Brother Douglas don't want him here on the sidewalk dirtyin' up the place. The customers don't like it."

"Hmm." The Chief of Police looked at Scooter, a quizzical expression on his face. "Mr. Douglas ever tell you that, Scooter?"

Scooter slowly rose to his feet. "Nah suh, he ain't never said nothing to me 'bout it. I's—"

"You calling me a liar, boy?" the farmer blurted in a raised voice. "You know whut happens to uppity niggers 'round here, don't you?"

Scooter cringed, backing away.

"Now, you just hold on right there, Charlie," the Chief said. "Last I heard, you're a farmer and I'm Chief of Police. I don't plow your fields, and you don't make the law. That's the way it is, ain't it?"

The farmer scowled, turned, and spat in the gutter. "Yeah, but there ain't no nigger gonna—"

"Didn't hear Scooter say anything except answer my question," Chief Bowen said. "You don't have a problem with him talking to me, do you?"

"Why no, Chief, you can talk to anybody you want to, but he's a—"

"Yes, I know. I also know I don't care. You see, as long as I run this town, and he stays out of trouble, he can be any place on the sidewalk he wants. It's public property. It doesn't belong to you or Mr. Douglas or me or anybody else in particular. It belongs to everybody. Now, why don't you go on in the store and do whatever you came to town for? That way, everyone's going to be happier."

The farmer stared, first at the Chief then at Scooter before stepping toward the entrance. "Someday, you're gonna git yours, Chief. You oughta know better than to take a nigger's side." Turning his back to the policeman, he continued, "That's what's gone wrong with this town. Too damn many nigger-lovers."

The Chief watched the door close behind the farmer, his cheeks flushed. *Some days, a colored man's side is the right side*. He looked at Scooter. "I do believe it's Monday, and you often shine my shoes to start the week."

"Yas suh," Scooter said, relief flooding his face. He knelt in front of the Chief and slide his box forward. "Put your foot up here, and I'll give you a shine that'll last 'til next Mondy."

The Chief complied, and the dramatic snare drum sounds Scooter produced with his shine cloth soon ricocheted along the block. Scooter's frequent glances toward the front door of Nolan Supply hardly interrupted the rhythm.

When Scooter finished, Chief Bowen said, "Sorry to have to say it, but it'd be best if you move on. That's Charlie, one of them Burnettes. That whole passel's mean as snakes and hates most colored folks, especially town coloreds. They ain't nothing but po' white trash. They need somebody to cuss 'cause they're so low. He's probably in there trying to make a problem with Mr. Douglas. I'd stay with you, but I have to get back to the station."

"Yas suh, I's moving," Scooter said, pocketing the dime the Chief gave him. He hung his box over the handlebar of his scooter. "I got to meet the Jedge anyway." He headed toward Main. Over his shoulder, he said, "Thank you, Chief. I don't mean no harm."

Chief Bowen watched Scooter push himself along the sidewalk. "I know you don't, Scooter, I know," he said in a quiet voice. He looked toward the door where Burnette had disappeared. "Someday, this is going to get too ugly to handle with just words." He sighed. "And I don't know who will win."

CHAPTER TWO

Daniel J. Jackson, Recorder's Court Judge for Nolan County, pulled into his reserved parking space and killed the engine of his two-tone, '53 DeSoto. He looked at his watch and smiled. It was eight o'clock, giving him two hours before his first case of the day. Opening the door, he took a deep breath, savoring the freshness of the crisp winter air. It was an idyllic March day, cold enough for a topcoat, hat, and gloves, but warm enough to linger outside. The high sky was as blue as a newborn's eyes, and the early sun made promises of brightness enough to cast shadows.

Exiting his car, he yelled across the parking lot, "Good morning, Deputy Smith. Light docket today. If the weather holds, might be able to catch up on our fishing."

"Maybe you, Judge," the white man said. "But not me. I gotta stay 'til five, no matter what. It'll be about dark by the time I get out of here."

Judge Jackson reached into the car and took out a paper sack. Holding it in his left hand, he walked onto Main Street and turned west. His face creased into a smile as he stared toward the business section of the town where he'd lived all his life. With few exceptions, it looked like it did when he was young—prosperous, growing, eagerly facing the future.

His smile turned into a grin. "Nothing better than living in a small town." He stepped out at a jaunty pace, tapping his cane along the sidewalk.

The cane was an affectation he acquired a year ago. He thought it made him appear serious, more judicial in stature. The paper bag didn't fit his picture of himself, but he needed its contents. Two blocks later, he was in the business area bounded by Smithwick

Street on one end and Haughton on the other. Dawson's downtown was a block long or block and a half if you counted the T-intersection with Valdese Street.

"Morning, Ben," he said to an elderly colored man as he walked in front of Willard's Shoe Repair. "How's Sarah's rheumatism doing?"

"Mawnin', suh," Ben said, his head lowered in a sign of respect. "She doin' alright. Just take her a while to git going ev'ry day. She be tickled pink you asked." He stepped into the gutter to allow the Judge to pass.

Judge Jackson walked on, nodding to the men and tipping his hat to the women. He prided himself on knowing the names of most of the people he met on the street. If a stranger approached, the Judge was apt to stop him and introduce himself. Behind his back, people smiled and called him their town greeting service.

"Morning, Mrs. Walters," he said, passing in front of Peele's Jewelers. "You're out mighty early."

"Morning, Judge Jackson. I'm getting my chores done. Gotta man coming to turn the garden today. Want to get it ready so the sun can warm it up. Be time to plant peas soon."

"Yes, ma'am. Early peas are the sweetest of the year. I was telling my wife this morning she should call Ol' Ned to come over with his mule and plow up the plot."

He moved on and a half-block later crossed Valdese Street. Passing in front of the Texaco station, he looked toward the corner and smiled at the sight of the colored man standing in the edge of the Belk-Tyler parking lot beside a battered scooter. "That boy," he said to no one in particular, "he's steady as clockwork. Every Monday I hold court, he's waiting for me." He crossed Main Street and called, "Scooter-Who?"

"Scooter-Hey," the waiting man responded.

"I trust you're feeling well today. How's your scooter doing?" He nodded toward the decrepit conveyance resting on the sidewalk.

"It be doing right good, Jedge. I gotta git me a new wheel for the back pretty soon, but it still gits me around. You sure be looking fine this morning. Shine?"

"Now, Scooter, you know that's why I walk all the way down

here. You give the best shoeshines in North Carolina."

"Jedge, you sure got a mouth on you to make a man feel good," he said through laughter. "I could meet you at the courthouse and save you all that walking."

"You trying to get me in trouble with my wife? She says I need the exercise."

"Shucks, I ain't gonna believe that. You in good shape for a man as old as you."

The Judge grimaced, but knew Scooter was too innocent to mean anything by the remark.

"You don't need no shine. They's already looking Sundy-mornin' good."

"You can touch them up. But here are the ones that really need help." He handed the bag to Scooter. "Can you do something with these old shoes? I found them in the back of the closet. I must have thrown them in there after working in the garden."

Scooter peeked into the bag, then took out one shoe. "Yas suh, they looks pretty bad. You oughta let me fix your shoes 'fore you put them away. That mud on them don't hep a bit when it sets there a long time. But you done said I be the best so I better do'm." He turned the shoe in his hand, gazing at it intently.

Judge Jackson looked at him, wondering about his age. Somewhere between twenty and thirty, he guessed. He didn't ask because, first, he figured Scooter didn't know, and second, he didn't want to embarrass him.

Scooter shoved his cap up, pushed his shoeshine box forward, and knelt behind it. "Put your foot up here and I'll change your shoes. Easier to shine if they's on your feet."

Scooter's box was homemade from rough plywood with a flat carrying handle that doubled as the footrest with a thin strip across it. Judge Jackson rested his left foot with his heel against the wedge. Scooter lifted, then slipped the shoe off, replacing it with the soiled one and carefully tied the laces. They repeated the process to get the right shoe in place.

As Scooter tied the second shoe, a middle-aged colored woman walked by. "You better fix the Judge's shoes real good. He a mighty important man here." She beamed a smile at Judge Jackson. "Mornin'. If Scooter don't do it right, you just let me know. I'll tell Aint Liddie."

Judge Jackson tipped his hat. "I'm sure he'll do fine, but I do appreciate your kind words."

"Yas'm, Miz Freeman," Scooter said. "I knows who the Jedge is. He gonna look good for court."

As she walked away, Scooter mumbled, "She a fine woman, but she do be bossy—always telling me what to do."

The Judge hid his smile behind his hand.

Scooter studied the leather for a moment, tilting his head first to the left, then to the right. He appeared to reach a decision, then pulled off his ragged cotton gloves and folded them into his box. He worked with a battered brush. After a few swipes, he stopped. "Them's so bad, I gotta use my special stuff." Reaching into his box, he pulled out a pint whisky bottle.

"Whoa, Scooter. You're not going to drink that right here on Main Street, are you? As an officer of the court, I'd have to call the police." The Judge chuckled to soften his words.

Scooter giggled. "Naw suh. You knows I ain't no drinking man. I found this-here old bottle and carry my secret cleaner in it for folks with shoes that need a little extry." He held the bottle up. "What kinda whiskey do it say this was?"

"Scotch. It's fancy. Not like the bootleg they make around here."

Scooter studied the bottle. "I ever git enough money, I gonna buy some for my cousins down by the river." He poured a trickle of the thick liquid onto his brush and resumed his brisk scrubbing. After a moment, he stopped and smiled. "That's better. That's much better." Satisfied with the left shoe, he asked for the right, and the Judge complied.

He gave it the same cleaning treatment as the other, then with a final cleansing swipe, said, "Put your left one back up, and lemme see if it's dry."

After the Judge switched feet again, Scooter felt the shoe and said, "Yep, it be ready for my super shine." From his box, he removed a tin of black polish, pried the cap off, then rubbed his fingertips across the wax, and spread it on the Judge's shoe. More wax, more rubbing. "See, that's my secret. I rubs th' polish with my hands in my special way, and your shoe just sucks it in. Makes the leather nice and soft, and does a real good shine."

As he spoke, he was busy working more polish into the leather using both hands. His touch was like a mother oiling her baby's bottom, gentle yet massaging. He called for the right foot and repeated the process. Next, he took out another brush and inspected it carefully. "Gotta be soft and clean. Can't put no dirt in that polish, or it'll leave scratches."

Judge Jackson smiled. He'd heard Scooter's spiel many times, but the soft, melodic tones of his voice made the story worth listening to each time.

Scooter worked with the brush, his hand moving so fast it blurred. When he stopped, the shoe reflected the overhead sun.

"That looks great, Scooter."

"Oh, we ain't finished yet. Gotta look better than that. You got Cousin Joshua for bootleggin' this morning. He give me heck if he see'd your shoes looking bad."

The Judge chuckled. "I'll be sure and tell him you did a good job."

Scooter put the brush in his box and took out an old rag. He examined it as a good craftsman checks his tools, held it in both hands, gripping each end, then bent and spat on the toe of the shoe. "Hang on, Jedge. Here come the ride." He began buffing, the rag dancing, his hands blurring as the cloth polished. He played it as a good percussionist plays a snare drum, producing many of the same sounds. At a point in the procedure only he understood, he stopped, spat again, then returned to the rhythmic slapping of the cloth.

"Wha'cha think? Good 'nuff?" The noise ceased, and Scooter looked up at the Judge.

Judge Jackson saw his head mirrored in the toe of his shoe. "Scooter, you're a miracle worker. Can you bring the other up to that level?"

"Ain't no problem, suh. I got the rhythm now."

Five minutes later, the Judge changed shoes again, and Scooter polished the first pair he'd worn. After Scooter was satisfied and released him, the Judge fumbled in his pocket and pulled out his change. "You still charging ten cents for a shine?"

"Yas suh, for the bad ones. But if that's too much, I'll take a nickel. And that pair you got on ain't worth more'n two cent. They was already shining."

"No, I think ten cents is fair. Here's two-bits." He handed Scooter a coin.

Scooter stared at the quarter, then pulled out the dime Chief Bowen gave him. "Sorry, suh. I ain't got no change for that."

"Now that does present a problem, doesn't it? Wonder what we can do about it?"

Scooter held the coin toward the Judge. "You kin just owe me."

"I have a better idea," the Judge responded, smiling. "It doesn't look good for me to walk down the street carrying a paper sack. You take the extra nickel and drop the shoes off at my house? Just put them inside the screened-in back porch."

"You ain't got to pay me to do that. It be what I do—I mean, favors for folks I like."

"I know," the Judge said, "but this is out of your way. And it's worth it to me."

"Yas suh, I'll do that then. I'll put'm right where you said." A big smile split Scooter's face.

CHAPTER THREE

While retracing his route up Main Street, Judge Jackson pulled his pocket watch from his vest. "Hmmm, only eight-thirty. Wonder if Henry's had breakfast?"

At the *Dawson Times*, he turned and entered. "Henry? You hiding in here?"

From the back came a voice. "Who wants to know?"

"Show some respect to your betters, you damnyankee," the Judge called. "How about some breakfast? Or, are you setting some earth-shattering story in type?"

"In Dawson?" The voice followed by the man entered the front room. "The most interesting thing that's happened around here in the past ten years was that fox killing Sam Gardner's chickens. I made that front page for two weeks."

Henry Flanagan stopped and appeared to study his visitor. He grinned and in a theatrical voice said, "My eyes are bedazzled by the brilliance of your splendiferous attire. You are an example of sartorial elegance seldom seen in this sleepy southern village." He bowed at the waist as his voice reverted to normal. "Obviously, you renewed your subscription to *Esquire* magazine. Camel hair topcoat open over a three piece suit, gold-tipped cane, homburg, and new shoes." His laughter interrupted his dissertation. "I should have acquired a law degree instead of toiling in printer's ink. I'd be a rich man like you."

He looked toward the rear then back at the Judge, a smile growing. "That's my new headline, *Judge Jackson, Fashion Model Under His Robes*. Eli, hold the presses, we're resetting the front page."

A colored man in his fifties stuck his baldhead from the back room. "Huh, what you saying? You know I ain't set no front page yet."

"Morning, Eli," Judge Jackson said.

"Morn'n, Judge," Eli said, rolling his eyes at Henry. "I mighta knowed you two was joshing one 'nother."

"I'm serious," Henry said. "Look at the Judge. He looks like he's ready for his wedding."

"I dressed this way to make Henry look bad," Judge Jackson said. "Of course, that's not hard. That jacket has more ink on it than his front page." He squinted. "And probably better news. Was that shirt white one time?"

Henry looked at his shirtfront as he wiped his hands on the smock leaving ten new trails of stain. He stuck out a hand to shake.

Eli walked back into the pressroom muttering to himself. "I got to 'gree with the Judge on that one. Mr. Flanagan look like he got his clothes at the town dump."

"And these aren't new shoes," the Judge continued. "Scooter worked them over for me. Wouldn't do yours any harm to have him come by."

Both men looked at Henry's shoes that had once been brown. Black splotches covered the toes and laces while the sides bore the scuffs of long wear with little or no care.

"He'd be a miracle worker if he could restore these," Henry said. "What the hell. I wear them because they're comfortable, not because they're pretty like yours. Pretty shoes aren't for working men. You probably take yours off while you sit behind the high bench." He grinned. "Hadn't thought of that before. Wonder if I could slip a camera in there and catch you in your socks. Probably have holes in the toes and heels." His chortle filled the office.

"You bring a camera in my courtroom, and I'll slap you with Contempt of Court and give you a week in jail." He paused. "Might improve the paper. Eli could put it out and print some worthwhile news."

Henry laughed. "Give me a minute and I'll go with you. Eli's setting up a new ad for Farmers Supply's semi-annual sale. You know, that's the one where they try to dump the stuff they couldn't sell at the last semi-annual sale. I'll be right back. Breakfast at Lucille's okay?"

"Good by me. Tell you what. I want to get a paper—"

"Take one," Henry said. "They're by the front door."

The Judge chuckled. "No, I want to know what's happening outside of Dawson. I'll swing by Flip's and pick up a *News and Observer*, then meet you at Lucille's. If you get there first, order me a coffee."

"Yeah," Henry said. "You're too hoity-toity to read a local paper, Mr. Recorder's Court Judge. You want coffee, you better run over there and order it because I might forget." Both laughed as the Judge walked out the front door.

The Judge crossed Main Street and entered Flip's Drugstore, one of only two places in town with a pharmacist. It was named for its original owner, Flip Matthews. Few of the customers knew his real name was Frederick. Young people assumed the store was named for the current owner, Flip Matthews Junior, but old-timers remembered that he was the third Frederick Albert Matthews. People in Nolan County didn't use fancy tags like the third or the fourth. If you had your daddy's name, you were a junior.

"Flip, the papers come in yet?" the Judge asked the man working in the pharmacy in the rear of the store.

"Yep, by the front window, just like always. Is it a new court session already?"

"Sure is."

"Good. We need something to get rid of the cabin fever around here."

"Easy for you to say. I'd rather be at Gardner's Creek," the Judge answered.

"Humph. You fish as bad as you judge," Flip said, a smile lighting his face.

Judge Jackson's court began every Monday except when Superior Court was in session. There was only one courtroom in Nolan County, and the two courts shared it. Superior Court had finished the previous Friday, clearing the way for Recorder's Court to convene on Monday.

When he wasn't holding court, the Judge could be found in his office studying, keeping up with changes in the law. His not-very-secret dream was to become a Superior Court Circuit Judge, and he was determined to be ready when it happened. However, it was an elected position, and everybody loved the incumbent.

In recent months, he had concentrated on the *Brown versus Board of Education* ruling handed down the year before by the U.S. Supreme Court. Essentially, it outlawed the separate, but equal school system used throughout the South. States maintained one school system for whites and a second for coloreds. So far, the ruling had only produced an over-abundance of jawboning, however, Judge Jackson felt certain the day would come when things changed and all schools opened to Negroes. The only questions that remained were how soon it would find its way into North Carolina, then to Nolan County, and how much turmoil it would bring.

In his heart, the Judge was ambivalent about the ruling. He believed he treated everyone the same, as everybody should. But sharing space with Negroes and having white children go to school with them was something else. He grew up in the South, and it was hard to go against his upbringing. However, the Supreme Court had based its ruling on the Constitution's guarantee of equal protection under the law, and he'd sworn to uphold those same laws. If he received the Superior Court position he coveted, he'd gladly lay his hand on the Bible and swear again. When he considered the future, his first hope was that no integration cases would come before him. But if they did, he promised himself he'd meet the challenge.

Flip walked from behind the small window that allowed customers access to the pharmacist. His sandy-colored hair was held in place by something with an oily sheen, probably Wildroot Cream Oil, one of the more popular hair tonics for men. He wore a light blue smock similar to a doctor's and a white shirt with a narrow, navy blue, knit tie.

"Nice outfit," the Judge said. "New slacks?"

"Yeah, picked them up at Belk's. Can't figure out what they're all about, but the kids love them." Flip turned and pointed toward his hips where there was a small belt starting nowhere and going nowhere.

"They'll never catch on," Judge Jackson said. "That little belt is just for decoration and they're way too tight. Besides, they don't have any pleats."

"They're pretty comfortable. Make me feel younger somehow. It's about time men's clothes changed some." He hitched up his pants. "Anything interesting on your docket, anything Henry can write a decent story about?"

"Nope. Much the same—couple of bootleggers, two coloreds cutting one another, speeders, reckless driving—the usual stuff. I should be finished in time to go after Beauregard Bass."

"I'm not gonna ask if you brought your fishing pole. I'm sure you did. But when dark falls, I suspect Beau will still be swimming in Gardner's Creek, and you'll be headed home with an empty creel."

"It'll happen. I'll get him. One day, old Beauregard will be mine, and he'll be sweeter for all the years it took to catch him. Might as well be today." The Judge pulled his watch from his vest. "Henry's over at Lucille's. Want to have breakfast with us? I have some time before court."

"Breakfast? I had that two hours ago. But I'll come over and have a cup of coffee. Wait while I tell Aunt Liddie where I'll be." Flip walked toward the back and called, "Aunt Liddie, come out here, please. I'm going over to Lucille's with the Judge. Watch the store while I'm gone. Anybody comes in, sell them what they want, or come get me."

"Yas suh, Mr. Mat'hews, I'll do that," an elderly, overweight, colored woman said, walking into the sales area. "Want me to do some dusting while y'all be gone?"

"No, just watch the customers. You've done enough for one morning."

Flip looked at the Judge and motioned him out the door. "I'm worried about her. She's been working here longer than I can remember. She's slowed down some, but she's got too much pride to give it up. If I could afford it, I'd give her a pension and hire someone else, but the best I can do is let her come in every day. Of course, it means I have to do more of the work, although she doesn't make it easy. She insists on doing the things she's done since my grandpappy hired her, but it's just too much."

"It's a shame she doesn't have any family left," the Judge said.

"Yes it is. She's outlived all her brothers, sisters and cousins. I figure she must be in her eighties."

They walked into Lucille's Café as Flip added, "Too bad she never married. She'd have children, grandchildren, maybe great-grandchildren to take care of her. She lives down by the river though. Those people take care of their own."

"Now I see why you were so slow," Henry interrupted from a booth along the wall. "Didn't say you were going to pick up the a-poth-e-cary."

"Listen to that," Flip said. "There he goes with them fifty-cent words again. Then he wonders why we don't let him forget he's a damnyankee. Can't a soul understand him."

CHAPTER FOUR

After shining the Judge's shoes, Scooter pushed his way up Main Street, then took a left on Smithwick, the brown bag holding the Judge's shoes secure under his arm. He felt proud to be trusted with such an important job. He kept repeating in a litany, "Put them on the porch, put them on the porch."

Ten minutes later, he was behind the Judge's house. He laid his scooter down, careful not to let his box spill, and walked up the three steps to the back door. He opened it and slipped the bag inside, then eased the door closed, not making a sound. Wearing a smile, he retrieved his scooter and pushed himself away toward the business section. "I done just what the Jedge told me to do. Reckon I earned that nickel."

Once back on Main, he stopped at the intersection of Valdese Street. "I wonder if that mean ol' Burnette be gone yet. Ain't nobody much out today." He took a few steps down Valdese, staring toward where he knew Burnette had parked. However, the curve of the street prevented a clear view even though the street was only a block long.

As he worked his way along the sidewalk, his friendly, "Scooter-Hey" elicited smiles and a return, "Scooter-Who," but no one needed his services. He passed in front of B L Restaurant, staring at the small take-out window in the front. As with the other white restaurants in Dawson, Scooter knew if he wanted service, he got it on the sidewalk in front of that opening. There were no Negroes cued up this early, but at lunch, there would be. The fifteen-cents hotdogs—two for a quarter—smothered in chili, mustard, and big chunks of chopped onions were a favorite of both races.

"Scooter-Hey," he called through the window.

"Scooter-Who?" sounded from the inside. "You coming back for lunch?"

"Yas suh, I gonna be here."

"Well, sing out, and I'll pile on the chili. Gotta take care of my special customers."

"Thanky, suh. I will."

Scooter went another few yards, then stopped. Charlie Burnette stood on the sidewalk talking to another man. Hardly breathing, Scooter retraced his route until he turned the corner onto Main Street. There, he leaned against the front of Eagle's Dime Store and took a deep breath. "Sure wisht I knowed why that man hates me so much." After resting a moment, he pushed off toward Smithwick Street. At the corner, he crossed and headed back west. There were still few people out, and fewer still that needed a shoeshine. His only customer over the next hour was Mr. Andrew McNeill who worked in Davis Shoe Store.

He dallied a moment in front of Belk-Tyler Department Store. "Shining ain't so good today. Maybe I kin do some yardwork." He turned right onto Haughton Street, down a block, then right again onto Church Street. The homes were on large lots with stately trees adorning the lawns. Azaleas sprouted around every house, and most yards had one or more magnolia trees. Dormant roses grew in front, and Scooter knew each backyard held a vegetable garden. Many of the buildings, all two or three-stories, dated from the previous century.

He smiled at the lack of activity. No one was raking or pruning. That meant there was work available, and he could do it. He took his time propelling himself down one sidewalk, then up the other, hoping to see an owner. He knew better than to knock on anyone's front door. Colored men simply did not do that.

"If I don't see no one soon, I'll have to go 'round back." Scooter hated going into people's yards because most of them had dogs. It seemed to him all white folks' dogs hated colored people. They were always coming after him. Many times, he saved himself by using his scooter to keep the dog at bay until the owner or a neighbor rescued him. Scars on his arms represented the times he'd been unsuccessful.

He started at the end of Church Street where the Methodist Church, built in the nineteenth century, stood and pushed himself past the Baptist and Episcopal Churches. Three blocks later, he turned and retraced his movement. Across from the Baptist Church, he saw a woman emerge from behind her house dragging a garbage can.

"Scooter-Hey, Miz Patterson," he called. "Can Scooter hep you?"

Mrs. Deborah Patterson, called Debbie since she was a little girl, looked up and said, "Scooter-Who? You sure can. You looking for work?"

"Yas'm. I's hoping y'all need some leaves raked or something."

"You came to the right place. It ain't easy being a widow-woman and keeping this big ol' house going all by myself. Put this can by the curb then come out back. I have loads for you to do."

Scooter watched her walk away. He felt good that she had work for him, and she had no dog. Her last one, a cocker spaniel, barked at him, but never tried to bite. Still, he was always nervous when working in Mrs. Patterson's yard until the dog died the previous year.

As Mrs. Patterson went behind the house, Scooter dragged the can to the curb, returned, and brought out two others. He then knocked on the screen door of the back porch.

..*

Mrs. Patterson was a comely woman, neither too fat nor too skinny, pleasant to look at. Her handsome, red hair was always neat, and she was never without a light touch of lipstick. Today, bright red was her color of choice. A few men had shown interest since the death of her husband ten years before, however she politely turned them away. She told her friends that at thirty-eight, she didn't need to raise another man.

"Com'in," Mrs. Patterson called to Scooter.

"No'm, I druther not. Tain't right for no nigger like me to come into a white lady's house. I'll wait here."

Mrs. Patterson appeared at the door. "Nonsense. This is my house, and I invite whoever I please. And right now, I please to invite you. Now, you come on in here and have a cup of coffee with me."

"Yas'm, if I have to." Scooter edged his way through the door held open by Mrs. Patterson, staying as far from her as possible. "Ma'am, I really don't think I outta be here. But a cuppa coffee do sound good."

"Fine. Now sit yourself down. I have a fresh pot perking. It'll be ready any minute." She walked to the stove where a percolator was busy bubbling away. She peered at the glass bulb on the top. "Yep, looks like it's ready."

She poured coffee into two china cups, put one in front of Scooter, then placed containers of sugar and milk, and a silver spoon beside his cup. "Help yourself."

Scooter stared at the coffee, then at her, a look of discomfort on his face, his hands firmly entwined in his lap. "Miz Patterson, I can't touch that. I ain't never seen nothing so fine as that cup. I scared to death I drop it. Ain't you got no ol' cup I can take in the backyard?"

Mrs. Patterson looked at him, stubbornness flashing from her hazel eyes before a look of understanding took over. "Yes, I have an old cup for you. It's a shame though that we can't sit down and have coffee like other people." She rose, took his cup, and poured it into a white mug. "If you want, you can go outside and pull out the rakes and clippers. I'll bring the coffee out there."

Scooter rose and almost ran out the back door.

..*

Debbie Patterson and Scooter raked side-by-side in the front yard. The winter's accumulation of leaves, twigs, and other debris made their task tedious. They quartered the lawn and created several piles in the first three quarters.

"Let's take a water break," Mrs. Patterson said, wiping sweat from her forehead. "Get the jugs."

Scooter ran to the hedges in front of the house and pulled out two water containers. One had a red top and the other, blue. Returning to her, he handed the blue to her.

She unscrewed the cap and took a long pull on the water. Only after she drank did Scooter open his bottle and drink. Mrs. Patterson sank onto the grass. "Sit down here, Scooter. We can rest a minute."

Scooter settled onto the lawn, keeping his distance from her.

"What's wrong with your leg?" she asked. "You limp when you walk."

"Ain't nothing really wrong with it. The left one's just shorter, that's all. It was born that way, and it ain't never caught up."

"That's too bad. Does it bother you?"

"No'm. I's used to it, and it don't matter a bit when I'm riding my scooter. Then I got one foot up and one foot down. Don't nobody know but me."

What an attitude, she thought. I whine when I get a blister on my heel from new shoes. He goes through life with a deformed leg and doesn't complain at all. Makes me question myself.

She took another drink from her jug. "What's your real name? I mean, I know everybody calls you Scooter, but you must have a real name." She stood and picked up her rake.

Scooter followed her example, then frowned as if concentrating. "I don't rightly know. Aint Liddie calls me honey sometimes, but don't nobody else call me that. Everybody just calls me Scooter." He reached with the rake and pulled in some debris.

"Stop with the raking. Think back as far as you can. What did people call you before you got your scooter?"

He put the rake down, then frowned some more. "I done had it a long time, but seems like afore I got it, I had a different name. I'll try to 'member." He picked up the rake and swept it across the grass.

Mrs. Patterson looked at him, shaking her head. "What a shame. What have we done to these simple people?" she said under her breath.

The frown lines on Scooter's forehead smoothed, and he turned, a smile lighting up his face. "I 'member, Miz Patterson. I 'member whut folks used to call me. They called me Hey Boy. They'd say, 'Hey Boy, c'mere,' or 'Hey Boy, fetch me some water,' or something like that. Yep, that's whut they called me, Hey Boy."

"That's good," Mrs. Patterson said, a look of resignation on her face. "I like Scooter better. Don't you?"

"Yas'm, I do. When somebody calls me Scooter, makes me feel good. Like I is somebody. And far's I know, ain't nobody else got my name."

She looked around the yard. "Look, you finish this area then load the wheelbarrow with what we raked up. I'll fix some lunch." She went into the house.

Scooter followed her instructions. By the time she announced that lunch was ready, he had finished the raking and dumped the debris along the curb, ready for pickup.

She invited Scooter in for lunch, but he repeated his protests of earlier in the day. They picnicked under a large oak tree that dated back to the Civil War.

She served sandwiches using chicken salad made fresh the previous evening. With them were fried potatos and sweetened iced tea. Scooter ate three sandwiches, all his potatos, and drank two glasses of tea. He used the tip of his finger to pick up the crumbs. All the while he insisted that one sandwich was enough. She sat at a picnic table nibbling as she watched his hearty appetite with a sly smile. Scooter sat on the ground several feet away. He refused to sit with her.

After they ate, they cleaned up the remains of the meal, and Mrs. Patterson took the dishes into the house. Scooter stayed away from the back door.

"Scooter, I take a nap after lunch," Mrs. Patterson said, sticking her head out the doorway. "I'm going inside. You just rest until I get back, then we'll work on the backyard."

..*

Scooter leaned against the oak tree and watched Mrs. Patterson disappear into the house. He fumbled in his shoeshine box and pulled out a six-inch long piece of wood that had the front half of an animal protruding from it. Cocking his head, he studied the carving, surveying it with a critical eye.

He reached into his box again and rummaged through its contents. Unable to find what he wanted, he took everything out. With loving care, he sorted the items. Brushes in one pile, tins of polish in another, and rags in a third. At the bottom of the box, he found what he needed, a small piece of well-used sandpaper. With a tender, almost caressing touch, he sanded the right front leg of the carving.

Laying the piece of paper on the bottom of the box, he picked up a rag. From inside the folds of the cloth, he pulled out a three-inch clasp knife and opened it. The blade was shorter than the handle by almost an inch with the end pointed like an awl. He tested its sharpness with his thumb.

"Hmm, reckin I ought to hone this afore I start." He looked around the area, then rose, and limped toward the back of Mrs. Patterson's property where he knew there was a rock garden. He picked up several rocks, examined them, then replaced them in the same spot. Finally, he found what he was looking for—a flat rock about three inches across.

Moving back into the shade of the oak tree, he sat and spat on the rock. In a circular grinding motion, he rubbed the knife blade against the stone, occasionally stopping and checking the edge with his thumb. When the stone dried, he spat on it. Finally, satisfied with the sharpness of the blade, he closed it and placed the knife on the old rag. A moment later, he had returned the stone to its former resting place.

Scooter leaned his head against the oak tree, picked up the knife and the partially carved stick. Holding it in the air, he examined it, turning it in his hand. Then he set to work. Carefully and patiently, he removed thin shavings, working on the head of the animal. After each cut, he used the sandpaper, rounding and smoothing, polishing the wood as a jeweler would a fine gem. An hour passed with Scooter engrossed in the carving. He was working with the sandpaper when the back door of the house opened.

"Okay, Scooter. I'm raring to go," Mrs. Patterson said, negotiating the steps. "Think we can finish the backyard before dinnertime?"

Scooter jumped, her voice surprising him. He folded the clasp knife, covered it with the rag, then stuffed the carving and the knife into his shoeshine box. Standing, he said, "Yas'm. I's ready when you is."

Mrs. Patterson looked at him. "What were you doing? Was that a knife I saw?"

Scooter dropped his head. "I wasn't doing nothing, ma'am. I just whittles a little when I have time. It was my stick. I brung it with me. Honest—"

"Oh, hush. I don't care about the stick. But I did see a knife, and knives scare me. Let me see it."

Scooter unwrapped the cloth and handed her the knife. "It's

mine, Miz Patterson. I found it at the dump. Honest. It was throwed away."

She opened the blade and tested it with her thumb, jerking away as soon as she touched it. "You know how sharp this is? My late husband didn't have a razor this sharp. Did you do that?"

Scooter's chin hung to his chest. "Yas'm. I keeps it as sharp as I kin 'cause it whittles better."

"You whittle? Show me."

Reluctantly, Scooter reached into his shoeshine box and handed her the carving he'd been working on.

Mrs. Patterson's look turned from a scowl to one of amazement. "Why, Scooter, it's perfect," she gushed. "Did you do this?"

Scooter's head stayed down as he shuffled from foot to foot. "Yas'm. It's just something I do when I's resting. It ain't even done yet."

"Do you have any that are finished?"

Scooter looked at her, his hands performing a dance all their own. "I gots one, but it ain't very good."

"Let me see it. I'll be the judge of how good it is."

Scooter rummaged in the box and came out with a wooden horse about two inches tall by three inches long. "Here's one I done last week. I ain't too happy with it, but I kept it anyhow."

Mrs. Patterson took it from him, turning it in her hand, examining it from every angle. "Why, Scooter, this is wonderful, so lifelike." She looked at its underside, then blushed. Its gender was evident.

"Do you have others?"

"Yas'm. Back at my shack, I gots maybe fifty. I been whittling a long time now. Sometimes, nobody wants they's shoes shined, and they ain't no yard work so I whittles." He looked at her, fear showing in his face. "Did I do something wrong? I didn't—"

"No, you haven't done anything wrong. I think you've done something really special. I'd like to see some of the others. In fact, will you sell me the one you were working on?"

"Ma'am, that one ain't finished yet. If you let me finish, I be happy to give it to you. I be mighty proud if you had it."

Mrs. Patterson returned the carving to Scooter. "You finish it. We'll set a price."

"Price? I don' know 'bout setting no price. I gits ten cent for a shoeshine. I reckon maybe a nickel or maybe even two cent for one of these. Do that sound all right?"

"No, Scooter, that doesn't sound right. Your work is worth more than that. You're setting yourself too low."

"Well, I don't know then. I ask Aint Liddie what she think."

"Good. You ask her. Then bring me the carvings to look at. I'm sure we can work out a deal."

CHAPTER FIVE

Henry Flanagan entered the newspaper office after breakfasting with the Judge and Flip. "Eli, anybody looking for me?" he called toward the room in the back.

"Nah suh. Been quiet as a church mouse. Even Miz Andrews ain't come by to complain about the boy throwing the paper in her roses," Eli said, walking into the front area.

Mrs. Christiana Andrews was Dawson's chronic complainer. It didn't matter what occurred, she found a reason to whine. On Wednesdays and Fridays, she fussed that the newspaper boy threw the paper into her rose garden. Often, she came to the office to show her scratches from retrieving it. If it was a delivery from Flip's Drugstore, it took too long, or the pills didn't look right, or they weren't needed any more. If it was a clothing purchase, the material was of poor quality or the dye would run. Every merchant had a Christiana story. They needed to add no embellishments, she provided her own. No one in town could remember when she was last satisfied.

On the plus side, or minus depending on point of view, Mrs. Andrews was also the town snoop and knew everything that was going on in Dawson. It was said that if Christiana didn't know, she'd make it up and still be right. Henry had used her several times to verify stories before publishing them. Her details were more complete than Henry's investigation developed.

"How's the ad coming?" Henry asked.

"It's done. Wanna see a copy?" Eli said.

"No, I trust you. Do you have anything else to work on?"

"Nah, suh," Eli said. "The paper's set for tomorrow 'cept for the front page and the editorial. You ain't writ that yet. That be all. We be caught up."

"Okay." Henry thought for a moment. "Take a long lunch. There's no point in your hanging around. Come back at one, and I'll have the first page. Most of it's done, but I'd like to have one decent story for top middle. Maybe I can pick something up at the courthouse." He paused. "I can't think of anything to put on the editorial page. Maybe we'll just use some letters to the editor. We've had some good ones recently."

"That's the truth, suh."

"I'll look through them," Henry said. "Now, you get out of here."

"Thank you, suh. That's mighty nice a you. You sure you don't have nothing else for me to do?"

"Nope, go fishing or something. I'll see you at one o'clock."

"Well, there might be a big old catfish down by the river," Eli said, moving toward the front door.

Henry entered his office and dropped onto a worn sofa. He lowered his face into his hands and sat for a moment before looking up. His expression was a mask of sadness as he surveyed the room. "So this is it. This is what I chased Germans all over Europe for—a two-bit newspaper in a one-horse town. Some days this whole damn place seems smaller than the foxholes I slept in." He walked to his desk and from the right bottom drawer took a bottle of vodka. "Dreams. I had such dreams. Now I only find them in a bottle." He opened the small refrigerator in the corner and pulled a tray of ice from the freezer section. "A little ice, two inches of vodka, fill it with grapefruit juice, and I'm magically transformed into the *Super-Editor* of the *Dawson Times*." He saluted the glass. "Be still, my heart." He took a long pull on the drink, frowning. "Not scotch, but it'll have to do. Can't have any of the old biddies in town smelling booze on my breath." He laughed, a dry sardonic chuckle.

Like most men in his age group, Henry Flanagan was a World War II veteran. He grew up in Brooklyn and enlisted in the Army at the age of twenty-five, the week after Pearl Harbor. In so doing, he walked away from a promising start as a newspaper reporter on Long Island.

He earned his spurs in the business by starting at the bottom as a teenager selling papers in his Brooklyn neighborhood. After high school, he landed a job as a copy boy and all-round gofer on a small paper and worked his way up to junior reporter. By age twenty-two, everyone said he was on his way when he landed the position on Long Island. Three years later, the Japanese attacked Pearl Harbor and Henry Flanagan's life took a sudden turn. He postponed his dream of becoming a top reporter, preferably for the *New York Times*, and enlisted in the Army. As with everyone else in the country, December 7, 1941 brought permanent changes to his life.

While fighting his way across Europe, he became friends with Bobby Joe Griffin, a man two years younger than Henry, from eastern North Carolina. Henry listened for hours to Bobby Joe's homespun humor and fell in love with the towns and villages he'd never seen. In the foxholes of Italy, France, and Germany, he didn't realize he listened, not with a journalist's ear, but with the ear of a man seeking a life. Bobby Joe died during the waning days of the war, and Henry decided to emigrate to Bobby Joe's home area.

"Bobby Joe, I sure didn't know how little your world really was when I used my mustering-out pay to buy the *Dawson Times*." He stared into his drink. "Here's to you, wherever you are." He tipped the glass and drank.

He took another look around the office then walked out, drink in hand, and entered the rear area of the three-room operation. The equipment stood idle. He ran his hands over the type tray loving the feel of the metal carvings. Newspaper work—his love, his mistress, and his Satan. There was nothing he would rather be doing. Of course, Dawson wouldn't be his first choice today. He preferred a major market like New York, but that was not to be. He had made his decision, and now he lived with it. He'd blown all his money buying the paper. Dawson had its pluses, though. No competition, and it wasn't exactly the end of the world, although on many days it seemed close. Reporting on the county fair and church bazaars had their own rewards—plenty of southern fried chicken and other delicacies kept his appetite sated. He rubbed the ample belly bulging over his belt as he thought about it.

Finishing his drink, he returned to the office and again opened the refrigerator. As he reached for the ice bucket, he stopped. "Oh, hell. I may as well try the courthouse. Maybe there's a story there. I need to hit the liquor store anyway."

..*

The two-story courthouse was old, but functional with a sign on the front lawn proclaiming it was completed in 1885. Old-timers told hand-me-down stories about the big party when they cut the ribbon. The Governor came to town to stand beside the Mayor with a large pair of scissors. Each held a handle and together they snipped the tape, officially opening the building. At that time, it was the most modern courthouse in eastern North Carolina. If the storytellers were believed, the crowd was huge that day—everyone claimed multiple ancestors who attended.

Since then, the courthouse had been in continuous use and, some said, continuous decline. The building had been red brick, but over the years, many coats of white paint hid its original color.

Henry stepped through the front door and stopped, looked left then right. On each side, a set of stairs led from the foyer to the courtroom on the second floor. The one on the left wore a sign reading *Colored.* The other side carried another sign, *Whites Only.* A hallway led to the rear of the building. Along the corridor were indications of separate, but equal, treatment of the races. A water cooler on the left was for *Colored*, while one on the right proclaimed *Whites Only.*

Henry turned to his right, went up the first few steps then stopped, frowning. "That's it. I'll write an editorial that will stir the pot." He grinned and continued his climb up the curving staircase to the second floor into the courtroom. There were two sets of benches with an aisle down the center. Again, coloreds occupied the left side, and whites the right.

Henry slipped into a seat on the back row, the only white spectator. On his left sat several Negroes. Judge Jackson was on the bench and a colored man Henry didn't recognize from the rear stood before the Judge. Henry pulled a stenographer's pad from his smock and listened.

..*

"Joshua, how many times have you been before me for bootlegging?" Judge Jackson asked from his raised position.

The colored man in front of the bench answered in a quiet

voice, "I don't rightly remember, suh—three, maybe four."

"Uh-huh. And how many times have I put you on the county chain gang?"

The colored man's head jerked up. "Two, suh. Once in the fall and once in the spring. I 'member them good. You ain't gonna do that agin, is you? It's March. Snakes is looking for food in them ditches. Ain't no fit time to be working there."

"Well, Joshua, seems like we have a problem here. Bootlegging is against the law. We even have a special name for it, Violation of Liquor Laws. And you're charged for the fifth time. When I asked how you pled, you said, 'Guilty.' That leaves me to come up with something that'll stop you from bootlegging."

"I sure sorry to be such a bother, suh." Joshua stared at his feet, his brow creased, his hands deep in his pockets. The bib overalls and blue chambray work-shirt he wore showed the effects of age, harsh cleaning, and a hot iron. His old brogans were beyond salvage, though. They'd seen too many tough days in the fields.

Judge Jackson looked down at Joshua, concern showing on the Judge's face. "How many children do you have?"

"Six, suh." The head stayed down although the feet shuffled.

"Does your mother still live with you?"

"Yas suh."

"What would happen to them if I sent you to the Prison Camp?"

"They'd git by as best they could, suh," he said. "Farmers be hiring hands soon to git crops in the ground. They all work in the fields, all except the lit'ist one. My woman's strong. She git by."

"I see." The Judge entwined his hands and rested his peaked forefingers against his lips.

The Negroes sitting along the front row on the left side of the courtroom were Joshua's family—wife, mother, and children from teenagers down to a toddler. There were several other Negroes sitting behind the family. One of the women rested her hand on the shoulder of Joshua's wife. Joshua's children stared at the Judge.

Judge Jackson pulled his hands from his face and smiled. "When I saw Scooter this morning, he asked me to mention him to you. He said you're his cousin. Is that right?"

Joshua looked up, curiosity reflected in his eyes, then lowered his head again. "Can't rightly say, suh. I's knowed him since he was borned, but he ain't no kin that I can be sure of. After his mama was kilt when he was real little, he growed up down by the river, a lot of that time at my place. I mean, it ain't that he's not my kin. Most of us down there is related in some way. River-niggers been there since Pres'dent Lincoln freed the slaves. We don't git along with the hill-niggers real good so we just stays amonst ourselves."

"So, if Scooter says you're kin, it may or may not be true. Is that right?"

"Kinda, suh. Down by the river, we calls ev'rybody cousin. If you wants to know 'bout Scooter, check with Aint Liddie at the drugstore. She practically raised that boy."

"Thank you, Joshua. Next time you see Scooter, tell him I asked about him. He's a good man." He picked up his gavel and slowly turned it in his hands. "Now, we need to find a way to keep you out of trouble. How much moonshine do you drink a week?"

Joshua stood a little straighter. "'Bout a pint, 'less there's something special going on."

"Special?"

"You know, like a birfday, or dinner on the grounds at church, or somebody has a baby. Special stuff like that."

"Hmmmm, I see." Judge Jackson turned to the bailiff. "How much do you drink a week?"

"I don't drink, Judge. I'm a Southern Baptist," the white man said.

"A pint seems like more than enough to me, including special occasions. It's sure more than I drink, or anybody I know." The Judge stopped talking and scribbled on a pad for a moment. "Help me with my math, Joshua. I believe two pints make a quart. Is that right?"

Joshua turned and looked at his wife.

She nodded.

To the Judge, Joshua said, "Yas suh. That's whut my woman says."

"Good. Now," the Judge looked at his pad, "there's four quarts in a gallon, right?"

Again, Joshua looked at his wife who nodded.

"Yas suh, that's right."

"So that means you drink between a half and a gallon of moonshine every month. Does that seem right?"

"Yas suh, I guess so."

"Okay, here's what we're going to do."

Joshua stopped fidgeting and stood still, looking straight at the Judge, worry lines creasing his forehead.

"You'll spend this week and the next eight weekends in jail. The Chief will let you out early on Monday mornings so you can work. You have a job, don't you?"

Joshua nodded.

"Where? Who are you working for? You have to talk to me. See that lady over there?" Judge Jackson nodded toward the Court Reporter. "She's taking down everything we say. She can't write down a nod."

"Yas suh. I try to 'member that. Lemme see. Monday and Tuesday, I be breaking land for Muster Whitcomb. He got thurty acres to plow. Then Wednesday and Thursday, I works for Muster Walder. On Friday, I spends the day hepping my woman in the garden—that is, unless something better comes up."

"Fine. You'll be out in time to get to the fields." The Judge wrote on his pad. "For the next year, the next twelve months, I'm going to ask the Chief of Police to have one of his officers check in on you at least once a week. If he finds you with more than a half-gallon of moonshine, he's going to let me know. After tobacco season in the fall, I'll have you right back where you're standing now. And if that happens, Joshua." He paused for emphasis. "I'll send you to the state pen in Raleigh. You've heard about that place, haven't you?"

Fear flashed across Joshua's face. "Yas suh, I's heer'd of it. I don't want to go there, Judge."

"Good. Do you understand what I'm saying?"

"Yas suh."

"Tell me."

Joshua took a deep breath. "You said if I haves more than a haf-gallon of moonshine, you gonna send me to Raleigh."

"Close enough." The Judge banged his gavel, saying to the deputy, "Take him away, Clyde. Give him one of your very best rooms."

Everyone laughed, including Joshua, as Clyde led him from the courtroom.

..*

Henry and Judge Jackson relaxed in chambers in the waning minutes of a thirty-minute recess.

"You have a unique approach to justice," Henry said. "Your handling of Joshua must be a first in the annals of the judiciary."

"What else can I do?" Judge Jackson answered. "Would it have been better to send him to the Prison Camp again while his wife and children go hungry? Joshua's a good man. He just likes his moonshine."

"Yeah, but he's still a bootlegger. Aren't you sworn to uphold the law?"

"Therein lies the dilemma, my friend. It's illegal to make white lightning in this state. Also, it's illegal to have it in your possession. Those laws are very clear. However, as a parallel, we have a maximum speed limit on the open road of fifty-five miles an hour. Yet everyday, I see people driving faster than that. When I ask state troopers and other law enforcement people about it, they tell me they don't bother to stop anyone unless he's doing at least ten miles above the limit. Are they wrong to put their own twist on the law?"

Henry sat silent for a moment. "I think I'll pass on that one. Sounds like a damned if I do and damned if I don't situation. Do you think Joshua will live up to his promise?"

Judge Jackson considered the question carefully. "Yes, I do. And if he doesn't, I'll do my best to send him to the state pen, exactly as I promised."

The room stayed quiet until Judge Jackson said, "It's a bad law, Henry—one I hope will get changed some day. I've talked to a couple of legislators about it. Why should it be illegal for a man to make liquor for his own use? Now, don't get me wrong. If Joshua was selling it, I'd throw the book at him. But as far as I know, he only makes enough for drinking and sharing with his friends. And for the life of me, I just can't think that's so terrible."

Henry leaned forward. "The law—"

"Just a minute," Judge Jackson said. "I can grow vegetables and give them away, sell them or keep them for myself."

"Yeah, but the law's not about gardens."

"Hold on. I'll get to the point. I can put those vegetables up and do whatever I please with them. I can make jellies, jams, and preserves. I can sell them alongside the road if I want to. But I can't make a gallon of hooch for myself. Henry, it just doesn't make sense to me."

"Judge, I'd never be dumb enough to argue the law with you, but somehow, I think you're kind of twisted on this one. Preserves and jellies aren't exactly the same."

"Okay, how about this one? I can plant a grapevine, harvest those grapes, and make wine for my dinner table. Or apples. I can buy apples and make hard cider. They're both alcoholic drinks. Why the difference?"

The Judge leaned forward. "Remember that we're only talking homemade here. Alcohol is not illegal in North Carolina. The state sells beer licenses for on and off consumption. I can go down the street to the state store and buy the finest brands. Heck, I bet a lot of people would be embarrassed if we stood outside the ABC Store and took pictures—some of our finest citizens." He smiled. "Including you and me." He turned serious again. "The Alcohol Beverage Control agency must drag in a ton of tax money. Yet, poor old Joshua, who can't afford the branded stuff, can't make a jug to share with his friends."

Henry chuckled. "You win, the law stinks."

"I know, and that's what gets under my skin. Look at Joshua. He's a good husband and father. He works all over the county. Every farmer I know says he's honest, hardworking, and dependable. He's never been arrested for fighting, beating his wife, or stealing. Hell, he's never even knifed one of his neighbors, or one of the hill-niggers, as he calls them. What I'm saying is he's a good citizen, a good husband, and a good father. Why should I put him in jail because he makes moonshine for his own drinking? I just can't do it anymore."

..*

Henry sat at his desk, a vodka and grapefruit juice on his left, thinking aloud. "I've been here ten years, but I'm still learning about the South. Guess the Judge's handling of that case is what they call *homespun justice*. He's right. Bootlegging laws don't make a lot of sense unless you're making it to sell." He sipped his drink. "That's my new editorial. Separate but equal has waited a hundred years. It can wait awhile longer."

He opened his steno pad, jotted key words, arranged them in the order he wanted, then lay down the pencil. Turning to his manual Royal typewriter, he rolled in a sheet of paper. After staring at it a moment, he began to type.

Today, this editor was treated to an example of how cold, hard words on paper are best interpreted by humans with a sense of justice. I have calluses from sitting on hard benches in courtrooms, but today's additions were worthwhile. I will not go into detail here—I am sure you will hear about it on the street—but I must state how fortunate we are to have an honest, caring person like Judge Daniel J. Jackson holding court for us.

Laws are written by human beings who do their best to make them living documents. However, one of the traits that makes each person different is interpretation of the written word. Some see the words and are commanded to take the harshest action possible. In this case, a long jail sentence, a large fine, or perhaps both might have been rendered. Others read those same laws and see an opportunity to act in a humane way. Judge Jackson saw the latter. That's not to say the culprit escaped unpunished. No, quite the opposite. Judge Jackson simply found a way to mete out justice with a soft touch rather than with a gauntlet. This Editor believes our community will be the better for it.

Thank you, Judge Jackson, for reminding me that Justice is supposed to be blind, that Justice is not based on color, that Justice can be applied with a touch of humanity. And for reminding me that all men are created equal.

CHAPTER SIX

Flip entered the drugstore, picking remnants of country ham from his teeth after breakfast with Henry and Judge Jackson. The room was narrow, only enough space for freestanding displays, a counter with barstools, and floor-to-ceiling shelves on the opposite wall. The right wall held a counter with enough space behind it for a person to work. Those who sat in front could purchase sodas and ice cream. Farther down were four booths where high school sweethearts courted, and other patrons chatted. Flip employed two teenagers to keep the ice cream and sodas moving on Saturdays. Monday through Friday, one student reported for work after school. Otherwise, he and Aunt Liddie served the customers.

Beyond the booths was a side door that opened into an alley, the entrance for Negroes. The front was for whites only. There were no signs posted, however it had been that way so long everyone simply knew. There had once been a small window opening into the alley from the pharmacist's cubicle. In those days, Negroes were not allowed in the store and placed their orders through that window. Flip's father closed it in 1942. He said if coloreds were good enough to fight for liberty, they were sure good enough to come into his store.

"Did y'all have a nice breakfast, Mistah Mat'hews?" Aunt Liddie called from her perch on a stepladder, feather duster in hand.

"What are you doing? Please, get down," Flip said, a tone of alarm in his voice. Even if she had been young, Flip would have been alarmed. Aunt Liddie weighed over two hundred pounds.

"Suh, these high shelves ain't been dusted in a long time. I's just reaching them."

"Thank you, but I'd feel a lot better if you put both feet on the floor. I'll get those top items. You work on the lower shelves."

"Now, Mistah Mat'hews, that ain't fair. Your gran'daddy hired me to keep this place clean, and you ain't letting me do that. I don't understan'. I diapered your fanny when you was a baby, and now you acting like I can't do nothing."

"I know, Aunt Liddie. I'm lucky you still run this place every day. But it makes me feel better when I see you with both feet on the floor. For my sake, please don't climb that ladder anymore."

"Humph. Stubborn white man," Liddie said, climbing down from the ladder. "You was stubborn as a chil' and you is stubborn as a man. I done tried, but I just can't make no dent in that hard head of yourn."

Flip chuckled. "Anybody come by while I was out?"

"Miz Christiana."

"Great. What was she complaining about?"

Liddie giggled. "She wanted you to know th' deliv'ry boy was late yesterday."

"Anything else?"

"Well, she wanted some Epsom salts. She sayed she was terrible constipated. But she say she'd come back when you got time to tend to your business."

"Why didn't you sell her some?"

"I told her I would. I even got down a box, but she said nah, she'd wait for you. I don't believe she trusts me."

"Not only you, Aunt Liddie. She doesn't trust anybody," Flip said, walking into his alcove. He looked through the window. "And stay off that ladder."

..*

Midafternoon was a slow time in downtown Dawson. Women were home preparing the evening meal while their men worked. The drugstore was empty except for Flip and Aunt Liddie. She dusted shelves as high as she could reach while throwing looks over her shoulder toward the back room. He had gone to the storeroom to pull out another carton of aspirin.

Henry strolled in and took a seat at the counter. "What's a fellow have to do to get a milkshake here?"

"Now, you hush your fuss, Mistah Flan'gin," Aunt Liddie said with a giggle. "You knows I's right here. Do you want a choc'lit one?" She looked around. "With extry syrup?"

Henry chuckled. "Yes, ma'am. You know I do. An Aunt Liddie special."

"What's all this noise out here," Flip said, walking in carrying a box. "Oh, I might have known. The local Yankee for his afternoon pick-me-up."

Henry looked at Aunt Liddie. "Don't you have some errands you can send him on? You know, like deliver a prescription to Mrs. Christiana?"

"Lawd, Mr. Flan'gin. You tryin' to get me in trouble? I believe he'd rather make you a milkshake than face her." She laughed, her rolls of fat shaking. "It mighty-fine to see two good friends like you joshing one 'nother." She shifted to Flip. "You come over here and set with yo' friend. I do them aspirin."

"I'll do that, Aunt Liddie. Pour me a soda, please." Flip slid onto the stool beside Henry. "Anything in the news racket?"

Henry grinned. "I saw the damnedest thing this morning. Dan handed down a ruling that has to be unique. Sometimes, he amazes me with his common sense." His grin grew. "Never expect such from a damn rebel."

"That's all you know," Flip said. "What did he do?"

Henry filled him in on the court session he witnessed and his conversation with the Judge. Then he reached into his pocket. "Here's tomorrow's editorial. Eli's setting it now."

Flip took it and read quietly. "It's good, Henry. And, the Judge sure deserves it, but you have one statement that people might take wrong."

"What's that?"

"This one." Flip read, "Justice is not based on color." He looked at Henry. "There's some folks might say you're taking the side of Negroes with that."

"Well, I'm not." Henry stopped, then frowned. "Maybe I am. Justice should be blind. There's nothing I know that says the law should treat one race different from any other."

CHAPTER SEVEN

When Liddie arrived for work on Wednesday, Scooter sat on the curb whittling, his shoeshine box by his side. The scooter leaned against the front window of the drugstore.

"Scooter-Hey, Aint Liddie," he said, rising to his feet. "I been waiting for you."

"Why didn't you come to my place if you wanted to talk to me," she said, puffing her way down the sidewalk.

"I didn't want to bother you whiles you was gitting ready for work." Scooter stopped and shuffled his feet. "You got a minute we kin talk?"

"Sure. Come on in while I git th' store ready for business." She took a key from her battered black purse and unlocked the front door.

"You got a key to the door?" Scooter asked with a look of disbelief. "I didn't know that."

"Yep, Flip Junior's gran'daddy give me this key afore he died. Said I was his partner and a partner deserved a key." Her eyes took on a faraway look. "He was a mighty-fine white man." A tear slid down her cheek. She dabbed at it with a coarse handkerchief then appeared to remember where she was. "I been opening this door every Monday through Saturday since. When I's buried, I wants this key in my casket. You make sure they do that."

"Yas'm, I shore will. I ain't never knowed no nigger what had a key to a white man's place and was his pardner. Ol' Mustah Flip musta thought you was something special."

"Naw, I just worked for him. That was his way of talking." Liddie unlocked the door and stepped inside.

Scooter hung back, cradling his shoeshine box under his arm.

"Maybe I better go 'round the side to the colored door. You gonna open that one?"

"Course I am. I does it all." She looked through the door, peeking up and down the street. "Ain't nobody lookin'. Come on in. Won't hurt nothing this time."

Scooter followed her in and watched as she moved around the store, turning on lights, then unlocked the door to the alley.

"You just hold on 'til I get some coffee started," she said. "Muster Flip like it ready when he walks in." She went behind the counter and washed out the pot. After measuring coffee into the basket and filling the pot with water, she placed it on a hot plate. "Now, what you want to talk about?"

Scooter hung his head. "I want to show you these and ask you which is the best." He reached into his shoeshine box and pulled out an old piece of towel and lay it on the bar. When he unfolded it, there were five carved figures—two dogs, two horses, and a sheep. Each was small enough to fit in his palm and intricately detailed.

"Where'd you git them?" Liddie asked picking up one of the dogs and a horse.

"I made them, I mean, I whittled'm. When I ain't got nothing else to do, I whittles."

Liddie looked at him with a skeptical eye. "Don't you lie to me, boy. You sure you did these?"

Scooter squirmed under her stare, took off his Brooklyn Dodgers baseball cap, and held it in front of his chest. "Yas'm, honest I did. I been practicing a long time. I never showed'm to you 'cause I didn't think they was good."

"So, why you showing me now?" Liddie asked, a scowl on her face.

"Miz Patterson caught me whittling and said she wanted one."

"Miz Deb'ra Patterson?"

"Yas'm."

"Boy, whut's wrong wid you? Don't you know Miz Patterson's a widder? Ain't nothing but trouble for you there. You stay away from that white woman."

"Aint Liddie, I didn't do nothing," Scooter said, staring at the floor. "I was working on her yard yesterday, and she caught me whittling after she give me lunch." He looked around, clearly uncomfortable, squeezing his cap into a ball. "She was mad 'cause I had a knife so I had to tell'er why I had it."

Liddie stared at him. "Whut kind of knife you got, and where'd you git it? You know you ain't got sense enough to carry no knife. Something happen and the po'lice gonna be all over you."

"I found it at the dump. It was all rusted and the blade had the end broke. I cleaned all the rust off with sand and sharpened th' blade so's I could whittle with it. I even put a point on it so's I could dig out the wood when I needs a hole."

"Where is it? You give it to me right now."

Scooter had never seen her look so serious. He flopped the cap onto his head, fumbled in his box, then handed her the knife. The cover on one side was missing, and rust stains showed where it had been. There had once been two blades. Now, there was only one.

"It ain't smart fer you to have no knife like this. Who knows you got it?"

"I ain't showed it to nobody but Miz Patterson. Maybe some people seen me whittling." The cap was back in his hands. "Why? Do it be bad to have it?"

A look of compassion took over Liddie's face. "Scooter, you ain't like other people, not even other colored folk. You don't see things like they do. You don't see what kin happen to you 'cause you's simple-minded." She placed her hand under his chin and gently lifted it. "Tain't nothing to be ashamed of. It's just the way things is. I took care of you after your mama died. I tried to hep you as you growed up, but you been growed a long time now. You oughta know that a nigger with a knife and a nigger what's seen with a white woman is looking for trouble. Don't matter what you're doing. It just be trouble." She ran her hand over his short kinky hair, her fingers parting the tight curls.

"I's sorry, Aint Liddie. I didn't mean no harm. Whut you want me to do? Miz Patterson said she want to see my whittlings."

The look on Scooter's face was one of misery. His cap was in danger of being shredded.

A tear slowly ran from Liddie's eye. "Show her. Miz Deb'ra be a fine white woman. Many's a time I seen her down by the river when somebody was sick, bringin' medicine, food, even a cake—

or jist stickin' her head in the door to say howdy. Everytime she come in this store, she stop and talk to me, ask 'bout my health and how you be doing. They's some mighty-fine white folks in Dawson, and I reckon she be one of the best. If she want your whittlin's, you give'm to her." She wiped the tear away. "Just knock on her back door. Don't you go in her house, and you be on your best behavior when you's talking to her. You understand me?"

"Yas'm."

She handed him the knife. "And don't you tarry. You gives her the carvings and gits away from there. After that, you makes sure your dealings with Miz Patterson is yard work."

"'Spose she wants 'nother whittling?"

"You tell me, and we'll talk 'bout it." Liddie pulled Scooter to her large bosom. "You's the closest I ever had to a child. You may not be too bright, and you's got awful big, but you's still my little boy. You just be careful, you hear."

"Yas'm. I understand."

"Now, you go on, I got work to do. Mustah Mat'hews be here soon." She stepped away, straightening stock on the closest shelf.

Scooter didn't move.

Liddie worked for a moment before realizing he was still there. "Whut you doing? I told you to git outta here."

Scooter put his cap on, then jerked it off. "I got one more I wants to show ya."

Liddie stared at him. "Whut's wrong wid you? You's acting funny." She frowned at him a moment then her look softened. "Okay, lemme see whut other one you got."

He looked into her face as he withdrew a figurine from his pants pocket, gingerly handing it to her. "It's a new one. I worked on it most all night."

Liddie looked at the carving, a smile spreading. "Why Scooter, it's like th' dog Miz Patterson . . ." She stared at him. "You made this for her, didn't you?"

"Yas'm. Did I do wrong?" He hesitated. "She always treats me so nice and yesterday, she said she liked my whittlin', and I really like her and—"

"Stop talking now, you ain't done nothing wrong." Liddie studied the carving. "It's real nice. I think she'll like it. I know I would. You just go on and give it to her." She kissed him on the cheek before adding, "But you just 'member whut I said."

Scooter gathered his things and left the drugstore with a grin on his face. Soon he was pushing himself down the street.

Liddie watched until he turned onto Valdese Street. "I just got a feelin' in my bones they's gonna be trouble. I hope that boy don't git caught in it."

..*

Henry Flanagan ate breakfast alone in Lucille's Restaurant. He slid a pat of butter onto the top of the hot grits Lucille served with his country ham and eggs.

The tables in Lucille's were old, carried the wounds of years of use, and wobbled on the uneven floor. "I made some cinnamon buns last night if you want one," Lucille said, refilling his coffee cup.

Henry quickly swallowed. "Yeah, heat one up for me. But hold it until I finish my eggs."

"You got it, Yank." Lucille moved to the next table pouring coffee and pushing the cinnamon buns.

Henry watched her walk away. *Damn. After ten years, I'm still a Yankee*. He sopped the last of his egg with his biscuit and sat back in the chair, looking around the room until he spotted Lucille behind the counter making coffee. "I'll have that sweet roll when you have time."

"Lucille, make that two, and one coffee, and put it on his check," Flip Matthews said as he walked toward Henry's table. "Might've known I'd find you here." Flip pulled out a chair and dropped into it. "Who's watching the news ticker? Might be a big story coming in."

"Sure, and you-all might elect a Yankee mayor, too."

"That's y'all, not you-all. Ain't you ever going to learn how to talk English?" Flip chuckled.

"Not bloody likely," Henry said. "Speaking of watching, who's minding the store?"

"Aunt Liddie's there. No matter how many times I tell her to come in late, she insists on showing up at seven and opening up. I walked by. She's in there with Scooter. Looked like they were sharing family secrets."

"How's her health holding up?"

"She's strong as an ox. Everyday, I'm scared something will happen to her, but everyday she surprises the hell out of me. You know she walks to work from down by the river. That's gotta be two-three miles—uphill."

Lucille delivered the cinnamon buns. They were six inches in diameter, three inches high and oozing with sugar icing. "Here we go, one for Flip and one for the Yankee. You want another one? Let me know now, and I can pop'm in. I got the oven at just the right temperature, and that old thing gets crankier by the hour."

Henry stared at the sweet roll. "Another one? Lucille, you know I'm on a diet. One's all I'm going to eat. Can't speak for the apothecary though."

"Diet." Lucille laughed. "That belly that's catching all the crumbs don't look like no diet to me. Last time you tried to diet, I damn near went broke. Nah, Yankee, you ain't dieting. I'll heat one up. Somebody'll want it."

Henry shot her a look that she deflected with a smile. "Somebody's gotta remind you the war ain't over yet."

..*

Henry walked into the front office of the *Times*. "Hey, anybody here?"

"Eli's in the back. Ain't seen Miss Mabel yet. Eli let me in and said I could wait for you."

Henry turned toward the corner where he kept a table and chairs for people wishing to place ads or conduct other business with the paper. "You're Reverend Turner, aren't you?"

"Yas suh. I'm right pleased you know who I am." He stood with his hat held in front of him in both hands.

"Don't be, sir. I'd be a poor newspaperman if I didn't know the leading citizens of both races in Dawson."

"They musta taught you that in them Yankee schools. Sure ain't no Southerner would say it."

"Oh, I'm not so sure of that. There are many nice people around here who see the person, not the color." Henry smiled and stuck out his hand. "Now, what can I do for you?"

Reverend Turner looked at the hand, then gingerly shook it. "I 'spect you just answered my question. What I was gonna ask was do you really believe what you wrote in the paper?"

"What are you referring to?"

"That editorial in yesterday's paper."

"The one about Judge Jackson? Yes. I meant every word of it. Sometimes the law needs a kind hand, and the Judge knows how to administer it with compassion. When he runs for Superior Court, I'm going to push him as hard as I can."

"Yessuh, I agree with that, but that ain't what I mean." He pulled a copy of the *Dawson Times* from his back pocket. "I mean this part." He unfolded the paper and read, "Thank you, Judge Jackson, for reminding me that Justice is supposed to be blind, that Justice is not based on color, that Justice can be applied with a touch of humanity. And for reminding me that the Constitution says all men are created equal." He smiled. "Do you really mean that last part about being equal, that justice 'sposed to be the same for colored folks as for whites?"

"Come with me, Reverend. I think we should probably have a nice, long talk."

They walked into the office and Henry settled into his chair behind the desk. Turner stood, his hat still in his hands.

"Please have a seat, sir," the newspaperman said. "Why don't you tell me exactly why you're here? Whatever you say will not leave this office unless you give me permission to print it."

"Thank you, sir. I'm sure you heard about that S'preme Court case, the one that says all chillun oughta go to the same schools."

"Yes, I'm familiar with *Brown versus Board of Education*. Basically, it says *separate, but equal* is unconstitutional."

"That's the one I mean. What you think's gonna happen?"

Henry leaned back in his chair. "Someday, maybe sooner than we expect, that ruling will be enforced. I just hope it can be done in peace."

"Uh-huh. And when that day comes, what side you gonna be on?" Reverend Turner's discomfort was obvious, but it was tinged with a look of determination. "Is your paper gonna back the colored man? Is you gonna write things like you did yesterday?"

Henry took a deep breath as he placed his forearms on his desk, his fingers intertwined. "Reverend Turner, I hope I'll do what's right." He paused, a pained look on his face. "But one of the things

I learned in the hedgerows of Germany is that sometimes the urge to survive takes over. You hunker down, cover your head, and cower, just hoping the barrage will end soon. It may not be a pretty reaction, and you might feel like sh—uh, bad later, but it happens. What I'm trying to say, sir, is I don't know, and I won't lie to you and say I do."

There was silence in the room as the two men studied one another. Reverend Turner spoke first. "Thank you for your honesty. I just kinda hoped we'll be on the same side. I been thinking I oughta preach a sermon on all men being born equal. I was gonna invite you to attend my church and then hope you might write one of them editorials." He stood. "It gonna take me a few weeks to get the words right. If you can see your way clear, I'd love to have you at 'leven o'clock services when I do. I 'preciate you listening to me. I 'spect you's a good man."

"You write that sermon, sir. I don't normally go to church, but I might make an exception for that. But if I can be so bold, don't get too fired up. Sometimes slow and easy is the best way for things to happen."

"Suh, we been slow and easy for a hun'erd years. I don't want nobody hurt, but it's time." He walked from the office through the vestibule and left the building.

"Damn, I need a drink," Henry said and reached for the refrigerator. "It's coming, and for the South, it'll be the War Between the States all over again." He pulled out the chilled glass, dropped in a couple of ice cubes and brought it up to halfway with grapefruit juice. The other half disappeared under vodka.

"Eli," Henry yelled. "Come in here, please."

"You call me, boss?" Eli said, shuffling into the room. "Did you talk to the Rev'nd?"

"Yes, I did. What can you tell me about him?"

Eli's forehead furrowed. "He's a mighty proud man. First one in his fam'ly to ever git any education. And he kin bring down the roof with his preaching. When he start in on sin, you just knows you goin' to Hell. Yas suh, he's a mighty-fine man."

CHAPTER EIGHT

Scooter limped out of the drugstore, shoeshine box in hand, a puzzled expression on his face. He enjoyed working for Mrs. Patterson and didn't understand Aunt Liddie's demand that he be so careful. "She wouldn't never do nothin' to hurt me. She likes me, she even give me coffee from one of her purty cups," he mumbled, picking up his scooter. He hung the box over the handlebar and slowly pushed away.

As he came abreast of the Watts Theater, he crossed Main Street, dodging his way through the two lanes of traffic. He stopped in front of the VicCar Theater. "Scooter-Hey, Big Man," he called toward a large colored man. "What you doing uptown? I ain't seen you in a long time?"

"Scooter-Who? How you be?" the man answered, waiting for Scooter. "I'm just killin' time. You still shinin' shoes?"

"Not yet, ain't nobody much aroun'. It'll pick up later, though."

Big Man's real name was Jeremiah Q Lincoln. The Q didn't stand for anything. His daddy bragged that the letter Q made his boy sound like a smart man.

Big Man gave Scooter a sympathetic look. "Well, while you're waiting, you kin give me a shine."

"What you mean? You ain't got no money for a shine, but I'll give you one on credit." Scooter put his box down and knelt in front of Big Man.

"Money? How 'bout this?" He pulled a roll of bills from his pocket and shoved it in Scooter's face. "What you think I do all the time? I'm making money, boy." He put his right foot on Scooter's box.

"Yeah, what you doin' fer it?"

"I damn sure ain't workin' my ass off in no fields. I ain't never gonna do that shit agin. Just look." He held his hands out to Scooter, palms down. "You don't see no dirt under my fingernails. Nope, them days is over fer me."

Scooter stopped spreading polish and looked at Big Man, confusion evident on his face. "How'd you git all that money then? How much you got there?"

Big Man looked around then leaned close to Scooter. "Runnin' bootleg. I run a load to Raleigh. Didn't have no trouble at all," he whispered.

"How you do that? You ain't got no car." Scooter returned to his rhythmic shining routine.

"Sure I do. That be it right there." Big Man pointed toward a 1949 Ford sedan parked nearby. "That's mine." He scanned the area. "It's got a special place in the back. I kin carry fifty gallons a shine, and it don't hardly sag a'tall."

Scooter stood and limped around the car, touching the doors, trunk lid, and hood. "That's purty. Where'd you git it?"

"I bought it from a white man in Bethel. Said he won't gonna run no more shine. Offered to sell it."

Scooter continued scrutinizing the vehicle. "Yeah, but where'd you git so much money. That must a cost a lot."

"Course it did," Big Man said. "You don't git no car like that without spending money. I don't worry 'bout money though. I got all I want, and they's plenty more where that come from."

Scooter stared at the car, then at Big Man, and returned to his task of shining his shoes.

When Big Man was young, everybody called him Jeremiah, but by the time he was twelve, he'd sprouted and was the biggest boy in school. Not only was he taller, but he outweighed everybody, and that included most of the teachers. Someone hung the name Big Man on him and it stuck. Today, it fit his six-foot-five, three hundred-pound body, and he reveled in it. He wouldn't answer if someone called him anything else.

Big Man quit school when he was thirteen, which was as well because he was only in the fifth grade. He spent the next fifteen years growing up and working at whatever jobs he could find. During the summers, he spent most of his time in tobacco fields—

planting, weeding, suckering, and breaking.

As his shoeshine rag snapped out its rhythm, Scooter stared at the car, feeling outmatched by Big Man. Finished, he stood. "I got a knife."

"Yeah. Whut kind?"

Scooter dug in his box and brought out the rag he used for wrapping. "Here it is."

Big Man took it and opened the blade. "You call this a knife. It ain't nothin', but an ol' broke—" He swiped his finger over the blade and drew blood. "Damn, that's sharp," he said as he sucked on his finger. "Almost as sharp as mine." He handed it to Scooter then reached into his pocket. "You look at this one."

He shielded his hand with his body and motioned Scooter to move in closer. Scooter stepped forward then jerked back.

Big Man laughed. "Now, that's a knife. I done kilt two men with that."

Scooter stared at the five-inch switchblade.

Big Man folded the blade, then pushed the button and the blade leapt out. Laughing, he refolded it. "Don't tell nobody I got it. The police might git too nosy. I'd have to hurt somebody."

"You didn't really kill nobody, did you?"

"Better not say no more." Big Man was quiet for a moment. "Say Scooter, I got an idea. Why don't you make a run with me? It gits kinda lonely driving up to Raleigh. I usually leave right after sundown. Once we drop the load, I knows a cupla women what likes a good time." Big Man stared at Scooter, a smile playing at the edges of his thick lips.

Scooter ducked his head. "I don't know 'bout that. You knows how Aint Liddie is. She be mad if she knowed I was talking to you."

"Liddie." Big Man spat on the sidewalk. "When you gone quit lettin' that old woman push you around? She ain't even your mama." He glared at the drugstore. "Shit, she's just an ol' uppity bitch what's black on the outside and white on the inside. She thinks she's hot shit 'cause she works for ol' man Mat'hews."

Scooter bristled. "Don't you be talkin' that way. She's my friend. She takes care of me." He paused, his mouth working with no words coming out. Then, he said, "She's important. She has a key to the drugstore. Bet you ain't never knowed no colored what's got a key like that."

"She do?" Big Man looked at the storefront. "I be damned. I'd a never guessed it. Anyway, you want to make some money, you come see me Sundy. Here's a dollar for the shine."

..*

Scooter watched Big Man drive away. "That's a nice car, but I likes my scooter better," he muttered, rubbing the handlebar. "You takes me everywhere I needs to be and don't use no gas."

The scarred scooter looked like it belonged in a garbage dump, which is where he found it ten years before. At that time, the foot platform was bent, and it had no rear wheel. Scooter straightened and reinforced the platform with wood, then searched the dump several times before finding a child's wagon with three usable wheels, adapting one to fit the rear. Eventually, the other two wheels were recycled as replacements. A discarded can of paint allowed him to paint it bright red. To others, it might look like junk, but to Scooter, it was the most beautiful vehicle in town.

He pushed his way to Church Street and made a circuit without seeing Mrs. Patterson. At the corner of Church and Smithwick, he looked toward Main Street and squinted at the clock on the tower above the town hall. "Only eight o'clock. Too early to knock on her door."

After propelling his way back to Mrs. Patterson's house, he stopped, removed his shoeshine box, placed it on the sidewalk, then sat on the curb. He noticed the shoelace on his left tennis shoe was untied.

"Gonna need some new shoes afore next winter," he whispered, then looked around, afraid he'd disturb someone. "It'll soon be time to go barefoot, but I better start checkin' the dump. Might take me awhile to git lucky agin. Most folks don't throw out they's old stuff 'til fall shoppin'. These shoes 'bout finished. They's got tears in them I can't fix and the soles near worn through. Wisht I could git some leather ones."

When he pulled on the lace, it broke. "Doggone't. I done got two knots in it." After adding a third knot, he retied the shoe.

Scooter's clothing was clean, but showed the ravages of wear and age. The denim of his dungarees had faded to a motley off-white, and red patches dominated both knees. The right rear pocket was torn at the bottom, but showed Scooter's attempts to repair it. The long-sleeve plaid shirt he wore matched the pants in cleanliness, but was in somewhat better condition. His belt was a piece of clothesline from the dump. He wore his old cotton jacket with ragged elbows and frayed cuffs. He pulled off his tattered Brooklyn Dodgers cap, re-shaped the bill, and ran his fingers over the logo before replacing it. "Sho' would like to see them Dodgers play. Mustah Flanagan says they's the best." He straightened his legs and smoothed a wrinkle that ran across his thigh.

When the fabric shifted, a tear along the seam on the side became visible. He turned and sifted through the items in his shoeshine box until he found a pipe-tobacco tin, lifted the top and shook out a large needle threaded with red yarn. "May as well fix this ol' tear while I's waitin'."

While stitching his dungarees, he studied the houses along the street. "Betcha these rich white folks don't have to sew they's own pants." The houses were two and three stories high, sitting on wide lots giving them large front and side yards. Some had wrap-around porches, some had porches across the front and one had a covered entranceway. From experience, Scooter knew that each had a screened-in back porch. All were of clapboard construction and painted white.

Although they were similar, they wore the distinct personalities of their occupants. Dogwood trees, a favorite in eastern North Carolina, grew in front of several. Others had pines, and there was an occasional oak tree. The house across from Mrs. Patterson had a huge weeping willow tree.

Scooter looked at the roof of Mrs. Patterson's house. "Don't know why nobody'd want a platform on top they's house." He referred to the widow's walk that Mr. Patterson added. Scooter had heard some of the old colored women whispering that Mrs. Patterson used to lay up there naked.

He continued stitching the tear in his pants while comparing the houses to the small shacks down by the river. "Wonder whut these folks do's with all them rooms. I gits along fine with my one room and my wood stove. Ain't nobody I know got nothin' as big as these, and we gits along fine. 'Course them ol' shacks'd look better if they was painted."

A voice interrupted his thoughts. "Scooter, why are you sitting out there?"

CHAPTER NINE

Standing, Scooter saw Mrs. Patterson in her front door. "Scooter-Hey, ma'am." A big smile split his face as he hid the needle by his thigh.

"Scooter-yourself. Come on 'round back. I have some coffee brewing. I'll bring you a cup."

"But, ma'am—" he said as she disappeared into the house. After tying the thread, he snapped it. "Aint Liddie say'd for me to stay away from her, but what kin I do? I hafta give her these whitlin's." He stared at her closed front door then looked at his feet. "I ain't sure whut to do."

"Scooter, where are you?" Mrs. Patterson's voice came from the rear of her house. "I have your coffee. Come on and get it."

He put his sewing tin in the shoeshine box, checking that the figurines were still there. Pulling off his cap, he scratched his head then replaced the cap, picked up the scooter and pushed his way to the rear of the house. "Reckin I better do whut she says. Ain't Liddie'll yell somethin' fierce if I don't do what a white woman says."

Mrs. Patterson stood on the screened-in porch, wearing a blue terry cloth bathrobe and fuzzy blue house slippers. Rollers filled her hair.

Scooter glanced at her, then looked down, embarrassed at her attire, knowing he wasn't supposed to see a white woman dressed like that.

"Here's a cup of coffee to get you started." She handed him the chipped mug he'd drunk from before.

He kept his eyes averted as he accepted it. "Thank you, ma'am." He rapidly backed down the rear steps, careful not to look at Mrs.

Patterson.

"Have a seat and work on your carvings or something. I'll bring you an egg sandwich in a few minutes."

"No, ma'am, I can't—"

Mrs. Patterson walked away from him.

He shuffled his feet, looked around and took a sip of the coffee. "Aint Liddie ain't gonna like this."

Moving toward the oak tree, he mumbled to himself. "Soons she come back out, I'll give her them whitlin's and leave." He leaned his scooter against the tree trunk and removed his shoeshine box from the handlebar. After setting the box and the coffee cup on the ground, he took out the rag holding the figurines and unrolled it. "Aint Liddie said I couldn't take no money. She didn't say nothin' 'bout coffee and a egg samwich." He sipped from the cup. "Oh, dis be some good coffee. Besides, I'm hongry."

He sat the carvings on the ground and carefully laid out the cloth, smoothed out the wrinkles, then placed the animals on the fabric, fingering each as he stood it on its legs. The cocker spaniel remained in its separate wrapping. After satisfying himself that things were exactly as he wanted, he sat with his back against the tree sipping the coffee. "Maybe this be alright. I'll have a samwich then give her the whitlin's and git outta here."

While he drank his coffee, his eyes were drawn to the garden. "Betcha it ain't been turned yet. Maybe if I shovel it, I kin earn that egg samwich. Aint Liddie'd like it a whole lot better if I work for it. That way, I bet she wouldn't be so upset."

He rose, walked to the garden and entered through the sagging wood-frame gate. "Yep, I was right." He sat his cup on the ground near the gate, insuring that it wouldn't tip. He walked to the shed, took out a shovel, then returned to the garden. With practiced efficiency, he began digging and rolling the dirt. Earthworms wiggled in the moist soil. His muscled arms and back barely flexed with the effort. He threw himself into it, immersed in the job.

"Scooter, where are you?" a voice from the direction of the house called. "Oh, there you are. What are you doing in my garden?"

"Just turnin' the ground. You don't mind, do's you?"

"Mind? No, I don't mind at all. But I have your sandwich. Come over here and eat your breakfast, and bring your cup so I can refill it."

Scooter walked to the picnic table where she waited for him. "I was just tryin' to make up fer you givin' me coffee and a samwich."

"Thank you, Scooter, but that wasn't necessary. Now, you just sit here and eat. Hope you like bacon. I put some slices in the sandwiches."

"Yas'm, I loves bac'n." Scooter saw three wrapped sandwiches on a plate. "You take yours first, then I'll take the one what's left."

Debbie chuckled. "Mine's in the kitchen, and I gotta get back to it before it gets cold. These are yours. I'll leave the coffee pot here." She headed toward the back porch.

"Ma'am, I can't eat three samwiches. That'd be wasteful."

"Eat what you want. We'll give the rest to the birds." She walked into the house.

Scooter looked after her then picked up a sandwich, unwrapped it and took a big bite. "Ooh, dat's good. White folks sure use a lot of bacon." Two bites later, the first sandwich was finished and a few minutes later, all three had disappeared. He sat back, licking his fingers. Lifting his cup, he drained it.

..*

Debbie watched through her back window as Scooter devoured the sandwiches, smiling at his obvious enjoyment. When he finished his coffee, she sat hers on the counter and walked into the backyard. "Now, Scooter, I believe we have some business to transact. Did you bring the carvings."

"Yas'm, I got'm right here." He walked to the tree and picked up the cloth holding the five figures. "Here they are." He passed them to her.

Mrs. Patterson looked at each of the figurines, turning it and examining with a critical eye. "They're perfect. I just love them. I want three—a dog, the horse, and the sheep. I'll give you fifty cents, no, a dollar apiece."

"A dollar? No'm, I can't do that. Aint Liddie'd skin me alive." Scooter stood with his cap in his hand as Mrs. Patterson continued to admire his carvings.

"Okay, how about I give you three dollars for all three."

"I don't know, ma'am. Aint Liddie said I should give you

whichever ones you like. I best do it that way or she'll git mad."

"So, you want to give me these three? Is that right?"

"Yas'm."

She stared at Scooter, wrinkles furrowing her forehead.

Scooter squirmed under her scrutiny, the baseball cap turning round and round in his hands.

Her face brightened. "Suppose I hire you to prepare my garden. Would that be all right?"

Scooter frowned and scratched his head, then worried the baseball cap like a rosary. Finally, he said, "Yas'm, that sounds good. I 'spose I could do that."

"Good. Here's what we'll do. If you do a real good job, I'll give you five dollars to work in my garden."

"Ma'am, that's too—"

She held up her hand like a traffic cop. "Scooter, you just hush. Didn't your Aunt Liddie teach you not to argue with a white woman? I said I'll give you five dollars, but you better do a good job. That soil had better be so fine, it dribbles through my fingers." Mrs. Patterson smiled. "And you give me these three carvings. Deal?"

"Yas'm," Scooter said as he hung his head, a chastened look on his face.

"Good. I'll be gone most of the day, but I'll fix you a couple of sandwiches for lunch before I leave. I'll be back early enough to fix a light supper before you go home. If you finish before I return, just whittle or something until I get here. I'll have your money then, and I'll pick up my carvings."

"Lunch? Supper? No, ma'am—"

"There you go—arguing with a white woman again. Am I going to have to talk to Aunt Liddie?"

"No'm, I be quiet."

..*

Scooter spent the rest of that Wednesday working in the garden. By four o'clock, he'd turned the soil, removing weeds and the roots of last year's crop as he went. Then he raked it down, and chopped out the dirt clods. He knelt and lifted up a double handful of the soil. When he opened his fingers, it sifted through. He smiled. "Reckin that ought to be fine enough for Miz Patterson."

He walked to the backyard faucet and rinsed his hands, neck, face and head. Sweat saturated his shirt and cap. He'd removed his jacket hours before.

Mrs. Patterson appeared at the back door and called, "Scooter, as soon as you get cleaned up, I have a pitcher of fresh-squeezed lemonade and some ham sandwiches. Bet you worked up an appetite." She walked to the picnic table and placed everything down. "Go ahead and dig in. I've got something to do inside."

Scooter poured a glass of lemonade into the old glass she left. "Oooh, that sure tastes good," he said after draining half the glass. "An', it's so nice and sweet. Miz Patterson use a lot more sugar than Aint Liddie." He finished the glass and poured another before picking up a sandwich.

Glancing toward the house, he peeked between the slices of bread. "Country ham. That's gonna be good." He took a big bite and chewed. "Ain't had no ham this good in a long time," he mumbled through the mouthful of food.

In a few minutes, he'd cleared the platter of sandwiches, emptied the pitcher, and retreated to the oak tree. With a contented sigh, he sat, leaned against the trunk, and took out his knife and a fresh stick. He began a fresh carving, a 1949 Ford sedan.

..*

Mrs. Patterson looked through the kitchen window and smiled. "That man works harder than anybody I know. Glad I picked up that package. I'll give him a few minutes to relax before I go out there. He gets so flustered when I talk to him." She returned to washing dishes.

When she checked again, Scooter appeared to be asleep. His back was against the trunk of the oak tree, and his head lolled toward one shoulder.

"Is that the picture of innocence? He's a man who gives his best to whatever job he's doing. I hear the men at church rave about the way he shines shoes. There ought to be a way to help someone like Scooter."

Returning to her chores, she was deep in thought. "I'll ask Pastor Green if he knows anyone that can help. If someone doesn't take an interest, he'll get old and die without ever really living. It's just not fair that we don't show more interest in the colored folks that live around us. Where'd we be without them?" She looked out the window again and saw that Scooter still slept. "Maybe the Pastor knows somebody that will give him a steady job, something that will put money in his pocket on a regular basis."

She dropped the dish she'd been washing, splashing her apron. "Why do I need the Preacher? I'll just do it myself. I bet everybody on this street could use a steady yardman."

CHAPTER TEN

Mrs. Patterson stood under the oak tree, smiling at Scooter. His soft snores blended into the sounds of early evening in North Carolina. "He's worn out. He works so hard and asks so little in return."

She reached to shake him, but stopped before her hand touched his shoulder. "Musn't do that. He'd absolutely panic." She retreated to the porch, opened the door, and slammed it with a bang.

"Okay, Scooter. Time to collect your pay," she called.

Scooter's new carving lay in his lap while his knife rested on the ground beside him. The hood of the Ford had begun to take shape under the sharp edge of his blade.

"Huh?" Scooter jumped, the carving flying from his lap. "I'm sorry. I didn't mean to fall asleep." He grabbed at his cap, and brushed at the shavings clinging to his pants at the same time, accomplishing neither. The cap dropped to the ground and he stooped for it, his foot barely missing his knife.

Mrs. Patterson turned away, a smile on her face, then picked up his knife and the stick. "A new one. What is this, some kind of car?" she asked, examining the piece of wood.

"Yas'm. I, I never done no car afore. Big Man got hisself one and I thought I'd try to carve it." The words were a nervous stutter and his cap took a severe mauling in one hand.

"I'm sure you'll do a good job on it just like you did on my garden." Mrs. Patterson handed him the stick. She closed the blade on the knife then gave it to him. "Better be careful. Suppose you'd stepped on this? It would cut right through the soles of your shoes." She walked toward the back porch. "I need a glass of water. I'll be right back." *I'll give him a chance to settle down.*

She walked into the house and looked through the kitchen window. Scooter stared in the direction she had moved. He appeared to relax, then brushed the shavings and sand from his pants. She saw him pick up the chips from his carvings and stuff them in his pocket. After he had policed the area, he sat beside the tree facing the house.

Satisfied he had calmed, she rummaged in her purse, left the house again, and walked into the garden. "Scooter, come here, please."

He jumped to his feet and ran to where she stood.

"You did a fine job on the garden. I don't think I've ever seen a plot so ready for planting. I'll expect you to come back and lay in the rows. Now, here's your money." She held out a five-dollar bill.

Scooter stared at the money. "Ma'am, that's too much. I can't take it. I don't even get that much for breakin' 'bacca all day." He squirmed, digging his shoes into the sandy soil. "Ain't never made no five dollars in one day in my whole life. Aint Liddie—"

"You did today. We made a deal this morning, and you did a fine job. Now take this money, and if Aunt Liddie gives you a problem, I'll talk to her."

"No'm. Please don't do that."

"Take it or I'll go straight to the drugstore right now."

Scooter reached, took the bills and shoved them into his pocket. "Thank you, ma'am." He turned to the tree, his head hanging, and reached for his box.

"Excuse me. Don't you have something for me?"

He spun toward her. "Oh, I's sorry. I forgot." From his box he took the three carvings and handed them to her. "I wasn't trying, I mean, I didn't mean to—"

"I know." She examined the figurines. "These are so good. I'm going to show them to my ladies' group. They'll love them. I'll sell all you can carve. Talk to Aunt Liddie and come up with a price. I need to know how much to charge.

"Now, we have some other business to discuss," she continued. "I was looking through some of my husband's stuff in the basement this morning and found these. I think he would have liked you to have them." She handed him a shopping bag.

Scooter looked inside and grinned. "Ma'am, they's new

dungarees," he said as he pulled them from the bag. "Look, they's dark blue and look how stiff they is. I ain't never had no new ones."

"Well, it's about time you did. Now, look in the bag again."

He did and his grin grew. "A shirt," he exclaimed, taking a plaid one from the bag. "And, it's new, too. It's got long sleeves and everythin'."

His grin died. "Ma'am, I can't take these-here things. I ain't done nothin' to earn'm."

"Scooter, you can be the most exasperating person I've ever dealt with," she said, her voice rising, fists planted firmly on her hips. "I told you these were my husband's, and I don't have any use for them. I want you to have them, and don't you argue with me anymore. I just won't allow it." She stamped her foot.

"Yas'm." Scooter's head dropped. "I take'm." He hesitated before adding, "But I see's the price tags on them."

"Enough about that. Now, we have something else to talk about." She arranged her face in what she hoped was a business look. "I need someone to help around this place. A man to do yard and garden work. I'll pay you three dollars a day. Are you free on Wednesdays?"

Scooter looked at her. "You mean you wants me to work for you ev'ry Wensdy?"

"That's exactly what I mean. And I'll throw in lunch."

"Three dollars?"

"Yes, three dollars. That's as high as I'll go, so don't try to bargain with me." A smile slipped through before Mrs. Patterson assumed her stern look again.

"No'm, I don't 'spect no more. It just—"

"Good. I'll see you next Wednesday, seven o'clock, bright and early. Don't be late. I'll make a list of all the work. Now, you'd better head for the river before it gets dark." She turned and moved toward the house, a wide grin on her face.

Mrs. Patterson took five steps before Scooter remembered and called her. "Ma'am, uh, I got one mo'." It came out in a nervous squeak.

She turned toward him. "One more what?"

"Another whitlin' I wants to show you."

"Why didn't you show it to me earlier? I've already picked my three."

"I don't mean for them three. I made this one extry."

She gave him a quizzical look. "Show me."

Scooter handed her the carving of the cocker spaniel.

She stared at it. Tears formed and drained from her eyes. It was a likeness of her dog. He had been a present from her husband when they were first married. The dog died after bringing her fifteen years of companionship. She swiped at her cheeks with the back of her hand.

Scooter stared. "Ma'am, I'm sorry. I didn't mean . . ."

Mrs. Patterson looked at him, wiping away another set of tears. She smiled. "This is the nicest thing anyone ever gave me. Thank you, Scooter. It looks exactly like Mr. Lee."

Scooter squirmed in fear, but said, "Muster Lee?"

"Oh, you didn't know my dog was named Robert E. Lee, did you? You probably only heard him called Bob. I'm going to put this in a special place on the mantle where everyone will see it. Thank you, Scooter. I shall cherish it forever." She walked to the back door, composed herself, then turned back. "I'll still see you next Wednesday." She entered the house.

Scooter stood. "I made her cry. I'm in big trouble. But she was happy . . . but she cried . . . I don't know, but this can't be good. I knows coloreds what make white womens cry goes to jail."

CHAPTER ELEVEN

The sun shone through a cracked window, waking Scooter at seven. He rolled off the thin mattress on the Army surplus cot, stood, stretched, and rubbed his back. Looking at the bed, he mumbled, "That ol' leg's wobbly agin. Every time I move, it feels like it wants to fall off. I needs a coupla blocks to set it on."

The frame was the result of a scavenging trip to the town dump. The mattress came from a neighbor. Scooter was its fourth owner.

He pulled a pair of dungarees over his ragged boxer shorts, walked outside and pumped a bucket of water from the hand pump on the edge of his neighbor's yard, then splashed his face. "Oooh, that water's cold. How kin it be so cold when the air be warm? Don't make no sense."

After returning to his shack, Scooter washed his face, neck, hands, and arms. He'd taken his Saturday-night bath the night before so he felt confident he could face the world clean. Dressing in the dungarees and shirt Mrs. Patterson gave him made him feel good. The pants were large, but he cinched them around his waist with a piece of rope. Turning the legs up two cuffs to fit his five foot six inch frame solved the length problem.

He pulled on his worn sneakers and settled the Brooklyn Dodgers baseball cap on his head, staring into a cracked mirror. "When Aint Liddie see me, she goin' be some surprised." He looked at his feet. "Wisht I had some better shoes though. Course if I works for Miz Patterson ev'ry week and saves my money, I'll have enough to buy some leather ones. That'd be nice. Ain't never had no new store-bought shoes afore."

He limped to the wood heater and opened the cast iron door. "Cold. Ain't a warm ash in there. Maybe Aint Liddie's got some coffee."

After a last look at himself in the mirror, Scooter grabbed his worn jacket and headed for Liddie's. He didn't bother to lock the door for two reasons. First, there was no lock and second, there was nothing worth stealing. He pushed his scooter down the dirt street, limping along beside it. His "Scooter-Hey" echoed as he spoke to everyone he saw.

At Liddie's house, he knocked on the front door before pushing it open and calling, "Aint Liddie. You up yet?"

"Course I'm up. Whut you think, I sleep all th' time? You ready to go?"

"Yas'm, but—"

"Where'd you get them clothes?" Liddie asked as he entered the kitchen where she sat eating breakfast.

"Ain't they somethin'? First time I ever had brand-new ones. How's I look?"

She stared at him, a smile shaping her mouth. "You looks good, honey. You looks just fine. Now, where'd you git them clothes?"

"Mz Patterson give them to me. She said—"

"Didn't I tell you not to take nothin' from that woman? Didn't I tell you to work for ev'rythin' she give you? Did you work for them?"

"Well, kinda. I worked in her garden yesterday. I turned the ground and got all the weeds out. Took me all day. It needed a lotta work."

"And she give you th' clothes cause you did that? Did she pay you, too?"

"Yas'm, she paid me fer th' work." Scooter's cap was in his hands, being turned and twisted.

Liddie scowled at him, then relented. "That's good. Now git yourself some breakfast. I wants to git a early start on Church. We gotta walk. Joshua's in jail."

"Yas'm, I want to talk 'bout that."

"Talk whiles you eat."

Scooter walked to the wood stove and spooned scrambled eggs into a tin plate, then picked up a homemade biscuit. He was relieved she hadn't asked more about yesterday, but his toughest argument lay in front of him. He sat at the table and spooned eggs into his mouth. "Do you reckin it'd be all right if I didn't go to church today."

Liddie's head snapped up. "Whut? Not go to church? Course you're goin' to church. We always goes to church."

"But," Scooter said. "It's only one Sundy. Pastor Turner won't mind if I miss one day."

"Ain't important what he minds or don't mind." She stood over him as he sipped his coffee. "Today's Sunday and fer as long as I remember, we been goin' to church on Lord's Day. An', we ain't gonna change nothin' today."

"But Aint Liddie—"

"But, nothin'. You goin' to church and that's that. Whut's so impo'tent that you wanna miss church?"

"I just got somebody I needs to talk to. I thought—"

"Hmph. If they's anybody you ought to be with, they goin' be in church, so you kin wait 'til this afternoon. Don't they go to church? Who is it?"

"Big Man. I needs to talk to—"

"You oughtn't spend time with that'un." Liddie sat beside Scooter. "I hears he's 'bout to get in trouble." She laid her hand on his. "He ain't our kind of colored. Why you need to talk to him?"

Scooter concentrated on his coffee cup. "It's jist somethin' tween us. I . . ."

A frown creased Liddie's forehead. "You's old enough to do whut you wants. You's at least twunty-five, maybe even thurty. But I wishes you'd wait 'til after church."

She flipped open her King James Version of the Bible and read,

And on the seventh day God ended his work which he had made; and he rested on the seventh day from all his work which he had made. And God blessed the seventh day, and sanctified it; because that in it he had rested from all his work which God created and made.

She closed the Bible. "That's whut it say in the Good Book, but if whut you got to do is more important than that, you go right on and find Mr. Jeremiah Q Lincoln."

..*

In Judge Jackson's three-story, antebellum home on Smithwick Street, the morning began differently. He awoke to the jangle of the alarm clock at seven, rolled from between crisp sheets, patted his wife on the fanny to wake her, and walked into the shower. When he finished and returned to the bedroom in a satin robe, a fresh cup of coffee sat steaming on his dressing table.

"Good morning, dear," he said to his wife, Jane, who was sitting at her dressing table brushing her hair. "Better get a move on if you want breakfast before we leave. I'd like to be at church by nine-thirty so I can look over the scripture before the class arrives. What should I tell Mrs. Luther to make for you?"

"I've already told her I'll be having a late breakfast. Remember, I told you Mrs. Fairchild is taking my class today. I'm going to have a long, hot bath, a leisurely breakfast and as much time as I want to dress. I'll meet you at church. You take the DeSoto. The Caddy's mine today."

"Now, I remember. You never did tell me how you trapped Mrs. Fairchild. You really should. I might want a Sunday morning off some day."

She chuckled. "I doubt it. You're such a goody two-shoes, the only reason you'd skip teaching Sunday School would be to attend services at some colored church." Her expression turned serious. "Anything new on this mess of letting them into white schools."

Judge Jackson sighed. "No, nothing in this area yet. I expect it'll take a few years before it filters down to where we'll be involved. So far, it's like the Supreme Court never made a ruling."

"Well, I hope the problems don't start until you're retired. It's stupid, and it's going to get people killed—coloreds and white people. Maybe we ought to think about moving up north."

"Up north?" Judge Jackson said with a grin. "Yeah, that'll work. Getting you out of Dawson would be harder than stopping Sherman's March to the Sea."

She sat on the edge of the bed. "Well, we need to do something. I don't want to see you going against white folks." She stared at him. "And I know you would. You and your precious love for the law. Sometimes I think you'd put me in jail just to prove you treat everybody the same."

The Judge laughed. "Better not test me." In a dour tone, he added, "Yes, I fear there will be trouble. I don't know what I'll have to do. But you remember I took an oath to uphold the law.

Somehow, I'll do it. If I can't live up to my word, I'll resign and grow tobacco."

"Tobacco? You?" Jane flopped backward across the bed, laughing. "Have you looked at your roses recently? You'd die broke."

The Judge continued dressing. "Okay, so I'll never make a farmer. How about a fisherman?"

Her laughter grew louder. "Fisherman? You, a fisherman? Was that the famous Beauregard Bass we had for dinner last night? Tasted a lot like pork."

That brought a peal of merriment from the Judge as he sat beside his wife. He pulled her to a sitting position, turned her head toward his, and kissed her lightly on the lips. "Mrs. Jackson, I love you, and I promise I'll find some way to take care of you. Of course, it helps that your daddy left you that tobacco money."

They laughed together as she hit him with a pillow.

..*

Flip Matthews' morning had its own auspicious start when Little Flip, actually the fourth Frederick Albert Matthews, bounded into the bedroom and dived across the bed. "Hey Dad, time to get up. It's almost eight o'clock and Sunday School starts at nine-thirty." Without taking a breath, he continued, "Mom, can we have pancakes for breakfast. There's syrup in the cabinet."

Lorrie Matthews looked at her eight-year-old son through sleepy eyes then turned her head toward her husband. "He's your son. You take care of him. I'm going back to sleep."

"Oh no, you don't," Flip said, pushing the covers back. "You're going to bounce out of bed and fix the men of the house a hearty breakfast. Pancakes and bacon sounds just right."

"Yeah Mom, pancakes and bacon," Little Flip echoed. "That sounds just right for the men of the house."

Lorrie rolled her eyes, but climbed out of bed. "Okay, but that means I don't have to go to Sunday School. Once I get you bums out of here, I can enjoy my morning."

Little Flip ran from the room as his dad said, "You drive a hard bargain, woman, but I guess the Baptist Church can make it one Sunday without you. You fix breakfast while I get cleaned up, then we'll rendezvous in the third pew at five before eleven. But don't be late. You know Pastor Green'll be looking for you."

..*

Debbie Patterson rolled over and squinted as a sunbeam found its way through the leaves of the oak tree outside her bedroom window and landed in her eyes. She scooted away from it and stretched, then patted the bed on both sides of her. "Tom, it's mornings like this I miss you the most. Why'd you have to die? It seems so stupid to die after the war was over. Why'd you step on that mine?" A solitary tear sneaked across her cheek.

She wiggled onto her side. "Tom, I've been thinking. Would you mind if I dated another man? I know I said I wouldn't, but . . ." She adjusted the pillow as she turned onto her back. "It's not like I have anybody in mind, but there must be a few single men around. Not for *that*. I mean, I've learned to live without it. Even though I do have wonderful memories of us. I get so lonely."

As she dressed for church the thought kept replaying itself. *I've been loyal for ten years. Do I have to give up my life because Tom stepped on a mine in France?*

She stared into the mirror, hung her head and said, "Tom, give me a sign. If you don't want me to share my life with another man, let me know. But if you don't mind, well . . . well . . . Find some way to tell me."

..*

Henry Flanagan's day began the same as any other Sunday. His eyes fluttered open and a bolt of pain punched from behind his eyeballs, causing him to sit straight up in bed. However, before reaching an upright position, he grabbed his head and lowered himself back to the pillow. "Oh God, that hurts." He took a deep breath hoping the oxygen would stifle some of the ache. It seemed to enhance it.

He swung his legs over the side of the bed and eased himself to a sitting position. Placing one hand on the bed for support while the other continued to hold his head, he stood. *Dammit, this is the last time, the very last time.* He took a step. *Ooh, it even hurts to walk.*

He fumbled his way into the bathroom, took four aspirin and a twenty-minute hot shower. *Only thing that's going to help this head is a little hair of the dog.* His stomach rumbled. *But first, I need something to eat.* His stomach lurched.

In the kitchen, he measured two cups of water into a saucepan and set it on the stove. After turning on the gas burner under the pot, he took out oatmeal, measured a cup and put it on the counter. While waiting for the water to boil, he assembled the makings for his recipe for a Bloody Mary—tomato juice, Worcestershire Sauce, Tabasco, A-1 Steak Sauce, lemon juice, salt, pepper, celery salt and a fresh bottle of vodka. He created the mix, then, as the last ingredient, cut it by half with vodka.

He took a sip and smiled for the first time that day. The water boiled so he stirred the oatmeal into it. After taking another sip of his drink, he placed two slices of bread into the toaster, put the butter on the counter, and sipped again while stirring the oatmeal.

Ten minutes later, he was at the table with the buttered toast, oatmeal with milk and sugar, and his second Bloody Mary. He ate little, but finished the drink. His headache had retreated to a dull throb, and he felt a pleasant buzz from the alcohol. "Nothing like a Bloody Mary to start the day," he said, his smile growing.

He stood at the kitchen counter mixing his third drink when he heard the voice.

Hank, what the hell're you doing?

Henry spun, looking around the room. "Who, who said that?"

Who do you think? You once told me nobody else ever called you Hank. Don't tell me you've forgotten.

"Hank? Nobody but Bobby Joe used that name. How'd you know? Who the hell are you?"

You can bet your sweet ass I ain't your conscience. You pickled that sucker a long time ago. But I didn't drag you all over Europe so you could screw things up when you thought I was gone.

"Bobby Joe? Is that you?" Henry turned all the way around searching the kitchen with his eyes. "Where are you? I can't see you."

Shit, Hank. Sometimes I wonder why I even try. I'm right here—here, in your head. What, you forgot what happened when we hit that pill box? That sonnavabitching Kraut wasted my ass. When that machine gun zeroed in, it was like a thousand baseball bats slamming into me. Damn shame that flamethrower wasn't a few seconds faster. Best part of that whole day was I watched that damn German fry.

Henry settled into a chair, his eyes wild, and his head swiveling, searching the room. "No, Bobby Joe. You're dead. I held you in my arms when you died. You were almost cut in half. I cried when the medic made me turn you loose."

Good. Now we're getting somewhere, Hank. Do you remember why I called you Hank?

"Yeah, my initials, HF. You said they were the same as Henry Fonda's, and his friends called him Hank."

Correct, my friend. Now, are you convinced who I am?

Henry continued to look around his kitchen. His eyes had lost some of the wild look. "You're a ghost?"

Ghost? Such a cold word. I don't like it. Let's just say I'm filling in for your conscience until it gets out of alcohol rehab.

Henry reached for his Bloody Mary.

Don't touch that glass. Why the hell do you think I'm here? You're digging yourself an early grave. Just look at you. You're forty pounds overweight. You don't exercise, eat right, or listen to your doctor. And booze, shit, you drank a fifth of scotch last night. And that was after sneaking vodka all day.

"You know about the vodka?"

Hell, everybody knows. You think you fool people with that grapefruit juice?

Henry held his head in his hands. "Why hasn't anyone said something?"

You dumb sonnavabitch. You're living in the South. If they like you, people will help, will cover for you. You might be a Yankee, but folks around here got a lot of respect for you. You put in ten good years. Don't ruin it with booze.

Henry reached his hands out, feeling the air. "I wish you were here, Bobby Joe. I need a friend, somebody I can depend on. What should I do?"

I am here. I never left you. I brought you home from Germany, didn't I? I found a newspaper you could afford to buy. I'm with you every day. I kept hoping you'd straighten out without me having to jump in.

You wanna know what to do. First, pour that drink down the sink, then do the same with all the booze in this place. Finish your breakfast. Take another shower. Get dressed in something that looks presentable. You're goin' to church.

"Church? I can't do that. I, ah, I don't have anything good enough to wear."

Are you arguing with me or making excuses?

"Excuses? Maybe so. Which . . . which church?"

Shit, I don't care. No wait, the Memorial Baptist Church. That's where Flip and Judge Jackson go. And, in case you've been too drunk to figure it out, you do have friends. If you'd get down off that damn Yankee horse, you'd find out fast enough that you have a lot of friends, and two of the best are Flip Matthews and Judge Daniel Jackson.

CHAPTER TWELVE

Henry rummaged through his closet looking for something suitable. Nothing he found met the definition of Sunday Best, the standard of a churchgoer's wardrobe. Everything was either ink-stained or too small.

After Bobby Joe's lecture, he showered again, and under the gentle prodding of the voice, brushed his teeth and gargled with a strong mouthwash three times. He hoped he'd buried the smell of alcohol.

After shaking out as many wrinkles as possible, he selected a pair of gabardine slacks, then found a dress shirt with only a couple of ink smudges and a tie with matching stains. Checking himself in the mirror, he mumbled, "This outfit just won't do. It looks like hell. I'll wait until I have some decent clothes."

Bullshit. You can shop next week. If that's the best you've got, people'll give you a pass today. They'll be so shocked to see you in church, they won't notice what you're wearing. I guarantee it.

In spite of himself, Henry searched the room, looking for Bobby Joe.

You're going to sprain your neck. I done told you, I'm in your head. Now get a move on. I want you walking through the front door at ten forty-five. Besides, if you do what I say, maybe I'll arrange a surprise for you.

* * *

Judge Jackson settled into his seat and leaned across his wife to shake hands with Flip. After the ritual greeting and some whispered good-natured barbs, each turned and surveyed the congregation as they took their places.

The pews closer to the pulpit housed attendees who had laid

claim to their seats years before. No member would sit in another's dedicated spot. If a regular churchgoer did not attend, the seat went unused. Only when someone died did positions change.

The last two center pews were empty so visitors could find a place without struggling through the congregation. On most Sundays, there were two or three people in the seats. The Pastor addressed them in his remarks, inviting them to attend again and become members of the congregation.

Flip reached across, interrupting whisperings between Jane Jackson and Lorrie Matthews, and nudged the Judge. "Look who just came in. Can that be our Henry?"

"What?" The Judge swiveled in his seat, looking first at one entrance then the other. "Hallelujah. This has to qualify as a small miracle. I gave up on him years ago."

"Something must have moved him because there he is. I'd recognize those ink-stained clothes anywhere. Think we can make room for him?"

"Sure," the Judge said, "I'll get him."

Lorrie and Jane rolled their eyes as Flip shifted to the end of the pew. Then they followed his example.

..*

Debbie Patterson had arrived a moment after the Jacksons and took her usual seat behind the Judge. After the customary "Good Morning," "Nice weather today," and "We need some rain," with the people around her, she opened the program and studied the musical selections for the service.

The opening hymn, *Rock Of Ages*, was one she knew and loved. She flipped to page 168 in the hymnal and hummed the tune. She prided herself on her singing and memorized as many of the songs as she could.

She saw Flip point to the rear, and she turned, following his directions. The disheveled man standing in the entranceway looked familiar, but his clothing reminded her of a day laborer on Saturday night. She returned to her study of the second song, but realized that Judge Jackson had risen and was walking up the aisle. Curiosity caused her to watch as he approached the man. They shook hands and the Judge led him toward the front of the church.

Debbie looked again at the man, surprised that the Judge would take an interest. She pretended to study the hymnal, but her ears strained to overhear the conversation between the two. As they arrived at the pew, she heard the Judge say, "Jane, Lorrie, I'm sure you remember Henry Flanagan, our bachelor editor of the *Dawson Times.* Henry has agreed to join us. This is his first time in our church."

Editor of the newspaper, she thought, and a bachelor. His first visit, and he sat in front of her. She remembered her one-sided conversation with her dead husband that morning. Was this the sign she asked for? If so, she wasn't overwhelmed. She closed her eyes, thinking, Tom, if you've sent this man because of what I said this morning, you could have done better. Or maybe not. This is Dawson and the pickings are slim in bachelors over forty. If he's your choice, I'll try.

As the service proceeded, she found herself distracted by thoughts of how to meet Henry Flanagan. From what she'd seen when he walked in, he wasn't ugly—well, not exactly. A good haircut would rid him of that shaggy farmhand look. He was overweight, but in a nice suit that wouldn't be so obvious. Besides, she could prepare meals that would melt the extra pounds. Maybe he'd enjoy walking with her. She loved to stroll the neighborhood in the evening, looking at flowers and trees and making small talk with the people she met. It would be more enjoyable with a partner. Walking was good exercise, too. It would help him slim down. She blushed as she realized how far her thoughts were taking her. She hadn't had thoughts like these since she was a teenager.

She decided to welcome him to the church when the sermon was over, then find an excuse to visit the paper tomorrow. Tom must have sent her this man, and she didn't intend to disappoint Tom.

..*

Henry squirmed in his seat, then forced himself to stop. His stomach grumbled, his hands shook, and he wanted a drink. He glanced at the Judge hoping he and the others didn't know how uncomfortable he was. The service continued through songs, meeting announcements, prayers for the sick, prayers for the healthy and seemingly, prayers for about everything else. Then the sermon began.

Henry questioned why he'd listened to the voice. This wasn't for him. What effect on his status in the community could attending church have? Little to none. He'd always be a Yankee outsider.

Quit fidgeting. You're acting like a three-year old.

Henry's head didn't move although he started, then controlled himself. He accepted that Bobby Joe had somehow infiltrated his mind.

Look around. Now, don't be too obvious, but see the people who come to this church? Every one of them knows who you are, and you've done business with most of them. They know you run the newspaper. They respect you and they'll help you if you give them a chance. Didn't the Judge come after you at the door when you were thinking about leaving? You're in good hands, but you gotta relax and let it happen.

Henry nodded, recognizing that Bobby Joe was right. He scanned the congregation, or as many of the people as he could without turning his shoulders. He felt like someone was staring at him, but if so, it must be from behind. Everyone he could see appeared to concentrate on the preacher.

The sermon ended, the pastor made his Call to Christ, and they began the last hymn. Henry looked at his watch. Two minutes before twelve. Things were right on schedule.

When the song ends, don't bolt for the door. Hang around and chat with people. A lot of folks will come over and tell you how glad they are to see you and invite you to attend again. They'll shake your hand and pat you on the back. These are your neighbors, the people who make up the community. If you want to belong in Dawson, these are the people who must accept you as one of their own. A Yankee, yes, but their own Yankee. Bobby Joe continued his string of instructions.

Henry cut Bobby Joe off, thinking, Okay, okay, I get the picture. I'll be gracious, smiling and friendly. Then I'm going home and have a double.

Oh no, you're not, the voice said. *The Judge'll invite you for lunch, and you're going with him and Jane. Also, Flip and Lorrie will come along. You'll be so busy this afternoon, there'll be no time for a drink. So relax and enjoy. Don't forget, I'm working on a surprise for you.*

The hymn ended before Henry could answer. Everyone milled in the aisles, making their way toward daylight. As Bobby Joe had predicted, men shook Henry's hand and slapped him on the back with vigor. Women touched him on the arm and smiled. He received so many invitations to come back next week that he lost count.

He looked toward one of the stained glass windows and saw Madonna and the Baby Jesus smiling at him. Her image changed to Bobby Joe. *That surprise is ready. Don't disappoint me.*

As he weaved his way up the aisle, another hand touched his elbow.

"Mr. Flanagan, it's wonderful to have you here this morning, and I hope you'll attend next Sunday. I'm Debbie Patterson."

Henry looked at her and the intensity in her deep blue eyes unsettled him. Fumbling for a response, he saw a flush rise from her throat and cover her face as she dipped her head. Words failed him. A beautiful woman stood in front of him, her light touch resting on his arm. He felt a warmth surge through his body that he hadn't felt for years.

Jane Jackson saved him. "Debbie, how nice to see you. I knew you were here because your beautiful voice carried the hymns again this morning."

"Thank you. You're very gracious. I just wanted to welcome Mr. Flanagan—"

"We're all going to lunch at Lucille's," Lorrie chimed in. "Why don't you join us? Flip is treating Mr. Flanagan to celebrate his coming to church."

"I am?"

"Yes, you are," Lorrie said without hesitation. "You know how Lucille's tables are set up. Six is a much better number than five."

"Well . . . I, ah . . . don't know. I hate to impose," Debbie said. "Are you sure I won't be in the way?"

"Of course not," Jane added. "We'd love to have you. I've been meaning to call you anyway. I wanted to ask about your recipe for that triple-fudge chocolate cake you brought to the last church supper."

"It's settled then," Lorrie said, turning toward Henry. "All six of us are headed for Lucille's. Let's walk. It's such a beautiful day."

How about that for a surprise? Bobby Joe said.

CHAPTER THIRTEEN

Scooter left the church as fast as possible after Pastor Turner said his Amens, Hallelujahs, and told his flock to go and sin no more. Even then, it took another thirty minutes for him to get away as Aunt Liddie chatted with everyone in the congregation, or so it seemed to Scooter. Finally, about one-thirty, he told her she'd have to go home without him because he needed to find Big Man.

His roll of cash intrigued Scooter. He promised himself he wouldn't get involved, but he was curious to know how Big Man got that much money—more money than he'd ever seen.

He pushed himself down Slate Street knowing Big Man often visited this area because of the availability of liquor. While Scooter had never taken advantage of the back-door sales, he'd heard stories for as long as he could remember. According to Joshua, hill-coloreds bought all they could at the ABC Store, then sold it at two to three times the cost. Joshua said many white folk went to Slate Street to buy through the back door.

He saw the car parked alongside the street with a group of Negroes lounging beside it. Big Man stood in the middle, seemingly holding court.

"Scooter-Hey," Scooter called as he pushed himself into the crowd.

"Scooter, your own damn self." Big Man was dressed in a see-through, short-sleeve, yellow nylon shirt, a pair of charcoal-gray wool slacks that looked new, and a gray homburg. A pair of black penny-loafers with shiny quarters in the slots, and a lime-green sports jacket completed his ensemble. "Boy, you gotta git some new rags. Don'cha know it's Sundy?"

Scooter's pride in his new clothes melted as he stared at his friend. "Oh, you's looking good. Wisht I could dress like that."

"You can, littl'un. You just team up with me, and I'll put you on easy street." He winked at the men in the crowd.

He took Scooter's arm and walked him away from the group, then looked around before adding, "I's makin' a run tonight. Give you fifteen dollars if you ride wid me."

"Fifteen dol— Why're you funnin' me? You ain't got that much money to pay me."

"Shit, Scooter. I done tol' you onct, I got all the money I need." He pulled a roll of bills from his right front pocket. "Here. Here's the fifteen right now." Shielding his bankroll with his body, he peeled off a ten and a five and thrust them at Scooter.

Scooter's eyes went large as he stared at the bills. "I don't know. Aint Liddie wouldn't like it."

"Aint Liddie. That ol' woman's messin' up your life. You gotta git out from under her. You gotta live, boy, and I'm just the one to help you. You ride with me, and you'll find out what life's really like. Fifteen dollars. How long it take you to make that much shining shoes?" He continued to hold the money out.

"I made five dollars yesterday, turning a garden." He didn't mention the carvings, afraid Big Man would laugh at him.

"Yeah, and at the end of the day, you was tired, sweaty, and dirty. For this money, you don't git none of them things."

Scooter stared at the money. "Alright, I'll do it." He took the bills and stuck them in his pocket. "From now on, I'm with you."

"Now you gittin' smart." Big Man clapped him on the shoulder, a grin on his face. "Let's go to my house and see if my little brother's got some clothes what'll fit'cha."

..*

At sundown, they drove out of Dawson headed for the bootlegger's house where they would load the moonshine. "You let me do the talkin'," Big Man said. "This-here man don't like town-coloreds and if you don't talk to him right, he gits real mean."

"You de boss," Scooter said. He was dressed in a pair of blue gabardine slacks, a long-sleeve blue shirt, a dark gray sports coat, and black, lace-up shoes. He'd never felt so fine even though the shoes were too small and pinched his toes. As he fingered the crease in the pants, he thought, I ain't never had no clothes like these afore. And Big Man's brother had a closet full of'm. Havin' money ain't bad. Wonder why Aint Liddie don't like Big Man.

The car pulled up a long driveway filled with mud holes to the rear of a one-story farmhouse. He blew the horn and a few minutes later, a large white man walked out the back door, wiping his mouth with his sleeve. "I done told you not to come at dinner time," he said in a nasty voice. "I know you ain't got no damn brains, but you better learn to read a clock if you gonna work fer me."

Big Man who had stepped out of the car, said, "I's sorry Muster Burnette, suh. I wanted to be here earlier, but I got held up." He raised his head. "Is the stuff ready fer me to load?"

"Yeah, but you gonna have to wait 'til I finish supper. Just sit your ass down in yo' car and wait." He re-entered his house.

Big Man got in his car and leaned back in the seat. "Dam' ignorant white trash. Thinks he's so dam' hot. One of these days, I fix'm." He pulled out his switchblade and played with it, flicking it open, closing it, opening it again.

Scooter stared at the knife then scanned the area. The house was better than anything down by the river, but it needed work. The back porch sagged and one of the steps was broken. The white paint, which at first glance had looked good, was peeling under the eaves, and mildew ate away at it around the cinder block foundation. The yard was full of potholes, some of them filled with stagnant water. Weeds appeared to be the major crop grown near the house. Scooter continued looking around and saw two tobacco barns, a mule corral, and some farm buildings that sagged under age and disrepair.

"Big Man," Scooter asked, "what we doing here? That be Muster Burnette, the meanest white man I knows. He don't like me. He skeers me."

"Just be quiet. I don't give a shit who he likes." Big Man flicked the knife open again. "He makes the shine, I hauls it, and the people in Raleigh pays me. That's what's important. With the money I's makin', I'd kiss his ass if he said to." He ran his thumb along the knife blade. "Course, one of these days when I don' need him no more, he might have a bad accident. Set still. He be back."

Scooter frowned and his mouth opened, then closed. He settled into the seat.

They waited for thirty minutes, little conversation between them. The time passed to the rhythm of the knife opening, closing, opening, closing.

Burnette came across the back porch, digging at his teeth with a tooth pick. "Pull your car down to the barn and be quick 'bout it. It's gonna be dark soon, and I don't want no lights. If you'd showed up before supper, we woulda had plenty of time before dark."

"Yas suh," Big Man said, subservience replacing his cockiness. He put the car in gear and followed Burnette.

Forty-five minutes later, with the moonshine loaded, Big Man and Scooter prepared to leave. Burnette leaned in the driver's window. "Now, you listen to me good, boy. You drive careful and don't git caught. If I lose this load, I'm gonna take it outta your ass."

"Yas suh."

"Do you 'member where you deliver the stuff?"

"Yas suh. I been there before."

"Then git on outta here. Tell'm I'll have 'nother load next week."

"Yas suh," Big Man said, rolled up the window, and drove away. "Dum' white trash som'bitch. He's gonna git his one of these days," he muttered.

Big Man drove carefully, keeping the speedometer hovering on fifty-five miles an hour, the speed limit. When cars wanted to pass, he pulled to the right as far as he could, and when he saw no oncoming traffic, flashed his lights to assist the trailing driver. When he needed to pass a slower car, he insured he had plenty of empty road, then crawled past at the speed limit. Big Man played the odds that obeying the law would not attract attention to him. The trip was uneventful until they entered the city limits of Tarboro.

"Shit," Big Man said, as the traffic light changed to yellow just before he entered the intersection. He looked into his rearview mirror. "Uh oh, we got company. You be quiet, Scooter. I'll do the talkin'." He pulled to the right and stopped.

A Tarboro police cruiser pulled in behind with its red light flashing. A police officer exited and walked to Big Man's side of the car. "Lemme see your driver's license," he said, flashing a light into the car. "Where you boys goin'?"

"Ah'm sorry," Big Man said, pulling out his license and handing it to the officer. "Thet ol' light changed so late, ah just couldn't stop." His dialect was thicker than usual.

"Yeah, I saw that. Are you Jeremiah Q Lincoln?"

"Yas suh. Thet's whut my daddy named me. Thet Q don't stand for nuttin though. Hit's just a Q."

"Hmmmm. What's your birthday, Jeremiah?"

"The twun'y-sebenth of Febwary, suh."

"What year?"

"Nineteen twun'y-seben. Ah members cause the year and the day is the same. Makes it easy."

"Yeah, I guess it does." The officer smiled. "Where you boys goin'?"

"We's headed fer Raleigh, suh. My ol' mammy's mighty sick, and I wanna see her agin afore she dies."

"And you?" the policeman asked, shining the light on Scooter.

"He come along to' hep me so's ah don't fall asleep, suh. Ah worked a full day in the 'bacca fields even though it be Sundy. Some folks ain't got no 'ligion, and ah has to work when I kin."

"Hmmmmm," the officer said, putting the light back on Big Man. "Says here you live in Dawson. What's your address?"

"123 Syc'more Street, suh. Hit's a little white house with two bedrooms. Ain't much grass in the yard cause of a big oak tree, and the roof leaks some, but it's all right fer a nigger like me."

"Okay, move on and drive carefully. Watch out for traffic lights. Be ready to stop no matter when it changes." The policeman stepped away from the car.

"Yas suh. Ah'll be kereful." Big Man pumped the accelerator and pushed the ignition button.

"Just a minute, boy," the officer said, turning back to the car. "Almost forgot. You got a taillight out. That's why I pulled you over. Better get it fixed. I'll give you a ticket if I see it again."

"Yas suh. Ah'll stop at the nex' station whut's open." The car started and Big Man pulled away.

When they reached the Tarboro city limits, Scooter let out a big sigh. "I was skeered to death. How'd you know whut to say?"

"These town cops ain't nothin', but uneducated white trash. All you gotta do is act dumber than they are and say, Yas suh a lot. Hell, he prob'ly can't write good enough to give a ticket." Big Man threw back his head and let out a loud laugh. "But, it don't hurt to be ready either. I had this waitin' where he couldn't see it." He held up the switchblade, the moon reflecting dully off the exposed blade.

Big Man stopped outside Tarboro and with Scooter holding a flashlight, replaced the burned-out taillight. "I always carry a extra one. I even got a headlight case one blows out. I shoulda checked before we left Dawson. But I was runnin' so late after messin' around with you that I plain forgot."

"I didn't do nothin'."

"Naw, I guess you didn't." Big Man smiled. "That white ass was prob'ly waitin' for a couple of niggers to come by. Okay, let's git on to Raleigh."

When they were on the road again, Scooter asked, "Whut would you have done if he'd found th' moonshine?"

"That woulda been the last thing he foun'. He'd be laying in the road back there, and we'd be right where we is."

"Oh," Scooter said in a subdued voice.

CHAPTER FOURTEEN

Debbie sipped her iced tea and stared out the window. It was a pleasant evening and couples walked along the street, some of them arm-in-arm. She envied the women. Loneliness seeped into her soul as she followed one particular couple with her eyes. "Tom, can you see that couple?" she said, speaking to her dead husband. "The one by the church. Don't they look romantic? Oh Tom, I want to be in love, I want to walk with someone who cares about me, someone who'll hold my hand and kiss me under the oak tree. Like we used to do before . . . before you went into the Army. I miss you so bad. I want you back." She paused. "But, if I can't have you . . ." She took another taste of tea, her eyes reflecting the light from the window.

A few minutes later, she rose, walked from the room, and climbed the stairs, letting herself out onto the Widow's Walk. She stood for a moment, looking over the neighborhood, smiling.

"People look much smaller from up here. Don't you think so, Tom? I feel like no one can see me, but I can watch everyone." A blush crept up her throat onto her face. "Remember when we came up here and . . ." The blush deepened. "I was afraid someone would see us, but you assured me no one could when we were laying down." She reflected on her memory as the redness receded. "That was one of our best times. If you were here now . . ."

She sat, tucking her legs under her, lost in thought. "Tom, did you give me a sign this morning? Did you send Henry Flanagan, or am I jumping to conclusions? Oh, Tom, I need to know. You have to help me with this. Give me a sign I can recognize."

She looked around the Widow's Walk, then between the railing supports to the street. "Guess you have nothing to say tonight."

Another couple walked into view. Debbie watched, a feeling of longing eating at her insides. They came abreast of the house as a puff of wind blew directly into Debbie's face. She blinked and rubbed her eyes with the backs of her hands. When her vision cleared, she looked toward the couple again and shook her head. The woman's hair was shoulder length, styled like Debbie's and was the same color. The man wore a wrinkled, ill-fitting suit. He brought the woman's hand toward his lips in a romantic gesture. Their heads leaned together as if blotting out the world. Debbie couldn't see their faces, but from the side, they looked . . . they looked like . . .

Another puff of wind hit her in the face causing her eyes to tear. When they cleared again, she looked back to the couple that now walked away from her. The woman had long hair, halfway down her back, much longer than Debbie's, and it was a different color. The man wore slacks and a casual shirt, no jacket. Debbie stared until they passed from view, then looked around again. "Tom, you're pretty sneaky. There's no wind tonight except for two little puffs in my face. Okay, I understand your sign. Now, I wonder if Mr. Henry Flanagan will cooperate."

..*

Henry sat at his kitchen table, a cold cup of coffee in front of him. "Bobby Joe, I need a drink. Maybe you ghosts can flit around without one, but I'm still alive, and I need a drink." He looked at the cup. "Coffee won't cut it. I need something that'll calm me down. I can't quit cold turkey."

Easy Hank. You don't need booze. Think of something else. How about Debbie Patterson? What'd you think? I thought she liked you. Bet you didn't expect my surprise to be anyone like that. Nice looking broad.

"She's not a broad. She's a lady who lost her husband in the war. Just like we lost—" He paused. "Sorry about that. Forgot for a moment you're one of the lost ones. But you shouldn't talk about her like that. And what do you mean, your surprise? I'm sure she just acted nice. I mean, Flip's wife pretty well trapped her into going with us."

Man, didn't they teach you Yankees nothing up north? A man might get trapped like that, but not a woman. She went because she wanted to. Didn't you notice how she smiled at you? No, I guess not. You were so busy running from her you didn't notice she was gaining on you all the time.

"Are you sure? You really think she liked me?"

Just do what I say. And the next thing I'm telling you is buy some clothes. Don't even sort that crap hanging in the closet. Send it straight to the dump. Now, get off your lazy ass and go for a walk. You need the exercise.

* * *

"I'm gone havta drop you off here," Big Man said as he pulled the car to the curb. "The men I deal with don't allow no visitors."

"Wha'chu mean? I don't know nobody here," Scooter said, looking around the residential neighborhood. "I ain't 'bout to git out." His voice reflected his uncertainty.

"Oh, settle down. You knows I ain't gonna leave you. See that house over there." He pointed toward a two-story clapboard house in need of paint. "They's a coupla women there what'll take care of you while I'm gone." He grinned. "You know whut I mean, don't you?"

Scotter's eyes grew large as he stared at the house. "Let me go with you. I'll stay in the car."

"I done told you. I can't. Them's tough people I deliver to. They'd take both us out back and whup our asses. You'll be okay. These are two fine ladies."

Scooter continued to stare at the house. "Okay, but you make sure you hurry. My Aint Liddie don't want me hanging out wid none of your women."

"Oh shit. I'm tired a hearin' 'bout your Aint Liddie. Come on." Big Man got out of the car and crossed the street.

Scooter watched from the car, then exited and caught up with his friend.

In the house, Big Man took the two women into the kitchen while Scooter sat in a ragged, overstuffed chair in the parlor.

After Big Man left, the women treated Scooter warmly, and gave him a late supper even as they cut smirking glances at him. Other than that, they left him alone, and he spent the evening in the same chair he'd dropped into when he entered the place.

When Big Man returned from his delivery, he produced a bottle of moonshine and offered it around the room. The women took long drinks, making horrible faces.

Scooter took the bottle then handed it to Big Man. "I don't want none a that. Can we go now?"

Big Man grinned, shaking his head. "You stay here." He passed the bottle to one of the women. "Come on, ladies. I'm ready for some fun." The three of them disappeared into the back room leaving Scooter in his chair.

Female giggling and Big Man's laughter drifted through the closed door. Later, Scooter fell asleep to the sounds of grunts, moaning, and the squeaking of the bed. Pictures of Big Man and the women filled his dreams interrupted by scoldings from Aunt Liddie.

CHAPTER FIFTEEN

"Good morning, Mrs. Andrews," Chief Bowen said, tipping his hat as Christiana Andrews walked past him on the sidewalk.

"Might be a good day for you. You didn't have to dig your newspaper out of the rose garden," she said without slowing her pace. "You just wait 'til I see that Flip Matthews. I'm gonna give him a piece of my mind. If he don't get that boy straightened out, I'm gonna quit taking the *News and Observer*." She walked on with a determined step.

Chief Bowen watched a moment, grinning. "If Flip's newspaper boy could throw straight, she'd be after somebody else. Maybe even me. That woman ain't ever been happy, and I doubt she'll ever be happy. In fact, I bet she's only happy when she's unhappy and making sure others are unhappy, too."

It was eight-thirty on Monday morning and Chief of Police Lowell Bowen was on his way to Lucille's Restaurant for coffee. He wore his uniform proudly. It was fresh from the cleaners and looked good even as it stretched to cover his paunch.

Albert, who ran the laundry on Main Street, learned the hard way how Chief Bowen expected his uniform. Several times the Chief walked into Albert's business and demanded the uniform be re-pressed, although it meant waiting in the changing room. Albert now did it right the first time and bragged, "I make the Chief's creases so sharp I cut my finger on one."

Chief Bowen looked right and left for Scooter, then glanced at his shoes dully reflecting the morning sun. "Where is that boy? He knows damn well I get my shoes shined on Monday. Suppose somebody sees—"

In the midst of the Chief's mumble, Scooter rounded the corner from Valdese Street. "Scooter-Hey, Chief."

Chief Bowen answered, "Scooter-Who?" then stumbled over an imaginary crack in the sidewalk, struck speechless. He'd never seen Scooter dressed as he was today. Instead of the ragged dungarees and shirt he usually wore, he was dressed in a nice, but wrinkled, pair of slacks, sport shirt, and dress jacket. Even his shoes were leather, not the torn sneakers he usually wore.

The Chief recovered his voice. "Where'd you get those clothes? You look like you're dressed for church . . . or your wedding." He laughed. "You ain't getting married today, are you?"

"Suh, you knows I don't got no woman." Scooter chuckled. "But if I had one, I'd want clothes like these."

"Where'd you get them?"

"They's Big Man's," Scooter said, pride in his voice. "I mean, they's his little brother's. Ain't they something?" He pirouetted so the Chief could see the whole outfit.

"Big Man?" The Chief frowned. "You mean Jeremiah Lincoln? Are you hanging out with him now?"

"Not 'xactly. I took a ride with him last night. That's all," Scooter said, his voice muffled by his hanging head.

"Where'd y'all go?"

"Uh . . ." Scooter stared at his shoes. "I druther you ask Big Man."

Chief Bowen studied him, then shrugged. "Okay, I'll do that. Now, how about a shine?"

"Yas suh, boss. I kin do that soon's I git my box. Got to git home, then I be right back." Scooter sounded relieved. "Twon't take me but a few minutes cause I kin pick up my scooter. And, don't you worry. I'll find you and give you a special shine 'cause you had to wait."

"Sounds good. Check Lucille's when you get back. I might be there." Scooter rushed away as the Chief added, "You might not want to spend too much time with Lincoln. I've got my eye on him."

Chief Bowen watched Scooter's back, muttering under his breath. "I'm sure Lincoln's running moonshine. I heard about that car he bought. Hell, half the troopers in the state know that car." He wiped his hand across his mouth. "Time to start charting Mr.

Big Man's doings. I want the shiner. Bring him down and the pipeline will dry up. A run on Sunday night? I'll be watching next week." He moved on turning the corner toward Lucille's. "I hope Scooter's not mixed up with him."

..*

Eleven o'clock found Debbie primping in front of her mirror. She'd brushed her shoulder-length hair until it shone. Finally, accepting that it looked as good as she could make it, she put her brush away and stepped in front of the full length mirror that hung on the back of her bedroom door. She wore a royal blue dress adorned with a string of pearls and a black belt cinched at her waist. "Nope, the pearls are too much, too obvious. Maybe my cameo pin." She spent the next ten minutes switching jewelry until she satisfied herself with a gold cross on a thin chain.

After a last look in the mirror, a pat of her hair, a tiny spritz of perfume, and a fresh glance at her watch, she departed the house and went left on Church Street. Her no-nonsense stride carried her to the corner of Church and Smithwick where she turned toward Main. She wore an enigmatic smile broken only by morning greetings to passersby.

Ten minutes later, after window-shopping to strengthen her resolve, she pushed open the door to the *Dawson Times*. Tom, don't let me down now, she thought walking to the receptionist counter.

"May I help you, Mrs. Patterson?" the receptionist, Mabel Ayers, asked.

"Yes, I'd like to see Mr. Flanagan if he's in. I have a classified ad to discuss with him."

"I can help you with that. I process all the ads for the paper. We can get the words down so it says exactly what you want, but don't run up the cost."

"Oh," Debbie said. "Uh . . . I guess that'll be okay. But I thought Mr. Flanagan did all that."

"No, ma'am. He takes care of the stories and such, but just gives a quick look at the ads. Now what is it you want to advertise? Just sit down over there, and we'll work it out." She came from behind the counter, and they settled at a table in the corner of the front office.

Debbie fumbled in her purse. "Here's what—"

The phone rang.

"Wouldn't you just know it? Every time I walk away, that thing rings. Excuse me." She pushed back her chair and began to rise. "Oh darn. I hate this chair. I lose more hose to it." She stood and examined the back of her right calf as the phone rang for the fourth time. "Yep, that splinter got me again. This paper ought to pay for my stockings."

The phone sounded again.

"Anybody going to answer that?" said a voice from behind them. "Mabel, you out there somewhere?" Henry Flanagan came through an office doorway, an irritated look on his face. "You know I like to have the phone answered by the third ring. What are you—"

A look of bewilderment captured his face. "Uh . . . hello, Mrs. Patterson. I . . . I didn't know Mabel was working with you. I mean, I would have answered the phone if I'd known."

Debbie stood. "Good morning, Mr. Flanagan. I have an ad to help Scooter. You know Scooter, don't you? He's that Negro that cuts shoes and shines grass and all." She stopped, realizing how badly she'd misspoken.

Henry grinned. "Yes, I know him. A rather unassuming young man. In fact, I was going to look him up today to see if he could do anything with these old shoes." He looked down at his ink stained brown shoes, blushing. "I mean, I only wear them for work, but . . ." His voice trailed away into embarrassment.

"Only thing gonna help them shoes is a new pair," Mabel said, hanging up the phone. "That was Mrs. Christiana. She wanted to know what time the paper's gonna be delivered. I told her, same time as every week—Tuesday and Thursday afternoons. Then I told her today was only Monday. Don't think she liked that answer too much. If I was you, I'd stay away from her for a while. She sounded real riled."

The tension between Henry and Debbie broke with their laughter.

"What would Dawson be without Mrs. Andrews?" Henry said. "She creates life where there is none."

"I know what you mean," Debbie chuckled. "I deal with her in my women's church circle. I don't think we've ever sponsored anything she liked. She even complains when we help the March of Dimes. Says it's not right. We ought to be helping something important."

"Will you look at the time?" Mabel said, smirking. "I can't believe it's so late. Henry, I'm going to take the phone off the hook and eat my lunch. I'll take care of anybody that walks in, but I ain't going to answer that phone. I made some chicken salad last night, and my sandwich'll get soggy if I don't eat it soon."

"Uh, okay," Henry answered, turning his head toward Mabel. "That sounds good."

"Why don't you get out of here?" Mabel said. "It ain't good to eat at your desk all the time. Is it, Mrs. Patterson? I happen to know Lucille's making her special chicken noodle soup. You know, the one where she uses those big flat noodles and lots of chicken. Some of the best I ever ate, and I'm a right good cook, myself. Go on down there and have some, Mr. Flanagan. You go with him, Mrs. Patterson. Lucille will put meat on your bones. You're skinny as a rail."

Henry and Debbie looked at Mabel whose size indicated she followed her own advice about eating. Henry's mouth opened. "I—"

"Go on now," Mabel said. "You're getting on my nerves."

Debbie stuck out her hand. "Guess we'd better do it, or Mabel will throw us in the street."

"Yeah, sounds like it," Henry said, accepting Debbie's hand. "We'll be back in a bit," he said toward Mabel. "I have a paper to put to bed."

They walked out the front door together, but not before Henry dropped Debbie's hand.

Mabel stared after them as they crossed the street. "I'll be damned. Who'd a thought it? Henry Flanagan and Debbie Patterson. Okay, Cupid, the first arrow landed, but you still got a lot of work to do."

..*

"What do you think of Scooter?" Debbie asked.

"Think? I never think of him." He hesitated and broke into laughter with Debbie following close behind. "You'd never know I make my living with words, would you?"

"I think you're cute," she said.

Henry ducked his head, afraid he'd blush. "Scooter was one of the first people I met when I came to Dawson."

"Really. How?"

"I'd just closed the deal on the newspaper and was walking down Main Street to admire what my GI Bill bought when he came riding up on that old scooter." Henry stopped talking and chuckled at the memory. "'Scooter-Hey, Mr. Yankee. Them shoes sho' need a shine,' he said. He was the first to call me a Yankee, at least to my face."

Debbie chuckled. "So, what did you say?"

"What do you think? I said, 'Well, you better put a shine on them.' And, he did. But not before he told me how funny I talked."

"Here's your soup and sandwich," Lucille said, placing a bowl and small plate in front of Debbie. She turned to a serving tray and repeated the act in front of Henry. "You two eat up now. If you want more soup, just let me know. Nobody leaves my place hungry, not even you, Yank." She elbowed Henry's shoulder.

"Debbie, I'm glad to see you out and about." Lucille winked at Debbie. "I might not have chose him, but the pickings are awful slim these days. I reckon a Yankee's better than nothing." She laughed, elbowing Henry again before walking away.

Henry ducked his head, his face turning red.

"It's obvious she respects you," Debbie said.

"Respect? Humph, I'd hate to be someone she didn't like."

"Wish I could have seen you with Scooter that first day," Debbie said. "That was what, ten years or so ago?"

"Yeah. Ten years this Fall. Right after I mustered out of the Army in September of 1945."

A look of sadness swept over Debbie's face. "That was the summer Tom was killed."

"Sorry. I didn't mean to bring back sad memories."

"Don't give it a second thought. There are so many wonderful memories of Tom that an occasional sad one doesn't hurt as much as it used to."

They turned to their meals, and other than commenting on how good and rich the soup was, the only noise at the table was an occasional slurp.

You're doing fine, Hank. But how long are you going to keep up this Mr. and Mrs. stuff?

Henry's head jerked before he regained control of himself. Not now, Bobby Joe, he thought. Get out of here. I'll handle it.

Sure you will. Okay, I'm tuning out. You're on your own. But don't screw it up.

Debbie lifted her head, pushing the soup bowl away. "I was wondering if you'd mind if I call you Hank. Mr. Flanagan is so formal, and you don't look like a Henry. You look more like a Hank. Has anyone ever told you that you have the same initials as Henry Fonda? I read in a magazine that his friends call him Hank."

Henry hesitated. "Ah, Hank is fine. I had another friend a long time ago that called me Hank. In fact, he said the same thing about Henry Fonda. I like the name." As he said this, he thought, Did you put her up to this, Bobby Joe?

"Good. Okay, Hank, you call me Debbie. That's the name I prefer, and all my friends use it." She smiled at him, touching his hand. "And, I think we're going to be friends."

Henry looked at their hands touching. Her fingers were warm, shooting heat into him. It was a pleasant feeling, and he yearned to hold them tight.

She withdrew her hand. "Good. That's settled. Let's talk about Scooter."

"Who?"

"Scooter."

"What about him?"

Debbie leaned forward in her chair. "I want to help him. He's such an earnest young man, such a hard worker. He deserves a better life than shining shoes and mowing grass. I'd like to see him get a decent job with steady pay."

"Why him? He's simple-minded."

"I know. But have you seen the woodcarvings he does? When was the last time he shined your shoes? Did you notice the determination he put into it? I tell you he's got more going for him than many whites around here that have steady jobs."

"What do you want me to do?"

"When I walked into your office, I had one idea. Now, I have two. First, I want to place an ad. There're a lot of people around Dawson who need yard and garden work done. You know, spring cleanup, gardens prepared. I've hired him for every Wednesday, and I can keep him busy one day a week until late autumn after the leaves fall. I'm sure there are at least four or five others in town who can do the same. That will give him steady employment until Thanksgiving. After that, I didn't know until we came to lunch. Now, I have a great idea." She paused and took a sip of her iced tea.

"How about some dessert?" Lucille said, striding up to their table. "I've got apple pie that was made fresh this morning. You want your usual double-slice with ice cream, Yank?"

Oh, no you don't. If we're going to get your weight down, you gotta give up dessert—starting right now.

Henry hesitated.

"I'll have to pass, Lucille," Debbie said. "This dress is fitting kinda tight."

"Yeah, I noticed," Lucille said. "I'll bet the Yankee noticed, too. Tight in all the right places. How about it, Yank? Pie and ice cream?"

Henry groaned. "I'll pass, too. Same problem with a different result."

"Well, hallelujah," Lucille said. "'Bout time you paid attention to your weight. Now, if you'd just buy some new clothes. I bet that shirt was one of the first things you bought when you got out of the Army." She walked away.

"What was that you said about her liking me?" Henry asked Debbie. "If she liked me any more, she'd bring out one of her butcher knives." He looked at his left sleeve and laughed. "She's right about this shirt though. If I could salvage all the ink in it, I could probably lay a pretty good newspaper. If I have time after I put the paper to bed, I'm going shopping. Now, what was your second idea about Scooter?"

"Thought you'd never ask," Debbie said, grinning. "I could suggest he become your wardrobe counselor or valet, but that probably wouldn't work. You two dress too much alike." She chuckled. "So, I simply propose that you hire him."

"Hire him?" Henry paused. "To do what?"

"I don't know. I just have the idea. You flesh it out."

"Now, Mrs. Patterson, that's not fair."

"That's Debbie. C'mon, Hank. There must be something he can do. Carry out trash, deliver papers, clean up the place, get ink out of your clothes, something. I didn't say you have to pay him much. Just enough to get by. Think about it, and you'll see it's a good idea."

"Why me? Why not Flip, or Louise, or any of the other people on Main Street? The *Times* is not exactly making me rich, you know."

"No good reason. It just seems right. And I know you'd be a good influence on him. He needs all the education he can get."

"Good influence?" He grinned. "Are you forgetting I'm the town-yankee?"

"Stop that. Everyone around here respects and likes you."

"Yeah, that's what you said about Lucille. Such respect could give me gray hair."

Debbie lay her hand over his. "I'm serious. Will you give it some thought? I think Scooter really is worth saving."

Henry withdrew his hand and rubbed his chin. "Is that why you had lunch with me yesterday? Is that why you're here right now? To butter me up to hire Scooter? If it is, that's pretty low."

"No," Debbie said, her face flushing. "It's not. I'm here with you because . . . because . . ."

The silence hung heavy between them. It was as if the entire restaurant had quieted to hear her answer.

"Because I wanted to be with you," she finished in a soft whisper. "I . . . I wanted to have lunch with you. That's why I showed up at the paper just before noon—hoping I could get you out of the office."

Henry continued staring at her, then dropped his eyes. "Please don't do this, Debbie. I'm not a worldly man. I don't know my way around women. If you're playing a game, you'll win simply because I don't know the rules."

"Oh, Hank," she said, a plaintive tone in her voice. "This isn't a game. I wouldn't have brought Scooter up if I'd known you might take it that way. I'm here because I want to be, and that's the only reason."

Henry fiddled with his napkin, then took another sip of tea. "I hope so because . . . well, I enjoy being with you, too." He blushed, refusing to look at her. "Will you have supper with me tonight?"

"I'd love to. And I won't mention Scooter anymore. I'll work with Mabel to place the ad I had in mind this morning."

Henry looked at her, a smile on his lips. "Don't give up so easily. If it's a package deal, you might convince me."

CHAPTER SIXTEEN

Henry Flanagan walked into Lucille's Café, several copies of the Thursday edition of the *Dawson Times* under his arm. "Lucille," he called, "hand these around to your fine patrons."

"You giving away papers?" she asked. "You feel all right, Yank? You ain't sick, is—" She stared at him, a smile forming. "Whooeeee, don't the Yank look special?" she said loud enough for everyone to hear. "Let me feast my eyes. Good thing you didn't get too much of a haircut, or I'd never known who you was."

"Oh, knock it off. You'd think I never wore new clothes before."

"Oh, yeah, I'm sure you have—you must have. Let me think. Hmmmmmm, nope. Can't remember the last time I saw you in clean clothes, much less new ones."

"That's not fair. My clothes are always clean." Henry laughed, settling into a chair with his back to the entrance. "Only problem was you couldn't tell because of the ink stains."

"You got it, Yank. Here let me get some napkins. Can't have you dripping egg yolk on that vest or those new pants." She turned toward the other customers. "Don't our damnyankee look good?" She smiled and said in a quieter tone, "Debbie's having a good influence on you. If she don't work out, let me know. I might ditch Lester." She punched him on the shoulder. "Now, what can I get you this morning?"

Judge Jackson came through the door, his cane making its distinctive sound on the wooden floor. "Lucille, has Henry been in yet? He's not at the paper so I thought he might be here."

Lucille grinned and nodded her head in Henry's direction.

Henry turned toward the door, then stood, beckoning the Judge to his table.

"Hallelujah," Judge Jackson said. "If my eyes don't deceive me, I am witness to a miracle."

"Enough, already," Henry said, grinning. "Everybody. Go back to what you were doing. No, wait. I may as well get it over with. I went to Belk's yesterday and bought five new work outfits, four dress shirts, five ties and two new suits. Now get off my back and eat your breakfast." He chuckled. "If any of you want my old clothes, stop by the paper." His laughter boomed and soon everyone in the restaurant joined him.

"How about shoes?" the Judge said. "Did you get new ones?"

Henry held his foot in the air. "Yes, two pairs, and ten pairs of socks. I'm not going to talk about anything else I bought, so don't ask. But I did *not* buy a phony cane."

Again, the patrons and workers joined him in laughter. The Judge flushed.

Following breakfast, Henry and the Judge walked down Main Street toward the newspaper office.

"Anything in court today?" Henry asked.

"Traffic cases. Come by if you want to catch up on your sleep. Oh, by the way, thanks for the editorial you wrote last week. You laid out justice the way it should be."

"My pleasure. You just keep ruling with your heart and your head rather than acting like a robot. I'll keep reporting."

Judge Jackson walked away, and Henry steeled himself for more comments on his attire as he pushed open the front door of the Dawson Times. He stopped on the front step, thinking, It's worth it. Debbie is worth every word of it. He entered, a satisfied smile lighting his face.

Hey, Hank, Bobby Joe here. You're making me damn proud I came back to help you.

..*

Scooter pushed his way down Main Street, careful to stay out of the way of the few pedestrians on the sidewalk. "Scooter-Hey, Miz Jacobs," he said as he passed her. "Nice day, ain't it?"

"Afternoon, Scooter. Oh, I'm supposed to say, Scooter-Who." She giggled and kept walking.

He'd had few customers today, but that was okay. He fingered the money in his pocket that Mrs. Patterson had paid him for working in her garden yesterday. Three dollars. And back in his shack, hidden in his special can, he had the five dollars she paid him last week and the fifteen dollars Big Man gave him. More money than he'd ever had before.

He paused and scratched his head. Who could he ask to count it for him? Couldn't be Aint Liddie. She'd have too many questions, especially about that from Big Man. Well, he had plenty of time. He knew he couldn't have enough for leather shoes yet. They cost too much.

Maybe after the weekend, though. Farmers with their families came in on Saturday for shopping and entertainment. A lot of them brought their Sunday shoes to have them shined for church the next day. He'd make good money Saturday to add to what he already had. Then, if he could catch up with Big Man, maybe he'd give him money to ride to Raleigh again.

"Scooter-Who?"

He looked and a grin spread across his face. He saw Big Man standing beside his car with Rodney. "Scooter-Hey." He moved toward them. "Whut y'all doing uptown today?"

Big Man waited until Scooter got close. "Jist hangin' round 'cause I can. My schedule lets me do 'bout whut I want. Today, I feel like actin' like it's Saturday. You know whut I mean. Farmers come in to spend they's tobacca money. Me, I's spendin' my corn money." He let out a loud guffaw and slapped Rodney on the back. "Ain't that right?"

"Corn money. Dat's a good'un," Rodney said. "That's jist whut it is. Money from corn squeezin's."

"Not so loud, you fool," Big Man said, grabbing him by the arm while looking around. "That damn chief police may be stupid, but he ain't harda hearin'."

Rodney jerked away, then rubbed his bicep. "How come you want to hurt me? I's jist funning', same as you."

"Ain't the same when you says it. You'd ain't go no sense of humor. It's funny when I say it." He turned toward Scooter. "Ain't dat right?

"I s'pose. If you says so."

Big Man let out a belly laugh and threw his arm around Scooter. "Well, what'd ya think of our trip to Raleigh? I tol' Rodney 'bout that cop in Tarboro."

"It was alright," Scooter said. "It was a good ride. You got a nice car. Bad part was sittin' around all night in them womens' place."

Big Man pulled out his handkerchief, wiped dust from the hood of his car, then winked at Rodney. "C'mon, Scooter. You gotta grow up one a these days. You're a man now, and you never had a woman."

Scooter's head dropped, a reddish tinge radiating into his brown coloring. He set his shoeshine box on the sidewalk and rummaged inside, coming up with a well-used piece of towel. "Here. You can use this," he said, holding the cloth out without looking at Big Man. "It's real soft. Work nice to shine yo' car."

Big Man took the rag and spat on it before scrubbing at bug-splatter on the grill. "I don't understand you, Scooter. You ain't simple, but you shore act like it most times. You shine shoes and stay in that ol' shack down by the river. You grub in white folks' gardens and haul they's trash. You mow they's yards with the sweat off yo' brow. And whut you got to show fer it? Nothin', that's what."

Scooter brushed at the thigh of his dungarees. "I got me some new pants and a new shirt, and I made five dollars last week plus my shine money. I do alright."

"Yeah," Big Man said. "Hell, I paid you fifteen dollars for one night, and I made a lot more than that. And you didn't git your hands dirty one bit. Look how clean my hands is. You see any dirt under my fingernails? Now look at yours. Ain't mine better than diggin' in the dirt?"

Scooter looked down, examining his fingers. He mumbled, "Yeah, but Aint Liddie say money that easy gotta be bad money."

Big Man shook his head. "Shit, I done told you. You's a man now. You don't have to do nothin' that *Aint Liddie* says. She's an old woman. You stick with me. You'll make lots of money, and I'll git you a woman at the same time. Be the best time of your life."

"Well, I wouldn't mind having a lot of money. I could git me some leather shoes. But I'm doing alright. I got me a job now, and—"

"Job. What kind a job you got?"

"I'm gonna work for Ms. Patterson every Wednesday, and she gonna pay me three dollars a day."

Big Man's laughter echoed up the street. "You jist fergit them three dollars. I'm puttin' you on the payroll." He looked at Rodney. "Meet my new bodyguard. Git him a weapon—a good'un. I want my man to be ready." He took a clasp knife from his pocket. "Let me see your hands, Scooter."

He held them out.

"Jist whut I thought. Look't them fingernails. Here." He handed over the pocketknife. "Clean'm. If you gon' be with me, you gotta keep your hands clean. I don't want to see no shoepolish and no dirt. You gon' be a gen'leman now."

..*

Liddie stood in the front of the drugstore, ostensibly dusting merchandise in the window. Her face wore a frown of worry as she stared at the threesome across the street. After a moment, she walked to the back of the store and waited until Flip finished with a customer.

"Now remember," he said, "take one three times a day—after your meals. That way, the pill will digest with the food and won't upset your stomach. Okay?"

"Shouldn't ought to have pills that make you sick," Mrs. Cooper said. "Seems stupid to me. Take a pill to get well that makes you sick. Next, you'll sell me a pill to fix me up from the pill you sold me that made me sick."

"Yes, ma'am," Flip said. "Right after meals, and you won't have any problems."

Mrs. Cooper picked up the bottle and dropped it into her purse. "I still say it's stupid."

Flip smiled and shook his head as she walked away.

"Mr. Mat'hews, you got a minute?" Liddie said.

"Of course. What's on your mind?"

"Scooter. He's across the street with Big Man and Rodney Roosevelt."

"Isn't he the one that was sent to the state pen for robbing a filling station?"

"That's th' one. He's a bad'un. Ain't nothin' but trouble. It worries me seein' Scooter with him and Big Man at the same time."

"I agree. Neither is good company." Flip walked from his cubicle to the front of the store. "Yeah, they sure look cozy, don't they? Think they're up to something?"

"I don't know whut to think. Scooter's a good boy, but . . . Whut you think I should do? You know Scooter ain't all that bright. Them two can talk him into anything."

Flip faced her. "Aunt Liddie, you raised Scooter from a little tyke. I can't believe he'd go bad after that. You'll just have to trust his upbringing."

"Humph, I druther trust a two-by-four on Big Man and that Rodney's behinds. And if they mess up my boy, I just might do that."

..*

"Afternoon, boys," Chief Bowen said, coming around the corner from Valdese Street.

"Scooter-Hey."

"Scooter-Who," the Chief said. "Weather's right warm for this time of the year."

"Yas suh, it is," Big Man said. "We's jist talkin' 'bout that, won't we, Rodney?"

"That's 'xactly what we wuz doin', Chief. Mighty warm for this time of the year."

"Everything all right here?" Chief Bowen asked. "You boys ain't getting into trouble, are you?"

"No suh, everything's fine," Big Man said. "Rodney's been tellin' us how bad it is in the penitentiary. Ain't that right, Rodney?"

"It's bad there, Chief. I ain't never goin' back. You ain't gonna have no more trouble with me."

"Nice to hear," Chief Bowen said, walking alongside the car. "Nice wheels, Big Man. Somebody told me you got this. Reminds me of a bootlegger's car I heard about. Seems he had a special tank in the back for hauling shine. Funny how folks'll go to so much effort to break the law."

"Yas suh," Big Man said. "Some folks ain't got no respect for the law. They ain't like me and Rodney and Scooter. We respects the law, don't we?" He looked from one to the other.

"I'm mighty glad you feel that way," Chief Bowen said. "You

see, one thing I learned a long time ago is lawbreakers most often get caught. Oh, they might get away with it for a while, but sooner or later, the law catches up with them." He rubbed his hand over the hood. "Yeah, sure looks like that bootlegger's car. Well, y'all boys have a good day." He walked away a few steps then stopped, and looked again at the car. "Yep, the kinda car I should keep an eye on. Scooter, you take care of yourself." He moved down the street.

Rodney said, "He knows, Big Man, he knows."

"Bullshit. He don't know nothing. Ain't smart enough to catch Big Man. He jist shootin' his ignorant mouth off."

"I don't know," Rodney said. "You better be careful."

"Git the hell off the sidewalk," Marvin Burnette said, coming out of the dime store. "You niggers know better than to block a white man's way."

Scooter stepped off the curbing to let him pass. Big Man and Rodney did the same.

"Y'all better not be making no trouble. Me and my brothers goin' be in town tonight. Might go to the picture show. Best you stay out of the way." He crossed the street, forcing Scooter to step aside again.

"Sonnavabitch," Big Man said when he was out of earshot. "One of these days, I'm gonna git him. I'm gon' slit him from his balls to his Adam's apple."

Scooter watched Burnette go into Flip's Drugstore, anger burning inside him, then turned toward Big Man. "How much money you gonna pay me?"

CHAPTER SEVENTEEN

Judge Jackson drummed his fingers, fluffed the sleeves of his robe, and leaned his head back, staring at the ceiling while tapping his lips with his left forefinger. His boredom was evident to everyone in the courtroom—everyone except the young attorney.

"Your honor," the lawyer said, playing to the few spectators, "my client is a deacon in his church, a pillar of the community. How can the state accuse him of reckless driving? How can the police besmirch his spotless reputation by issuing a ticket for twenty miles an hour over the speed limit? I ask you . . ."

Judge Jackson rolled his eyes, wishing they'd teach young lawyers when to shut up. If there was such a class, the man in front of him flunked.

"My client drives for his church, delivers food to the poor. It would be a malfeasance of justice to . . ."

The Judge looked around, hoping for a distraction and saw a deputy approaching the bench from the side.

The deputy cupped his hand at the Judge's ear and whispered, "Sir, there's a man from Raleigh here to see you. I put him in your office. He said he'd wait."

The Judge nodded, then returned his attention to the attorney who showed no indication he'd ever finish.

"Your Honor, the mercy of this court owes my client—"

"My dear friend," Judge Jackson said, cutting him off mid-plea. "You've spent twenty minutes telling me what an upstanding citizen Mr. Sutherland is. I have no arguments with his contributions to the community, nor do I question his love for his wife and children. You didn't mention it, but I bet he has a loyal canine trained to guard his family. However, the issue here is one of reckless driving and speeding." He rapped with his gavel. "Guilty. One hundred dollars fine. See the bailiff." He stood. "We'll take an early recess. Court re-convenes at one o'clock." Judge Jackson left the chambers.

..*

The door to the office was open, and the Judge saw a man sitting in his chair. As he moved into the room, the man sprang to his feet and came around the desk.

"Judge Jackson?"

"Yes. Who are you?" He looked the man over as he stepped forward. Well-dressed in a three-piece, navy pinstriped suit. Shined wing tips and a red tie that matched the stripe in the suit. Not bad, the Judge thought. Must be a defense attorney. "And how dare you sit at my desk. I hope you have a good reason for interrupting my court. I don't take lightly to lawyers who—"

"I'm Howard Terollian, staff attorney to the governor." He stuck out his hand in the age-old tradition.

The Judge stopped in mid-tirade. His demeanor changed, not subservient, but cooperative. "Interesting. Why are you here?" He shook Terollian's proffered hand.

"The governor asked me to visit you." Terollian continued as if accustomed to ignoring admonishments. "He insisted it be in person. How much time do we have?" He settled into a visitor's chair.

The Judge recaptured his desk and glanced at his watch. "About twenty minutes. If you need more time, we can talk over lunch."

"We'll see. As you have probably heard, Judge Leggett is getting up in years and his health has been slipping. The Governor believes he might retire before the next election. If so, the Governor will be looking for a quality candidate to replace him, someone well-versed in the law, someone with a reputation for fairness and knowledge." Terollian paused, staring at Judge Jackson. "And of course, someone who supports the Governor and is electable. He wouldn't want to squander political capital on an appointee who would not work hard to be re-elected. That would reflect badly on him, wouldn't it?"

Judge Jackson's attempt to hide his surprise failed. "So you came to me? I didn't know he'd ever heard of me. Is he looking for input on a potential replacement? There are several—"

"Well, yes. He is compiling a list." Terrolian's brow wrinkled, then he smiled. "But my assignment is to feel you out for the position, not ask your opinion on others."

The Judge stared at him, settling back in his chair. Could his ears be failing him? After all these years, could his dream be coming true? "The . . . the Governor wants to appoint me?"

"I didn't say that, not exactly. He has a short list, and you're on it—near the top, I can add. He's heard good things about you."

"I'm flattered." Judge Jackson took a deep breath, hoping he could keep the anxiousness out of his voice. "You may report to the Governor that I am interested . . . very interested. And, if he appoints me to a Superior Court position, it'll take a platoon of marines to rip the robe off me."

Terollian chuckled. "Maybe I'd better not use that one. The Governor served a hitch in the army. But I'll let him know you'll fight for re-election on his ticket. That is right, isn't it?"

The Judge leaned forward resting his elbows on the desk. He knew his next words might sink him, but he'd sworn never to sacrifice his honor for gain—not even the position that inspired him to attend law school. "Tell the Governor, I'll campaign hard for myself and any others who put the interests of the people first." He sighed. "As far as I know now, he qualifies."

Terollian stroked his chin. "You're an interesting man, Judge. I'll report your words to him . . . exactly as you said them."

..*

The Judge's eyes stayed locked on his door long after Terollian took his leave. He had politely refused the Judge's invitation to lunch with the excuse he had another stop to make, and the Governor expected him in Raleigh that night. He promised someone would contact the Judge soon, then pulled the door closed as he left.

The Judge rubbed his palm across his face, barely believing what had happened. For years, he'd dreamed of someone on the Superior Court bench retiring so he could run for the position. Now there was a possibility of an appointment—and by a man he respected. He had voted for the Governor, and was pleased at the job he was doing. If he ran for re-election, he'd pull the lever for him again.

He leaned forward, reaching for the telephone, a smile taking over his face, chasing away all thoughts except *Superior Court Judge Jackson*. Jane'll never believe it, he thought.

The phone rang, causing the Judge to flinch and jerk his arm back. *Never fails to scare the pants off me*. He answered, "Judge Jackson."

"Are you coming home for lunch?" Jane Jackson said. "I have to be out of here by one, so you'd better let me know now."

The Judge smiled. "Yes, I'm coming home. I'm on my way. Make something special. I have big news?"

"What, what news?"

"I'll tell you when I get there."

"Daniel J., if you don't tell me right now, you'll pay. You know I don't like to wait. I'll . . . I'll make tuna sandwiches."

"Oh no. You know I hate those." He chuckled. "Of course, they do work to keep the young lawyers from getting too close to the bench. Nothing like tuna breath to keep them behind their tables. Be patient, my dear. I can't leave until I hang up, so I'm cutting you off. By the way, I sure love you today." He dropped the phone into its cradle and stood, glancing at the doorway while removing his robe. *Hope I wasn't too blunt with Terollian.*

..*

Fifteen minutes later, the Judge walked into his house and called, "Jane, come out here. My news has me busting at the seams."

"I'm in here making tuna sandwiches. Bring it in here."

He rushed into the kitchen and in a flow of words without breathing, or so it seemed, told her about Terollian's visit.

"Oh, Danny, that's wonderful." She threw her arms around his neck and hugged him. "You've worked so hard." She leaned back and stared into his eyes. "You've earned it."

"Let's not get too fired up. I'm not booking the country club for the celebration yet. But . . . ah, dammit, I really want this."

"Then I want it for you." She grinned. "I can't wait to tell the girls. They'll turn green with jealousy. All day I've been dreading this afternoon's circle meeting, listening to Christiana complain and Edna talk about her operation. Now I'll top them all." She kissed him on the cheek. "Daniel J. Jackson, I'd propose to you if you weren't already married."

"Slow down." He tightened his arms around her, holding her closer. "It's not fact. I may not get the appointment. I'm only on a list. So you best not be bragging to the girls yet."

"Party pooper. I can at least start planning. When the word comes, we'll throw the biggest bash in the history of Dawson." She paused, her face screwed up in thought. "I'll have to go to Norfolk for a new dress." She stepped out of his embrace. "Let me see. What color's best for the bride of a Superior Court Judge? Maybe royal blue . . . or purple. That's it, purple. Isn't that the color of royalty?"

"Hold it right there, your highness. Before you ascend the throne, you have to feed the anointed. What's for lunch?"

She squealed in glee. "Chicken salad sandwiches. Mrs. Luther made it fresh this morning. Now, is that appropriate or not? Your favorite. Your place is set. I'll get you a glass of tea and a couple of sweet gherkins. Nothing's too good for my man today."

Judge Jackson glanced at his watch as he pulled out his chair. "Gotta rush. I have to be back on the bench in twenty-five minutes. Can't let my guard down now."

"Oh, pooh. Can't you take a few minutes from your precious law to have lunch with your wife? Sometimes, you drive me—" She grinned and shook her head.

The Judge was busy chomping a mouthful of sandwich.

She sat at the table and placed her hand over his, the one not stuffing food into his mouth. "It's okay. We'll talk tonight."

..*

Jane left her church circle meeting before Christiana Andrews finished her litany of complaints. She rushed through the door calling, "Mrs. Luther. Where are you? We have to set tonight's menu."

Mrs. Luther came in from the kitchen. "What you mean, Mrs. Jackson? I done started supper. You said this morning—"

"Forget what I said. I changed my mind. We have to fix Mr. Jackson's favorites. You start one of your triple-layer chocolate fudge cakes. I picked up some thick-cut porkchops. You can fry them, and stew tomatoes with fresh corn. You know how he loves those."

"You want I should make biscuits. He do love my homemade biscuits."

"By all means. Now, what kind of potatoes . . . or maybe rice? Yes, porkchop gravy and steamed rice. He'll love it."

Mrs. Luther chuckled. "I don't know what y'all got goin' tonight, but I be glad to fix the best supper I knows how. Then I'll just git on outta here so y'all can enjoy one another." She winked and headed toward the kitchen.

"Now, Mrs. Luther," Jane said, a slight blush rising. "Oh, I almost forgot. Put this in the fridge." She passed her a bottle of wine.

Mrs. Luther looked at the bottle, then at Mrs. Jackson. "Uh-huh."

..*

Judge Jackson pushed back from the table. "Ummmm, I'm too full to move. If I had known you'd carry on like this, I'd have called the Governor myself."

"Not every day my man comes home with such big news. You keep bringing, and I'll keep the kitchen fires banked."

"Oh, yeah. That I'd love to see—you tending the hearth."

"You know what I mean. I'll have Mrs. Luther take care of it. She's really good, you know?"

The Judge laughed, walked behind his wife, leaned over, and kissed her on the cheek. "We could take the rest of the wine with us."

"In a few minutes." She looked up at him. "This afternoon, while Christiana was droning on and on, I got to thinking." A frown creased her forehead. "If you get this appointment, you'll be gone a lot, won't you?"

"Yes, I'll be on the bench in several counties here in the northeastern section of the state—riding the circuit. Sometimes it'll be Nolan County but other times, it'll be elsewhere. That'll mean I'll be away from home, maybe for weeks."

She frowned. "And you'll be in the middle of this mess of putting coloreds in our schools, won't you?"

Judge Jackson lifted her hair and kissed the nape of her neck. "Let's not talk about that now."

She shoved her chair back, banging his knees, and stood. "We have to. We have to talk about this before you're appointed. You know how I feel. I . . . I can't go against my upbringing." She sniffled. "You won't, will you?"

He pulled her against his chest. "Jane, I love you, and I'd really rather not discuss this now."

She pushed away. "Well, *Judge*, *I* want to discuss it." She stepped a couple of feet away, her hands on her hips, fingers down. "Two people live in this house. I'm one of them, and I won't be ignored. We talk, or you sleep on the couch."

He sighed and returned to his chair. "Please sit down." He paused, and when he spoke again, it was almost a whisper. "We have talked about this. You know I swore to uphold the law, and you know how the Supreme Court ruled. If such a case comes before me, I'll listen, then rule in the best way I know how."

Jane stiffened and gripped the back of her chair, her knuckles white. "Have another slice of cake. It's the last damned one I fix for you." She strode from the room, her back stiff, and her head high.

"Please don't . . ." Judge Jackson watched her leave, then sighed, and rubbed his forehead. After a moment, he took a sip of wine and looked toward the ceiling. "Lord, I'm going to need all the help you can give me." He emptied the glass. "Ah hell. Maybe I won't be selected."

BOOK TWO

CHAPTER ONE

October 1955

Superior Court Judge Daniel J. Jackson pulled into his reserved parking space and killed the engine on his two-tone '53 DeSoto. He looked at his watch and smiled—eight, giving him two hours before he had to be on the bench. He opened the door and took a deep breath, savoring the freshness of the day. It was an idyllic October day, cool enough for a jacket, but warm enough to enjoy the beautiful autumn changes. Around the parking lot, the leaves on the trees danced in a light breeze reflecting the colors of the rainbow—reds, oranges, yellows, the green of those that had not begun to change, and the brown of those ready to fall.

Exiting his car, he yelled across the parking lot, "Good morning, Deputy Smith. Nice to see you again. You didn't catch old Beauregard Bass while I held court in Beaufort County, did you?"

The policeman laughed. "No way. He's still waiting to strip your hook. Glad to see you back. Anything good on the docket today?"

"Don't make me think about it. We start the State versus Alonzo James. I'll have lawyers preening like peacocks all day."

"Glad I don't have the duty," Smith said. "It's not too bad once the trial starts, but watching them select a jury is about more than a man can bear."

"That's what I meant," Judge Jackson said, chuckling. "I miss the days when I could escape early to feed Old Beauregard his supper." He moved toward Main Street, stopped, and called back to the Deputy, "Have you seen Scooter recently? I'm hoping he's around to do my shoes."

"Not today. He gave me a 'Scooter Hey' from his bicycle one day last week. Can't remember what day it was." He hesitated and rubbed his chin. "Don't think he had his shoeshine box. Somebody told me he's about quit shining shoes."

"Yeah, that's what I heard, too. I worry about that boy."

"Ain't much need to from what I see. He's sure dressing better. And that bicycle must've cost him forty, fifty dollars."

"That's what I mean," Judge Jackson said, walking away. His face creased into a smile as he stared toward the business section. Spending time away from Nolan County made him appreciate his hometown more. Riding the circuit to the other county seats was nice, but there was something about Dawson that was special. As he sauntered along at a jaunty pace, tapping his cane on the sidewalk, his smile grew.

"Morning, Ben," he said to an elderly colored man. "How's Sarah's rheumatism doing?"

"Mawnin', suh," Ben said, his head lowered in a sign of respect. "She be hangin' in there. Fixed a big feed at the church last week. Proves she kin do it when she wants to. Glad to see you's back in town. I tell her you asked. She be tickle pink." He stepped into the gutter as the Judge passed.

He reached the traffic light at the corner of Smithwick and Main and stopped. "Probably no point in walking down to Haughton. I doubt Scooter's there." He crossed the street and peered through the window of Joe's Barbershop on the first floor of the Dawson Hotel.

Joe Strawbridge, the proprietor and sole barber, unlocked the door. "Morning, Judge. Come on in. You must be looking for Slim." He swiveled toward the rear of the shop and called, "Slim. Git out here. Customer."

A colored man in his fifties came out of the back, set his broom aside, and walked to the shoeshine chair. "Mornin' Jedge. Guess you couldn't find Scooter."

"No. Have you seen him?"

"Naw sir. Not in a few days. Last I seed, he wuz with Big Man, and they wuz both struttin' like they's white boys. You want I should shine yo' shoes?"

"Yep. Give me what you've got."

"I do's the best I can. I ain't no Scooter though."

"You're good enough."

"Judge," the barber said, "if you don't mind, I have some work to do in the back. Hope you have a real nice day. Slim, If anybody taps on that glass for a haircut, tell'm we open at nine."

..*

Liddie stopped dusting a shelf when Scooter pushed through the side door of Flip's Drugstore.

He didn't exactly swagger—his limp prevented it—but he carried himself in the manner of a proud man. "How you be, Aint Liddie?"

She stared at him. "I see you still spendin' Big Man's money."

"Ain't these purty clothes?" He twisted and turned in front of the mirror behind the soda fountain. He wore a Hawaiian print, rayon shirt under a lime-green sport coat and gabardine slacks. His feet were clad in penny loafers with quarters in the slots. The sole of the left shoe was thicker to compensate for his shorter leg. On his head, tilted at a rakish angle, was a gray homburg with the front of the brim turned down. "You gotta admit these be better than them ol' rags I used to wear."

"I ain't gotta admit nothin'. I don't know where you and Big Man gittin' all that money, but I know it cain't be good. I done told you to stay away from him. Something bad's gonna happen to that man, and I don't like you being with him."

Scooter chuckled. "You been sayin' that a long time, and it ain't happened yet. He knows whut it's about."

"You mark my words. He goin' to jail." Her face softened. "I hope you ain't with him when it happens. You best remember where you come from."

Scooter's eyes bored into her. "I remember. I remember being hongry and wearing rags. I remember ridin' that ol' scooter in ragged shoes. I remember bein' cold in the winter and sweatin' like a field hand in the summer. Yas'm, I remember. I remember shinin' shoes fer ten cents, an' grinnin' for the white folks. Don't havta do that no more. I got money." He pulled a roll of bills from his pocket, a ten on top. "See this. That's whut working for Big Man got me."

Liddie glared at him. "Blood money, liquor money, whorin' money, who knows whut kinda money." A look of sadness took over her face. "Maybe you better go. You a hill-nigger now. You ain't from the river no more. I don't know you." She turned to the shelf and wielded the feather duster like a whip.

"I'm sorry, Aint Liddie," Scooter said. "I don't mean to hurt you. But I ain't gonna crawl no mo'. Big Man tol' me to stand up, and I is."

Scooter stared at her broad back, then, with his head down, moved toward the front door. He almost bumped into Debbie Patterson who was entering.

"Scooter," Debbie said. "Don't you look nice. I've missed you these last Wednesdays. Have you quit working for me?"

Scooter looked at her, his face in conflict. Then he glanced at his hands and squared his shoulders. "Yas'm, I have. I don't do that diggin' in the dirt no more. You gon' have to git yo'self another man. See." He held out his fingers. "No dirt."

"You 'pologize to Miz Patterson," Liddie said striding toward them. "Ain't no need for you to be so sassy."

He pushed the door open as Liddie added, "I sorry 'bout that, Miz. Patterson. He . . . he ain't hisself these days. He sound more like Big Man ev'ry time I see him."

Scooter sneered and stepped onto the sidewalk.

..*

Debbie watched as Scooter picked up his bike and limped away in an angry stride. "Yes. He has changed, hasn't he?" She hesitated. then looked at Liddie.

Liddie's eyes shone with tears. She pulled a rag from her apron pocket and blew her nose. "I's so worried 'bout him. Whut I gonna do? He's the closest thing I ever had to a son."

"I don't know. I wish I did. I like Scooter, and thought he was my friend. I tried to help him. Now . . ."

"I 'preciate it, Miz Patterson. You a good woman."

I'll ask Hank, ah, Mr. Flanigan," Debbie said. "Maybe he'll have some ideas."

"Hi, Debbie. Nice to see you. What brings you uptown so early?"

She turned to see Flip calling from his pharmacist cage. "Hello. Just felt the urge to get outside this morning. My feet brought me this way so I figured I might as well pick up a new lipstick." She hesitated, glancing at Liddie, then looked at Flip. "Have you noticed the difference in Scooter?"

"Hasn't everyone?" he answered. "Seems like most of the people that come in here comment on it. What do you think?"

Debbie glanced at Liddie again, feeling uncomfortable talking in her presence. "I think he has a lot of talent that needs direction. Remember those figurines I gave you to sell back in the Spring? They were so good. Now I guess he's pretty much quit whittling."

"Yeah. Three dollars a piece, and I had no problem selling them. A salesman from Raleigh bought one. Said he'd love to represent whoever did them. I talked to Aunt Liddie and Scooter about it, but he was already under Big Man's spell. Far as I know, he hasn't done any more." He hesitated, switching his attention to Liddie. "Sure wish he would. There's money to be made for both of us."

"I talk to him, but he say he ain't got time. He too busy bodyguardin' Big Man." She sneered, "He say that a hard job. Most folk couldn't handle it. He mighty proud a that job."

"Yeah, I guess he is," Debbie said. "Shame though. He does have talent with that knife. I was thinking one time he might be able to set up a business. You know, hire others to do the basic carving, then he could put on the finishing touches—those extra lines and nicks that make the animals come to life."

"Good idea," Flip said. "Talk him into it, and I'll be his agent. But somehow, I don't think it's going to happen now."

"Don't be too hard on him," Liddie said. "This th' first time in his life he ever had anythin'. The first time he ever had real shoes and purty clothes. Soons he git over havin' a few dollars in his pocket, he'll come aroun'. I know he will. He be a good boy."

"I hope so," Flip said. "But right now, I wouldn't put money on it. He's feeling too full of himself."

"Don't be so negative, Flip," Debbie said. "Aunt Liddie knows him better than anyone." She glanced through the front window and saw Scooter and Big Man talking on the other side of the street. "Of course, easy money is a powerful draw."

..*

"You're late," Big Man said. "I spected you at my house at seven o'clock. Cain't you read that fancy watch you bought?"

"Easy, Big Man," Scooter said. "I wuz tired this mornin'. I jist decided to git some extry sleep. Ain't nothin' happened, has it? You's safe, and now I be here."

Big Man appeared taken aback by the words. "That ain't the right kinda answer. I hired you to do what I say. If that ain't workin', you might not be the right man."

"Ease on down," Scooter said with a shrug. "What's a coupla hours. You need me, all you gotta do is whistle. The scoot-man will come runnin'."

Big Man stared at him. "You keep up this attitude, and we's gone have a hard talk real soon. You gittin' too big fer yo' britches. Don't make me put you down." He slipped his switchblade from his pocket and snapped the blade open, holding it along the seam of his pants. "I can cut you jist as fast as I cut that nigger in Raleigh that messed with me."

Scooter's eyes grew big, and his bravado melted away. He tore his attention away from the blade and looked down, shuffling his feet. "Put that thing away. I's sorry. I was jist funnin'. You da man. Ain't no need to git out no knife. You da boss. I do what you say."

"That's more like it. Now we got that straight, you come on round to the house, and I'll tell you what I been thinking. It's time for the Big Man to grow." He paused, eyeing Scooter. "If you plays your cards right, I'll take you along. More money than you ever dreamed of."

"I's as good as on the way." Scooter didn't hesitate. He jumped on his bicycle and peddled away. When he looked back, he saw Big Man watching him, a grin on his face.

CHAPTER TWO

Judge Jackson stepped down from the shoeshine bench. "Slim, if you get much better, Scooter's going to lose his standing in the town. That's a mighty-fine shine." He fumbled in his pocket and came out with a quarter. "In my judicial opinion, that's a twenty-five cent shine. You keep the change."

"Don't know nothing 'bout them ju . . . ju . . . whatever you said, but I 'preciate the tip."

The Judge stood by the front window watching the sun reflect off the toes of his shoes. "You earned it."

Chief Bowen tapped on the front door, and Slim opened it. "Muster Strawbridge say we open at nine. 'Course, he didn't know you was comin' by." He stepped aside so the Chief could enter. "I tell him you here. He in the back doing paperwork."

The Chief walked in and dropped into one of the barber chairs. "No, don't bother him. I saw the Judge and thought I'd let him do a little politicking. You do know, don't you, Slim, elected officials like him have to work at getting re-elected all the time? I mean, it ain't easy being everything to everybody. Might wangle me a cup of coffee out of him if he wants my vote enough. 'Course if he don't, I may run against him next election."

Slim laughed. "You havin' fun with me and the Jedge, ain't you?"

The Judge chuckled. "Now that'd be a pickle if he ran against me. Who would you vote for, Slim?"

"Lawsy, Jedge, don't you do that. It'd be too much for my po' ol' head. Ain't no way a man could choose between you and the Chief." He shook his head. "Uh-uh. I better git Mr. Strawbridge. If y'all wants to talk politics, you know how much he love it."

Slim disappeared into the back room, and Chief Bowen turned his attention on the Judge. "It was you I came in to see. Do you have a few minutes?"

The Judge looked at his watch. "Sure, Lowell. Walk with me up the street. I still need to catch breakfast."

Joe Strawbridge stuck his head out of his office. "Haircuts at nine. Working on my damn quarterly tax. One of these days I'm going to send it all to the gov'ment and ask them to let me have what's left after they take what they want. Sure be easier." His head disappeared into the room.

The Judge and the Chief laughed as they walked out. Slim chuckled and locked the door behind them before picking up his broom.

..*

"Judge," Chief Bowen said as they walked along West Main Street, "you know I ain't got the kind of education you got, but I have a problem that has me twixt a rock and a hard place. I mean, I want to enforce the law, but it seems to me that sometimes a man has to follow his conscience. Don't you think so?"

"Lowell, with an introduction like that, I could answer about anything, and neither of us would know what we were talking about. If I understand right, you seem to have some kind of dilemma about your job. Am I right?"

"Yes sir, I do."

"Okay, instead of skating all around it, lay it on the line so we both understand. But before you do, remember that if we talk about a person who might come before me in the courtroom, I'll have to recuse myself."

Chief Bowen studied the Judge as they walked. "I know. And that's one of the reasons I haven't talked to you before. You're the best we have, and I don't want to do anything that will hurt you on the bench."

"Thank you," Judge Jackson said, touching the Chief on the arm. "I appreciate that vote of confidence. However, if I can help, that's part of my job, too. What's your problem?"

Chief Bowen took a deep breath. "I know you think a lot of Scooter, and so do I. But right now, I fear I may have to bring him in. I suspect he's doing some things that will get him arrested." He grinned a weak grin. "In Dawson, that'd be almost as bad as locking up the Mayor." His grin grew. "In fact, some folks would like it better if it was the Mayor." He smiled at the Judge.

The Judge chuckled. "I hope you're not asking me to comment on the qualifications of our good Mayor Jimmy James. He's been in the job for twenty-five years. I prefer to think he's learned it by now. And if not, maybe a few more elections will help him."

"Naw, Judge. That ain't where I'm headed. It's Scooter. That boy is mixing in things he shouldn't, things that might be getting worse by the day. Have you seen the way he's dressing? He's getting a lot of money from somewhere, and he's not doing the jobs he used to do. My problem is I'm wondering if I should look the other way. I mean, can I bust the folks he's running with without arresting him?"

The Judge took several steps without saying anything. "Lowell, you know the answer to that. You have to use an even hand when you apply the law. Remember, there's a blindfold around the eyes of the Lady of Justice. She doesn't see friends or enemies, people she respects or people she hates. And you can't either. If you have something on Scooter, you have to get a warrant—all personal feelings aside." The Judge stopped and took Chief Bowen by the arm. He stared into the Chief's face. "Is he breaking the law?"

"We're still building the case. The Raleigh police tell us moonshine is pouring into the city, and lots of it comes from Dawson and Nolan County. The Sheriff and I are cooperating, taking a hard look at some suspicious characters. We don't have it firmed up yet, but we're pretty sure Big Man is hauling. You've seen that car of his, haven't you? A bootlegger's car if ever I've seen one. And Scooter is riding shotgun for him."

"I see. What about the suppliers, the people making the hooch?"

"That's why we're going slow. We have some hunches, but not enough to set up a raid." He looked sad. "Arresting Scooter would be like arresting my own flesh and blood. I mean, he's shined my shoes almost every week since I got this job." He paused. "Well, he had until recently."

Judge Jackson frowned. "The law is the law. Your job is to apprehend those who break it, and work with the District Attorney to convict them." He patted the Chief on the shoulder. "Don't know if that's what you wanted to hear, but that's about all I can say."

..*

Scooter and Rodney joined Big Man in his living room. It was small, and the furniture looked like city dump discards or, at best, Salvation Army. There were two easy chairs and a couch. Filmy curtains, filled with dust, hung over the front and side windows. It was obvious no woman lived there.

Rodney dropped into one of the chairs, then jumped up. "Damn. You know you got a spring sticking up?"

"Don't bother me none," Big Man said through a giggle. "I don't set in that chair."

Rodney shifted to the sofa, settling in beside Scooter. "What'd you call us over here for? I got better things to do than sit around and git jabbed in the ass. I don't appreciate this. No, I don't appreciate it one little bit." He glared at Big Man.

"Tough shit," Big Man said. "You want to leave, jist git the hell outta here, and don't come back. I can find ten more to replace you, and they prob'ly be better men." He paused, his eyes locked on Rodney. "Any day you think you got more than me, you jist try me." He drew the switchblade from his pocket and flicked it open.

"Now, don't be gittin' all uppity on me," Rodney said. He made a show of rubbing his butt. "I jist shot my mouth off 'cause I got stabbed in the ass. You knows I's with you." He looked at Scooter who sat without saying a word. "We's with you. Ain't we, Scooter?"

"I am," Scooter answered in a soft voice staring at the knife. "I cain't speak for you."

Big Man's eyes stayed locked on Rodney. "Don't give me no mo' shit, you hear? Before I tell you my idea, you gotta swear you won't tell nobody. This is big, I mean, bigger than anything you ever heard. Whole lot bigger than that penny-ante shit got you sent to Raleigh. If you shoots your mouth off, either one of you, jist know I'm gonna be all over you. Won't matter how careful you are, I'll be there when you least expect it . . . and you'll die. Understand?"

Scooter nodded.

"C'mon, man. You knows you can trust me," Rodney said.

"No, I don't," Big Man said. "But you better know I'll kill you if you cross me." His eyes bored into Rodney.

"You an' me," Rodney said. "You an' me all the way."

"Better be. Now here's the plan. I talked to some folks in Raleigh where I delivers the shine. They don't care who makes it as long as it's clean, taste good, and don't make nobody sick. So, I'm thinkin', why should I haul for some white bastard when I can haul for myself? You followin' me on this?" He looked toward Scooter.

Scooter glanced at Rodney, then nodded. He had no clue what Big Man was talking about, but wouldn't admit it. Big Man was in a foul mood. He'd already pulled that knife twice.

"So," Big Man continued, "here's what we gonna do. We'll find us some sharecroppers and set them up makin' shine. Rodney, that your job. I got a couple in mind already, but I figger we can use five, maybe six. That way we'll have enough to make runs to Raleigh 'bout every day. My friends will help me git everything we need to start. Once we get it goin', we'll be in tall cotton. Won't take long before we pick up some more cars, maybe some trucks, and hire drivers." He grinned. "Them damn rednecks be out of business 'fore they know what's happenin'."

"Yeah," Rodney said. "That's the kind of thinking I likes. I already know some boys whut'll love it. They—"

"Slow down, boy. I'll tell you when. That's somethin' we'll talk about all in good time. Before you shoot your mouth off, you best make sure you're talking about people what makes good stuff, and knows how to keep quiet. I don't want no worthless niggers in this. So you might as well fergit most a yo' friends. I ain't about to go down on no bootlegging charge."

Rodney's mouth opened but Scooter shut him out. "What about me? What I gone be doin', takin' care of you?"

"Not quite. You be my number one bodyguard, but I got another job for you. You gonna be my enforcer. Somebody step out of line, you make sure they jump back fast."

He looked at Rodney. "We need guns. Don't git them from around here. Look up yo' old friends from prison, but make sure they don't owe the man. We'll need pistols and huntin' rifles, and I want Scooter to have a sawed-off shotgun. If we havta shoot, I wanta be ready." He stopped, appearing to think. "Better get some brass knuckles, too. Oh, and switchblades for each of us—four, maybe six inch blades. Can you git all that?"

"If you got the money, I can find stuff," Rodney answered. He turned to Scooter. "You ever shoot a gun—any kind of gun?"

Scooter lowered his head. "No. I ain't even held one." He looked at Big Man. "But I can do it if somebody teach me. You gonna show me?"

"Don't you worry. Once we gits them, we'll practice at the dump. Lots of big rats down there for targets." Big Man hesitated. "I been thinking. If you gone be my number one, you oughta move in here. I wants you to sleep with that shotgun by yo' side. Once we start messing with these ol' rednecks, it might git rough."

"Big Man," Rodney said, eyeing Scooter, "if it's gonna git rough 'round here, maybe I oughta stay with you."

"I kin protect him," Scooter said, his eyes flaring. "You just do whut you're told. Git me them guns, and I'll do the rest."

Big Man guffawed. "My ol' man used to say, don't mess with no wasp nest. You done broke that rule, Rodney. You ain't careful, Scooter might do more than buzz yo' head. Now, do like he said and git the guns. I got faith in him." He turned toward Scooter. "Let's go to yo' shack and git yo' stuff. You can have my little brother's room. He's movin' out."

CHAPTER THREE

Judge Jackson walked into the *Dawson Times*. "Henry, you back there?"

"No. I'm in New York, getting ready to attend a Dodgers game. Where do you think I'd be?" Henry stuck his head out of his office. "Come on back."

"Oh, man. Proves one more time you can take the Yankee out of the North, but you can't take the North out of the Yankee. No respect for their betters," the Judge said loud enough for Henry's ears as he entered the office. "So, any news worth printing?"

"Depends on you. Superior Court starts today. Do you have a headline for tomorrow's paper?"

"Only if you identify me as an *anonymous source*. On second thought, I'm not saying anything. You need to earn your keep. Come to court and get your news the hard way." He looked at the clothes tree in the corner. "That Dodgers cap is ready for the city dump. I don't remember it hanging there. Where'd you dig it up?"

Henry rested his hands on his desk, his fingers interlaced. "I hung it there as a reminder of how messed up things are today. That's the cap I gave Scooter several years ago. He loved it, wore it everywhere, all the time. But he brought it back to me. Said he didn't want it anymore."

"Yes, I remember his wearing it. But what's the big deal?"

"He's one of Debbie's rescue cases. I agreed with her he was worth helping. Suddenly, he goes big-time and doesn't need anyone's assistance. Debbie washed the cap, and I hung it there hoping he'll come by one day to retrieve it. Another example of how things are changing too fast." He sighed. "Speaking of which, anything percolating down the law chain about Negro rights?"

"Nothing yet." The Judge dropped into the visitor's chair. "But, sooner or later, there's going to be a case, and when it happens, the reverberations will be felt all over the south."

"How about the Till Case in Mississippi?"

"Emmett Till?" The Judge looked at the ceiling. "I wish I could say that case is an aberration, but it's not. Young colored man whistles at white woman. Taken out, mutilated, and murdered. Happens far too often. It's happened here in Eastern North Carolina, although I'm happy to say, not recently. But it'll happen again. As long as we have males and females, we're going to have flirting. Color of skin only slows it down."

"But this time, there's been some stink about it. Why? Because Till's from Illinois?"

"Chicago, isn't it? And look at the time frame. Till allegedly whistled on August twenty-fourth. He disappeared on the twenty-eighth, two white half-brothers were arrested on the twenty-ninth. Till's mutilated body was found on the thirty-first. On September sixth, the same day Till was buried in Illinois, the accused were indicted by a Grand Jury. Sounds to me like the authorities were on it from the first minute. They knew who did it, brought them in, and took them to trial without any problem." The Judge paused, collecting his thoughts. "The trial started on September nineteenth. There was no doubt those two guys killed Till after doing some really horrible things to him. They even ripped out one of his eyes. But four days later, the jury—all white males—found them innocent. It only took an hour and seven minutes to reach the decision, and one of the jurors bragged they took a break so they wouldn't be too fast." He paused. "How'm I doing? Pretty rotten form of justice, isn't it?"

Henry nodded. "Sounds like you memorized the case file."

"No, but I'd love to read it. The question is, will this slip by as another example of race relations in the South, or will it lead to something bigger than what we've seen."

"There's been some outrage in the New York newspapers," Henry said. "Only time will tell. But there's another movement that could have a bigger impact."

"What?"

"Bus boycott in Montgomery, Alabama."

"Yeah? When did it start?"

"Hasn't, yet. But word has it a group of Negroes are all set to break the city busses if they don't change their policy of coloreds having to sit in the back. One of the leaders is a woman named Jo Ann Robinson. She's not some field hand, she's educated, a professor at Alabama State College, but more important for our conversation, she's a member of the Women's Political Council in Montgomery, and that's the group ready to roll. She says she has at least twenty-five businesses ready to support her. They're waiting for the right excuse to get things moving."

"Doesn't sound like much," the Judge said. "I'm more concerned with the mess-ups in the justice system."

"If they raise a stink with the busses, it'll end up in court. What're we going to do when things like that come to Nolan County?"

The Judge pinched the bridge of his nose. "I wish I knew. But I can tell you this. Once it starts, things will never be the same. Neighbors will build fences between their homes, relatives will argue different sides, and families will be split—the effects of the Civil War all over again. I don't know how the *new* South will look, but I'm betting the skin tone will be a lot darker. The day of absolute white rule is drawing to a close."

"Shouldn't it? Shouldn't we have Negroes on the police force, helping govern as town councilmen, even judges? Don't we call ourselves a country where anyone can rise to any level? And school segregation. What possible reason is there for having white children in one school and colored children in another? If nothing else, look at the wasted tax dollars. And anyone who believes they receive equal education hasn't walked the hallways of the schools. I have. The white schools get the best, by far the best. The coloreds are being short-changed in every department."

The Judge stood. "Hey, I didn't come here for a philosophical discussion. Want some breakfast?"

"Coward." Henry chuckled. "But breakfast sounds good. Do my reactionary image good to be seen with a Superior Court Judge. Give me a minute to let Eli know I'm leaving."

..*

The Judge and Henry walked west on Main Street, headed

toward Lucille's. "So, how's Jane doing?" Henry asked. "Debbie says she's the reigning queen of the church pew."

"She loves my being a Superior Court Judge. Remember the party we threw—I should say, she threw. She loved my appointment. I only wish she viewed the ramifications in the same light."

Henry watched his shoes moving forward, one step at a time. "I heard she's not thrilled that you may have to rule on integration."

"Off the record?" the Judge said.

"Not only off the record, but the promise of a friend."

"She threatened to leave me if I rule in a pro-integration manner. Her upbringing is firmly separation. Some nights, she gets so aggravated with me, she sleeps in the guestroom."

"As you said, families will be disrupted."

"Yeah. I speak from personal experience."

They covered a half block in silence, then the Judge said, "How are things with you and Debbie?"

Henry smiled. "Couldn't be better. She is one sweet lady."

"Will I hear wedding bells soon?"

"Slow down. So far, she's done a wonderful job of slimming me down, redoing my wardrobe, and showing me how great life can be. But marriage? I don't know about that one. Every day, I ask myself do I love her enough. Does she love me enough? Are we strong enough to make it work? Maybe it's beyond my comprehension. Look what you're going through."

"Don't judge it by my current situation. I have no regrets. Jane and I have been very happy. Of course, there have been bumps along the way, but we survived those, and we'll make it through this one. Her threat of divorce is only that, a threat."

"That's not how you sounded a minute ago."

"Don't get me wrong. It hurts to have her in the guestroom, and to quarrel with her. But I have every faith we'll survive this and be closer because of it."

The Judge walked on, apparently deep in thought. "Marriage, a good marriage, is more than a spur of the moment thing. It's a joining of the spirit, just as you join the flesh. It's two different personalities melding into one, two people standing as one. That doesn't mean there won't be disagreements." He smiled. "Jane and

I have had some doozies, worse than the one we're in now. But it's temporary. Love transcends the present. Love lives in the past, the present, and the future. Love accompanies you to the grave, then survives after you're gone. Take Debbie as an example. I'm sure she still loves Tom. But the very fact of her love for him means there's room for you."

"You had me until that last," Henry said. "What do you mean?"

"I mean the best proof of the ability to love is having loved. The very fact she loved Tom proves she has the capacity to love you. I've known others like Debbie who entered a new relationship that was stronger because of the earlier loss."

"What does that say about me?"

The Judge stopped and tapped Henry on the arm. "Quit thinking so much and listen to your heart. Go ahead and ask Debbie to marry you. If you two are truly in love, everything will work out. My only warning is, be sure you're in love with her and not simply in love with love. And vice-versa, of course. Too many people today don't understand the difference."

Henry stared into space, then looked into the Judge's face. "I've never heard love and marriage explained so simply, yet so completely. Maybe I should hire you to write a marriage counseling column." He chuckled. "Seriously, thank you. However, you voiced one of my concerns. Am I in love with Debbie, or to use your expression, in love with love? It's been so long, I'm afraid to find out the truth."

The Judge stepped off, and Henry fell in beside him. "I can only talk about Jane and me. You and Debbie have to find out for yourselves."

CHAPTER FOUR

THOUGHTS FROM THE EDITOR

I've been the editor of your paper for almost ten years, and I am pleased you allow me this privilege—and I do consider it a privilege to live among you and publish the Dawson Times. I moved here straight from the battlefields of Germany (figuratively, not literally). During the war, I served with many fine men. Skin colors covered the spectrum of the citizenry of our country. Most were some variation of white, meaning from a European heritage. However, there were also Indians (red), Orientals (yellow), Latinos (brown) and yes, even Negroes (black). When the shells fell and the agony of the battlefield threatened to overwhelm me, I lost interest in skin color. I fought to save myself first, and those around me, second. I discovered that bullets and shrapnel have no prejudices. They rip and tear flesh with no consideration of skin color. And the blood that flows is red, the same shade of red.

When I first arrived in Dawson, I was bothered by the Whites Only and Coloreds Only signs, the separate facilities wherever I went, the little windows in the fronts or sides of restaurants through which Negroes could be served. But as I lived with you, those things became commonplace and, all too soon, I accepted them as normal.

Today, I was at the Courthouse, our symbol of justice. When I entered, I automatically turned to the right, the Whites Only stairwell. Upstairs, I sat on the right, the Whites Only side. Later, I drank from the Whites Only water fountain—in the building where justice is purported to be blind. Does anyone see anything wrong with the picture?

Last year, the US Supreme Court ruled that our treatment of school children in a separate, but equal manner is illegal. I have no insight as to how long the ruling will take to reach Nolan County. I only know that when it happens, it will be right. Not right because it is the law of the land, but right because we are all humans together.

This year we celebrated the one hundred seventy-ninth anniversary of the founding of our nation with its government emphasizing equality. The Declaration of Independence says . . . all men are created equal . . . The battlefields of Europe were my proof. All that is left is for us to accept it. I pray we will.

Henry rolled the paper out of the typewriter, laid the sheets on the desk, and read his final draft aloud. A smile formed. "Should have done this years ago." He turned toward the door. "Eli, come in here, please."

Eli took the copy from Henry and looked at it. "You sure you wanna run this, Mr. Flanagan? Gonna cause a stink."

Henry looked into Eli's eyes. "Yes, I'm sure. And if it stinks, we'll just burn some candles. Set it front page, center, above the fold."

"All right, suh. I'll do it." Eli shuffled from the office, a smile playing at his lips.

After giving the editorial to his typesetter, Henry leaned back in his chair. *That felt good. About time I stood up for what's right.*

He rocked forward when he heard, "Mabel, is Hank hiding in his office?"

"Yeah, he and his trusty typewriter. He just gave Eli some copy so he might have accomplished something today." Both women laughed as Debbie's heels clicked on the floor announcing her path to the office.

She tapped on the doorframe. "Hey, good looking. You about ready for lunch?"

"Only if there's a beautiful Southern Belle to break bread with me." He rose, walked to the doorway, and kissed her on the cheek. "Look at this." He handed her a carbon copy of what he wrote.

As she read, a frown formed. "Are you sure?"

"I'm sure. What's the problem?"

"This will hurt you. You've been here long enough to know Southerners get angry when outsiders tell them what's best. And you've been here long enough to know you're still an outsider. Some of our good citizens will think you're interfering."

"So be it." Henry shrugged.

"Listen, I'm not slimming you down, teaching you to dress, and falling in love with you so you can become the local pariah. Be sure. Running something like this could cost you the paper." She crossed her arms over her chest. "It could get you a visit in the middle of the night."

"Debbie, aren't you being a bit melodramatic? This is 1955, not 1875."

"Hank, you've been here ten years, but you haven't learned much. People who mess with race relations make themselves unpopular. I just want you to know the hornets' nest you might be swatting."

Henry paused, reflecting on her words. "My intellect says you're right, but my conscience says I have to do this. The editorial is only the first. Honey, can't you see that things must change? Dawson. Nolan County. North Carolina. The South. Progress cannot be denied. The Supreme Court has ruled. It's only a matter of time. Any government that doesn't comply, will see federal troops in the streets. Is that what you want?"

"You know better. You might be right, but I'm scared for you. I've only had you for a few months. I don't want to see you tarred, feathered, and ridden out of town on a rail. If you're sure you want to do it, I'm with you."

Henry pulled her into his arms. "Thank you. I knew I could count on you."

"Ah, 'scuse me, Muster Flanagan." Eli stuck his head in the door.

Debbie stepped away from Henry, a blush rising.

"I hates to bother you, but are you really sure? I done read it good now and, I mean, it might be the best thang you ever wrote, but—"

"Dammit, Eli," Henry said. "Yes, I want it set exactly like I wrote it, just where I said. We'll bar the door and stand together."

"You the boss, suh. I just hates to lose my nice job when somebody burn de place down." Eli walked toward the pressroom mumbling. "Now where's an old man like me gonna fin' another job like this, workin' for a boss like him?"

"Don't cuss, honey," Debbie said. "He's only worried about you—same as me."

..*

Debbie's prediction proved correct. The *Dawson Times* hit the street on Thursday morning at seven a.m. By noon, Mabel had fielded twenty-seven calls, twenty of them complaining about the editorial. Ten were from advertisers. Seven of those canceled their next ad. Home deliveries were still to come.

Mrs. Christiana Andrews was the first home delivery through the door. She came in screeching at Mabel. "One time, the very first time the boy puts the paper on the porch, and this is what I see on the front page. What's the matter with you people?"

"Good afternoon, Mrs. Andrews. Is there something you want to talk to me about?"

"You? No, not you. Get that damnyankee out here,"

Henry overheard the conversation from his office. "Ah, crap." He swallowed, stood, put on his suit jacket, and walked out. "Mrs. Andrews, how are you? Is there something you need?"

"Need, yes? I *need* to cancel my subscription. If you're gonna start pushing niggers down my throat, I don't *need* your paper." She spun and stomped out.

Henry stared after her, frowning, then turned toward Mabel. "Tell Eli to run another two hundred copies. I feel like everybody's going to want one."

..*

Charlie Burnette pushed back from the table and rubbed his belly. "Twarn't too bad a supper tonight. Woulda been better if the biscuits hadn't tasted like they was made from cement. I mighta broke a tooth. What'd you do with the paper? You did remember to pick up a copy, didn't you?" Under his breath, he mumbled, "Be just like that ignernt bitch to forget."

Alice Burnette, wife of Charlie Burnette, flinched. "I might have throwed it in the trash already. I thought you read it." She ran her hands down the sides of the faded, worn dress she wore. Her shoes were drab, but matched her hair, which hadn't seen a hairdresser in years. She attempted to style it, but couldn't hide the premature gray that dimmed the once brown tresses. Split ends were the best part of its condition.

"Well, woman, I didn't. What the hell you think I give you money for? I'll tell you when you can throw things out. I done told you I want that paper beside my plate waitin' fer me when I come in. So whatever you done, git it. And it better not be messed up. You oughta know better than mess with the paper until I read it. Maybe you need another lesson in who runs this house." He glared at her. "I need to see if there's anything about cotton prices. 'Course, I doubt it. That damnyankee prob'ly ain't found out we grow cotton yet."

As she scrambled from the kitchen, he muttered, "Don't know why we can't get a Southern paper here. Oughta run that sonnavabitch outta town on a rail."

His wife returned with the paper, folded so the front page didn't show. "Charlie, don't you need to check on the still? You were in the field most of the day. Somebody mighta been there."

"Ha, ain't nobody gonna screw with my still. They know I'll track'm down and kill'm. Now, hand me that damn paper and pour 'nother cup of coffee."

Charlie grinned as she lay the paper on the table, her hand trembling. "You're learning a little respect, ain't you? 'Bout damn time."

"Charlie, you mind if I visit Shirley a bit tonight? I ain't talked to her in a coupla days. If it gits too late, I could stay over there."

"Hell no, you ain't goin' to her house. Ev'ry time you talks to that sister of yourn you come home with some uppity bullshit. She puts ideas in your head that ain't good for you. Last time, you come home with that shit about me giving up the farm and moving into town. Git a job in a store, you said. I had to put the strap on you before you quit talking 'bout it. Naw, you stay away from her."

"Yes, dear," she said, pouring his coffee. "Be careful, it's real hot. If you don't mind, maybe I could go for a walk. I need some fresh air."

"What's the matter with you? You stay right here and clean up this kitchen." He rubbed his crotch. "By the time you git finished, I'll be through with the paper, and we can go to the bedroom."

"I got kind of a bad headache tonight. Some fresh air might help. Then, when you finish with the paper—"

"Cain't you hear? I said, clean up this place. Git these damn dishes outta my way." He leered. "I kin cure your headache one way or the other—the strap or what you really want."

"Whatever you say," she answered in a sad, fearful voice. "You're my husband. I'll clean up, then wait for you in the bedroom."

Charlie Burnette stared at his wife's back. "You damn right I'm your husband. That means you do what I say. Don't you fergit it. I put the food on the table and the roof over your head. Now clean them dishes and be quiet about it. I'm gonna set on the porch and read the paper." He rose and walked from the room.

He pulled his rocker around to catch the light from the bare overhead bulb and opened the paper. The editorial caught his attention, and he began reading, his lips moving with the words. At the end of the first paragraph, he stopped and rubbed his eyes. "Damnyankee thinks he oughta git a ribbon for goin' to war. He don't have no idea how tough it was back here tryin' to make ends meet. Sonnavabitch wouldn't last a day in the tobacco field."

Sipping his coffee, Charlie flipped the paper up and continued reading. "What the hell?" he screamed, dumping the hot coffee into his lap. He jumped up, brushing at his pants with one hand and flinging the paper with the other. The cup and saucer shattered on the rough boards of the floor. He danced around, yelling obscenities into the evening air. "Who the hell does he think he is? Somebody's got to learn that som'bitch a lesson, and I'm just the man to do it."

He raced toward his pickup. "I'll get Marvin, and we'll pay him a visit. A few whops up alongside his head'll teach him something. Justice be blind, my ass. Justice be white, and it's 'bout time that bastard learned it."

..*

Martha Burnette placed the wet plate into the dish-drainer, then reached into the soapy water. She washed another dish, dipped it in the rinse water, and placed it alongside the first.

Dogs barking caused her to look through the window. Marvin's pack of hounds raced toward a vehicle turning into the yard. Twin beams of light bounced, then stopped.

Hurrying into the front room, she saw Charlie Burnette rushing toward the house. Her hand popped to her mouth as she retreated to the kitchen, her other hand clenched into a fist. She saw rage on Charlie's face and knew it would infect Marvin. She wanted to run, to get away before they started drinking, before they got drunk, before . . .

The front door burst open. "Marvin. Marvin, get out here. We gotta do somethin' about this."

Martha peeked through the door and saw her husband enter the room from the hallway fastening the galluses on his overalls. "What you yellin' about? Man can't even get comfortable in his own home. What got your dander all riled now?"

"The damn newspaper. You seen it? We gotta stop that damn-fool yankee or he's gonna ruin the whole county. He's trying to rile the niggers."

"Slow down. Let me see what you're carrying on about."

Charlie handed him the paper, and Marvin stared at it. "Too many words. I ain't in the mood." He yelled toward the kitchen. "Martha, git out here and read this to me."

She swallowed, but the lump in her throat wouldn't go down. She walked into the room. She could have been the sister of Alice Burnette, but wasn't. However, her looks, demeanor, and the fear in her eyes mirrored Alice. "What is it, Marvin? What you want me to read?"

"You tell her, Charlie."

Charlie pointed to the editorial then stomped around the room mumbling under his breath.

When she began to read, both men sat, Charlie leaning forward on the edge of his chair. At the end of the first paragraph, she paused, afraid to go on, hoping she wouldn't have to.

Marvin said, "Hell, ain't no news there. We seen enough nigger blood to know it's red."

"Hush," Charlie said. "Martha. Keep readin'."

As she continued into the editorial, her eyes grew more fearful, and she glanced at her husband frequently. What she saw was not reassuring. Marvin's face was turning red, a sure sign of anger. When she finished, he grabbed the paper from her hands and crumpled it.

She stepped away from him, but he gripped her arm. "Git my

jug. I gotta think on this."

She flinched. "Maybe you shouldn't. You—"

"Dammit, woman. How many beatings you need to teach you not to back-sass me? Git my shine and two clean glasses. Then git the hell outta my sight."

She hurried from the room, picked up his moonshine jug and two glasses, and delivered them to Charlie and Marvin. Then she left the house, taking to the dirt road, and walking away. She'd wait until he was asleep before she went home. There'd been too many whippings and rapes when he was drunk. "Not tonight," she prayed, "please don't let him hurt me again tonight."

..*

Three hours later, Charlie and Marvin Burnette drove down Main Street, the pickup truck weaving from side to side. The hour was late enough that the street was empty. Charlie was behind the wheel while Marvin hung out the passenger window yelling and slobbering into the night.

It had taken two hours of liquid courage to get them ready for the trip, their threats gettin more generalized as their words became more slurred. Only when they depleted Marvin's *private stock*, did they decide it was time. The truck bed held large rocks, rags, and a can of kerosene they had gathered while still sober enough to function.

Charlie stopped in front of the newspaper, jumping the curb with his left front tire and knocking over a parking meter. He stumbled out, dropping to his knees as his feet hit the sidewalk. "C'mon, Marvin. We gotta burn this place to the ground." He giggled, struggling to stand.

Marvin got out and circled the truck, staggering while holding onto the bed with his right hand. At the tailgate, he reached in and grabbed a big rock with both hands. "First, we gotta make some air holes. Burn better if it get some air." He heaved the rock through the front window, tumbling forward as he did so.

"Yeah, good idea," Charlie shouted, following his brother's example. He also fell on his face as the rock crashed into the glass.

They rolled onto their backs laughing.

"Yeah, we gonna make this place look like the fourth of July," Marvin said. "Wisht we had some hot dogs."

"More air holes," Charlie said, struggling to gain his feet.

A police car pulled up, and Chief Bowen jumped out. "What the hell you people doing? Marvin, Charlie, that you? Get your asses up."

They staggered to their feet, leaning on one another, blinking and squinting as if trying to see who had spoken.

Marvin said, "Oh, it's you, Chief. Stay out of this. We gotta job to do. This old newspaper gonna burn. You shoulda shut it down, but you didn't. Now we gotta do it." He wobbled to the truck and picked up another rock, turned and threw it. "We gonna turn this piece of shit to ashes."

Chief Bowen shook his head, leaned into the car, and keyed the radio. "Get everybody on duty up here to Main Street. We may have a fight on our hands. The Burnettes are drunk and disorderly again." He replaced the microphone and leaned against the car. "You boys put them rocks down now, or you're gonna take a whipping when my men get here. Which is it gonna be?"

"Go to hell. You ain't nothing but a white nigger," Charlie said. "I'm gonna bust you like I shoulda done a long time ago." He threw a rock through the windshield of the police car, then whooped in laughter. "Hey, Marvin. Lookit that. The Chief's windshield done broke."

Marvin pointed at the can of kerosene. "Yeah, bet it'd burn just like this ol' newspaper."

Chief Bowen glanced up the street at his approaching backup. "I'm real sorry you boys are acting like that." He reached through the window of his cruiser and came out with his nightstick. "Down on the sidewalk, both of you, spread-eagled. Don't make me hurt you."

Charlie's laughter grew louder. "Hey, Marvin, he don't want to hurt us. Ain't that rich?" He stepped toward the Chief. "He don't—"

His speech mutated into a scream when Chief Bowen cracked him across the shins. He crumpled onto the sidewalk, moaning.

"Marvin," the Chief said in a commanding voice. "Do what I told you."

Marvin stared at his brother. "You done mess with the wrong folks." He pulled a six-inch rock from the pickup with both hands and lifted it upward, extending his arms to throw it.

Chief Bowen sighed and jabbed the end of the nightstick into Marvin's gut, sinking it about four inches into his paunch.

Marvin's hands grabbed for his stomach as he heaved, vomit spewing onto the street. The Chief jumped backward, missing the flow. The stone he'd been holding crashed down onto Marvin's head, dropping him to the sidewalk.

"Not in the book, but effective," the Chief said, walking around the puddle to Marvin's back, then kneeling and cuffing his hands behind him.

"Damn, Chief, you didn't have to hit me like that," Marvin moaned, blood trickling across his forehead. "We's just having a little fun. I wouldn't a let Charlie burn the newspaper office. My head hurts awful bad."

A second police car arrived, followed by a third. The officers jumped out and cuffed Charlie who sat rubbing his shins and blubbering.

"They're going to have some nasty hangovers when they face the Judge in the morning," Chief Bowen said. "Take'm in and book'm. Drunk, disorderly, threatening a police officer, damage to personal property, damage to a police car . . . Ah hell. Check the book and use anything you find. I'm plain tired of these two assholes." He looked at his car. "One of you take this in. I gotta let Henry know what his editorial did for him and this town. I'll take your car, Oakley."

He took a few steps, then turned back. "You're on duty the rest of the night. Christopher and Oakley, post yourself right here in front of the newspaper. The rest of you keep a sharp eye on Main Street. Somebody by the radio at all times." He nodded toward the Burnettes. "There might be more like them. Nothing good is gonna come from this."

..*

The door opened under Chief Bowen's pounding, revealing Henry on the other side. "It's bad enough you woke me, but did you have to wake everybody in the building? What's up? You bring me a headline?"

The Chief stormed into the room. "I'm bringing you a dose of reality. I headed for your office this morning, but got sidetracked. While it might not have changed anything, at least I would've had my say before now."

"Have a seat. I suspect you're somehow riled about my editorial. Is that it?"

Chief Bowen shook his finger in Henry's face. "Riled? No, your paper riled me this morning. Now I'm so damned mad I could break something. Just who the hell do you think you are? You think because you lived here a few years, you have a right to mess with the people and traditions of the South—traditions that evolved over two-three hundred years? I had hope for you, I really did. I have hope for the future, hope the races can come closer together. You can't rush it. It will take time, and it will take patience on both sides. The Judge is doing it right. You're . . . you're—"

"What happened?" Henry dropped onto the couch, a deep sigh shaking his body. "Something must have set you off. What have my words caused?"

Chief Bowen walked to a chair and sat, then bounced to his feet and paced. "For starters, they got your office busted up, the front windows broken out. I arrested the Burnette brothers for throwing rocks. They had kerosene and rags in the truck. If they'd started a fire, the whole business district might have gone up."

"So you come here to yell at me because they're fools?"

He spun on Henry. "There you go. Sure, they're fools. But they're local fools. They grew up here. They might be the worst, but there's a lot of folks who don't hanker to share with Negroes. They're quite happy with the way things are. You got to understand that and quit pushing."

Henry studied his hands. When he spoke, his words were soft, almost humble. "Lowell, you're a local, too. You grew up here. Yet, you know that what I wrote is true. I've seen you with both races. You're fair, you're even-handed—or as even-handed as you can be." He stared into the Chief's face. "I bet if you could choose between the Burnettes and most of the coloreds in town, you'd go with the coloreds."

Chief Bowen flared. "See, that's the difference between me and you. I took an oath to uphold the law of the town, county, hell, the whole country. And I work hard doing it. It don't matter a hoot what I feel inside, only what the law books say. If the legislature said tomorrow all men had to be bald, I'd buy a set of clippers. The day comes when I can't enforce the law, I'll resign. That's the way it is with my job. One side or the other—ain't no middle ground, no grays, either right or wrong. But you, you think you're so damned special because you can write whatever you please, anything that feels good. You own the paper so you stick anything in it you want. You don't stop and think of what might happen. You just set behind your desk and type."

Pausing, the Chief took a deep breath, squeezing his eyes shut. When he spoke again, his voice was under control. "Your words mess with people's lives. They could get somebody killed. Suppose you'd been working late tonight when the Burnettes came to call? And what happens tomorrow and the day after? We ain't had a colored man lynched in this county for as long as I remember. I sure hope that piece of shit you wrote don't cause the next one."

The Chief turned toward the door, then stopped, his gaze lowered. "Sorry I blew up, but how I feel personally don't change a thing. I'm not like you. I can't do things simply because I feel like it." He hesitated. "I have a squad car in front of your place. Things should be alright 'til morning."

CHAPTER FIVE

Henry's stare stayed locked on the door Chief Bowen slammed when he left. Thoughts rushed pell-mell through his head, none taking serious form, rippling like a pool when raindrops fall. However, a few basics swam to the surface. Was Chief Bowen right? Was he meddling in something he didn't understand, and making it worse? He loved Dawson and didn't want to hurt it. He loved Debbie, and she was part of the area and its heritage. She supported him, didn't she? Could she love him if he lost the respect of her friends?

He squeezed his eyes shut remembering her words from Wednesday when he showed her the editorial. *This will hurt you . . . Some of our good citizens will see this as interference . . . It could get you a visit in the middle of the night . . . People that mess with race relations make themselves unpopular . . .*

He realized she'd given him good advice, which he ignored in his zeal to change the world. She never said she agreed with him. She warned him. Not once had she said she believed as he did.

Segregation was wrong. Deep inside, he knew it, but what did he know about the impact of sudden change? Nothing. Exactly nothing. Yet he'd charged in like a clumsy knight-errant, a modern day Don Quixote.

Debbie? Would she stay with him in the face of the backlash by the Burnettes, and maybe others? He wanted to call her, but the hour was too late. He'd find out tomorrow if he'd lost the woman he loved.

May as well get dressed and check the damage, he thought. There'll be no sleep tonight.

..*

Henry stood in front of his office, Officer Oakley beside him.

The policeman said, "We swept as much of the glass out of the way as we could. Don't want people hurt."

"Thanks," Henry said. He peeked through the window at the mess. "Looks like I have a clean up job on the other side. Do you know any glass workers? I want these replaced and lettered as soon as possible—tomorrow, uh, today, if it can be done."

"Try Dawson Glass Company. Don't know how much inventory they keep, but they're the only one around that works with big sheets."

"Of course. Guess my head's not working. They advertise with me . . . well, they did. I wonder how many will drop me now."

Oakley looked over his shoulder at his car where Officer Christopher sat. "Mr. Flanagan, I read what you wrote." He frowned. "It sounds good on paper, and I don't disagree with you, but things been this way a long time. None of my business, but if I was you, I'd tone it down a bit. Chief Bowen might not be driving by the next time."

"Yeah. Guess I was lucky."

"They might come after you—not your paper." Oakley walked to his car, opened the door, and climbed in.

Henry sighed and entered the building, his chin resting on his chest. After turning on the overhead lights, he looked around, frowned, and shook his head. He retrieved a broom and dustpan from the back room and began sweeping the shards of glass into a pile.

"Ain't no fittin' job for the editor," Eli said, coming through the front door. "You give me that broom. I bet you got some writin' to do."

"Word travels fast, doesn't it?" Henry said, handing over the cleaning tools. "How'd you hear?"

Eli chuckled. "Ev'rybody down by the river know. Don't know who started it, but won't surprise me if some a my neighbors be here soon."

Even as he said it, Aunt Liddie hustled her bulk through the door. "Ooooh, what a mess. Now, Muster Flan'gan, don't you worry 'bout nuttin. Joshua be here soon with some plywood, and Paster Turner's out roundin' up folks to help. Did they hurt anything 'cept the windows?" She walked to Eli. "Give me that broom. You don't know nothin' 'bout sweepin' no flo'. You git in the back and set whatever our newspaperman writes."

Eli smiled. "Good idea, Aint Liddie. I git everything ready."

"Hold on, you two," Henry said. "What makes you think I feel like writing?"

Both stared at him.

"You ain't gonna let that white trash scare you, is you?" Aint Liddie said. "I thought you had mo' backbone than that."

Henry looked at her, then heard hammering. Looking toward the broken windows, he saw a piece of plywood going up, a group of black hands supporting it.

"Nice evening, ain't it?" Pastor Turner said, peeking through the opening. "Weather's right warm for this time of year."

Shaking his head, Henry retreated to his office wondering what to do. He took two sheets of onionskin, two pieces of carbon paper, a sheet of bond, and slipped the package into the typewriter. He stared at it, praying for inspiration. After a moment, he typed.

It's one a.m., and I'm in my office. Outside, I hear the noise of hammers nailing plywood over what were the front windows of the Dawson Times. I wrote an editorial, a voice from this newspaper—my voice—that provoked an attack. Fortunately, our fine Police Chief, Lowell Bowen, intercepted the gutless scum that hides in the blackness of the night, and prevented more damage than broken glass.

What kind of vile things could I have written that caused such a reaction? Am I a writer that can foment revolution? Am I another Thomas Paine? He wrote, These are the times that try men's souls. His words inspired his fellow revolutionaries, those who went against insurmountable odds in 1776. The result was the United States of America.

Oh, I'd love to claim to be his modern incarnation. But it is not so. I'm only a humble scribe that sees things as they are and knows they are wrong. With that knowledge, I had the audacity to state that justice should be blind. In the past, I have also pointed out that the U.S. Supreme Court ruled that separate but equal schools are unfair and in violation of the laws of our land.

I know the fair-minded citizens of Dawson and Nolan County of both races will read my words with an open mind and nod in agreement. Bigots from both sides will declare me unfair, not understanding, a meddling Yankee, and other uncomplimentary things. So be it. I wrote it. I stand by it.

He rolled the paper up to reread his words.

Debbie burst into his office. "Are you alright," she said, not waiting for an answer. "I'm so damned mad I could spit. What idiots . . . they'd better not have hurt you . . . how dare they attack your paper . . . Are you sure you're okay? If they hurt one hair on your head . . ."

Henry stood, laughing as Debbie sputtered disconnected threats against the Burnettes and words of care for him. Her outrage bubbled over. He'd never seen her in such disarray. The dress she wore was mis-buttoned, causing it to hang longer on one side. She had on mismatched shoes and no makeup. Her hair looked like a bird's nest.

"What are you laughing at? Don't you realize—"

Henry came around the desk and kissed her. "Damn, I love you, Deborah Patterson. Will you marry me?"

"Why are you laughing? Those rednecks could have—" She stared at him. "What did you say?"

He grinned, surprised that he'd asked. But it felt good, and moreover, it felt right. "I'm thinking I'll be safer if I keep you on my side. So I proposed marriage, Mrs. Patterson. Of course, it's also true that I'm madly in love with you."

"Well . . . why . . . what . . ." Her mouth kept moving but no words came out. "You want to marry me?"

"Yes, more than anything I've ever done or will ever do in my life. I want you to be Mrs. Hank Flanagan." He took her hand and knelt. "Will it help if I repeat it from here? Okay, my dear Debbie, will you—"

"Get up. You look silly down there. I just can't believe . . . I mean, I don't . . . Yes. Oh yes, Hank, I want to marry you." She threw her arms around his neck.

"Do my ol' ears hear what they says they hears?" Aunt Liddie stuck her head in the doorway of the office. "You and Miz Patterson gitting hitched? Oh, that just be the best thing yet." She stopped and sniffled, large tears on her brown cheeks. "I sho' hope y'all do it where I can see. I loves weddings, and yours be most special."

Henry grinned. "Aunt Liddie, I'll make sure you and all my friends are invited. I want everyone to—" He stopped, his forehead wrinkling. He looked at Debbie. "That can't happen can it? There's no place we can be married in front of all the people of Dawson. Even our wedding must be segregated."

"Don't you worry yo' haid 'bout that," Liddie said. "I jist peek through the window." She blew her nose in a rag she dug from a pocket.

"Well, isn't this a homey scene?" Judge Jackson said, leaning against the doorway of the office. "Here, I thought I'd find the *Dawson Times* in ashes, and instead, I find Henry and Debbie cuddling in public, Aunt Liddie not doing much of a job of chaperoning, and the front getting boarded over. And from the looks of some of that plywood, I don't want to know where it came from."

Debbie unwound her arms, blushing. "Sorry, Judge. I didn't hear you come in. Hank just—"

"Proposed," Henry said. "And my second proposal of the night goes to you, Dan. Will you be my best man? If it hadn't been for you, I'd have never found the courage."

"I'm honored," Judge Jackson said. "Have you two picked a date?"

"Oh my," Debbie said. "The wedding party. I have so much to do. A date? No, no, we don't have a date . . . do we, Hank? I mean, do you have a special day? Soon, though. But far enough away that we can plan a big wedding. Is the Baptist Church okay? Where should we have the reception? A dress. I have to order a dress. Maid of Honor. Oh, my gosh, who? We need to talk to—"

"Excuse me, Judge." Henry gathered Debbie into his arms and stopped her rambling with another kiss. "Now my fiancée, go home and get some rest. I have work to do."

"Yas'm, he be right," Liddie said. "You needs yo' beauty sleep. You looking right rough."

Debbie's hand flew to her hair. She looked at Henry, love shining in her eyes. "As long as I know you're okay, I'll go home. I love you, my stubborn newspaper editor. But please, please don't write anything else that will cause more people to come after you." She kissed him on the cheek, then allowed Liddie to lead her from the room.

The Judge watched them leave. To Henry, he said, "Looks like you took our talk to heart."

"Yes, plus tonight let me know how fast life can change." Henry's eyes followed Debbie as she walked through the front door. *What will she think when she sees my new editorial*?

Henry and the Judge walked to the front of the building and studied the plywood going up. "You best stand back, Judge, Muster Flan'gin," Pastor Turner said, chuckling. "Some a the little pieces of glass go flyin', no matter how careful we is. When Aint Liddie won't in there tellin' you what to do, we kept her busy with that broom and dust pan. But even with that, I wouldn't walk around barefoot for a while."

"I promise to wear shoes," Henry said, smiling. "You're doing a great job. I sure appreciate it."

"Ain't nothing, suh. We ain't never had nobody around here like you. We appreciates a white man what can see things from our side some. You gonna write another them pieces?"

"I'm thinking about it, Pastor. I sure am."

The Judge who'd been inspecting the window covering turned. "Maybe we ought to talk, Henry. Let's go back to your office."

"Excuse us, Pastor," Henry said. "When the Judge wants to talk, I listen." He tapped the Judge on the arm and headed toward his office.

The Judge closed the door behind them, then sat opposite Henry. "How do you plan to respond to what happened tonight?"

"The only way I know how—with words. Want to see them?" Henry picked up a copy of his latest editorial and handed it to his friend.

The Judge read in silence. When he finished, he said, "It's an excellent piece, but you've attracted a pack of wild dogs. Throwing more red meat at them might not be the best idea." He looked at the paper again. "Under normal circumstances, I wouldn't recommend you change a word."

"Normal? I guess you think it's too strong for these abnormal times."

The Judge's voice came out soft, almost embarrassed sounding. "Yes. That's exactly what I think. Dawson is a powder keg. It won't take much of a spark to set it off." He waved the paper. "This could do it."

Henry frowned. "I have a responsibility to the town, a responsibility to call it as I see it. Especially when the law agrees with me."

The Judge leaned forward, his eyes intense. "I'm not here to argue with you, Henry. You know we see things pretty much eye to eye. But there are many ways to a final destination. Ask yourself this. Do you want to see the North Carolina Highway Patrol walking the streets, or even the North Carolina National Guard? How do you feel about a curfew? How about people being stopped and searched if they're carrying packages or acting *strange*? How about arrest powers being liberalized so *suspicious* people can be held in jail?" He leaned back in the visitor's chair, a sad look on his face. "All those things could happen, and maybe more if we're not careful. Rushing into equality of the races could bring chaos. Think about integrating the schools. Where do you get the classroom space? Build new schools. Where do you get the money to build new schools? What will be the psychological impact on small children being thrown together in a world foreign to them? And, how will the students act toward one another. It's easy to say let's do it. Doing it is another issue."

"Wow. That's a ton you dropped on me. What do you think I should do?"

"Walk slower. Take baby steps. You'll get to the same place, but maybe without side effects."

Henry leaned back and stared at the ceiling. "My gut says you're right while my heart screams you're too cautious. When I was in combat, I learned to trust my gut. I will now. I'll keep my typewriter quiet until we see what progress is made." He paused. "However, like you sooner or later, I have to follow the dictates of my conscience, no matter where it leads."

"You won't be sorry," the Judge said. "It's going to happen in our lifetimes. Let's hope it's with a minimum amount of blood."

CHAPTER SIX

Raymond Clayton of Dawson Glass company scratched his head, staring at the windows of the newspaper office from the inside. "I'm sorry, Mr. Flanagan, I don't have nothing in stock that will fit that. Biggest sheet I got will only cover about half. Probably take me a week, two weeks to get it the right size. It'll be best if I send the measurements, and let the distributor cut it."

Henry frowned. "Well, if that's the best you can do."

"Yes sir, that's it. I don't stock big sheets. Too much can happen with the coloreds I hire. They ain't always the most careful, you know? When somebody needs a big piece, they let me know in advance, and I order it. Works real good 'cept when we have a hurricane or some good ol' boys get a bit liquored up." He paused. "Sorry, sir. I didn't mean . . . uh . . ."

Henry smiled. "It's okay. Just take the measurements and get the glass as fast as you can."

"One thing I can do, I can put up some fresh plywood. That stuff looks pretty bad. I have some sheets in the warehouse."

"Hmm, hadn't thought of that. Let's take a look." They walked outside, and Henry smiled at the mismatched, overlapping, multi-colored, dingy pieces. "You have a point, Ray. Doesn't look too professional, does it? But I have another idea."

That afternoon, Henry and Eli stood in front of the building admiring their handiwork. A new plywood sign hung alongside the entrance.

Dawson Times
Still in Business

..*

"See what happens," Big Man said. "You git one a them do-gooders down here, and somebody gonna bring him down."

Big Man and Scooter stood across the street from the *Dawson Times*. Big Man's face was mostly grin.

"Muster Flan'gan be a nice man," Scooter said. "He give me a Brook'n Dodgers hat." He frowned. "Wisht I still had it. I kinda like that ol' thang."

"See. That's what I mean. He give you a piece a trash he prob'ly gonna throw away. If he cared, he'd a got you a new one. You was right to give it back to him."

"It was still a nice cap," Scooter muttered.

"That ain't important." Big Man pointed at the storefront. "What you got here is some good ol' boys puttin' that damnyankee in his place. Anybody goes agin the whiteys git they balls handed to them. Way I hear it, that ol' man Flanagan lucky the Chief come by. Next time, they make sure the place burn to the ground—with him inside."

"I heered he writ us coloreds be the same as whites. Is that what it was?"

"Something like that. Stupid, that's what he is. Everybody know ain't no colored man gonna be treated like no white man. We gotta take what we want." Big Man rubbed his chin. "Like you'n me. We knows, and what we wants is money. When I gits our whiskey stills going, we gonna be rich."

Scooter shuffled his feet. "You be smarter than me, and I don't mind having 'nough money so I don't have to work so hard. I's right happy workin' for you."

Big Man stared at the plywood across the windows of the *Dawson Times*. A sly smile grew from a small grin into a full-fledged face-filler. "You know, Scooter. I'm thinkin' we just might make some money outta this." He paused. "Yeah, I gotta think on this. I betcha all them coloreds just looking for somebody to tell'm they's as good as white folks." He turned and started up the street toward his car. "I knows a coupla fellows in Raleigh might can help. Maybe I'll stop in to see them next week. Yep, might make you'n me a little richer."

"What you talkin' about?" Scooter said. "I don't see no way to make money. Just them Burnettes and their friends acting like they always do. They hates us."

"Don't you worry 'bout that. I'll do the thinking for both of us. C'mon. Gonna send Rodney to Raleigh today to get the guns."

..*

"Marvin, one a these days I'm gonna learn not to drink that stuff you make. It gives the worst hangovers I ever had." Charlie sat on the edge of the jail bunk, his head in his hands. "Reckon we could git some aspirin. I'm dyin'."

"Oh, shut up, Charlie. My head's as bad as yours. Do you know how I got this cut?" He fingered a shallow slash running down from his hairline across his forehead. "Way I 'member it, this whole thing was your stupid idea. Now we got the Chief on our backs. You shoulda knowed he'd be all over us for tryin' to burn up the newspaper."

"I didn't see you come up with no better idea. We just got unlucky. He happened to come by at the wrong time. Next time, we'll do better."

Marvin looked around, then whispered. "What you mean next time? You got an idea?"

"Yeah. To start with, we won't drive right down the middle of Main Street." He gripped his head again. "Man, I gotta have some aspirin." He stood and walked to the cell door. "Toby? You out there? Man, I need some help."

An officer rounded the corner. "What do you want, Charlie? You're the biggest whiner I ever seen." He grinned. "You're worse than the blackest sharecropper I get in here. What is it?"

Charlie's eyes flashed anger. "Watch your mouth. You best remember where you come from. Your daddy and my daddy were neighbors. We growed up together." He said in a more conciliatory voice, "Can you get me some aspirin? My head is busting. 'Bout four for me . . . and you better bring some for Marvin, too."

Toby chuckled. "Yeah, big, tough men. Way I heard it, you thought you were pretty bad last night. I'll check on the aspirin. Don't die 'til I get back." He wandered away.

Charlie heard a door open, then close. "Damn som'bitch got the big head since he become a cop." He turned to Marvin. "I'm thinking we went after the wrong target. That ol' newspaper didn't do nothing to us. It was that Yankee that runs it. When we get outta here, maybe we'll just pay him a midnight visit. Maybe we oughta grab him and one of his nigger friends, and let folks know how things are."

Marvin leaned into Charlie and spoke in a quiet voice, "How? What you thinkin' about?"

"How 'bout a double necktie party? I bet we can get lots of folks to show up. Maybe burn a cross. How 'bout that ol' nigger that works for him?"

"Damn, Charlie. You crazy? They'd put us under the jail and throw away the key."

"Not if we blame it on the Klan. I got the beginnings of a idea. Give me time to work on it."

..*

Chief Bowen sat, elbows on his desk, his head resting in his hands. *What have we started here?* He looked at the ceiling. "Lord, don't let this be what I'm afraid it is. If Flanagan keeps writing that stuff, the Burnettes will keep going nuts. Next time, they might have help. A lot of people 'round here like things just the way they are."

There was a knock on the door, then Toby stuck his head in. "Charlie and Marvin are whining somethin' bad about their hangovers. Okay to give'm some aspirin?"

The Chief smiled. "Serves them right. Bastards kept me up most of the night. I'd almost trade their headaches for a good night's sleep. Yeah, let'm have the aspirin." He chuckled. "But you might want to put some rock and roll on the radio—loud."

Toby withdrew from the room leaving the Chief with a shrinking smile. He picked up the newspaper and looked at the editorial again. "Dammit. Sometimes you can be right at the wrong time."

CHAPTER SEVEN

Scooter walked beside Big Man, scanning the area like Big Man taught him. He thought it was silly since the only folks on Main Street were people he'd known all his life.

"Scooter-Who?" Pastor Turner said, approaching the two of them. "How're you, Big Man?"

Scooter ignored the Pastor and kept sweeping the area with his eyes. Not that he thought it necessary, but that was his job.

"Mornin', Pastor," Big Man said. "I was hopin' to bump into you."

"Well, you did. What can I do for you?"

Big Man looked around, then in a quieter voice said, "Did you read the paper the other day—that stuff 'bout justice bein' blind?"

"Yeah. What about it?"

"I was thinkin' Muster Flan'gan writ a mighty-fine piece. And it'd be a shame if we don't support him. Scooter and me was talkin' this morning we oughta go by his office, and tell him what a fine man he is. Wasn't we, Scooter?"

"Huh?" Scooter looked at Big Man wondering what he meant. They had never discussed anything like that, but knew he had to agree. "Ah, yeah, that's what you said."

"See," Big Man said. "Scooter and me thinkin' it's time we stood up and did our duty. And that is help our brothers git justice. To help them understan' that we's all equal under God's eyes. Scooter come up with the idea we ought to partner with you. We could—"

"I only have one partner, but He always has room for another. What do you have in mind?"

Big Man looked around. "This ain't a good place to talk. Too many white folks around."

Pastor Turner stared at him. "Them don't sound like the kind of words I need to hear. But if you wants to come by the church in about two hours, I be there." He smiled. "Hardly ever too many whites there."

"Yes sir." Big Man smiled. "Me and Scooter just might do that. We's got some business first, but if we get finished in time, we'll stop by the church." He tipped his hat. "Mighty-fine to see you agin, Pastor Turner."

He tapped Scooter on the arm, and the two of them stepped off.

"What was that all about?" Scooter asked in a soft voice. "We ain't never talked 'bout nothin' like that."

"We must have," Big Man said with a laugh. "You said we did. You don't lie, do you? Now let's git around to Rodney's."

..*

Pastor Turner watched Big Man and Scooter climb into the car and pull away. His expression showed how puzzled he was by the conversation. While he knew the Lord told him to give the benefit of doubt to sinners, he wasn't sure that was a good idea with Big Man. Something about him got in the way of feeling charitable.

He wondered about Scooter though. The man he saw today had little resemblance to the one he'd watched grow into manhood. Anyone carrying Big Man's dirty laundry was up to no good. Maybe Aint Liddie could explain it.

He walked through the alley beside the drugstore and let himself in the *Coloreds Only* side door. Aunt Liddie stood behind the counter, her bulk squeezed front and back. There were no customers.

"You got a minute?" he called to her.

"Hi, Pastor Turner. I always got time for a man of the Lord. Let me give Mr. Flip his milkshake. I be right back. You just take a stool."

He walked to the counter and sat as she bustled to the rear of the store with the milkshake, then returned. "You want something? Maybe a ‘nilla shake. I make a mighty good one."

The Pastor chuckled. "I know you do. But I's more in the mood for a strawberry."

"I kin do that." She grabbed a cup and began dipping ice cream. "What you got on your mind? You got the look of a man what's been thinkin'."

"You shore you ain't married. You read a man like a wife."

"Oh, git on with you. You just somebody that keeps his feelings on his face. That's what makes you such a good preacher. We can always see how much you believe in the Lord."

Pastor Turner laughed. "Guess I can't argue with you there." He told her about the conversation he had with Big Man while Scooter stood by. "Do you know what they might be up to? Has Scooter said anything?"

Liddie's head hung. "He don't hardly ever talk to me no more. He done been bit by the greed bug. Big Man got money, and Scooter want it. I's right worried 'bout that boy."

"I'm sorry to hear that. I hoped you might know something. Guess the best thing to do is see if they come by the church."

Liddie poured the milkshake into a glass and set it in front of the Pastor. "Nice and thick, just the way you like'm."

He looked at it, then tried to stick a paper straw in. It bent. "Reckon you better give me a spoon 'til this thing softens a little."

..*

When Big Man parked in front of Rodney's house, Scooter said, "You think he got the guns?"

"He better. I give him the money, and he went to Raleigh yesterday."

"I knows," Scooter said, not happy with the idea. He supposed being a bodyguard meant knowing how to use a gun, but that didn't change how he felt. And that was scared.

Big Man pounded on the front door. "You in there, Rodney? Git yo' black ass out here."

After two more poundings, the door opened, and Rodney stood holding his pants up with one hand. "Why you wakin' me? Shit, I didn't get home 'til damn near daylight."

"Ain't my problem," Big Man said. "You git what I sent you for?"

"Told you I would, didn't I?"

Big Man peeked through the open door. "Dammit, git outta the way and let us in. Anybody else here?"

Rodney stepped aside. "I don't know. Told you I was asleep."

"You damn well better find out. I ain't paying you for a bunch a lip. Thought you knowed that."

"Okay, okay, don't git all upset. Set down, and I'll check the house."

Big Man and Scooter walked into the living room while Rodney went from room to room.

"Ain't nobody here," Rodney said, joining them.

"Show me the guns."

Rodney dropped into a chair. "Shit, you don't think I'd bring them here, do you? I ain't that stupid. My ol' lady'd be all over me before I could git'm in the door."

Scooter looked at Big Man and saw he was getting angry. He shrunk into the couch cushion. He'd seen him mad before. It wasn't pretty to watch.

"Alright, wise ass," Big Man said. "Where the hell is the stuff?"

Rodney laughed and slapped his thigh. "At yo' house. I put'm under yo' house."

"What?" Big Man jumped to his feet. "You stupid ass. What you mean, my house?"

"Easy, friend, easy. Ain't no problem. It was still dark when I got back to Dawson. I didn't want to wake you so I stopped by and shoved'm underneath your place. Don't worry. They's behind a pillar. Can't nobody see them."

"Scooter," Big Man said, "if you was half as stupid as him, I'd shoot you, but not 'til I cut yo' nuts off. Rodney, git your clothes on. That stuff better be where you left it."

"Damn," Rodney said. "You the most suspicious som'bitch I ever worked with. Just set tight while I git dressed."

Twenty minutes later, they were in Big Man's kitchen. Rodney had recovered three burlap-wrapped parcels from under the house. He dumped the first one. Three .38 Police Specials and three boxes of shells clattered onto the table.

"Ain't they purty?" Rodney said. "Almost new and ain't got no record behind them." He looked from Big Man to Scooter and back. "C'mon. You know I done good with these."

"What else you got?" Big Man said. "Scooter, pick out the one you want."

Scooter looked at the three guns, then picked up the one closest to him. He held it by the handle, not sure what to do with it.

"Shit," Rodney said. "That some bodyguard you got."

"Shut yo' face, and show me the next bag," Big Man said.

Rodney scowled, then grunted as he picked up another package and lay it on the table. "You gonna like these." He unrolled the burlap, revealing three sawed-off, double-barreled shotguns, several boxes of shells, and three sets of brass knuckles. "Ain't they sweet?"

Scooter watched Big Man and mimicked the smile he saw break across his face. He glanced at the revolver in his hand then back at the shotguns, his stomach feeling queasy.

"Yeah," Big Man said, his white teeth shining. "That's more like it. That's what we need. Ain't it so, Scooter?"

"They's mighty purty."

"Wait'll tonight," Big Man said. "We'll do some shooting at the dump. You cut lose with one a these babies, you see what they do. Rodney, get us some good flashlights. We's goin' rat hunting tonight. When we finish, Scooter gone be the most frightenin' bodyguard around."

"That ain't all I bought," Rodney said. "I think you gone like this, too." He shook a third burlap bag upside down—three four-inch switchblades and three sheath knives tumbled out.

"These are good," Big Man said, picking up a switchblade. "But what you gonna do with them others, play Boy Scout?"

Rodney grinned. "Feller in jail told me 'bout this. See, we wear them around our legs under our trousers—you know, strap'm above the calf."

Big Man looked serious, then slapped him on the back. "Good thinkin'. I knowed I picked the right man. What you think, Scooter? Here, pull up your pants leg. Let's see how it works."

Scooter frowned, but put his foot on a kitchen chair and followed instructions.

"See, here's how we do it," Rodney said wrapping the leather strap around Scooter's leg below the knee, then buckling it. "I bought these narrow belts, cut them off, and punched new holes. Looks like they was made for the leg, don't they?"

"That's too tight," Scooter said. "My leg'll go to sleep."

"Oh, hell, try it," Big Man said. "Walk 'round a little."

Scooter did a couple of turns around the kitchen. "Feels alright.

I kin wear it, I reckon."

"Good for you, my man," Big Man said. "Give me that'un with the longer belt. I got a big leg to match my name."

Rodney handed him a sheath knife. He strapped it on, then followed Scooter's example of walking around the room. "Damn, that feels fine. You really done good."

Rodney beamed.

Scooter picked up a switchblade, pushed the button, then jerked when the blade leapt into position. He ran his thumb along the blade. "Ain't very sharp."

Laughter boomed out of Big Man as Rodney frowned.

"Shit, I reckon you can sharpen it," Rodney said.

Scooter glared at Rodney then switched his attention to Big Man. "You tol' Pastor Turner we go by his church if we have time. Do I have time to put an edge on this piece of crap Rodney brought?"

"Take yo' time and do it right. Here, do mine, too. Guess the ol' Pastor gone have to wait 'til I gits time for him. Gittin' these knives and guns right is mo' important than what I wants to talk to him about."

..*

Flip was quiet at dinner, pushing his food around, eating little.

"What's wrong, dear?" Lorrie asked. "Something wrong at the store?"

"Huh? Oh, sorry. No, the store's fine. It's—"

"You should've seen me playing football at recess, Daddy," Little Flip said. "I scored five touchdowns. I'm gonna be good."

"I'm sure you are," Flip said, smiling at his son. "After all, I made all-conference my senior year."

Lorrie intervened. "If you're through, young man, you can start your homework. What do you have tonight?"

"Ah, Mom. I only got a little 'ritmetic and a few words."

"That's arithmetic. Now, get down and get started. I'll be in to check on you in a bit."

Muttering under his breath, Little Flip left the room.

Lorrie watched him, a smile in her eyes, then turned to Flip. "Okay, what's up? Something's eating at you."

Sighing, Flip ran his hand over his face. "I'm worried. We're living in an age of change and the changes might not come easy."

"What do you mean?" Lorrie's features darkened as if reflecting her husband's mood.

"This integration stuff. You saw the paper the other day. Henry's getting the coloreds all riled up, and some of the white folks aren't taking it so good. There's talk about stopping it before things go too far."

"What kind of talk?"

"Somebody could get hurt, maybe bad."

"Have you told Chief Bowen?"

He looked at her, his eyes beseeching her to understand. "I can't. If I do, everybody will take their business somewhere else. You know we don't have much of a profit margin now. If I lose my white customers, I'll have to close the doors."

"But—"

"But nothing." He stood, his voice resolute. "What good would it do? All I know is gossip. Telling the police won't stop anything, but if the town loses the drugstore, who really loses? The whole town. That's who. My store is needed, and I won't do anything that might cause it to close. My granddaddy started it, and I have to pass it to Little Flip. That's my family tradition."

"Suppose—"

"Forget it. We're not getting involved. I shouldn't have told you. And don't you tell anyone what I said. We're staying out of this mess. It's between Henry and the others. Ain't none of our business." He strode from the kitchen through the living room and into the night, the front door slamming behind him.

..*

Jane walked into the kitchen where Judge Jackson ate alone, and sat at the side of the table. "It was better when it was hot. If I'd known you were going to be so late, I would have rearranged my schedule."

"It's okay. I'm not very hungry." He smiled. "My fault. I should have called."

"Yes, you should," she said, a pretend-stern look on her face. "Did you have a meeting?"

"No, I was trying to catch up. Things are changing so fast, it's hard to keep up."

She frowned. "Anything you want to tell me?"

He hesitated. He'd been studying the reactions across the South toward the Supreme Court ruling. Maybe this time, he could make Jane understand why it was so important. "I was looking at some of the things going on in Virginia. They're taking a strong stand against integrating the schools."

"Oh, how so?"

Was that interest he saw? "Senator Harry Byrd, he's the strongest politician in the state, pretty much calls shots and gets what he wants." He unfolded a sheet of paper laying beside his plate. "Listen to this. I wrote it down. *If we can organize the Southern States for massive resistance to this order I think that in time the rest of the country will realize that racial integration is not going to be accepted in the South.* Those are Senator Byrd's words."

"Is he making any progress?" Jane asked.

"Yes, he seems to be. Governor Stanley appointed a commission last year to study the *problem*. They called it the Gray Commission, named for State Senator Garland Gray. Anyway, it came up with the following. First, amend the laws concerning school attendance so no child is required to attend an integrated school. Second, set aside funds for tuition grants for parents who oppose integrated schools. And third, local school boards should be given the authority to assign students to particular schools."

He laid the paper down and frowned. "Of course, that last one simply means Negroes to Negro schools and whites to white schools. And the others, well they pretty much speak for themselves—maintain the status quo, keep the children separate. If the state legislature passes these laws, it'll be thumbing its nose at the Supreme Court."

"How about other places in the South?" Jane said. "Anyone else showing any backbone?"

He studied his wife. "It's starting. Coloreds asserting what they see as their constitutional rights and whites trying to pass laws to stop them. Little flames popping up here and there, but before it's finished, there'll be full-fledged fires everywhere."

Jane sighed. "All because the Supreme Court couldn't keep its nose out of the South's business. Can't the President and Congress do something about it?"

"No. In our form of government, it's the Court's mandate to interpret the Constitution in the cases brought before it. They did, and now it's the law of the land."

"Well, somebody's needs to do something. It's just not natural for niggers and whites to be together. You know that. You grew up here. It doesn't matter what Yankees in Washington, D.C. think."

The Judge rubbed his eyes. "Honey, can't you see that it doesn't matter how we grew up. Until last year, the court had not heard a case on separate but equal. Now they have, and things are different. It's not about you and me. It's about giving everybody in the country equal rights."

"That's your shorthand for saying you'll take the nigger's side, isn't it?"

"Please, Jane. You know I find that word offensive."

"Well, I find it offensive they're ruining my marriage, my town, my life." She stood. "I find it offensive we have to change everything we've known all our lives because they want to go to school with white children. And I find it offensive that my husband defends them while turning his back on his friends." Her voice had gotten louder with each word. "That's what to hell I find offensive. I'm sleeping in the guestroom. The door will be locked." She punctuated her speech by stomping from the room.

The Judge watched her disappear, a soul-searing sadness in his heart.

CHAPTER EIGHT

Alice Burnette carried the coffeepot into the living room and set it on the table in front of Charlie. As she filled the cups, she considered the ten men who had come to the meeting called by Charlie and Marvin. She knew them from church and other community activities and knew they thought like her husband. Nine were farmers, and the tenth ran a small store catering to farm families.

"Don't forget the milk," Charlie said. "I know Claude likes his coffee white, just like his women. Ain't that so, Claude?"

"Most of the time," Claude Atkins, the storeowner, answered. "But there's them times when that brown stuff is right nice. Oh, 'scuse me, Mrs. Burnette. I didn't mean—"

"It's alright," Alice said. "I'm used to it." She glared at Charlie. "My husband says the same thing."

"That's the truth," Charlie said. "A man has needs and sometimes it takes a little more to satisfy him." He looked at Alice. "Hurry up with that pouring. We got business to discuss here."

She emptied the pot among the ten cups. "I'll make more. It'll take a few minutes to perk."

"Good. You do that. Now get out of here. This is man's work."

Leaving the room, she insured the door did not close all the way. She'd never known Charlie to be as agitated as he had been since he got out of jail. All he talked about was fixing things. He and Marvin had sat in the living room drinking coffee two nights previous, talking about who to invite to the meeting. Once they made up their minds, Charlie called her in to write down the names, five on one piece of paper and five on another. Then each brother took a list, saying they'd contact them. Tonight, the ten men had appeared, and she believed nothing good could come from it. After starting a fresh brew, she stood by the doorway.

"Has everybody got coffee?" Charlie said. "Y'all set to listen?"

She heard murmuring.

"Me and my brother asked y'all to come here cause we got a problem."

Alice peeked through the small opening and saw Charlie gazing around the room at the men.

"This here's serious," Charlie said, "and it concerns the nigger problem and that damnyankee newspaperman. We picked y'all 'cause we think you feel the same as we do. But if we's wrong, leave now."

"Git on with it," Claude Atkins said. "You know we'll stand with you on most things."

"I know you will, Claude. How 'bout the rest of you?"

Chairs squeaked, and Alice heard mutterings she couldn't understand, but goose pimples raised on her arms. She feared they'd do whatever Charlie and Marvin wanted.

"Here's what we got," Charlie said.

There was silence in the room.

"Marvin and me been thinking we oughta burn some crosses. You know, like the Klan does. Put the fear of God in them darkies before they get to feeling too big for their britches."

"Where?" Claude said.

Claude glanced at Marvin. "The lawn of that Rev'nd Turner's church. You know, the one on the edge of town."

"That all?" Claude said. "I've known you two long enough to know you're too goldurned mean to stop once you get started. You ain't talking just crosses, are you?"

Charlie walked over and stood in front of Claude. "You're right, but for the wrong reason. If we don't stop things before they get out of hand, they'll be no stoppin' them. There's enough nigger-lovers 'round here that we have to do whatever's necessary. If we let'm get started, it'll be twice as hard to get the coloreds back in line."

"I didn't hear no answer," Claude said. "What you got in mind? I ain't about to buy no pig in a poke."

Charlie smiled, then yelled, "Alice, that coffee ready yet? We got empty cups in here."

She scrambled away from the door and crossed the small kitchen to the stove. "Almost. Another minute." She felt like she had to know what they were planning. As she watched the bubbling of the coffee, she strained to hear.

"Marvin, get the coffee, will you?" Charlie said in an agitated voice. "That damn woman's slower than a coon-whipped hound dog."

She picked up the pot and headed for the door only to be met by Marvin.

"I'll take it in," he said. "You got some cake? The boys might like somethin' sweet."

"Yeah, I'll bring it in."

She moved to the counter and picked up a chocolate cake she baked that afternoon. About three-fourths of it was left. As fast as she could, she pulled out plates, forks, and a cake knife, then headed for the living room, hoping she hadn't missed too much.

As she pushed on the door, she heard Charlie saying, "I figure he's perfect. We grab him, take him out to the church, work him over a little, then burn a cross. The word'll get around in a hurry."

He saw Alice and quit talking. "What you want, woman?"

"I brought the cake."

"Well put it down and git outta here. I done told you, this is man-talk."

She set the cake and utensils on the coffee table and hurried back into the kitchen, again leaving the door open a crack.

She heard movement indicating the guests were getting cake and more coffee.

"I don't know 'bout messing around no nigger church," Marvin said. "Might be better—"

"Close that door good," Charlie said. "I don't want that bitch hearing nothing she don't need to know. Naw, wait. Tell her to come in here. She's always whining about seeing her sister. I'll git her out of here. Then we can set down and do some serious talking." He grinned his power grin. "I'll even let her take the truck."

She rushed to the sink and plunged her hands into dishwater as the door squeaked open.

"Charlie wants you," Marvin said.

Ten minutes later, Alice drove toward Shirley's house wondering what to do with what she'd heard. If she told anyone and Charlie found out, he'd kill her. But, if she didn't tell anyone, somebody else might die. Her mama had always said Shirley was the smart one in the family. Maybe she'd know what to do.

..*

Big Man glared at the eight men seated in his living room, wearing what he called his *ugly face*. They fidgeted, looked away, or both—all except one. He met Big Man's eyes stare for stare.

Rodney sat in a chair tilted against the wall in the corner, a smile playing at his lips.

"You 'bout the stupidest-looking group I ever seen," Big Man said. "Rodney, where'd you find this bunch? You shore they smart enough to make moonshine?"

Amos, a small man with skin black as midnight, snickered. "Git on with it. I got better things to do than watch you strut. And talkin' bout smarts, I knowed your daddy 'fore he killed hisself with that shine he made. Fool poisoned his ownself. I figger the weed don't sprout far from its daddy."

Big Man glared at him, his fists clenched. "You and me can talk later." He turned his attention to the group, and after a beat or two, said in a practiced voice, "Now, Rodney say he briefed you." He pranced back and forth across the room waving his hands. "But just in case he didn't do so good, or you too stupid to unnerstand, I'm goin' through it agin." He stopped and stared at the assemblage. "But before I start talkin', you gonna meet my enforcer."

He turned to the hallway. "Scooter. Come in here."

Scooter walked into the room armed like a desperado from the Old West. On each side, he had a thirty-eight stuffed in his belt, and a sheath knife hung below each pistol.

Amos snorted.

Big Man gazed at him. "You think this is funny?" He cut his eyes from one man to the next. "Some of you might think you know Scooter. But let me tell you, that was the old Scooter. The new one will cut your heart out if I tell him. If you want to feed the catfish in the river, all you gotta do is cross me. You unnerstand?"

Amos laughed aloud. "You tellin' me Scooter is your badman?

Shit, I knowed him his whole life. You really got me scared." His laughter boomed.

The others in the room looked at Amos, some of them with smiles.

"You a damn fool what's makin' a mistake. You on the edge of cutting yourself out of easy money. But before I throws you out on yo' ass, we gonna take a little trip to the dump—all of us. Scooter, get the guns. Amos, you ride with me."

Forty-five minutes later, they stood alongside the road that cut through the town's refuse disposal area. Everything from kitchen garbage to tree trimmings lay around them. It covered two acres of land that once had several gullies cutting through. The gullies had disappeared under tons of rubbish years ago. Now, a bulldozer operator worked two days a week pushing the fresh dumpings into hills. The smell was bad where the fresher trash lay, but bearable in the older sections. Huge rats roamed throughout, feeding and breeding at will.

Big Man held a large flashlight. "You ready, Scooter?"

"Yas suh."

Big Man turned on the light and swept the area. A pair of beady red eyes appeared in the beam then disappeared into vapor as a boom sounded. The light found a second pair of eyes, and they disappeared the same way.

Scooter broke open the sawed-off shotgun, pulled out the spent shells, and shoved in two new ones without uttering a sound.

Big Man grinned in the dark as he turned to the eight men. "Amos, you can leave. But remember, I knows where you live. And I knows yo' wife, yo' children, and yo' mother. You open your mouth to anybody, and lotsa people gonna end up like them rats. You unnerstand me?"

Amos stared. "What you mean? I wants to git rich like the others."

"You messed up. I don't put up with nobody what laughs at me. And if you laughin' at Scooter, you's laughing at me. Git on your way."

"But I ain't got no car."

"Then you better start walkin'. Anybody else want to back talk me?" Big Man shined the light into each face. "Good. We gonna go back to my place, and I tell you the plan. But before we go, two things you better know. Rodney told you what I'm gonna do, but even he don't know how. Only me 'n Scooter knows that. So once I tell you the details, you're in. Cross me, and I tell Scooter to kill you." He paused, looking from man to man. "And he'll blow your ass away as fast as he did them rats. Won't you, Scooter?"

"Uh-huh."

"I ain't walkin' nowhere," Amos said. "You brung me here, you take me back." He stepped forward, his fists clenched.

"You still here? I told you to leave. Scooter, help Amos on his way."

Scooter pointed the shotgun at Amos.

"Who you think you are, Wyatt Earp? You don't scare me. You jist a dummy like you always been."

Scooter lowered the gun, pulled back the hammer on both barrels, then pointed it at Amos again. "Want me to kill'm, Big Man?"

"Amos?" Big Man said.

Amos ran.

Big Man watched Amos until he was out of sight in the darkness, then turned to the group. "The second thing is you call me Mr. Q—and that's all you call me. My daddy give me Q for a middle name, and I likes it. You my employees now. That means you call me Mr. Q. The only persons what can call me Big Man is Scooter and Rodney. You don't unnerstand, you stay here." Again, he shined the light from face to face. "Rodney, git my car. Time's a wastin'."

Everyone piled into their vehicles.

Once back at his house, Big Man laid out his plan for taking over the bootleg whiskey business. The seven men who'd followed him from the dump listened without interrupting. He explained that he expected each of them to produce a delivery once a week. "I'll supply ever'thing you need. You make it, and I pay you twenty-five dollars a load. Anybody got a question?"

"Spose we git caught?" Jeremiah, a light-skinned Negro asked. "Spose the revenuers or the Sheriff finds our stills. Who gonna git us out of jail?"

Big Man laughed. "You stupid enough to git caught, you pay."

He frowned. "And if you git caught, you better know to keep yo' mouth shut. You talk to the man, you die."

"Where we gonna do all this?" Abel said. "You pickin' the spot?"

"Shit, you dummies got to do something," Big Man said, smiling before turning serious. "You knows them farms you sharecrop better than anybody else. Find yo'self a hidey hole in the woods. Make sure it's a good'un, and that's where you make the stuff. 'Course, you gonna take me and Scooter and Rodney there, in case you decide to git funny with my makin's."

..*

Amos walked alongside the highway, seething at the way Big Man treated him. "Shit. All I's doin' was funnin'. Asshole ain't got no sense of humor. But he gonna pay for treatin' Amos this way. I'll just wait, and when he gits everythin' running, them stills might have some accidents." He chuckled. "I bet his stuff won't taste so good with ashes in it." He stopped walking and laughed, slapping his thighs in his mirth. "Yeah, a few of them stomachaches that ashes cause, and he won't have many customers." He straightened and continued his trip with a much lighter step. "Folks'll run from his shine."

He walked another hundred yards, then a smile split his face again. "Or maybe somebody tell the Sheriff when Big Man's carrying a load."

CHAPTER NINE

Thanksgiving was a special time for the people of Dawson and Nolan County, the foremost holiday for the gathering of families and friends. Almost without variation, each table held a turkey, a baked ham, a large bowl of chicken salad, and every kind of vegetable grown in Eastern North Carolina. Before the main meal, there were nuts, homemade cookies and candies, fresh fruit, and other goodies to whet the appetite. And of course, desserts were legendary—pecan, pumpkin, sweet potato, and apple pies, and cakes of every description.

Then, as if Thanksgiving had been a dress rehearsal, Christmas repeated the extravaganza—the same foods in larger quantities. Families with small children stayed home so Santa could visit, then gathered later in the day with three, four, and sometimes five generations. After holding their stomachs at Thanksgiving and moaning they'd never overeat again, they repeated it at Christmas dinner.

Henry and Debbie were the guests of Judge Jackson and Jane for Thanksgiving, then returned the favor for Christmas. In each instance, the size of the group and the amount of food required stretching the tables with extra leaves. Children's tables were set up close enough for adult supervision, but far enough away for cousins to enjoy themselves. While Henry had attended other holiday festivities as a guest, this was his first as a member of Debbie's *family*.

A few of her relatives overpowered him with their *acceptance*, especially her favorite, elderly Aunt Maddie, who squeezed him to her bosom and said, "You just don't know how thrilled and relieved we are that you proposed to Debbie. We were afraid she'd never find another man. I mean, it's been over ten years."

"Uh, thank you," Henry said. "She's a very special lady, and I'm so happy she accepted." He edged away, wondering whether he'd been complimented, or if she thought he was Debbie's last hope.

After eating, the men retired to the living room with their cigarettes, cigars, and pipes while the women congregated in the kitchen and dining room. Henry listened politely as they drank coffee and spoke about what Eisenhower would do during his second term, how good or bad tobacco prices had been—depending on who told the story—how the Yankees were ruining baseball by winning too much—a favorite line of Dodger fans—and assorted other subjects. Obvious by their absence were comments about integration, equal rights for Negroes, and the newspaper business.

Debbie approached from behind, tapped Henry on the shoulder, and whispered, "All this smoke is getting to me. Want some fresh air?"

Henry turned to her and mouthed, "Please." To the men, he said, "Excuse me. Debbie's sinuses are bothering her."

The conversation continued unabated. The room had separated into Dodger fans and Yankee fans arguing the merits of their stars.

Henry took her hand and led the way from the room. Once through the front door, he said, "Thank you for rescuing me. Think we can escape? My apartment is much quieter. And no one smokes there."

She squeezed his hand. "What a wonderful idea. Only one problem. I'm the hostess, and you're the host. We'd be disgraced if we abandoned the Judge and Jane to my relatives." She looked around. "But we could slip around back and steal a kiss."

"Wonderful idea, soon-to-be Mrs. Flanagan. A snuggle is definitely in order—much better than Alka-Seltzer for that overstuffed feeling. How long before someone misses us?"

She pulled him down the steps and around the corner. "Aunt Maddie will be the first. I figure five minutes at the most. She's quite taken with you." Debbie giggled. "She said if she was twenty years younger she'd give me a run for my money."

Henry tried to look aghast. "Twenty? How old did you tell her I am? Even if she dropped forty years, I'd still choose you." They reached the big oak tree, and he pulled her into his arms. "I love you, Mrs. Patterson."

"And I love you, Mr. Flanagan."

"Yoo-hoo," Aunt Maddie called from the back porch. "They're out back, ladies. What are you two doing? You'll catch your death of cold. Want I should bring your coats?"

Debbie said, "We're fine, Aunt Maddie. We'll be there in a few minutes. Get the ice cream out, and we'll have some with cake as soon as it softens enough to scoop."

"Oh, you mean you want to be alone? Well, why didn't you just say so? Heck, I was young once. I remember how it was." She giggled, then in a softer voice said, "Want I should get all these people out of here so you can *really* be alone? Of course, in my day, we waited 'til after the wedding." Her laughter spiraled upward.

"*Aunt Maddie*. You mind your manners," Debbie said. "We're coming in to be *with* our guests. Don't you dare send them home." She turned to Henry. "If we don't get inside right now, my reputation in the family will be lost forever."

Henry kissed her. "Her suggestion sounds good to me."

"Not until I'm wearing a wedding ring." She kissed him back. "Or later tonight after everyone leaves—whichever comes first. Now let's get inside."

They entered the house through the back door, disengaging hands as they stepped into the kitchen. Debbie opened the utensils drawer while Henry continued into the living room.

Judge Jackson tapped him as he walked by and whispered, "Got a minute, or are you really interested in Mickey Mantle versus Duke Snider?"

Henry looked at the men who were deep into baseball statistics. "I'm all yours. What's on your mind?"

The Judge steered him out the front door and stopped on the porch. "I want to ask you what's on the wires about the doings in Montgomery, Alabama. Things have been so busy, this is my first chance."

"I assume you mean the bus boycott. Not too much. Some woman named Parks refused to give up her seat to a white man back on December first. The bus driver called the police, and they arrested her. The Negroes of Montgomery responded by boycotting public transportation. We heard before they were waiting for the right moment. Guess they think this is it. Nobody seems to think it'll amount to much."

"So you don't think anybody'll get hurt?"

"I didn't say that. I learned last fall not to guess what hotheads will do. I'm sure Alabama has as many as we do."

"Yeah," Judge Jackson said, pacing. "What about leaders? Who's heading up this thing?"

"Well, the NAACP is out front. The Parks woman has apparently been a member, even a local officer, for a long time. But the number one name is a young Baptist preacher from Montgomery." Henry chuckled. "His name follows Southern standards, three of them—Martin Luther King."

Judge Jackson appeared to think. "The coloreds in the South find their strength and their leaders in the church. Martin Luther, eh? Well, if he's as strong a leader as his namesake, we'll be hearing a lot more about him."

..*

1955 ended on Saturday in an unspectacular way with quiet parties and church services. Eastern North Carolina was not prone to loud celebrations for any occasion, and the end of the year was no exception. At midnight, illegal fireworks banged and an occasional louder boom—dynamite—could be heard. Chief Bowen instructed his deputies to keep an eye on things, but wear earplugs unless the noise and celebrations became excessive. Most of the time, a police car driving through the neighborhood was enough to stop unlawful explosions.

The Jacksons, Matthews, and Henry and Debbie spent New Year's Eve together, then attended midnight service at the Baptist Church. They made plans to have lunch the next day after Sunday services. All night Debbie wore a grin, promising big news on the first day of the New Year.

"What's she talking about, Henry?" Judge Jackson asked. "New Year's Eve is no time for keeping secrets."

"Yeah," Flip said. "You know I hate games."

Henry slipped his arm around Debbie. "She said if I tell you, she'll break off the engagement, then sue me for breach of promise.

My happiness is at stake here. My lips are sealed."

1956 dawned cold and clear with people preparing for worship services. Negroes and whites celebrated the birth of the New Year the same every year. They attended church then went home to prepare black-eyed peas for supper. Legend said the peas brought good luck. Also, couples visited neighbors and friends, but there was a significant change from normal visits. Superstition had it that if a woman crossed the threshold first, bad luck would follow the occupants throughout the year. So each time a front door opened, the man entered first.

The three couples from the previous night met in front of the Memorial Baptist Church.

"Okay, Debbie. Give," Lorrie Matthews said. "You promised to tell us today."

"After church," Debbie answered, looking proud. "I'm not giving up my secret until I've had a chance to thank God for leading me to Henry." She squeezed his arm and pecked him on the cheek.

"Oh brother," Jane said. "This woman is in serious love. Wait 'til they've been married six months. That attitude will change. She'll be anxious to share with us and cut him out."

"Hey," Judge Jackson said. "Do you do that?"

"All the time." Jane's eyes flashed from smiling to serious, then back. "I have more in common with my female friends."

Everyone laughed, but the Judge's chuckle carried a nervous edge.

..*

After the church service, they went to Lucille's Café for lunch, ordering their usual fare.

Lorrie pushed her plate away. "That's it. I'm not waiting any longer. My black-eyed peas are soaking in cold water. I have to get home. Either tell, or I'm going to come around this table and choke it out of you."

"Yeah," Jane said. "Enough with the secrets. I'll hold you while Lorrie does her thing."

"Secrets? Did I hear somebody say secrets?" Lucille said, putting dirty dishes in a large pan. "I'm all ears. I won't tell anyone. Let me in on it." She pulled a chair to their table and sat.

Henry let out a loud laugh. "You, Lucille? Hey, if I didn't have you and Mrs. Christiana as competition, I could get a paper out with some firsthand news."

"Oh, hush, Yankee. Just because Debbie cleaned you up and shrunk you down don't mean you get to interrupt Southerners." She punctuated her insult with a good-natured laugh.

"Okay, okay," Debbie said. "Here it is. Henry and I are getting married." A grin spread across her face.

Everyone stared at her, their faces in question marks.

"Huh?" Flip said. "That's not new. We've known that for a month or more."

"Yeah, but you don't know when," Henry said, his grin almost as big as Debbie's.

"I wish you had attended law school," Judge Jackson said. "Then, if you pulled this kind of stuff in front of my bench, I could hold you in contempt of court. Since you didn't, enlighten us. When?"

"The second Sunday in June, the tenth," Debbie said. "I always wanted a June wedding and now, Hank is giving me one. Isn't that wonderful news for the first day of the New Year—new love, new marriage, new family? Also, my two Matrons of Honor, that'll give us lots of time and more excuses to shop for *new* dresses."

"Are you having it in the church?" Lucille asked.

"Yes. Two o'clock in the Memorial Baptist Church. Pastor Green will perform the ceremony."

"I guess more congratulations are in order," Judge Jackson said. "So, congratulations, Debbie. Congratulations, Henry. It's been so long I'd forgotten those kind of decisions are a big deal." He reached across the table as if to shake hands, but jerked the hand back. "Ouch."

"What's wrong?" Henry asked.

"Jane buried her elbow in my ribs."

..*

Scooter and Rodney sat in Big Man's living room. It was three o'clock on New Year's day. Big Man said it was the perfect time for a meeting—the beginning of a New Year, the beginning of a new life. He took a long pull on the bottle of cheap bourbon, then passed it to Rodney. "I'm drinkin' to nineteen-fifty-six. This is the year we gits rich. Before it's half over, we gonna be rollin' in money."

"Sounds good to me," Rodney said, then took a large swig from the bottle before handing it to Scooter. "As long as them folks in Raleigh keeps drinkin', we gonna be fine. I jist feels it in my guts."

"Yeah, but we gotta get things movin'," Big Man said. "I'm already behind schedule. I promised stuff for New Year's Eve and didn't deliver. They had to go some place else. That better not happen again." He paused, glaring at Rodney. "They don't forgit when somebody lets them down." He looked at Scooter. "Don't jist stare at that bottle. Take a drink and pass it."

Scooter took a sip, then frowned, forcing himself to swallow. "They oughta put some sugar in this stuff."

Laughing, Big Man grabbed the bottle and turned it up, chugging several large swallows. "Aaaahhhhh, that's good, Scooter. You gotta learn to drink like a man, not like a little girl."

Rodney laughed. "Yeah, Scooter. Let me have that bottle. I'll show you how a man drinks. Better break out another one. This'un will be gone in a minute."

"I don't take no shit from you," Scooter said, pulling his switchblade from his pocket and flicking it open. "You better watch yo' mouth, or Big Man gonna need somebody to take yo' place."

"Easy, little man, easy," Rodney said, eyeing the knife. "I jist funnin'."

"I don't like yo' jokes," Scooter said.

"That's enough, Scooter," Big Man said. "Put the knife away. I need Rodney. If the day ever come, I don't need him no more, I'll give him to you." He guffawed as Rodney's eyes grew large. "Now for you, Rodney, I shoulda knowed better than to let you pick the bootleggers. Them's got to be the dumbest niggers any man ever had to put up with."

Rodney turned the bottle up and emptied it in several deep swallows. "Git 'nother bottle. And don't blame me. Took you forever to get the supplies. Then how's I 'spose to know they'd mess up the first batch."

"Cause that's why Big Man pays you," Scooter said. "That's why."

Big Man laughed. "You tell'm, Scooter. But this time, he's kinda right. My boys in Raleigh drug their feet. Now they screamin' for the shine. Damn near serves'm right it ain't ready." His face hardened as he stared at Rodney. "That is the last time I don't deliver though. We make the first run tomorrow, or I have yo' ass."

"Don't you worry," Rodney said, eyeing Scooter who continued playing with his switchblade. "It'll be ready."

"Good. We gonna make three runs a week. You and me'll trade off the drivin'. You pick somebody to ride with you. Cops so stupid they think drivers go alone. Two people ain't so suspicious."

"Three a week?" Rodney said. "Ain't that takin' a chance? Ain't but two ways I know to git to Raleigh, and that car of yours stands out."

Big Man bristled. "Yeah. Don't you think I knows that? How you think I'm gonna git enough money to buy another car if I don't run that stuff as fast as I can? We need more wheels, but that takes money, and most of mine is tied up in them stills. Cain't go to the white man's bank and get a loan for bootleggin'."

"Easy, Mr. Q," Rodney said, using the title Big Man demanded from his still operators. "I's just pointin' it out. You tell me when to drive, and I be behind the wheel."

"You bet yo' sweet ass, you will. Monday's mine. You got Wednesday. I gotta check with the Raleigh boys on what's best after that. It'll be Thursday or Friday, and you can drive that one, too. Now I finally got this operation movin', I got another idea I been meanin' to follow. Don't we, Scooter?"

Scooter looked at him, his face a question mark, but he knew better than to disagree. "We shore do. I reckon Rodney can take care of the drivin'. Don't take much brains for that."

Rodney glared at Scooter. "Look who's talkin' 'bout brains—the shoeshine boy." To Big Man he said, "Jist tell me when. I'm yo' man."

CHAPTER TEN

Midafternoon on Tuesday, Big Man stopped his car alongside The Holy Spirit Evangelical Church. It was a dingy-white clapboard building needing a fresh coat of paint. The roof was missing shingles and looked like a strong breeze would take the rest of them. Sand and winterkill weeds with occasional clumps of brown grass in no certain pattern filled the lawn. The remains of flowerbeds rested beside the steps leading to the front door. One word summed up the picture, poverty.

"Better leave the guns under the seat, Scooter. But carry your switchblade. You wearing a sheath knife around your leg?"

"Yeah. I got both of'm." He pulled the .38 out of his waistband and placed it under his seat. "I'm ready when you is. But how come we're goin' to see Pastor Turner?"

"Listen and learn, little buddy. I got a idea that'll make us some money—you, me, and the preacher."

"Do I have a part in yo' plan?"

"Like always. Let's go."

They got out of the car and walked to the rear entrance of the church. Big Man knocked, causing the door to rattle in its frame, then stuck his head in. "Pastor Turner, is you here?"

"In the office. Come in if you have business with the Lord."

"That's why we here," Big Man said, moving into the small office. "It's Big Man and Scooter."

The room was no bigger than eight-by-eight with a small, scarred desk occupying the middle, and four folding chairs leaning against the plaster wall. Several pictures of Christ hung in cheap frames.

Pastor Turner stood, his straight-back chair bumping against the wall. "Good to see you, Big Man—and you, too, Scooter. 'Course, I'd rather see you in the congregation on Sunday mornings when we gather to worship God."

"Yas suh," Big Man said. "We been talkin' 'bout that. And we's thinkin' we oughta turn over a new leaf. Maybe next Sunday we be there."

"Scooter," Pastor Turner said, fixing him with a stare, "you used to come with Aint Liddie. Now she comes with Joshua and his family. I 'spect she'd rather have you bring her."

Scooter had stopped in the doorway. He looked down and shuffled his feet. "I don't see her so much no more. I—"

"He lives at my place now, suh. We's business partners."

"So I heard," the pastor said with a last look at Scooter whose head was still down. "What can I do for you?"

"I heared on the radio they's got the boycott in Alabama. And that got me to thinkin' 'bout things 'round here. 'Member last fall when the paper had that piece on everybody being equal and justice being blind and all? I talked to you on Main Street right after it."

"Yes, I remember," Pastor Turner said, a suspicious tone in his voice. "You said you were comin' in then, but you didn't. Why you here now?"

"Well, Scooter and me was talkin', and we figger that's what the folks in Alabama tryin' to say. All of us be the same. Don't matter what color our skin. Ain't that right, Scooter?"

"Uh-huh," Scooter said, his eyes locked on the floor.

"Anyway," Big Man continued, "we bettin' the good folks 'round here could use somebody to help them boycott like down there."

Pastor Turner settled at the desk and rested his elbows on it. "Have a seat and tell me more."

Big Man grinned and flipped open a folding chair. "Sit down, Scooter. We need to tell our plan."

"I stay here."

Big Man concentrated on the Pastor. In his most earnest voice, he said, "Here's all you got to do. You start preachin' on Sundays and at prayer meetin's on Wednesday nights. You tell'm the Lord don't mean for us to have so little and the white folks so much.

You tell'm the Good Lord says justice is blind, He wants us to do the boycott, and we oughta git started on it right away."

"Uh-huh," Pastor Turner said. "Where do you and Scooter fit in?"

"Well . . ." Big Man ducked his head and rubbed his hand across his face as if embarrassed. "Well, somebody's got to show them how. And me and Scooter, well, we could do that. I figger we could charge five dollars a piece for the boycott, then split it three ways."

"Three ways? You must mean a third for you and Scooter, a third for me, and a third for the Lord. Is that right?"

"Uh . . . the Lord. Yeah, that's what I was thinkin', alright. The Lord oughta git a cut." He frowned. "How 'bout we do it by fours? Me, you, Scooter, and the Lord."

Pastor Turner grinned and shook his head. "What you're really saying is you and Scooter . . ." he looked at Scooter who did not return his gaze, ". . . ought to make money from this. Is that right?"

Big Man bristled. "Of course. If we puts our time in it, we should make something. I mean, we's businessmen."

Leaning back in his chair, Pastor Turner said, "You need to come to services. If you did, you'd find out it's not about what you want. It's about what the Lord wants." He smiled. "And right now, I believe the Lord wants you to leave so I can work on my sermon for next Sunday. We hope you'll come and hear it." He stood. "Scooter. Aint Liddie needs you. She's old and ain't got too much time left. She still thinks of you as her son."

Scooter's head snapped up, but he didn't meet Pastor Turner's eyes. He turned and left the building.

Big Man watched Scooter leave, then said, "He don't need her no mo'. I takin' care of him."

The Pastor frowned. "That's what worries me. Y'all come to church Sunday."

Big Man joined Scooter in the parking lot. Both wore a frown. Once in the car, Big Man said, "That one stupid man. If he thinks I gonna give him two-thirds when I do all the work, he crazy. Screw him. I don't need him or his church."

"Shouldn't oughta say things like that about a preacher," Scooter said. "Pastor Turner be a God-fearin' man."

..*

Pastor Turner stood at the window watching Big Man's car leave the parking area. "Lord, forgive me, but that's gotta be one of the sneakiest colored men in Nolan County. Imagine him tryin' to make money off the poor folks of my church." He chuckled. "He don't even know what boycott means. If he did, he'd know we ain't got nothing in Dawson to boycott."

Returning to his desk, he said, "I wish I knowed some way to break Scooter away from him. Cain't nothing good come from that, and I'm afraid it's going to be the death of Aint Liddie." He looked at the papers he'd been working on before Big Man and Scooter's arrival. It was his Sunday sermon. He had planned to talk about turning the other cheek. He picked up his pencil and tapped it where he'd stopped writing, staring at the words. "The Lord talked about *out of the mouths of babes*. Nobody ever going to confuse Big Man with a baby, but he might have said something. Maybe it's time for Negroes to be more choosy 'bout when to turn the other cheek. Maybe it's time for me to take a stand for my congregation. Last year, I told Muster Flanagan I was going to preach on all men being born equal and invite him to church. I ain't done it yet. This comin' Sunday will be the first time, but it ain't gonna be the last." His eyes turned upward. "I might need Your help on this, though."

..*

It was Friday, mid-morning with the temperature hovering in the mid-forties. The sidewalks weren't empty, but little socializing took place. Lucille's Restaurant had more than its usual number of customers, most of whom drank coffee and discussed the cold snap that had descended on Dawson. The smell of bacon sizzling on the grill and fresh coffee brewing tantalized the customers. The outside air meeting at the window with the warmth inside created a layer of moisture that beaded its way to the sill, leaving crooked paths through the condensation. Henry and Flip sat at a table near the front window

"What? You fellers ain't got a job no more?" Lucille said. "All you have to do is sit here and drink my coffee? I can't make no money that way. Order some food, or I'm going to throw you out in the cold."

"You're a hard woman," Henry said. "You know everything on your menu is fattening. I have to get in shape for the wedding."

"Take up walking then, Yank. I heard it's good for pudgy waistlines."

"Pudgy?" Henry said to Flip's laughter. "I used to be pudgy. Now I'm . . . I'm . . . svelte."

"You're what? I don't know what that means, but I know pudgy when I see pudgy. And you're pudgy. Now have one of my cinnamon buns, then go for a long walk."

Flip had a firm hand on his stomach as the belly laughter continued. "I love it, Lucille. Pudgy. That's a great description."

"Yeah, and what are you ordering?" she said. "Your coffee makes me the same money as his."

"Uh, how about a fried egg sandwich?" Flip answered. "Wrap it up and I'll take it with me for lunch. Aunt Liddie's been alone in the store long enough."

"Alright," Lucille said. "I'll make two. You owe her one for covering for you while you sit here and gossip."

"Men don't gossip," Henry said. "We were exchanging views on the world situation. Why just a moment ago, Flip was predicting the next move by the communists."

"Sure, Yank. I'll fix three egg sandwiches for you. You can surprise Mabel and Eli by being nice for a change. Is that coffeepot in your office working? Maybe I should pour three coffees to go. I'm sure they'd love a cup."

"Just the sandwiches," Henry said. "That way I won't have to come back here for lunch."

Lucille's laughter cackled out. "If not today, you'll be back tomorrow. You ain't married yet. You need me." She yelled toward the short order cook. "Five hen fruits on white-T. Make one dry. The editor's on a diet." She refilled their cups, then headed toward another table. As she moved past the window, she did a quick wipe with her hand towel.

Henry watched her move through the customers. "That woman is a town treasure. They should put up a statue—"

A tapping on the front window caused Henry and Flip to turn. Pastor Turner stood out front bundled in a worn black topcoat, a gray fedora, and gloves. He mouthed something and pointed at

Henry.

"Excuse me, Flip," Henry said. "Watch my sandwiches if they come before I get back. Looks like the preacher wants to talk." He walked out the door. "You want me, Pastor Turner?"

"Yes sir. I got something I want to talk to you about. I was goin' to your office when I seen you in Miss Lucille's. When you plan to be in?"

"Give me a few minutes. What's it about?"

Pastor Turner looked around the street. "I druther not say out here. I'll meet you at the paper." He walked away.

Henry followed him with his eyes, a frown creasing his forehead. Then he went inside the restaurant.

"What's up?" Flip asked.

Henry told him and saw his face turn from one of camaraderie to worry. "What?" Henry said. "You know something I don't?"

"No, but I'm hoping he's not putting his nose in this equal rights stuff." He stood and headed toward the door. "I'd better get back. Aunt Liddie's there alone."

"Hold on, Flip," Lucille called. "Your sandwiches are almost ready."

"Uh . . . okay." He walked to the counter. "Can you rush it along? I really need to get back." A moment later he was out the front door with two sandwiches wrapped in wax paper.

Lucille carried a brown bag to Henry who wore a puzzled expression. "What happened to Flip?" she asked. "He ran out like he had a nest of hornets in his britches."

"Not sure." He shrugged. "Guess you played on his conscience, and he had to get back to the drugstore."

"Uh-huh," Lucille said. "Maybe, but it'd be the first time."

A few minutes later, Henry walked into the lobby of the *Dawson Times* and saw Pastor Turner sitting on the edge of a chair in the corner. "Go ahead in my office. I'll be right with you. I have to pass out these sandwiches, or Lucille will never forgive me." He pulled one from the bag and handed it to Mabel.

She stared at it. "Christmas was last month. I figured I'd have to wait another twelve months before you gave me anything else. Hmmm, egg sandwich, no bacon, no cheese. I am truly blessed."

"Eat it or pitch it," Henry said with a pretend-growl in his voice.

"Here. Give this one to Eli." He gave a second to her, then went into his office with the third.

Pastor Turner stood near the desk.

As he put the brown bag down, Henry said, "Have a seat, my friend. What can I do for you?"

Displaying nervousness, the pastor settled in the visitor's chair. "Mr. Flanagan, do you remember a talk we had last year 'bout me preaching on justice being blind?"

Henry leaned back, folding his hands over his stomach. "Yes. That was after I wrote about Judge Jackson's brand of justice."

"Yes sir, that's when it was. I told you when I done it, I was goin' to invite you to my church. Well, this Sunday is the time." He hesitated, his eyes everywhere except on Henry. "Will you come?"

Henry took a deep breath then blew it out through his mouth. "You know I have the utmost respect for you and your people. You know I think you've been treated bad in the South, and I don't believe in *separate but equal*, the *colored only* fountains, *colored only* windows—all that stuff. But things are different now. I'm engaged to Debbie Patterson. She grew up here. If I—"

"I believe you, suh." Pastor Turner stared at the floor, shuffling his feet even though he was seated. "I jist thought . . . I means, I kinda hoped . . ." His voice faded away to a whisper. "I shouldn't a bothered you." His hands worked at one another.

Henry leaned forward, resting his forearms on his desk. "Stop that. Don't you do that old colored shuffle with me. You know I support you."

"Yas suh." The tone was subservient, slave to master. "I knows you do—"

Henry slammed his fist down with a loud crack. "Enough. One thing I can't stand is the way you people act like cowed dogs anytime a white man disagrees with you. We're equals, so don't pull that on me."

Pastor Turner's head snapped up, his eyes blazing. "Then come to services Sunday. I'm gonna preach it twice—eleven and seven." He stood. "It's awful easy to write a bunch of words. It ain't so easy being one of us." He walked out of the office, his chin held high.

A moment later, Mabel peeked in the door. "What did you do? That colored preacher looked like you made him drink turpentine."

"Maybe worse. I might have fired the first shot in the war between the races."

CHAPTER ELEVEN

Henry and Debbie cuddled on the couch in the parlor of her house. They'd had a delightful baked chicken dinner with homemade biscuits, snap beans, and tomatoes, canned from her garden in the late summer. While there had been no candles decorating the table, it was as romantic a meal as Henry could remember. Wine and candlelight were vastly overrated. Love was the only stimulant he needed.

He nuzzled Debbie's neck. "What are we doing Sunday?"

She squirmed under his caress. "Sunday school, church, maybe lunch with the Jacksons and the Matthews. If the weather works, we could walk around town?"

He sat up. "In January? I think not. I may have grown up in New York, but that doesn't mean I like cold weather. I had more than enough of that in France and Germany."

She smiled. "Oh boy. Now that you have me hooked, the truth is coming out. When we get married, I suppose I'll have to stay indoors from November through the end of March just because my husband doesn't want to be chilly."

He kissed the tip of her nose. "Very funny, Mrs. Soon-to-be Flanagan. You're well aware that the ceremony will admonish you to love, honor, and *obey*." He pulled her to him in a close hug. "Five more months. If I didn't love you so much, I'd be irate that you conned me into waiting until June. Every moment without you as my wife is a lifetime."

"Uh-uh. It's a headache night. All that sweet talking's not getting you anywhere." She paused. "But don't stop. I have been known to change my mind."

Henry chuckled and nibbled on her earlobe.

She jumped. "Quit that. Not fair. You know how that affects me."

"Uh-huh. And I plan to do it for at least the next hundred years."

"That's all? Then what? Divorce? I'll be scandalized. No one in town will speak to me. I'll be a scarlet woman."

"Maybe not scarlet at a hundred thirty years old. Maybe only a faded maroon."

"Humph," Debbie said flipping her hair. "So much for romance in the man I love. He already sees me as old and worn out." She pulled his lips to hers.

The kiss flamed every emotion in his being. When she broke free, he said, "Never old, my dear, never worn out. You'll always be young, beautiful, and desirable." He shook his head, fighting the desires that surged in him. "If you do that again, I'll forget what I want to talk to you about."

"Can't it wait?" Debbie said, snuggling into his chest. "Let's put on some soft music and let the evening go wherever it chooses. I have a new Sinatra LP."

Henry sighed, frowned, and forced himself to ignore his libido and her wonderful idea. "Pastor Turner came to see me today."

"Huh?" Debbie said, pushing herself off Henry's shoulder. "Of all the men I've known—all two of them—that may be the most romantic thing ever whispered in my ear. Makes me feel like the three hours I spent in the kitchen this afternoon and the hour I spent making myself gorgeous are paying off. Do you have any other words of love to lure me into the bedroom?"

Henry laughed. "Sorry, my dear, but this is eating at me. My heart and my head are both battling for control. Which one would you help win?"

"You ask me, a woman? Don't you know that everyone says women have no brains? They follow wherever their heart leads them." She grinned and kissed him on the chin. "Ooh. You need a shave."

Henry rubbed his face. "One of the prices of being a fiancée, my love. That ring on your third finger, left hand saves me the need for a second shave of the day." He laughed and pulled her head down, kissing the top of it.

"Okay, I give," she said. "What did Pastor Turner want?"

Henry straightened up on the couch, then spoke in a serious tone. "He's preaching on equal rights Sunday. He invited me to his service."

She bounced away from him. "He what? Hank, that's crazy. White people don't go to Negro churches."

"I know." He paused, his brow wrinkled. "But why? Are there two different Gods? Is there One for white people and Another for coloreds? Why can't I go to his church? Why shouldn't I go?" He stared into her eyes. "Why can't *we* attend services at The Holy Spirit Evangelical Church?"

Debbie's mouth fell open. "You're joking?" She returned his stare. "You can't . . . I can't . . . we can't go to his church."

"Why?"

"It's . . . it's just not done."

He pulled her to him again, and her head returned to his chest. "If there's only one God, worshipping Him has nothing to do with skin color. The First Amendment to the Constitution grants me freedom of religious choice. It doesn't say a thing about whites to white churches and coloreds to colored ones." He sighed, a sound that originated in his soul. "I'm going Sunday evening. I have to. If not, I'm a hypocrite. And I'd rather not have to go through life knowing I ran from what I believe."

Debbie sat up again and folded her hands in her lap. "I love you, Hank. Talk to me. Let me into your thinking."

He stared at his fingers, rubbing the tips with his thumbs. "Last fall, I wrote an editorial that I believed in very much. It riled a lot of people and the Burnettes tried to burn the paper. I wrote another one, not as antagonistic, but saying I would stand by my position. When I showed it to the Judge, he gave me some advice. He told me not to rush it, equality will come. He said I would only make it worse by stirring the races. I listened to him and did not run it. I also quit writing such editorials even though I believe as strongly now as I did when I published that last one."

He looked at Debbie and there was a pleading tone in his voice when he continued. "By attending the service, I can report it as news—and it is news, big news. A colored preacher, a man of God, is standing up for his people. He's not the first, and he won't be the last, but he's the first in Nolan County. I'd be a lousy newspaperman if I ignored it." His voice softened. "I'd be a pretty lousy human being if I didn't follow my heart. It led me to you, and now it's telling me to honor Pastor Turner's invitation."

Debbie's voice was heavy with emotion. "I won't marry a man who disgraces himself in front of me and my friends. I—"

"Debbie—"

"Hush and let me talk. I didn't interrupt you." She paused as if gathering her thoughts. "As I was saying, I won't marry a man in disgrace . . . unless I'm in disgrace with him. *We* will attend the Negro church Sunday evening." Her smile grew into a chuckle. "I may even call around and see if anyone wants to go with us."

..*

On Sunday night, Henry, Debbie, and Judge Jackson sat on the back pew of Pastor Turner's church. The seats, constructed from rough-hewn timbers, weren't comfortable, but were better than standing. A few splinters raised their heads, but most were either smoothed by the many rear ends parked on them through the years, or snapped away by bored congregants looking for something to do during long sermons.

There were no stained glass windows depicting pictures of Christ or the Madonna and Child, only ordinary panes, some of them cracked. Handmade wooden crosses adorned walls needing a coat of paint. A few of them had a carved figure of Christ mounted thereon. The floors creaked when walked on, enough to make one wonder how soon a footstep would punch its way through. Only the dais and the crucifixes showed richness, not the richness that money brings, but that of the many hands that had touched and caressed them over the years. The wood appeared to glow from an inner beauty.

The whites fidgeted under the glances of the colored attendees and nodded when the Pastor acknowledged their presence. The collection plate that passed in front of them held more pennies than silver—no bills. When the sermon began, Henry pulled out a pad and took notes in his peculiar form of shorthand.

Following the service, Pastor Turner stood at the front entrance and shook their hands the same as he did every congregant exiting. He may have worn a deeper smile for them.

They stepped into a group of smiling faces, each one thanking them for attending and inviting them to come again.

Liddie pushed her way toward them. "Let me through here now. Y'all step aside. I gotta give my friends a hug." She pulled Debbie to her huge bosom in a fierce embrace, then went after Henry. "I knowed there was good in y'all. I jist knowed it. C'mere, Judge. I owes you a hug, too. Y'all's the best friends a colored person ever had. I shore wisht Scooter could be here to see this. It might restore his faith in the Lord."

"Aint Liddie," Eli said, stepping up to them, "you don't quit squeezin' so hard, you's gonna hurt somebody." He removed his hat and held it in front of him. "Mustah Flanagan, I always said you's a fine boss. Now, I'm gonna tell ever'body, you's the finest they is. Miz Patterson, Jedge, y'all make me 'bout the happiest man in Nolan County tonight."

"Thank you for coming," Pastor Turner said, joining the growing group. "It means a lot to me and my flock to have you here."

"You preached a fine sermon," Debbie said. "I'd like to come back some time."

The others nodded in accord as the Pastor beamed. "You're welcome anytime, anytime at all," he said.

..*

At seven on Monday morning, Henry sat at his desk. A smile played at the corners of his mouth. "Who, what, when, where, how," he murmured. "Stick to the basics. It's a news story. Keep your emotions out of it."

He layered bond paper, carbon paper, and onionskin and rolled it into his typewriter. "Let me see. Headline. *Colored Pastor Fires First Shot in War of Equality*. No, too melodramatic. *Colored Pastor Preaches on Equal Rights*." He stared at it. "That's better. Not as confrontational. Don't want to bring the Burnettes out from under their rocks." He flexed his fingers and began to type.

Sunday, at The Holy Spirit Evangelical Church, Pastor Jeremiah Turner preached a sermon on the inequality of separate but equal, a culture the U.S. Supreme Court has declared unconstitutional. In his morning and evening services, he told his congregations it was time for colored people to stand up and demand they be treated the same as whites. He warned that some

Negroes might be hurt, but the laws of the land were on their side.

Pastor Turner said, "We might have to give some of our blood before the white man gives us what is ours, but that's the way it's always been when folks seek to reclaim what's rightfully theirs. You remember how Christ stood up to the Money Changers and chased them out of the temple, how the Jews stood up to the Pharaohs, how Moses led his people out of Egypt rather than let them be treated like trash. That's what we got to do—stand up for what's right. And what's right is colored folk got to be treated the same as white folk."

The attendees rose at the end of the evening service and gave Pastor Turner a standing ovation.

Henry rolled the paper up and read what he had typed. At the end, he smiled. "Not as strong as I'd like, but it meets the basic rules of journalism. Report the facts and keep your ego out of it. No one can accuse me of stirring things this time."

He frowned. "Of course, this may put Pastor Turner in the gun sights of the Burnettes or others like them. I hope the reverend considered that before he wrote his sermon."

He rose, walked into the outer office, and poured a cup of coffee. His mind floated above the scene, seeing everything, yet seeing nothing. The wrinkles on his forehead displayed the reason—worry about what he'd written. "Too strong? Too weak? I need to get a pair of independent eyes." He sipped his coffee. "Maybe I should run it around to Debbie's and have her look at it. She has good instincts."

"Who you talking to?" Mabel said, coming through the front door. "And what're you doing here so early? I like this time to settle in, especially on Monday, before you and Eli mess up my day."

"Good morning," Henry said. "How was your weekend?"

"Fine. Me and the family went . . ."

Henry walked into his office, not realizing Mabel was answering his question. He sat and stared at the article. "Damn, Henry. You wrote it. It's a good news article. Print it." He leaned back in his chair. "Okay, that's what I'll do." With a smile, he returned to his coffee and other stories that had to be ready for Eli when he arrived.

CHAPTER TWELVE

Jane rolled her shoulders, easing the tension. "That takes care of the business of the food collection committee for today. We're all set for the announcement. I think we did a right good job this year." She looked at the women in the room—Debbie Patterson, Lorrie Matthews, Christiana Andrews, and Edna Leggett. "There's plenty of coffee left, and I'm drooling over that beautiful double-chocolate cake Debbie brought. I say we adjourn the meeting and cut it."

They had stayed after the regular meeting of the Memorial Baptist Church Women's Circle to iron out the last details of the church's Food for the Poor program. They sat at a conference table in a meeting room of the church annex where they'd covered everything from asparagus to zucchini.

The previous year, they accumulated enough to divide among fifty families. The committee set a goal of seventy-five this year. Distribution of the food would be on Valentine's Day. Jane was chairperson of the committee, having held the position for the last five years. Members came and went but she knew she could always count on Debbie and Lorrie. Christiana and Edna were recent additions.

"We'd better eat that cake," Debbie said walking to the table where it rested. "This is Hank's favorite. If I take it home, he'll have at it, and that would break his diet."

"Humph," Christiana said, her customary look of disapproval lining her forehead. "Maybe slimming him down wasn't your best idea."

"What on earth do you mean?" Lorrie said. "He looks great. And he certainly dresses better since Debbie captured his heart."

She grinned at Debbie. "If I'd known there was such a good looking man under all those ink stains, I'd have introduced him to my sister a long time ago. Hmmmm, wonder if it's too late. He's not married yet."

"Don't you dare," Debbie said, chuckling and waving the cake knife at her. "He's mine. I have him hogtied, and he's not going anywhere except the altar beside me."

Everyone giggled except Christiana, who said, "The stuff he's doing these days, I'm surprised you're bragging about marrying him."

The levity disappeared as the others stared at her.

"Okay," Debbie said, bristling, "what's on your mind? If you have something to say about Hank, just say it." She walked back to the conference table and sat in a chair opposite Christiana.

"Don't think I need to. That piece in the paper yesterday says it all. Going to a nigger church. What kind of man is he?"

Debbie flushed and half-rose from her chair.

Lorrie forced a laugh. "Sounds like a newspaperman that goes where the news is. Isn't that right, Debbie? I bet he's at the office right now thinking up his next big story."

Debbie settled back into her chair and appeared to think for a moment. "I'll tell you what kind of man he is. He's the kind that loves people, all people. He doesn't think it's right for anyone to be treated like dirt just because their skin is a darker color." She stared at Christiana. "And he's the kind who will take his fiancée with him to a colored church to hear a stirring sermon by a good preacher. I went with him Sunday night." Her eyes dared Christiana to say anything else.

Lorrie and Edna gasped while Christiana glared.

"Could we change the subject?" Jane said. "This is hardly a subject for the ladies of the church to get into a dispute about. We all know men do the dumbest things. Why, you might not believe it, but Dan went with Debbie and Mr. Flanagan. I wouldn't go, but my man has a mind of his own whether I agree or not. I'm not proud of it, but nobody's going to badmouth him. This is still a free country. People can do what they want." She looked at Christiana, then shifted her gaze to Lorrie and Edna. "In fact, I've been thinking I may go with him next time."

"Well. I never . . ." Christiana huffed, rising. "Obviously, you won't need my help in the future. Edna. Let's go." She headed for the door.

Edna stood, looking at Debbie and Jane, her eyes downcast. "I'll pray for you." She followed Christiana.

Lorrie's head swiveled from the door to Debbie to Jane. "You girls sure know how to end a meeting with a bang. Did you really go to the colored church, Debbie?"

"Yes. And any doubts are now dispelled. If Christiana and Edna are against it, it must be the right thing to do."

Jane said, "No. It was stupid and can only lead to trouble. I'm so mad with Dan I haven't spoken to him since he left the house Sunday evening. But I'll be damned—"

"Jane, we're in church," Lorrie said. "Your language."

"Sorry, but I'll bet the Lord feels the same as me. I won't let that hypocrite badmouth my husband, Henry, or Debbie. She just gets under my skin so bad. All she does is gossip and make up stories. But don't think I agree with it. No way. Debbie, y'all are asking for trouble. And you're hurting this town. What will our country be like if we have the races mixing? How soon will it be before we have little half-colored children running around? What then?"

Lorrie shook her head. "It's happening just like Flip said it would. Friends turning against friends. Please, ladies. Let's not argue. We've never had any trouble before. Can't we forget it and do things like we used to? All these changes don't have to effect us."

Without taking her gaze off Jane, Debbie said, "Nothing can be like it used to be. Dawson is changing, and we have to change with it. Those who stay stuck in the past will miss the future."

..*

Alice Burnette watched through a crack in the door as her husband, Charlie, paced in front of the men assembled in his living room. "It has started. If we don't move soon, we may as well paint our faces black. Them and their nigger-lovin' friends gonna take everythin' we worked for. Y'all saw the piece in the paper. Now that damnyankee is glorifyin' that nigger preacher. If we don't take action, who knows what'll happen next? Marvin, what you think?"

His brother rose from his chair. "You know I'm with you. We

got to nip this in the bud. I say, nip it in the bud before it gits out of hand."

"Alright," Charlie said. "You heard Marvin. It's time for the county KKK to show its stuff. All we gotta decide is where to burn our first cross and what nigger we gonna bring out to watch. I say the front of that church that damn editor went to. We do that a coupla times and they'll git the message."

"Charlie," Claude Atkins said, rubbing his hand across his mouth. "I been thinkin'. What you're talkin' about is sure to land us in jail. Now I don't mind buggin' darkies some, but it ain't worth doin' time. This stuff 'bout pickin' one of them up . . . Well, I ain't sure about that. I mean, you and Marvin might go to the prison camp yet from when you tried to burn the newspaper office. If you leave, who's gonna be the bosses?"

Junior Cooper raised his hand.

"What?" Charlie said while glaring at Claude. "This ain't no school. You don't have to raise your hand."

Junior stood. "I'm like Claude. I got five children. If I go to jail, who's gonna take care of them and my woman? Who's gonna plant my crops?" He hesitated. "Maybe we oughta talk some more. This Klan stuff could bring the law down on us."

"Looks like we got two chicken-shits here," Charlie said. "They're 'fraid of the po-lice." He shook his head. "If this is the best we can do, the niggers and the Yankees will take over. It'll be like reconstruction all over agin. My granddaddy told me about it. White men had to walk in the gutter while niggers took the sidewalks. White women hid in their houses behind locked doors. And there was a lot of them women got raped by the burrheads. Is that what you want? Niggers in your bedroom mo-lesting your women. Junior, three of your chil'en's girls. How many high yaller grandchildren you want?"

Adam Adams spoke up. "I ain't sayin' you're wrong. But I kinda feel like Claude and Junior. We oughta wait 'til somethin' happens. A preacher shootin' his mouth off in church ain't worth gitting throw'd in jail. I say we watch, and be ready if somethin' real happens."

There were nods from the other men in the room, all except Charlie and Marvin. Charlie said, "From what I see, the rest a y'all lost your guts, too. You mark my words, you's gonna wish you'd followed me and my brother. Something bad is goin' to happen. And when it does, me and Marvin is goin' to be ready. I 'spect you'll be right there with us saying we should have done it sooner." He paced another circle, staring at each man as he passed in front of him. "Next time ain't gonna be no talk. I'll be takin' my gun."

Alice moved away from the door, breathing a sigh of relief. The group had turned against her husband's plan. That meant he'd have to give up his crazy ideas, and she wouldn't have to go to the police. She didn't want to turn him in, but Shirley, her sister, said she had to before he hurt somebody. She stuck her hands in the dishwater that had cooled while she eavesdropped. The smile that crept onto her face looked as foreign as an oasis in a desert. *He ain't much, but he is my husband, and some day we might have babies. Wouldn't be right to send him to jail.*

She heard the front door open and went back to peek into the living room again. She saw everyone except Marvin filing out.

"Alice, git my jug," Charlie called.

She cringed, wondering if she could pretend not to hear, or if she could slip out the backdoor without his knowing. If they started drinking, Charlie would get her in bed and . . . She loved it when he was sober, but he was so mean when drunk.

"Woman, you in there? You better do what I say. I ain't in no mood for your crap tonight."

She rushed to the sink and buried her forearms in the water, back to what was familiar, what her mother trained her for since she was old enough to stand on a stool and work in the kitchen. She recognized the signs. He was showing off for Marvin—showing how mean he could be, how he ran his house. "I'm washing dishes," she called. "Maybe you could—"

"Dammit. Do what I say."

The phone rang in their party line ring—two shorts. She relaxed as she heard Charlie cross the living room and pick up.

"Hello," he said, followed by silence. "Who are—" More silence. "Ain't no way. That nigger wouldn't do that." . . . "Are you sure?" . . . "If you right, they's gonna be one less troublemaker in Nolan County." . . . "I 'preciate you letting me know." He hung up.

Alice took Charlie's moonshine and two glasses into the living room, her heart banging in her chest. "Who was on the phone?" she asked in her softest voice. "Was it for me? I'm 'specting a call from Shirley."

"Naw. Man-business. Gimme that stuff." He was mad, the cords in his neck standing out. A vein pulsed in his forehead.

She handed him the jug and glasses. With a tremor in her voice, she said, "I might go over to Shirley's. Is that alright?"

"I don't give a damn what you do. Git out of here." He poured a glass of moonshine. "Marvin, we got a problem. That call was from some damn coon. Wouldn't tell me his name, but he said that nigger driver of ours is doublecrossing us. Said he won't be here Sunday to take a load. He's making his own stuff and stealing our customers."

"That cain't be," Marvin said. "He's too stupid. Naw, he got to be wrong." He paused. "If he's right, what we gonna do?"

Charlie frowned, passing the jug to him. "Pour your own. We'll see if he shows up Sunday. If he don't, I'm gonna take care of him." He appeared to think as he sipped his drink. "You know, Marvin, this might be just what we need to get the folks 'round here moving."

Alice frowned and rushed from the room. What was happening? What could she do? She couldn't turn her husband in for threatening to hurt a colored man. The police would laugh at her. She had to talk to Shirley. She would know. She would advise her. But one thing was sure, this was not a good night to be in the house with Charlie.

She wondered if she should call Martha. Tell her to get out of the house before Marvin came home drunk and mad with the world. Charlie and Marvin were two from the same litter--meaner than rabid skunks when they were drunk, and much worse when they were both drunk and mad. She'd call from Shirley's.

First, she had to get away. She headed for the back door, opened it, then let it close without a sound behind her, thankful she'd oiled the hinges that afternoon. She considered taking the truck, but decided against it. He might hear her. She skirted the house, careful to stay out of the light cast through the windows. He could always change his mind and call her back if he saw her. With a last rush, she made it to the road and walked away as fast as she could.

Maybe she shouldn't come back. Maybe she'd never return. Could she do it? Would she do it? The worry lines in her forehead smoothed, and she smiled. Shirley would know what to do, and how to do it.

CHAPTER THIRTEEN

On Sunday afternoon, Big Man called a meeting of his partners—Scooter and Rodney. Low clouds, the color of dirty snow, carried a threat of rain while temperatures hovered in the low forties. Adding to the misery was a blustery wind that cut through layers of clothing and turned ears and noses red. No one lingered on the streets, and greetings were a quick hello-goodbye. It was one of those dismal days when almost everyone locked the weather outside and bundled near a heat source.

Rodney pounded on Big Man's front door, then hunkered against the siding. "Hurry up in there. I'm freezin' my ass out here." He held his worn topcoat closed at the throat and appeared to shrink inside it.

Big Man opened the door and eyed him. "You one sorry sight. Git in here 'fore we let the heat out."

Rodney rushed through the doorway and made his way to the upright stove in the living room. "You shore pick lousy days to have meetin's. A man could catch his death out there. I much rather be home with my woman. Good afternoon for gittin' some."

"With three kids runnin' 'round the house? Shit, you better off here. Every time you git near yo' woman, you knock'er up."

Rodney cut him a look, but didn't say anything. He opened his topcoat and stepped closer to the stove. "What you want? I got things to be doin'."

Big Man walked to his chair and sat. "Sit down. You, Scooter, and me got business to talk."

"Soon's I warm up."

Big Man scowled. "Now. I ain't got all afternoon to waste on you. You don't want me to sic Scooter on you, do you?" He glanced at Scooter who leaned against a wall.

Rodney held his hands over the stove another moment then followed instructions. He dropped onto the edge of the chair closest to the heater. "Okay, I'm here."

"I ain't feelin' so good. This cold's gettin' to me. You gonna have to make the run tomorrow night." Big Man blew his nose into a red handkerchief laying on the table beside his chair. "Just tell the Raleigh folks I'm sick and sent you instead. They don't care who drives. I'll give you the drop off place." He blew his nose again. "And come right back after you deliver. I needs the money. Spent all my ready cash on the last load of supplies."

"You ain't broke, is you?" Rodney said. "I ain't got money for the gas."

"I got enough for that, but the rest of my money's in a safe place. Can't trust people in this neighborhood. They steal you blind." He took out his billfold and handed Rodney a twenty. "Put the change with the two-hundred you get for the shine." He glared at him. "And don't try to shortchange me."

Rodney laughed as he took the bill. "You knows me better than that. I wouldn't mess with your money. I's a honest man."

"You half-right—the part about I know you. That's why I warned you." He stood and walked to the door. "Now get outta here. Me'n Scooter got some talkin' to do."

Rodney glanced at Scooter whose face was noncommittal. "What you got to say to him I can't hear? I'm a equal partner, ain't I?"

Scooter came off the wall and took a step toward Rodney. "Right now, you's gone. You heard Big Man. Don't make me throw you out."

Rodney stood and made a show of buttoning his topcoat, then pulling on his gloves. As he moved toward the door, he glared at Scooter. "One a these days, I'll let you try." He slapped Big Man on the shoulder. "Want me to come by here after I git the load?"

"Naw. Just head on out. Who you takin' with you?"

"Don't know. I'll see one of my girlfriends later. Wife'll have to watch the kids so she can't go. Won't be no problem. I knows lots of women."

"Just make sure she keeps her mouth closed. She talks, and

Scooter shuts her up. Same rules for her as for you."

"Damn. Don't you ever git tired of remindin' me?"

"Nope. Now leave. I gotta rest."

Rodney stepped through the door that Big Man held open, hopped off the porch, and walked away at a fast pace.

..*

Big Man watched through the window, and when Rodney turned the corner, said, "Okay, he gone. Sit down, Scooter. We gotta job to plan."

Dropping into the chair Rodney had vacated, Scooter said, "I thought you was sick."

"Oh, I gotta little cold, but it take more than that to stop me. 'Member that preacher we went to see? You hear what he done last Sunday?"

Scooter scratched his head. "No, what?"

"He stole our idea. That's what he did. And I don't take it lightly."

"I don't unnerstand. What idea?"

"Damn, Scooter. Sometimes you so stupid, I cain't hardly believe it. He preached about our idea to lead the coloreds so we git equal rights."

"Uh-huh. I ain't got no problem with that. What's yours?"

"They's money to be made, and it were our idea. That's my problem. Ain't right he git rich when we thunk it up. I'm gonna talk to him."

"When?" Scooter said, frowning.

"I'd do it tonight, but he's preachin', being it's Sunday. That's another reason I give tomorrow night's run to Rodney. We gonna pay that preacher a visit and explain what's what. When we finish with him, he'll know you and me is running things."

"Spose he don't agree?"

Big Man laughed, a huge belly laugh. "He'll agree. If he don't, he gonna have a hard time turnin' the pages in his Bible with two broke arms."

"You think you gonna hurt the preacher?" Scooter said, his frown deepening.

Without looking in Scooter's direction, Big Man said, "Let's just say he gonna see things our way. Us three will be partners when we finish talkin' to him."

"Uh-uh," Scooter said.

Big Man looked at him with a puzzled expression. "What's that mean?"

"It means, uh-uh. Ain't gonna happen."

Big Man stared at Scooter, noting the ugly look on his face. "Maybe you don't unnerstan'. If we gonna make money on this equals business, that preacher's gotta learn who runs things. That's what we gonna do. We gonna teach him a lesson. I hope he learns fast so we don't have to hurt him too much."

"Uh-uh," Scooter said. "Ain't gonna happen."

Big Man stood, walked to Scooter, and towered over him. "What you mean? If I say it happens, it happens."

Scooter stared up at him and in a calm voice said, "Ain't gonna happen. We ain't messing with Pastor Turner."

"Who the hell you think runs things here? You do what I say."

"We ain't messing with Pastor Turner." Scooter pushed himself out of the chair and rose onto his toes. "Ain't no way you gonna do nothing to him. He's a man of God, and I ain't gonna let you or nobody else hurt him."

"Damn you, Scooter. Who—"

"Yell all you want to. Ain't gonna change my mind. We ain't seein' the preacher. I'll kill you before I let you mess with him. Aint Liddie says he's the best man she knows. That means he's the best man I know. I don't know what he's doing, but we ain't messing with him." Scooter's hand hovered over the .38 in his belt.

Big Man's eyes flicked to Scooter's pistol, then he walked to the couch and sat, a laugh bubbling out. "You're somethin', really somethin'. I turned you into a killer, now I gotta live with you." He looked around the room deep in thought, knowing Scooter continued to watch him, his hand never relaxing. "Okay. You win. We won't bother Pastor Turner." He chuckled. "I love you, boy. This is the first time you proved I done right by hiring you."

Scooter relaxed and sat in his chair, but his eyes never left Big Man's face. "I ain't shore what you talkin' about, but we ain't messin' with Pastor Turner."

"Alright. We jist take tomorrow night off then. Hep this ol' cold git better."

..*

Rodney sat tall and proud as he cruised Main Street, his right hand resting on the steering knob while his left caressed the smoothness of the wheel. Big Man's car made him feel powerful, the equal of anyone he met. He'd picked it up from the house a few minutes prior, but couldn't resist the urge to *drag Main* before picking up the moonshine. After that, he'd swing by Beulah's house, then head out to Raleigh.

Shifting his hands, he rubbed the dashboard, then fiddled with the radio dial, changing stations while marveling at how good it made him feel. A few more trips and he'd have enough saved to look for a car for himself. Not one as grand as this, but something he could use to pick up women. He grinned. There were only two major criteria—it had to run, and it had to have a big back seat. Such a ride would be as satisfying and a whole lot cheaper than the rooms he sometimes rented. Of course, it meant he had to watch how much he spent on partying, and make sure his wife didn't find out. If she knew, she'd nag him for money to take care of the kids. He groaned. Damn snot-nosed kids. Why'n hell did she get pregnant all the time? They were her problem, not his.

His mood changed when he thought of the night ahead of him. Big Man had said come straight back after delivering the goods and collecting, but what he didn't know wouldn't hurt him. Rodney had other plans. He knew a motel on Route 64 that catered to coloreds and rented rooms cheap. He planned to spend a few hours there. When he spoke to Beulah earlier in the day, she'd given him her look that said she was ready to party.

The bottle of hooch under the driver's seat guaranteed Beulah would be cooperative, and he'd be mellow and grinning tomorrow. While he preferred the state stuff, it was more expensive than bootleg. Besides, it was good enough. Only reason he wasted time with Beulah was because she was so good in bed. She might be ugly as bad concrete, but she knew how to please a man. He smiled. That woman knew tricks his wife would never try, plus she knew better than to get herself pregnant. He'd made it clear he wouldn't take care of any kid of hers.

Rodney drove up the mudholed lane to the sharecropper's house, stopped in front, and honked the horn. He looked around, disdain showing on his face. The building had never seen paint and leaned to the right like a giant hand had given it a push. From where he sat, Rodney could see broken boards in the sagging front porch. And he knew the inside was no better—probably never finished, cracks in the walls big enough to let roaches and rats come and go as they pleased.

Rodney shuddered. He'd never let himself get trapped into that kind of living—no running water and a two-holer privy out back. That didn't mean Ezra didn't work hard. Rodney knew he did—from sunup to dark, raising crops for the market. But half of every penny he made went to the owner of the farm. If it weren't for the bootleg whiskey Big Man sponsored him to brew, Rodney suspected the family would go to bed hungry. Even at that, there were probably nights there was nothing to eat. He'd rather go back to prison. At least he had three meals a day, a cot to sleep on, and clean clothes to wear.

Ezra came to the door and looked around the area. Apparently satisfied at what he saw, he called, "Pull 'round back to the barn. Me'n the boys'll meet you there."

Rodney complied, and the farmer and his two teenage boys joined him. He popped the trunk. "Git on with it. I ain't got no extry time for you." He leaned against the rear fender while they loaded the moonshine into the hidden compartment. In less than thirty minutes, Rodney was on his way.

The sun settled behind him as he headed toward Dawson to pick up Beulah. In spite of Big Man's admonitions to use back streets, Rodney couldn't resist *dragging Main* again. He came into town on West Main Street and worked his way into the business area, driving slow so everyone could see him. He had the window down and waved at the colored folks on the sidewalk, a grin wrapping his face.

..*

Chief Bowen drove toward Lucille's Café figuring he'd catch an early supper, then head back to the office. A couple of days during the week, he liked to hang around the station until the town went to bed. It let his officers know he wasn't too important to share night duty with them. And of course, if something happened, he was there until it was over. It was such a night when he had aborted the

Burnettes' attack on the newspaper. It had started as staying the evening and turned into an all-nighter.

He was thinking about Lucille's homemade soup when he saw the '49 Ford coming toward him. He recognized it as Big Man's and wondered who was driving, clearly not the owner. As it passed, he saw Rodney and noticed it rode heavy in the rear. On an impulse, he wheeled into an alley, then sped through the back lot, keying his mike. "Get someone on Main Street and flag down a black '49 Ford headed east. Suspicion of hauling illegal liquor. Move fast."

He took the next driveway and came out onto the street two cars behind the Ford. The traffic light at Smithwick Street turned red, and Rodney obeyed the signal. Chief Bowen tapped his siren then pulled left into the oncoming lane which was clear of traffic. He went into the intersection, angled in front of Big Man's car, then stopped.

Officer Oakley jogged up as the Chief climbed out. "What's up?"

"Maybe nothing, but come with me." He walked to the Ford. "Rodney. Good to see you. Do you know your brake light's not working?"

"Naw suh, I didn't know. Is you shore? Big Man take good care of his car. He lent it to me for tonight. I didn't check 'fore I drove off."

Chief Bowen moved to the back of the car and knelt as if studying the light. His real intent was to look at the rear tires so he could judge the weight in the rear. Looked heavy to him.

He nodded to Oakley, then said, "You better come check, Rodney. I swear it didn't come on when you stopped for the light. Officer Oakley, maybe you could put your foot on the brake while Rodney watches with me. We can't be too careful about brake lights. Somebody could run right into you if they don't know you're stopping."

Rodney got out of the car and walked to the rear as Officer Oakley crawled into the driver's seat.

"Okay, hit the brake," Chief Bowen called. "See, Rod—Well, I'll be darned. Guess I was wrong. It's working now."

Rodney knelt beside the Chief. "I shore be pleased it's alright.

Can I go now?"

"We better look at the other one," Chief Bowen said. He signaled Rodney to follow as he shifted his position. "Okay, hit the brake." He watched then said, "Looks fine. Sorry Rodney, guess I made a mistake."

"Chief," Officer Oakley called from inside the car. "You might want to look at this."

Chief Bowen walked to the driver's window.

Officer Oakley handed a bottle out. "Bumped this with my foot. Smells like moonshine."

The Chief sniffed then turned to Rodney. "Is this yours?"

"Ah . . . uh . . . what is it?"

"I think you know. Having illegal booze in your possession is enough to revoke your parole. Maybe I ought to take you in so we can talk."

"Please don't do that, sir. I don't want to go back to Raleigh. Can't I do something to change your mind? I do 'bout anything to stay free."

"Well," the Chief said, "I might feel better if you let me search the car."

"Ain't my car. I jist borrowed it. I don't know what's in there. You look all you want to. But if you finds anything illegal, it be Big Man's, not mine."

"Officer Oakley, ride with Rodney. Bring the car up alongside the station. We'll see why it's setting so heavy in the rear."

It only took a few minutes to find the trap door in the trunk and reveal the moonshine in the secret compartment. The Chief stared at it, then at Rodney. "This looks pretty bad for you. Guess I'm gonna have to book you. Then we'll have a long talk about who it belongs to, and how it got there."

Rodney's head hung. "Ain't mine, but if I can help, I will. Why in the world would Big Man lend me his car filled with this illegal stuff? I jist don't understand that boy sometimes."

The Chief turned to his officers. "Inventory and log it. Then put it in the evidence room. Rodney and I will get a cup of coffee while you do that. Come on in after you get the final count." He spoke to Rodney. "You can drink a cup with me, can't you?"

"Yas suh. I be mighty proud to set with you, Chief. And a cup of coffee'd go good on such a chilly evening."

Two hours later, Chief Bowen knew the details of Big Man's bootlegging operation and was making plans to pick him up. Rodney sat, moaning his fate in a jail cell.

CHAPTER FOURTEEN

Clyde Lincoln, who lived in Big Man's neighborhood and looked up to him, knocked on the front door of Big Man's house. Clyde watched the area and reported anything that looked suspicious to his twelve-year-old eyes. He loved it when Big Man smiled, patted him on the head, and thanked him. Sometimes, he would get a quarter, and one time, fifty cents. That was even better than a pat on the head.

"Hey, my man," Big Man said. "What's got you knockin' on my door tonight?"

"I seen your car. The po-lice was talkin' to Rodney."

Big Man squinted at him. "When? Where?"

"First on Main Street, then they took it up beside the station. I followed them, sneakin' in the shadows so they couldn't see me. When the Chief took Rodney inside, them other cops searched the car. They found some jugs of stuff."

"Shit," Big Man said. "What else did you see?"

"That's all. It was a lotta jugs and they took them inside." He flinched as Big Man's face got uglier. "Did I do somethin' wrong?"

"No, you done fine," Big Man said. "But that Rodney done done us bad." He began to close the door, his expression worried. "Oh, sorry. You're my main man. Keep them eyes open. Here." He handed Clyde a dollar.

As Clyde headed down the steps, Big Man called him back. "Wait a minute." He fished in his pocket. "Here's another dollar. If you see any police cars coming down the street, you run as fast as you can to the back door and tell me. Okay?"

Clyde's eyes were huge as they stared at the two bills in his hand. "Yas suh, I can do that." He hesitated then held the second bill out. "You don't have to pay me no more. I never had no two dollars before. I don't know what to do with that much money."

Big Man's worried expression flashed a smile. "You jist do what I asked. It's worth it to me."

"For you, I's all eyes and ears. Ain't nothin' gittin' by me."

Clyde turned to leave, but Big Man grabbed his arm. "One more thing. You willin' to do me another, ain't you?"

"Anything you want."

"I might leave. I ain't shore yet. If I do, and you see the cops, tell'm I been gone all day. Okay?"

"I can do that."

"You're a good man, Clyde. When you gits a little older, I'm gonna cut you in on my business."

Clyde's grin filled the night as he dashed down the steps to his house three doors away and climbed a tall oak tree. It was his *watchin'* tree. He'd built a perch high up in its branches that allowed him to scan the neighborhood. Nothing would slip past him.

..*

"Scooter. Get out here," Big Man called. "We got a problem."

"I's right here," Scooter said, coming in from the kitchen. He held a ham and mayonnaise sandwich in his hand, a large bite missing from one side. "Who was at the door?"

"Clyde. That damn Rodney got caught with the 'shine. They musta locked him up. Either that or the som'bitch run out on me. I need to know what he told'm."

"How we gonna do that?"

"Don't know. Clyde's watchin'. If he sees anythin', he'll come runnin'. Meanwhile, you and me better git ready to take off. How much money you got?"

Scooter turned his pockets inside out. "Five dollar and twenty-five cents. That's all."

"Shit. I ain't got but ten. That last bunch of supplies took all my ready cash." Big Man dropped into a chair. "Give me a minute to think. Go in the kitchen and finish yo' supper."

When Scooter was out of the room, Big Man walked to the fireplace, removed a brick, and stuck his hand in the hole. He fumbled around then withdrew a five-dollar bill. "I shoulda known better than to use all my money. Now we got to git to Raleigh so I can git some outta the bank. This is a fine mess." He frowned. "I ain't whipped yet. Damn cops ain't gonna git me. There's always 'nother way." He returned to his chair and sat, his mind racing.

Five minutes later, his face in question, but with a small flicker at the corners of his mouth, he rose and walked to the kitchen door. "Scooter. Come in here."

Scooter came into the room carrying a sandwich identical to the one he'd had before except it hadn't been bitten. "What?"

Big Man eyed the sandwich. "First, give me that. You can make yo'self 'nother one. Better hurry. We might have to haul out of here fast."

They moved back into the kitchen where Scooter laid out the loaf bread. "Make a bunch," Big Man said. "I'm hongry, and I don't know when we'll have time to eat next."

As Scooter spread mayonnaise, Big Man said, "Didn't you tell me one time your Aint Liddie's got a key to the drugstore?"

Scooter, who was reaching for the ham, hesitated. "Yeah. Mr. Mat'ews granddaddy give it to her. Why?"

"If Rodney talked, we gotta have money to git out of town. Even if he didn't, the damn po-lice will prob'ly keep my car so we need cash to git another one. That drugstore takes in a lot of money, and I'm bettin' the cash drawer's full." He paused. "Or maybe there's a safe. You ever see a safe when you been in there?"

Scooter shrugged as he took a bite of sandwich.

"Don't matter. If it's in a safe, we might be stuck on the money, but we can steal stuff to sell. All we needs is enough to pay somebody to take me to Raleigh."

Scooter chewed, looking like he was thinking over Big Man's words. "What you mean, take you to Raleigh. You ain't plannin' to leave me, is you?"

Big Man stared at him, then smiled. "Naw. You knows I wouldn't do that."

"Better not try." Scooter took another bite of the sanwich. "I don't want to rob the drugstore."

"What wrong with you?" Big Man flared. "Maybe you'd like to set on the front step and wait for the Chief. Maybe you want to go to jail where they'll use you for a girl. Huh? Is that what you want?"

"You knows I don't want that."

"Then, boy, you better wake up. We don't git our asses out of town, the Chief's gonna roll us up and stick us in a cell. How long you reckon yo' friend, the Judge'll give you?"

"He was good to my Cousin Joshua last year. Might not be too bad."

"Damn, you the dumbest nigger I knows. Beside you, Rodney look like a high school graduate. That judge'll lock us up and throw away the key." Big Man took a deep breath, trying to control himself. "Now, pack all them sandwiches in a bag and be ready to move if Clyde knocks on that door." He pointed toward the rear entrance. "Cause if he do, we're out of here." He paced, watching the door. "Naw. I ain't waitin'. We's wastin' time. Git the guns. Put'm in that gunnysack in the bedroom. We's leaving now."

..*

"Murphy," Chief Bowen said, "when we leave, call the Sheriff and give him the sharecroppers who're doing the bootlegging. He can hit their stills while we pick up Big Man. By morning, we should have this whole operation rolled up." He looked thoughtful. "And after that, stay off the phone. I want those lines available at all times."

"Yo, Chief. You can count on me."

Chief Bowen looked at the five other officers he'd called in. Four of them were off duty and he'd had to wait for them to dress. "Okay, two to a car. "Oakley and I will come in from opposite directions on Sycamore. Jones, you park on Slate, then cut across to watch the back door." He hesitated. "Everybody carry a full load. Rodney says Big Man's got a bunch of guns in the house. He also says he turned Scooter into a killer. Don't be taken in by the innocent young man he used to be. Be ready to drop him if he does anything funny." He looked from face to face. "Any questions?"

"You authorizing use of force on Big Man, too?" Oakley asked. "And anyone else with them?"

"Yeah. But be careful. I don't want anybody hurt. This is a bootlegging operation. Let's not treat it like a capital crime. Check your loads."

Each man pulled his revolver and made sure it carried six

rounds, then checked his shotgun. After that, they tested their hand-held radios. Everyone signaled with a thumbs up they were ready.

"Okay, one last thing and we're on our way. Stand by." Chief Bowen walked to his desk and picked up the phone. He dialed Judge Jackson's home number. When the Judge answered, he briefed him in a minimum number of words.

"Sounds like you have probable cause to bring Big Man and Scooter in," the Judge said. "Why're you calling me?"

"Cause I don't want some fast-talking lawyer springing them before I finish the booking. I have no doubt Big Man will run if he gets a chance."

There was silence on the line. "So you want somebody to deny bail. Is that what you're asking?"

"Pretty much," the Chief said.

"That's tough on a bootlegging charge. I'll have to think that one through real hard. Better come up with something else."

"I understand. Thanks, Judge." He hung up and looked at his men. "Take Big Man's house apart. I want anything you can come up with. Let's get it done."

..*

Big Man cut across backyards and through hedges, careful to avoid pools of light. Clouds covered the sky protecting him and Scooter from the moon's glow.

"Where we goin'?" Scooter asked from behind, lugging the gunnysack filled with weapons.

"Hurry up. I's heading for the cab stand on Washington. We'll git Zeke to take us to yo' Aint Liddie's place. Then, after we git the key, he can drop us off on Main Street."

"S'pose he ain't there. He might be on a run." Scooter stopped, switched hands, then limped faster to catch up. "Slow down some. These guns is heavy."

"Stop talkin' and save yo' breath, and they won't be so heavy. How long you reckon it'll take the Chief to put his people on the street lookin' for us?"

"Pro'ly not long. Why don't we just skip Aint Liddie and git out of town?"

"Cause we need money. I done told you. Now shut up." Big

Man huddled alongside Dawson Furniture Store and peeked around the corner, scouring Washington Street with his eyes. "Ease on up here. We gotta cross the road. Run as fast as you can. Soon's we git to the other side, duck in the alley. You can stay there while I git Zeke."

"Alright, if you say so. But I still don't like botherin' Aint Liddie."

"I don't give a shit what you like. Do what I say."

..*

Clyde alerted as a car turned onto Sycamore Street. He peered into the darkness trying to see. The car moved at a deliberate pace, its headlights off, then stopped.

He looked in the opposite direction and saw another vehicle using the same technique. That was two police cars. He was sure of it. He didn't need anymore to know what to do. He scurried down the tree and dashed around his house, then cut across yards to Big Man's.

..*

Chief Bowen whispered to his driver, "Stop here. I see Oakley's car. Let me check the others." He keyed the microphone. "You in position, Jones?"

"Yeah. I'm on Slate, opposite Big Man's place. Any time you're ready."

"Roger. Dismount and cut through the yards until you can see the back door of Big Man's place with a clear field of fire. Let me know when you're there."

"Roger. Out."

"Oakley," Chief Bowen said, "hold your position until Jones comes back to us."

"Roger."

The seconds ticked away as beads of perspiration pooled on Chief Bowen's forehead. Butterflies of fear fluttered in his stomach. He rubbed his palms on his thighs knowing they'd be slippery with sweat. This was his nightmare—approaching a suspect's house in the dark, a suspect who could be sighting along a barrel at this very moment. He bit his lip and stared at the radio willing it to speak.

"Chief. Jones. I'm in position. If he comes out the back door, he's mine."

The Chief let out a long breath. "Okay, let's do it."

He got out of the car and stepped behind a tree, his eyes searching for movement. None. "Let's go. Slow and easy. I don't want any shooting."

"Chief," the radio crackled. "Jones. There's a kid at the back door. He's acting wild, pounding as hard as he can. What you want me to do?"

"Give it a moment. If no one comes to the door, grab the kid. Probably a lookout. We're moving to hit the front door." He searched the darkness again. "All units. Let's go."

Dashing across the street, he saw Oakley and his partner doing the same. They ran up the steps as a foursome. "Open up. Police," Chief Bowen yelled, slapping the door with his open hand. It swung inward.

The four policemen jumped to the side and froze against the wall. The Chief hesitated, then dropped to a knealing position. He inched his head into the opening, then jerked it back. "Nothing," he whispered. "Too damn dark. Give me a torch."

Oakley handed him a flashlight.

He lay on his stomach, took a deep breath, and slithered into the doorway.

"Nobody home, Chief."

Chief Bowen pulled back and sat up against the wall. "What the hell?"

"It's me, Chief. Jones. I got the kid. He says the house is empty."

CHAPTER FIFTEEN

"Okay, son," Chief Bowen said, "tell me again."

"Muster Big Man ain't been home all day. I been watchin', and he ain't been here."

Chief Bowen, Officer Clark, and Clyde were in Big Man's kitchen, the noise of searching coming from the rest of the house. As instructed, his officers were taking the place apart searching for contraband.

Clark leaned against the sink, his arms crossed. On the surface, he appeared relaxed, like he wasn't noticing the play between Clyde and the Chief. However, closer scrutiny would reveal he was ready to bolt into pursuit if the boy ran.

The Chief paced behind Clyde who sat at the table. "Uh-huh. So, if you knew there was no one home, why were you beating on the back door?"

Clyde's eyes teared, and he wiped them with an angry hand. "No reason. I's jist doin' it."

The Chief stopped and examined the child, his eyes soft. *Just a poor, scared kid.* He took a deep breath. "I'll give you a reason. Okay?"

Clyde wore a frightened yet sullen expression. He sat up straighter. "You do what you want. I ain't tellin' you nuttin more."

The Chief picked up the chair across from him, turned it, and sat on it backwards. He rested his hands on the top of the back. "I think you were on Big Man's payroll. He paid you to watch for people who might be looking for him. In fact, son, if I went around the neighborhood, I bet I'd find a perch you built to watch from." He scratched the back of his hand. "How'm I doing?"

"Told you I ain't saying nuttin. Big Man's my friend, and I ain't rattin' him." A large tear squeezed from his eye. He backhanded it.

"Yep, you told me," the Chief said, looking around. "Want something to drink? Clark, see if there's anything in the fridge. I'm sure he won't mind sharing with his good friend, Clyde."

Clark moved to the refrigerator and swung the door open. "I see a RC Cola. How about that?"

"Good. Open it for the boy. He looks thirsty. Any food in there?"

"Hmmm. Yeah, there's a couple of ham slices and a few pieces of bread. Bread's open like somebody tossed it in. But it could probably be used for a sandwich."

"How about that, son? Would you like a ham sandwich with your RC?"

Clyde scraped his fingernail against the top of the table, his eyes down. "Yas suh, I is kinda hongry. I was up that tree—" His head jerked up. "You tryin' to fool me, ain't you?"

"No, son. If you don't want to talk, I'm not going to make you." He looked at Clark. "Fix him a ham sandwich. Put some mayonnaise on it if you can find any."

"I druther have mustard," Clyde said. He looked at Clark. "And can I have two slices? I likes that store-bought'n ham Big Man gets."

"Yeah," the Chief said. "That'd be better. Use mustard if you can find any." He glanced at Clyde who was engrossed in watching Clark. "Ah, heck. Make two. He's a growing boy."

Twenty minutes later, Chief Bowen had learned everything that Clyde knew, and guessed they'd only missed Big Man by a few minutes. He told Clyde to go home and warned that if he saw him again that night, he'd lock him up. Clyde's departure left little doubt he did not intend to spend the night in jail.

When Clyde was out of earshot, the Chief called his team together. "Okay, what'd you find?"

Oakley was the first to speak. "Some shotgun shells and .38 caliber bullets. No guns though."

Christopher added, "Coupla jugs of hooch, probably homemade."

"Anything else? Anything we can use to park them in jail for a while?"

No one spoke.

"Okay, if that's all we have, we're stuck with it. When we find them, I'll put it with what Rodney said, and what we found in Big Man's car. Then I'll hope some lawyer doesn't get them out before I finish the paperwork." He studied his officers. "C'mon, guys. Give me something."

Still no one spoke.

After a moment, the Chief said, "We'll split up and canvas the town. I want Big Man and Scooter found tonight. If we don't have them by morning, I'll bring in the Sheriff and the Highway Patrol, but it's not serious enough to involve them yet." He pulled his revolver and checked the cylinder. "Right now, I want them. It's our job. That's why the town pays us. Any question on that?"

"Uh, Chief," Clark said. "What else is there? I've never seen you so intense."

He lowered his head, then looked up. "You're right. I am intense. Tonight, I interrogated a twelve-year-old boy that Jeremiah Q Lincoln, aka Big Man, is well on his way to corrupting. I remember a naïve young man who shined shoes, took care of people's yards, and anything else he could do. He was a pleasure to spend time with. Now, according to Rodney, he's a trained killer. Yeah, I'm intense. I want Big Man, and I want him bad. Anything else?"

"Not me, Chief," said Clark.

"I'm ready," Oakley said.

The others stood mute.

Chief Bowen checked each of them. "No? Okay. Remember, they're dangerous and probably armed. Here's how we'll split the town."

..*

"Pull over here," Big Man said.

Zeke pulled his taxi to the side of East Main Street. "Where you goin'? I can take you in."

"No, we get out here. You turn around and wait for us. We be back in 'bout ten minutes, won't we, Scooter? Leave the bag here."

Zeke eyed them. "I spect you two ain't up to nothin' good. Best you pay me now."

"Damn you," Big Man said. "You got no right to say that."

"I got every right I need. It's my cab, and if you want it here when you git back, you pay me now. Five dollars."

"That's highway robbrey."

"Five dollars, or I'm goin' up the hill."

Mumbling under his breath, Big Man fumbled in his pocket and produced a five-dollar bill. "You better be here. If you ain't, I knows where you lives."

Zeke smiled. "Save that for somebody what's scared of you. You ain't nothin' but a fat boy." He took the money. "Just don't take too long. I might decide I got better things to do."

Big Man and Scooter got out and the taxi pulled away. "Bastard better be here when we git back," Big Man said. "I'll cut his balls off and stuff'm down his throat."

Scooter looked at him, then at the departing car, a thoughtful expression on his face. "Uh-huh."

They moved away from the street into the shantytown, working their way toward Liddie's place. When they were close, Big Man stopped and held Scooter by the arm. "Remember now, all you got to do is git her to open the door. I take it after that."

"You ain't gonna hurt her, is you?"

"'Course not. I'm gonna git the key, then we leave. All you got to do is stan' there." He studied the expression on Scooter's face. "You don't even have to stay inside if you don't want to. You can keep watch outside."

"Uh-huh."

A few minutes later, they were on the front porch of Liddie's house. "Call her," Big Man said. "Knock on the door and tell her you're here."

Scooter eyed him. "I ain't so shore bout this. Let's just go break in the drug store."

"Listen, dummy. We break in, there prob'ly be a burlar alarm. Cops be all over us. We open the door with the key, and it won't go off. You unnerstan'?"

"How you know there's an alarm? You hardly ever been in there."

"Do what I tell you, dammit. I ain't got time to worry with you. You jist bein' hard to git along with, that's all. Ain't I steered you right so far?"

Before Scooter could answer a voice from inside the house said, "Who's out there? You better git away from my porch."

"Tell her," Big Man whispered, glaring at Scooter. "You either tell her, or I'm gonna bust in the door."

"Don't you hurt her."

"I won't. Now talk to her."

"It's me, Ain't Liddie. Scooter. Me and Big Man."

The door opened. "Well quit standin' out there wakin' up the neighbors. Git in here." She eyed Big Man. "What y'all doin' down here."

"We jist come to visit," Scooter said, his head hanging as they entered the house.

"There wuz a day I'd a believed you," Liddie said. "But that day passed when you started hangin' out with him." She pointed at Big Man. "Now I figger you's in trouble and come runnin' home."

Big Man shoved his way past Scooter. "We ain't got no problem we can't handle. Course you can help us with it." He motioned to Scooter. "Close the door."

"Leave that door open, boy," Liddie said. "If y'all up to somethin', I want the neighbors to hear."

Scooter put his hand on the knob, his face reflecting pain. "Jist git it done, Big Man. I'll watch outside." He walked out the door, pulling it closed behind him.

Liddie stepped close to Big Man and stared up into his face. "I hopes you rot in hell for what you done to that boy. And if I could speed up you gittin' there, I would."

"Shut up, old woman," Big Man hissed. "I don't like you no better than you like me, so jist give me the key to the drugstore, and I'll be gone."

Liddie's eyes flashed to her purse sitting on a scarred coffee table. "What key? I ain't got no key."

Big Man laughed. "Shore you ain't. Maybe you ain't told enough lies to be good at it." He tried to step around her.

She spun and grabbed the purse. "Git out of here. You git out of my house. I don't want you here." She started toward the door.

Big Man grabbed her arm with one hand and jerked the purse away with the other. "You ain't goin' nowhere." He pushed her toward a torn upholstered chair. "You always had a fat mouth, and

I'm tired of hearin' it. You don't shut up, I'm gonna smack you good. Now sit down." He drew back his hand in a threatening gesture.

Liddie bobbed at the waist, and her hand went to her chest. She settled into the chair. "What you gonna do?"

"None of yo' business," Big Man said, fumbling in the scarred, black, patent leather bag.

"Do Scooter know what you're doin'?"

Big Man laughed. "He not only know, it was his idea. That's a right smart nigger you raised." He took out a change purse and opened it. "I can use this." He pocketed a five and three ones. "You got any more money 'round here?"

"No. Now gimme my purse."

"Keep yo' mouth shut unless I ask you a question. Where's that—Awwww. I bet this is it." He pulled a key from the bottom of the handbag and held it up, a dingy string hanging from it. "What you say, old woman?"

Liddie's right hand dug under her left breast, the fingers working. "I got nothin' to say to you. Git Scooter back in here. I got to hear from him this was his idea."

Laughter rang across the room as Big Man shoved the key in a pocket. "Ain't no chance, you old bitch. He do what I say now. He don't give a damn 'bout you." He tossed the purse into her lap. "I told him I wouldn't hurt you, and I won't—unless you piss me off too much. So jist set there while I search the place. You strike me as the kind puts her money in a coffee can."

..*

Scooter closed the door behind him as he stepped onto the porch, tears stinging his eyes. Aunt Liddie's words rang in his head. *There wuz a day I'd a believed you, but that day passed when you started hangin' out with him. Now I figger you's in trouble and come runnin' home.* She knew, she had to know, but she always had. Aunt Liddie was the smartest woman he'd ever known. Everybody said so. Everybody always told him how lucky he was she took him in when his mama died.

He sat on the edge of the porch, his head down, tears falling in the dirt around his feet. He wiped his eyes, then sniffled, thinking, Can't let Big Man see me like this. Big Man say I'm a man, say I ought to make my own decisions, say I be as good as anybody. Scooter didn't need the Supreme Court to know he was equal. All he needed was Big Man's word. Big Man taught him to shoot, taught him to be a killer. Big Man was his friend. Yet, Scooter wondered if he really could kill another man. Sure, he'd shot rats, and was good at it. Hardly ever missed any more. But a man—or a woman. A woman? He'd never thought about killing a woman. Suppose Big Man told him to kill Aunt Liddie. What would he do? The tears renewed their cascade toward the ground.

Scooter had no idea how long he sat, his mind racing uncontrolled from memories of before Big Man to memories after Big Man took him in. He had nice clothes, a bicycle, and money in his pocket. No need to scavenge at the dump for shoes that white folks threw away. He was a man, and nobody messed with him. Yet, he remembered the days when he shined shoes for ten cents, and the nice people who paid him. He took pride in how he could make the worst pair of shoes mirror the sun. Now he was proud . . . What did he have to be proud of? He did what Big Man said. When Big Man said get up, he got up. When he said, eat, he ate. When he said, let's go, he went. Did that make him a better man than he was when he did yard work, when he raked leaves with Miz Patterson, when folks told him what a nice person he was?

He shook his head and the tears fell harder. Didn't matter. Big Man said the police wanted them. Didn't matter that he once took care of Chief Bowen's shoes. If they found him, he was going to jail. That's what Big Man said, and Scooter had to believe him. He didn't have anything else.

Scooter rubbed his hands down his face, then ran his forearm under his nose. Time to act like a man. He stood and walked to the door of the house. Pushing it open, he stuck his head in. "Ain't you ready yet, Big Man? You find the key?"

Big Man turned toward him, then back at Aunt Liddie. He hesitated. "Yeah, right where you said it was—in her purse. I got it. Let's go."

Liddie's eyes bored into Scooter as her fingers continued to massage her chest, her face creased in pain. "Please don't—"

"We're out of here," Big Man said. "Good bye, old woman. Next time you see me on the street, you better step in the gutter and let me pass."

The tears leapt into Scooter's eyes again, and he hurried away as Big Man came through the door, pushing it closed behind him. If either heard the thump from inside, he didn't acknowledge it.

CHAPTER SIXTEEN

Charlie Burnette's truck bounced into Marvin's mudholed driveway. "Damn. That brother of mine don't pay attention to nothing no more. A feller could bust his spine in these damn holes." He pulled close to the front porch and blew the horn.

The front door opened, and Marvin stuck his head out. "Just a minute. I'm eatin' a piece of cake."

"Piece of cake, my ass. Get your coat and let's go. I don't plan on this takin' all night."

Marvin's head disappeared, then reappeared a moment later. His mouth was full of cake as he struggled into his winter corduroy jacket. He jumped off the porch and climbed into Charlie's truck.

Martha Burnette came onto the porch. "Where you going, Marvin? When you gonna be home?"

"Tell her none of her business," Charlie said. "You need to take charge of your own house."

"Don't tell me what to do," Marvin said, scowling. "I can handle my woman." He leaned from the window. "Ain't none of your damn business. I'll be here when I get here." He pulled back inside the truck. "Let's go."

Charlie drove toward Dawson. "Did you get Big Man's address?"

"Naw. Have to ask somebody. None of the folks I saw know where he lives."

"Shit. Guess we can go by the police station if we have to. They oughta know."

They drove without conversation for several miles, then Marvin said, "What's your plan? What we gonna do?"

"Do? We gonna pick up that nigger and put some knots on his

nappy head. There's a coupla hoe handles in the back. When we finish with him, he'll give up the bootlegging business."

"Sounds good to me." Marvin reached into his coat pocket and pulled out a piece of cake wrapped in wax paper. "Want a bite?"

"No wonder you so damn fat. All you do is eat."

"Naw, that ain't all I do. Ask Martha."

"Shit. I git more in a week than you do in a month."

They pulled into the downtown area of Dawson as Marvin licked his last finger.

"Well, looky there," Charlie said. "We done pulled in behind one of Dawson's finest."

In front of them, a police car inched its way down the street. The driver shined his spotlight into the shadows of doorways and the alleyways between businesses.

"Must be looking for somebody," Marvin said.

"Damn, you so sharp tonight, I'm afraid to touch you. Prob'bly draw blood."

"Go to hell."

Charlie laughed. "Think I'll stop him. He might know where Big Man lives." He eased up close to the policeman, blew his horn, and blinked his lights. Nothing happened, so he repeated the actions. The car in front pulled to the side and Charlie went alongside him. "Ask him where the darky lives," he said to Marvin.

"Hey, do you know where the nigger they call Big Man lives?" Marvin called.

"Who wants to know?"

"Me. Marvin Burnette."

"Move in front of me and pull over."

Charlie did, then watched as Officer Oakley walked to his side of the truck. "Hey. What's going on? Why you searching the alleys?"

"I'll ask the questions," Oakley said. "Why are you two on the prowl for Big Man?"

"We's gonna kick some sense in his hard head."

Oakley grinned. "Looking at you two, it might go the other way. He might just kick the shit out of you. What do you want with him?"

"Need to talk to him. Free country, ain't it?"

"Depends." Oakley stared at Charlie. "But if you find him, tell him to do everybody a favor and turn himself in. He can't get away."

It was Charlie's turn to stare. "So . . . y'all after him, too?"

"Yep. And we'll get him. Just a matter of time."

"What you want him for?"

"Can't say that's any of your business. Tell him what I said, though. Now you need to move on. If I was you, I'd go home. Tonight's not a good night to be seen with Big Man." Oakley walked back to his car, opened the door, and got in.

"We'll tell him if we find him," Charlie said to his back, then started the truck and drove off. "Shit. Ain't this a damn mess? Wonder what he done to git the police on his tail. We'll wait and see how this plays out." He did a U-turn and headed back the way he came.

..*

Judge Jackson couldn't get Chief Bowen's phone call out of his mind. While he loved the law, he knew it often gave too much benefit to the criminal. As the Chief explained Big Man's case, there was little doubt he should be in jail. Anything different was an invitation for him to run. And if he ran, it meant money to track him down and bring him back for a trial that, worst case, would put him on probation. No matter how you split it, the taxpayers and the underpaid policemen lost.

He sipped his coffee, then ate the last bite of his chocolate cake. Jane had gone upstairs thirty minutes or so before, saying she was tired. He stared at the steps a moment, then shook his head. What could he do to help her understand?

He climbed to the guest bedroom and tapped on the door. "Jane, I'm going out for a while. Can I bring you anything?"

"No. I'm going to bed early. Don't wake me when you get home."

With a frown and a deep sigh, Judge Jackson turned away and walked to the closet. He donned his topcoat and hat and left the house. Each day, he hoped, even dreamed, that Jane would change her mind and return to the master bedroom. However, it appeared she was more than willing to live apart under the same roof. He could only wonder why his married life had turned out so opposite what he yearned it to be. Yet, he couldn't compromise his principles to please her. Not unless he stepped down from the bench—and that was not in his plans.

He drove to the police station and walked through the private entrance, stopped and listened, knowing someone had to be on duty. The Judge sniffed, his nose crinkling at the odor of sweat, fear, and a tinge of BO left by past prisoners. "Who's got the duty?" he called, walking toward the front of the station.

"Who's there?"

"Judge Jackson." He turned the corner into the dispatcher area. "Hey, Murphy. So you're stuck here while the Chief has all the fun."

"Yeah. Hardly seems fair. But I'll remind him the next time something good comes up. What brings you in?"

"Curiosity. How's the Chief doing? Did he find Big Man and Scooter yet?"

"Nope. They missed them at his house. Now they're working their way street to street. Chief's determined to get him."

"I see. Mind if I hang around?"

"No sir. I'm glad for the company. How about some coffee?"

..*

As the Judge entered the police station, Big Man and Scooter climbed into the backseat of Zeke's taxi. "Good thing you waited," Big Man said. "Save me havin' to come after you."

Zeke chuckled. "You ain't figured it out, have you? You ain't got nothin' what scares me. My motto is, Long as you pay, I be where you say. Where you want to go?"

"One of these days, you gonna git yours," Big Man snarled. "Take us to the back lot of Main Street. We got business there. You can wait 'til we finish."

"I bet you got bizness. I drop you behind the movie, but I ain't waitin'. You two up to no-good, and I don't want no part of it. When you git caught, you ain't never heard of me. This ride's for free."

"I always knowed you won't worth a shit," Big Man said. "Scooter and me don't need you. We kin take care of ourselves."

"Glad to hear it," Zeke said. "Before this night's over, I'm thinkin' you gonna need takin' care of. You just remember, you ain't seen me." He started the engine and drove up the hill.

At Smithwick Street, Zeke turned right, then took a left into the unpaved parking and unloading area that serviced the stores. When he reached the rear of the movie, he stopped. "You can get out here. Take yo' bag with you. And if I'm ever dumb enough to let you in my cab agin, you better not bring no shotguns."

Big Man said, "What you doin' checkin' at my stuff."

"My cab, my bizness. You don't like it, walk."

Big Man stared at him. "You gonna wait for us?"

"Done told you I ain't. Don't need to repeat myself."

"When this is over, you 'n me gonna have a long talk," Big Man said as he followed Scooter out of the car. "You might not like it, either."

Zeke laughed and slipped a pistol from under his seat. "You come on, Big Man. Any ol' time. This is my friend, Satan, and Satan don't like you no better'n I do." He put the car in gear and drove away.

"What you gonna do 'bout him?" Scooter asked. "He shore talk big."

"Nothin' right now. We got other business." He ducked into the shadows, then headed toward Flip's Drugstore. "Bring the bag."

When Big Man reached the back of the store, he stopped and fumbled in his pocket, then pulled out the key he took from Liddie. "Here, give me the bag. Take this and go 'round front. Unlock the door, then come open the side door. I be waitin' for you."

Scooter stared at the key. "Why don't you use the key? I kin wait for you."

"Cause, dammit, I be the boss. You want to work for me, you do what I say."

Scooter stared into his face, as if trying to see beneath his dark skin. "Uh-huh. You don't scare me no more than you did Zeke. I figure you's 'fraid to go. The Chief might be out there."

Big Man's hand flicked like the tongue of a rattler, grabbing Scooter's shirt. "Listen, you little fart. Get smart with me, and I'll rip your gut."

Scooter heard the flick of a switchblade and recoiled, but stood his ground. "Give me the key." He took a couple of steps, then turned back. "One of these days, you gonna pull that knife on me, and I'm gonna shove it up your ass."

He hurried down the dark alleyway. When he reached the sidewalk, he stopped and peered around the edge of the building, then froze. There was a police car and a pickup truck in the street with an officer beside the truck. He looked like he was talking to someone. And that someone might be one of the Burnettes. "Big Man ain't gonna like this." He returned the way he came.

"What you doin' back here?"

"Po-lice out there—cross the street."

"Are you messin' with me?"

"Naw. And they's talkin' to the Burnettes. Go check if you don't believe me."

He glared at Scooter, then did as suggested. When he returned, he said, "Damn. That changes things. Can't hardly rob the drugstore with the cops right there. And we shore don't want to put up with them brothers tonight. Give me a minute to think. We still need money to git to Raleigh."

Big Man walked to the back of the drugstore and sat in the shadows leaning against the wall. "Gotta get my hands on some cash." He crossed his arms on his knees and laid his head on them. "That damn Rodney. He better hope they put him in solitary confinement. When I see him, he gonna bleed. No car, no cash, and the po-lice after me. Must be a way."

"Big Man, you all right? What we gonna do now?"

"Do? We gonna—" He stopped. "Wait. Yeah. That's what we can do."

"Huh?"

"The woman you used to work for. She lives around here, don't she?"

"You mean, Miz Patterson?"

"How the hell do I know her name? All I know is you said you worked for her."

"Gotta be Miz Patterson. She live on Church Street, right near here."

"Let's visit her. I bet she keeps cash in the house . . . or maybe some jewels we can sell."

..*

Five minutes later, Big Man and Scooter stood across the street from Debbie's house, huddled in the shadows of an oak tree.

"That's her house, the one right there," Scooter said, pointing.

The white, antebellum home stood out in the moonlight. The soft glow of the moon gave it a look of majesty, a throwback to the nineteenth century.

"Lights are on," Big Man said. "She must be home. We stay here a while to see who's walkin' around. I don't want no surprises."

"Ain't you worried somebody'll see us? I mean, we's right out in the open."

"Good thinkin'. See how much you learned from me." Big Man looked around. "We'll move over to the church. If we wait there, we be alright."

They jogged down the street and into a doorway on the side of the annex. Big Man examined their position. "This is good. Ain't nobody gonna spot us here." He settled onto the step. "You keep a watch. I'm just gonna close my eyes a bit. You see anybody moving in her house, you let me know."

Scooter glanced at him, shrugged, and turned toward the house. From where he stood, he could see into the front two rooms. The light was brighter in one than the other.

Thirty minutes later, Scooter's eyes burned, and Big Man's soft snores made him feel like giving up his vigil. He rubbed his hands across his face, then stared. Two people appeared in the room with the dimmer light. As his eyes focused, he realized one of them was Mrs. Patterson, and the other might be the newspaperman. They disappeared from view, then the front door opened.

Scooter nudged Big Man with his foot. "Wake up. Something's happenin'."

"Huh. Wha?" Big Man rose beside him. "Who is that, and what's he doin'?"

"I think it's Mr. Flan'gun, the fella what does the paper, and it looks like he's leavin'."

As he said it, Henry stepped onto the front porch holding Debbie's hand. They kissed, then he walked down the steps, into the street, and turned away from Big Man and Scooter.

"We'll wait a bit for her to settle down," Big Man said. "Then we go 'round back."

CHAPTER SEVENTEEN

Thirty minutes passed as Big Man and Scooter watched Debbie's house.

"How long we gonna wait?" Scooter asked. "All this settin' in one place is makin' me tired."

"When I say go, we go," Big Man said, an edge in his voice. "What's your all-fired rush? I knows you ain't got no hot date."

Scooter stared at him. "Sometimes you don't know as much as you think you do. I gotta girlfriend."

"Sure you do. Wait. See that." Big Man pointed toward Debbie's house.

Scooter followed his finger and saw Debbie pass in front of a window dressed in a housecoat, then the light went off. The second room darkened, drawing his attention back to the window. Staring, he saw illumination, probably from another part of the house. "Look like she goin' to bed."

"That's jist what I been waitin' for. Let's go. Leave the bag in the doorway, but give me one of the pistols."

"What you need a gun for to see Miz Patterson? She ain't gonna mess with you."

"Damn you, Scooter. You gittin' too big for your britches." He paused, taking a noisy breath. "Okay, forget the gun. I still got my knife."

They scurried across the street and dashed into the shadows on the side of her house.

"Here's the way we work it," Big Man said. "We go 'round back, and you knock on the door. When she ask who it is, you tell her it's you, and you need help. Tell her you cut yourself, or somethin'. She'll come to see what's wrong, and I take it from there."

"I ain't sure I likes this. You ain't gonna hurt her, is you? Do we have to mess with her?"

"Naw. We don't have to. We kin go right down to the po-lice station and tell'm to put us in jail. Then, 'cause the Judge likes you so much, we can ask him to send us to Raleigh. I mean, that's where we tryin' to git to, ain't it? 'Course, when we gets to Raleigh, they ain't gonna let us go to the bank. They gonna slam the jail door, lock it, and throw away the key." He glared at Scooter. "Would you rather git to Raleigh that way, or my way?"

"You right," Scooter said, frowning. "Guess we gotta do it. You ready?"

"Go."

Scooter moved alongside the house—keeping his head below window height—turned and climbed the back steps. The screen door was unhooked. He eased it open and walked onto the porch with Big Man close on his heels. Once he got to the rear door of the house, he waited for Big Man to come alongside, then whispered, "Where you gonna be?"

"Right here," Big Man said, slipping to the side of the doorway. "You knock nice and loud."

Big Man pressed his back against the wall where he'd be out of sight as Scooter banged on the door. "Miz Patterson," Scooter called in a plaintive voice. "You in there, Miz Patterson?" He put his ear against the door.

"Who's out there?"

"It's me. Scooter. I need hep, Miz Patterson."

Big Man grinned and whispered, "You doin' good—real good."

"Scooter? What kind of help? I . . . I'm dressed for bed. What's wrong?"

"You been hurt," Big Man whispered.

Scooter grimaced, but said, "I hurt myself. I'm bleeding. Please hep me."

Big Man strained to hear. Nothing. "Agin. Tell her agin."

"Miz Patterson. I ain't got no place to go. Please hep me. I be hurtin'."

"Just . . . just a minute."

Big Man heard footsteps, a key turned, then the door opened a couple of inches.

"Scooter? Stand where I can see you."

Big Man moved with a speed that belied his size, slamming his shoulder into the door. It popped open, a safety chain landing on the floor. He followed the swinging door into the room.

Debbie screamed.

"Shut up. Ain't nobody gonna hurt you 'less we have to. All we want is yo' money."

Debbie's eyes were huge as she looked between Big Man who stood in her kitchen and Scooter who stayed on the porch. Her hand was at her throat, holding her white bathrobe closed. Her hair was in curlers, and she wore fuzzy house slippers. She took a deep breath, appearing to summon courage. "Scooter. You lied, didn't you?"

"Yas'm. I jist—"

"Shut up. You best listen to me, woman. How much money you got here? Scooter, go to the front window and watch the street. Miz Patterson's gonna show me where she keeps her cash." He eyed her. "If she don't, I might show her a good time."

Debbie's hand flew to her mouth.

Scooter grabbed Big Man's arm. "You ain't gonna touch her. I kill you first."

Big Man glowered at him. "Watch yourself, boy. You do what I tell you."

"Not 'til you say you won't mess with her."

"Dammit." Big Man hesitated. "I won't. Okay? Not if she gives us enough money to git out of town. Go watch the street."

Scooter edged past the two of them and headed toward the front of the house.

Debbie's eyes followed Scooter, then returned to Big Man. "I only have ten, maybe fifteen dollars. You stay here. I'll get it."

"Ain't no way. Where you goes, I goes."

"No. It's in my bedroom. I won't have you there."

"You ain't got no choice. I go where I please. Now git on down the hall."

Debbie didn't budge.

"Move, dammit. My patience is runnin' out." He shook his fist in her face.

Debbie turned and walked into the hallway, then took a right into a bedroom with Big Man on her heels.

He went to the bed and ran his hand over the covers. "Them's right nice. I ain't never took a woman in a bed that fancy."

"Here's my billfold," she said, pulling it from her purse, a tremor in her voice.

Big Man took it and shoved it in his pocket. "That takes care of that." He eyed her as she inched her way toward the door. "What's your rush? I knows you like it. I seen that newspaperman leavin'. Hell, I can make you forgit—"

Debbie swung her purse, catching Big Man alongside the head, knocking him onto the bed. She dashed out of the room.

"You bitch," Big Man howled. "You gonna pay." He scrambled to his feet, but slipped on a scatter rug, almost going down. "Shit." Gathering himself, he tore after her. "Scooter. Watch the front. The bitch's gittin' away."

He heard a bump from the kitchen and headed in that direction, turning in time to see her run through the rear entrance. The screen door of the porch slammed, then he heard a cry.

He raced out and saw Debbie sprawled at the foot of the steps. "Gotcha now, bitch," he yelled as he sailed through the door and off the porch. He grabbed her arm. "Git up. You gonna find out what happens to a woman what hits Big Man."

Debbie wrenched away, her arm coming out of the sleeve of the bathrobe. She spun, leaving Big Man holding the robe. As she tried to run, he grabbed a handful of her flannel nightgown and yanked. It ripped down the back. She stumbled forward and fell, face first, then rolled onto her back. Big Man stepped forward, towering above her as he straddled her legs. He stared at the torn edges of her nightclothes.

"Well, well. Ain't this something?" he said. "Let's see what we got here." He grabbed the front of the gown and jerked, the material tearing and pulling free, leaving her naked. He threw the gown to the side. "Them's right nice." He reached for her breast.

"Big Man," Scooter screamed. "What you doin'? You stop right now."

Big Man turned toward the voice and saw Scooter on the back porch. "I told you to watch the street. She wants it. She gonna git—"

A jolt of pain surged through him, dropping him to his knees onto her legs. She had kicked him in the groin, and the ache was excruciating. Through the fog of pain, he realized she would run, and he couldn't allow that. His left hand held his nuts while his right dove into his pocket and brought out his switchblade, flicking it open in one motion.

Debbie scooted against the ground, trying to escape the weight pinning her. "Let me go," she screamed. "Scooter. Help me. I helped you. Please help me."

Big Man leaned forward and slapped her. "Shut up, bitch. Ain't nobody can help you. We gonna have some fun, then you's dead meat." He breathed deep, banishing the pain from his mind. Lucky for him, her foot had caught mostly thigh. With great effort, he moved his hand away from his groin and reached again for her breast.

She slapped at it, raking her nails across the back of his hand. "Scooter. Scooter. Help me."

Big Man laughed, the pain easing. "Shit, woman, you'd do better calling to the Almighty. Scooter ain't—"

He tumbled to the side as Scooter slammed into him.

"I tol' you no, you ain't—"

Big Man grabbed Scooter by the face and pushed him away. "You stupid—" He looked for Debbie who was scrambling to her feet, trying to cover her nakedness with her hands. "Hold on, bitch. You ain't goin' nowhere."

He rose, grabbing Debbie by the arm and throwing her onto the ground. "Stay there. I'll git back to you."

He turned toward Scooter who charged at him, head down. He backhanded Scooter across the face, but he kept coming, blood surging from his eyebrow.

"No, Big Man, no," Scooter screamed. His eyes were wild, his arms flailing, his body out of control.

Big Man grabbed him by the throat, twisting to allow Scooter's momentum to carry him past. His hand a blur, he slapped him several times, then hit him with a solid right. Scooter crumpled, blood pouring from his mouth and nose.

He tossed Scooter aside like a broken toy, then saw Debbie on her feet again. She'd picked up a rake and was swinging at his head.

"I'll kill you," she screamed.

He ducked and threw up his arm. The tines dug into his forearm, drawing blood. He wrenched the rake out of her hand only to see her grab a hoe. Without thought, he launched himself at her, the switchblade in an attack position. It found her and drove into her chest.

"Hank," she cried.

He pulled down on the knife and blood spurted, splashing his hand, face, and chest. He stabbed again as she fell, then dropped after her, the knife slashing through the night air. There was no sound other than his grunting as he stabbed her repeatedly, geysers of blood covering him and the ground beside them.

..*

Big Man sat back, his rage dissipating, leaving him limp. He looked at Debbie's body, realization dawning. He'd killed a white woman. He knew what happened next. Whites would hunt him like an animal and when they caught him, butcher him like a pig at hog-killing time. They might even hang him by his heels to bleed out.

Panicking, he stood, desperately looking around. He had to get away, had to escape Dawson. But how? He had no money. He looked toward Debbie's house, wondering if he should go back after her purse. No, he had her billfold. He had put it into his pocket before she hit him. He scanned the neighborhood. Someone might have heard her screams. They might call the police.

Lights. Were there any lights on? He looked from house to house. No. Each one remained dark.

From under the oak tree, Scooter groaned and tried to sit up. Big Man walked over and kicked him in the head, and Scooter dropped back to the ground.

"Gotta think." He pulled Debbie's wallet from his pocket and checked the bills compartment. Twelve dollars. Not enough. The drugstore. He still had the key. He'd break into the drugstore like he'd planned. There had to be money there. Then he knew a man who would drive him to Raleigh. Fifty dollars. That's all he needed. Fifty dollars.

He ran alongside Debbie's house and stopped, checking the street. Couldn't have anyone see him now. The guns. They were across the street. He could steal a car and drive himself. Or force someone else to do it. Yeah, that was it. Rob the drugstore, then put a gun in someone's ear and make them take him to Raleigh. That was his salvation.

He looked back to where Debbie's body lay. Suppose someone came along before he was out of Dawson. Remembering Scooter lying against the tree trunk where he'd tossed him made him smile. Scooter was his out. He had been his patsy all along. Now he'd do it one more time.

He returned to the backyard and looked at Debbie. The knife was still in her. He pulled it free, walked to Scooter, wiped the blade on Scooter's shirt, put it in his hand, and closed his fingers around it. "I said you gonna save my life some day. This be the day."

Checking both ways, he ran across the street and grabbed the bag of guns. Ramming his hand inside, he pulled out a .38 and stuck it in his waistband. Then, with the bag in hand, he hurried past the church into the parking area behind the businesses on Main Street.

CHAPTER EIGHTEEN

Chief Bowen cruised Main Street, shining his spotlight into the alleys and doorways. He listened with growing frustration as each car and each officer on foot reported finding nothing. He hoped to catch Big Man before he went to ground, before someone chose to hide him from the white officers. It wasn't happening.

He debated calling in the Sheriff, but hated to do it before exhausting all avenues. He knew he'd lose control of the case, and the Mayor would have him on the carpet in the morning explaining why. Even in police work, politics raised its head, and the Mayor didn't like anyone dictating to him in *his* town.

He keyed his microphone. "All units, report."

One by one, his officers reported no sightings, and no one who admitted seeing Big Man or Scooter.

The only hope came from Officer Christopher. "I questioned Zeke, the guy drives that broken-down taxi. He swears he hasn't seen Big Man in days, but my gut says he's lying. Do you want to talk to him?"

"Yeah," Chief Bowen said. "Bring him in and put him in a room alone. Let him sweat. Maybe by the time I get there, his memory will have improved."

The Chief released the button, then re-pressed it. "Oakley. Swing by the jail and talk to Rodney. Ask him where Big Man's hideouts are. Insist that he tell you." He hesitated. "I'm going to make one more swing around downtown. Then I'll hit the station. Day shift, come on in. Clock out and get some sleep. I'll need you ready for the street in the morning. This is taking longer than I expected."

..*

Officer Murphy pushed the microphone away and leaned back in his chair. The dispatcher area was quiet, the conversation between the Chief and his officers at a lull.

"Sounds like things ain't going too good, Judge. Not as easy as we thought it would be. That Big Man—"

"We?" Judge Jackson said, smiling. "You mean you helped Lowell plan this?"

"No, I didn't mean that. But you gotta admit, he don't sound happy."

"I agree. Think I could use your mike?"

"Course, Judge. All you gotta do is push this button to talk, then release it to listen. Heck, I could teach— Ah, 'scuse me, sir. I didn't mean . . ."

"Relax, Murphy. No offense taken." Judge Jackson keyed the microphone. "Lowell, you out there?" He released the button.

The mike stand almost bounced with the quick response. "Who is this? Murphy, you'd better not be goofing off."

"Easy, Chief. It's me, Dan Jackson. I'm here with Murphy, listening in on your adventure. Take it easy. If you spot either of them, don't let your frustration get the better of you."

Chief Bowen chuckled. "Good think you're not Catholic. You'd have me call this off and come in for confession."

"No, but I don't want you to do anything—"

"Easy, Judge. Everybody on the force is listening in." He hesitated. "Stand by. I'll be there in a few minutes. Out."

The Judge leaned back, staring at the microphone. "You work for a good man, Murphy. I hope you know that."

"Yes sir."

The phone rang.

"Dawson Police, Officer Murphy." He frowned and pulled a pad of paper toward him, then wrote some notes. "Yes, ma'am. How long ago was that?" He listened. "I'll get a patrol over there soon's I can. Might be a few minutes though. Everybody's out right now." . . . "No, ma'am. You stay inside. We'll be there." He hung up.

Murphy chuckled. "Mrs. Biggs on Church Street. Said she heard something coming from Mrs. Deborah Patterson's yard. She calls at least once a week. Always hearing strange noises from her neighbors. Wants somebody to check it out. Wha'cha bet, it's a pack of cats. First night I worked the desk, she called, and I scrambled a patrol on high priority. Of course, by the time they got there, whatever she heard was gone. When the boys came back in, they gave me a mouthful. Said she's been hearing things for years."

The Judge smiled. "Do you get many of those calls—false alarms, I mean?"

"Yes sir. And every time I send an officer on a wild goose chase, they rib me good." He hesitated, drumming his fingers on the desk. "I'll let the Chief pick somebody this time."

..*

Chief Bowen turned onto North Smithwick, then took a left into the area behind the stores on Main Street—the back lot as everyone knew it. He slowed and crept along, playing his lights on the trash cans, rear entrances, and loading docks. A few cats scattered under the glare, and a pack of dogs barked at him. Otherwise, all was quiet.

There was no illumination other than the moon and firelights above doors. They made it harder to see because of the shadows they cast. "You could hide a Sherman tank back here," he mumbled as he slowed, inching along.

Something caught his eye. Was it a movement? He stared, then swung his car in that direction, flicking the headlights on high and pointing his spotlight. No, nothing. May as well continue through the area and exit behind Belk-Tyler. There, he saw it again. A furtive movement near Flip's Drugstore. He sped up and shined his beam where he thought he'd seen the motion. Yes, the shadow of a man, a large man. He gunned the engine and raced forward, then slammed on the brakes with Big Man illuminated in the headlights.

"Halt. Police," Chief Bowen yelled, swinging open the door to his squad car, and jumping out. "Stay where you are. I've been looking all over for you. You're under arrest."

Big Man tugged at his waist.

..*

Scooter opened his eyes, then closed them against the headache that pounded. He touched the back of his head and felt a knot the size of an egg. What happened? Where was he, and why was he sleeping under a tree? Where was Big Man? What was in his hand? His knife? He didn't remember pulling it. No, not his. He could feel his on the side of his leg—uncomfortable, but he wore it because Big Man said he had to. Why did he have another one? He slipped it into his belt.

As his head cleared, he remembered where he was, and why he was here. It was Miz Patterson's yard, and— Miz Patterson. Memory flooded in, and with it, a picture of Big Man standing over her. And she was . . . was . . . He covered his eyes. He'd seen a naked white woman. That could only mean one thing—the lynch rope. She'd tell. All his life he'd heard stories about coloreds that messed with white women. Fear grabbed him. In spite of the pain in his head, he leapt to his feet and ran, but tripped, falling face forward into the dirt. He reached back to see what his legs and lower body lay across and felt skin. He didn't want to look. His head twisted, as if with a mind of its own. Even in the darkness, he saw the pale sheen of her, the whiteness of her body. And the contrasting darkness of the blood that had poured from her wounds.

Again, he jumped to his feet, but again went down. When he touched whatever wrapped his ankles, he felt fabric. A new picture formed—Big Man ripping Miz Patterson's robe off. Scooter stood, holding the material at arms' length, terrified, his eyes darting between her mutilated body and her robe. Then his respect for her intervened and, with great reverence, he covered Debbie's naked form.

Dropping to his knees, he prayed, "Oh, Lord. I knows I turned my back on you. But hep me if you can. I need a sign."

He kept his eyes pressed shut, and his hands clenched in the prayer position. *Aint Liddie. She'll hep me.*

He stood, tears raining, then ran from the yard, intent on making it to the river and sanctuary. Aint Liddie'd know what to do. He smiled through the tears as he ran in the middle of the street in his off-gait manner, favoring his short leg. He stopped. *Whad'd Big Man teach me? Stay in the shadows where nobody can see me*. He changed his path. *Aint Liddie, I'm coming home.*

..*

Chief Bowen yelled, "Freeze, Big Man. Lay down on the ground." He reached for his handcuffs, but in his peripheral vision saw Big Man's hand come up, and a flash. An object struck the door of his car, and a cracking sound echoed through the night. He dropped to the ground, fumbling to draw his weapon as another thump sounded above him. He recognized the sounds. There had been too many such occasions on the islands of the Pacific during his service in World War II. Too many thumps into objects near him. He leveled his pistol, steadied his aim, and fired. He could hardly miss as Big Man stood straight-on to him, pointing his gun with both hands. Chief Bowen fired again.

Big Man's gun fell and his hands floated downward as he crumpled, settling to his knees before tumbling forward onto his chest.

The Chief held his position, watching the body, his weapon aligned on it. There was no movement. But he knew better than to rush forward. Playing possum was a trick known worldwide. His best friend had made that mistake on Iwo Jima, and it had cost him his life. Chief Bowen watched and waited, counting to himself. When he reached one hundred, he knew it was time. He was sure he'd hit his target, and that meant Big Man needed medical backup. He couldn't wait any longer. It wasn't humane.

Without taking his eyes off the body, he reached into the car and pulled down the microphone and keyed it to transmit. "This is the Chief. I'm in the back lot behind Flip's Drugstore with Big Man. I had to shoot him. Get a doctor here—*now*."

"You got it," Murphy said.

In the background, Chief Bowen heard a telephone dialing. He grimaced. Murphy had left the mike open again.

One car bounced through the ruts coming in from the Haughton Street side while a second from North Smithwick skidded to a stop beside the Chief. The other halted, its headlights further illuminating the body between them.

Big Man did not move. Signaling his men to stay where they were, Chief Bowen approached in a crouch, his gun at the ready. Reaching the body, he knelt and felt for the carotid artery, then waved the others forward.

"No pulse," Chief Bowen said. "Back off until the doc gets here. He has to make the call."

CHAPTER NINETEEN

Judge Jackson joined the group around Big Man's body, breathing hard after running from the station. "Are you okay, Chief?"

"Yeah. Nothing hurt but my pride. I underestimated him. Oh, and a couple of holes in my car."

"Did you see Scooter? Was he here?"

The Chief hesitated. "No, I didn't see him. To be honest, I didn't think about him. Staring down the barrel of a pistol spitting bullets will do that to you."

"Don't take that as criticism. I was just asking."

"No problem, but you have a good point. Parker, you and Christopher search the alleys. Be careful. He's most likely armed. Consider him dangerous."

"Chief, you need to look at this," Oakley said from where he knelt beside Big Man. He held a billfold. "It was on the ground. Probably came out when he fell."

The Chief took it and flipped it open in the beam of the headlights. "Oh no."

"What is it?" Judge Jackson asked.

"Debbie Patterson's wallet. What was he doing with it?"

Oakley played his light over the body. "He's pretty much covered with blood. I don't think it's all his."

The Judge turned white. "Murphy got a call about a disturbance in Debbie's yard. You don't suppose . . ."

"We'd better find out," the Chief said. "Oakley, secure this scene. I'm heading to Church Street."

"I'm going with you," Judge Jackson said, jumping into the Chief's car. "Pray this is a wasted trip."

..*

Judge Jackson jumped from the car before it stopped moving.

"Hold up, dammit," Chief Bowen yelled. "We don't know what's out there. Last thing I need is you getting hurt."

"Sorry. You're right, but can you hurry? I'm worried about what we might find."

The Chief closed alongside him. "Me, too. I'll take the lead." He looked toward the house. "Debbie's lights are on. Let's hope she has insomnia." Flashing the beam around, he headed toward the front door. "We'll knock before—"

"Wait," the Judge said. "Shine it that way again. I thought I saw something near the tree."

Chief Bowen glanced toward the front door, then said, "Where?"

"Toward the backyard. A bit to the right, between us and— Oh, no."

A mound of white lay in the light. A hand protruded from it. They advanced, each lost in his own thoughts.

..*

As Chief Bowen, Judge Jackson, and several officers watched, Doctor Rogerson examined Debbie's body where it had fallen in her backyard. He pulled a blanket over her and stood. "She's been stabbed so many times, I can't count them in this light. I'd say death was pretty much instantaneous. She didn't suffer long."

"Big Man?" Judge Jackson asked, staring at the Chief.

"Best I've got. He had her wallet."

"Scooter?"

"Won't know until I talk to him." The Chief sighed. "Maybe he'll come out when it gets daylight. I don't want to think he was part of this. But we have a witness that puts them together earlier in the evening. Doesn't look good for him."

"Yeah," the Judge said. "If he took a part in this, he'll have to pay." He forced his eyes away from the blanket-covered body. "Somebody has to tell Henry."

"Oh, God." Chief Bowen's chin rested against his chest. "The grief never ends, does it? I don't suppose . . ."

Judge Jackson looked at him. His mouth opened, then closed, and he swallowed. "You have your hands full, don't you? I mean,

Big Man, now Debbie. I'll get Jane, and we'll see Henry. I can't imagine his reaction." He started toward the street, then returned to the Chief's side. "My best bet is Scooter went home, down by the river. Maybe he walked away before Big Man . . ."

"You might be right. I'll send a patrol." He hesitated, rubbing his hand across his face in a weary motion. "You know we'll have to treat him as armed and dangerous."

"Be as easy as you can . . . please. I still think there's good in that boy."

"Maybe." He turned to Oakley. "Take the Judge wherever he needs to go. After that, put together a patrol to hit the shacks down by the river. Don't take any chances, but don't be any rougher than you have to be."

"I understand, Chief. I remember the way he was before he teamed up with Big Man."

Chief Bowen watched them walk away. "I hope you're right about Scooter. Something good needs to come out of all this horror."

..*

The alarm woke Henry from a troubled sleep at six. He rolled over, punched the button, and swung his feet to the floor. All night, he dreamed of Debbie. They walked along the edge of a river, not the Roanoke with its dirty, turbid color, and fast-rushing water, but one that was clear, moving in a languid manner, beckoning to the romance in them. A boat appeared, moored beside a walkway. He helped her into it, her laughter trilling and echoing off the surface as hummingbirds swooped past their heads. But when he lifted his leg to step in beside her, the boat was not there. It was in the center of the stream, rushing away from him. Debbie called to him once, then was gone.

He shook his head and ran his hands through his hair, wondering at the strangeness of the dream, then shivered in the morning chill of his apartment. He wasn't superstitious, but this one bothered him. Why would she disappear? He pulled on his robe, thinking, I'll call her later, and we'll have a good laugh over it. She found humor in so many things and never failed to bring him into her happy world. Again, he marveled that one so beautiful, so perfect would agree to be his wife.

There was a soft knock, followed by louder, more insistent rapping. Henry doubled back from heading toward the kitchen to fix coffee. He checked his robe, tied it closed, and opened the door. "Judge. Jane. What brings you out so early?"

"Can we come in?" the Judge asked, the look on his face telegraphing how serious he was.

"Sure. I have a feeling—" The dream popped into Henry's mind, Debbie drifting away, disappearing. "Debbie? Is she alright?"

Jane walked past Henry to the sofa and sat on an end cushion. "Come, sit down." She patted the center of the couch.

The Judge took Henry's arm and led him toward Jane. "We have bad news. Sit with us while we tell you what happened."

Henry looked from one to the other, then followed the Judge's lead. "Tell me, Dan," he said, sitting beside Jane. "Is it Debbie?"

"I'd rather cut off an arm than have to—"

"Dammit, tell me."

"Debbie's dead. We found her body during the night. She was stabbed to death in her backyard."

"Stabbed? How? Why?" Henry's face sang of incredulity and intense pain. "But I saw her last night. She was fine. I . . . I don't understand."

"I'll get you a glass of water," Jane said. "Maybe a cup of coffee will help."

"I haven't made any yet," Henry said. "That's what I was about to do when you knocked." His voice was flat, the tone of one in denial and shock. "I'll make some now."

"No, I'll do it." Jane stood and walked into the kitchen.

Henry leaned his head back on the sofa. "Last night, we talked about the wedding. She's so excited. Dan, you'll never know how indebted I am to you and Jane. Debbie is the most wonderful thing that ever happened to me. When I'm with her, I'm so happy. It's like I was only a shadow before, moving from one patch of sunlight to another. Now I feel fleshed out, complete. Is that how it is with you and Jane?"

The Judge glanced toward the kitchen where Jane watched the pot on the stove. "Yes. I know what you mean. We have that same thing, that quality that fulfills the other."

Henry continued in a monotone. "She's going to wear blue, you know. Said she wouldn't feel right in white. She wore white when she married Tom." He paused. "If he hadn't died, I wouldn't have Debbie. Is it wrong to be glad he didn't come home? She asked if I minded if she doesn't wear white. Can you imagine that, asking if my feelings will be hurt? She's the most perfect woman alive." He grabbed the Judge's arm, his face a mask of sadness. "She can't be dead. I can't lose her."

Tears burst from Henry like a sudden summer thunderstorm.

"Jane. I need you," Dan called.

She returned to the room and sat on the couch, pulling Henry's head to her bosom. As she rubbed his back, she said, "We'll let the coffee cool and settle for a minute. It might be weak, but it'll be okay."

Henry sat up and dried his eyes. Jane handed him a tissue, and he blew his nose, then took several deep breaths. "Thanks. I'm ready for some coffee—and an explanation. Don't leave anything out."

Over the next three hours, Judge Jackson told and retold the story, as he knew it. Henry listened, asking an occasional question. Much of the time, he kept his eyes closed as if not wanting to face the reality of it. Jane made breakfast and insisted they all eat. Henry showered and dressed, going through the motions like an automaton.

At nine-thirty, the phone rang and the Judge answered, "Flanagan residence, Judge Jackson speaking." . . . "Yes, Mabel, what you heard is right." He glanced at Henry. "No, he won't be coming in today. You and Eli do whatever needs to be done." . . . "He's doing okay. Jane and I will stay with him." . . . "I'll tell him what you said."

He hung up and turned to Henry. "That was Mabel. She heard and wants you to know how sorry she is. Eli, too. She said the phone's ringing off the hook with folks crying about Debbie. They'll keep the office open. You can stay here with Jane and me."

CHAPTER TWENTY

When Flip arrived at the drugstore at seven-thirty, he was surprised to find the front door locked. Usually, Liddie was there by seven, opened the store, started coffee, and prepared the place for the business day. He peeked through the window. No sign of her. Unlocking the door, he thought, I'd better get someone to check on her. She might be laid up in that shack of hers.

As he entered and turned on the lights, the phone rang. He hustled to the back and picked up the receiver. "Flip's Drugstore."

"Did you hear yet?" a female voice said.

"Hear what? Who is this?"

"Christiana Andrews. All the money I spend in your place, and you don't know me?"

"Sorry, Miss Christiana. What is it I'm supposed to have heard?"

"Debbie Matthews. You know she went to that *colored* church. Now she's dead."

"What are you talking about?"

"One of *them* raped her and stabbed her to death. I hear he left her naked in the backyard after he'd had his way with her. Cut her face off. I can't tell a man the other parts he slashed and mutilated. It'll be a closed casket."

"Are you sure? Where'd you hear this?"

"Never mind, but you can bet it's true."

Flip dropped into the chair beside the phone stand. "Have you heard how Henry's taking it?"

"Humph. That nigger-lover. I have no sympathy for him. He's the reason she's dead. If he'd kept his nose out of things he don't understand, this would never have happened."

"Well, I can't disagree with you. Sorry, but I have to go. I'm here alone, and customers are coming in. Thank you for calling." He hung up, then dialed his home.

When Lorrie answered, he said, "It's begun. This mess between the whites and coloreds claimed its first victim. I just heard someone murdered Debbie last night."

"No. That can't be. I just saw her yesterday. Not Debbie." She continued with denials and sympathetic comments for several more minutes before Flip cut her off. He repeated Christiana's story, then said, "Keep the doors locked. Don't open one until you know who's on the other side." He paused, rubbing his brow. "Has Flip Junior left for school yet?"

"No, he's dawdling over breakfast again."

"Okay, drive him to school, then come to the store. Aunt Liddie didn't come in, so you can help me here."

"I was going to bake cakes for the church raffle."

"Do what I say. I don't want you and Little Flip caught up in this. I told you it would be neighbor against neighbor. Damn Henry and his meddling."

"Alright, if you think it's best."

"I know it's best. This town is going to turn upside down, and I don't want it to fall on my family. We're not going to take sides. We'll stay out of it."

..*

At ten, there was a knock on Henry's door. Judge Jackson rose, walked across the room, and answered it. Chief Bowen stood there, preparing to knock again. "May I come in? How's Henry doing?"

Lowell followed the Judge into the room, walked to Henry, and touched his shoulder. "I don't have the words to tell you how sorry I am. Debbie was a wonderful person. She'll leave a big hole in Dawson."

"And in my life," Henry said. "Thanks for coming by. What happened? Do you know yet?"

"I think we pieced it together. Well, I should say, we have an idea of how it might have occurred." He rubbed his stubble, then wiped at his eyes. "It was a long night. I'm on my way home to grab a nap, but wanted to stop by and let you know where we are."

"Have a seat," Jane said. "All we know is what Dan saw last

night."

Lowell pressed on his temples. "Headache. Do you have any aspirin?"

Henry started to rise, but Jane said, "I saw some in the kitchen. I'll get them." She rose and left the room.

Chief Bowen took a deep breath. "We picked up Scooter last night. As the Judge suggested, he had returned home to the river. My officers found him at Aunt Liddie's house." He paused and appeared to blink back tears. "Another tragedy. She's dead, too. Oakley said Scooter was sitting on the floor with her head in his lap. Doc says it was probably a heart attack, and she'd been dead for several hours. My guess is Scooter found her that way."

"Here's your aspirin and water," Jane said, rejoining them. "Liddie, too? That's terrible. She was a saint. This is a night no one in Dawson will ever forget." She looked at her husband. "I'll check with Mrs. Luther and ask her about the viewing. We'll send a wreath, of course."

Chief Bowen said, "Mrs. Luther?"

"Our maid," Jane said. "She attended the same church as Aunt Liddie."

Judge Jackson nodded. "Also find out who's taking care of her. She didn't have any relatives that I know of. And I doubt she saved much money. Flip couldn't pay her much above survival level. Maybe the church can help. Pastor Turner might know. Could you—" He stopped himself. "No, I'll ask him. You just see what Ms. Luther knows."

"Let me know what you find out," Henry said. "I'll publish a eu—" He took a deep breath and wiped his eyes. "I'll publish a eulogy for her."

"I'm sorry," Chief Bowen said, "but I'm about out on my feet. Let me finish so I can get out of here and get some rest. I have to be back in the office soon. There's another ton of paperwork waiting for me. Plus the Mayor wants to see me this afternoon."

"Of course," Judge Jackson said. "Sorry we took off on a tangent."

"Oakley got Scooter up while Christopher woke a couple of neighbors and told them about Aunt Liddie. Scooter had a knife in his belt. The handle was bloody, and the blade showed blood residue. Scooter's clothes had a lot of blood on them. So Oakley and Christopher brought him in."

"Scooter killed Debbie?" Judge Jackson asked. "That's—"

"I didn't say that," Chief Bowen said. "Although I thought it at first. When Oakley showed me the knife, there wasn't much else I could think. Then he told the rest of it. When he searched Scooter, he found a sheath knife strapped alongside his shin. It was identical to the one he had in his belt. Scooter said the first knife wasn't his and claimed to know nothing about it. Well, that was Oakley's interpretation since Scooter didn't say much of anything. He nodded for yes and shook his head for no. When Oakley asked him if the knife was his, he shook his head no."

"Did you check Big Man?" Henry asked, appearing to become more alert with the telling of the story.

Chief Bowen looked at him. "Yeah. As soon as Oakley brought Scooter in and told the story, I checked on Big Man. He wore the same kind of rig on his lower leg. The sheath was empty."

"So?" Jane said.

"My guess is Big Man killed Debbie and left Scooter behind with the murder weapon. At that point, Scooter probably panicked and ran to Aunt Liddie's. She raised him, you know." He paused. "If I'm guessing right, he must have been terrified. And finding her dead . . ."

He paused. "When we caught up with Big Man in the back lot, he was carrying a bag full of guns." He snorted. "He had enough to start World War III."

"Does Scooter have anything to say?" Judge Jackson asked. "Would it help if I talked to him?"

"Right now, he's sleeping—or he was when I left. When Oakley brought him in, he was such a mess I asked the doctor to give him a pill. I'm hoping when he wakes, he'll talk to me." He appeared to think. "Yeah, it might help if you were there. He has—well, had—a lot of respect for you."

"Consider it done," the Judge said. "What time?"

"Come by about four. I should be finished with the Mayor by then, and Scooter should be awake." He stood and addressed Henry. "Sorry I don't have more. But I'll keep you informed as best I can. Should I give Scooter any message from you?"

Henry looked up at him. The tears were gone, leaving rage behind. "Yeah. Tell him I hope he rots in hell, and I'll do everything I can to put him there."

"Henry," Judge Jackson said, his eyes flaring. "What—"

"What do you expect me to say. Maybe wish him a happy birthday? That son-of-a-bitch killed my Debbie. He may not have done the stabbing, but he and every colored around here killed her." He stood and began to pace. "All she ever did was nurture them, care for them. And what did she get in return? They killed her."

"Easy," Chief Bowen said. "We don't know for sure—"

"For sure? *For sure*? You stupid ass. What we know for sure is Debbie was murdered. What more do you need? And we know a damn nigger did it." He looked at his friends. "Now, if you don't mind, I'll ask you to leave. I have a newspaper to publish—maybe a special edition."

..*

Henry sat at his desk staring at his typewriter. Rage filled him—rage and bitterness toward Debbie's murderers.

He had rushed to the office as soon as Dan, Jane, and Lowell left his place. Mabel met him at the door babbling through tears. He brushed her aside, rushed into his office, and closed the door. He had to write, had to do it before he lost his edge. He had to do it while the pain was fresh, while he could tell the whole world how miserable the whole Negro race was. They killed Debbie, and he'd use his paper to destroy them. Equal rights? No way. He'd do whatever he could to stop its happening in his lifetime. They could return to the jungles of Africa where such behavior might be acceptable.

He loaded paper into the typewriter, then lay his forehead on his crossed arms on the carriage. Tears dripped onto the keys. An image of Debbie flashed into his mind, the way she looked when he kissed her goodnight. It seemed a lifetime ago. It was a lifetime. A life filled with happiness and expectation had turned into sorrow of boundless depth. She was delicate, defenseless, and so incredibly beautiful. Her eyes had shone with the happiness they shared. He loved her with very fiber of his being. Yet, when she needed him, he'd been asleep, dreaming of the wonderful years ahead. He failed her. Not only last night, but before that when he supported those who murdered her. His shoulders shook with guilt and sadness.

With physical effort, he lifted his head. *The pen is mightier than the sword.* It was his opportunity to prove the truth of that adage. He'd raise his pen and strike back at the scum who took her life. At the same time, he'd work to ensure no other white woman met Debbie's fate. He'd bring the coloreds to heel, put them in their place. He began to type.

Last night, two despicable human beings, representatives of their whole race, murdered Mrs. Deborah Patterson, my fiancée. They struck in darkness matching the color of their skins, the color of their souls. Was it a random killing by two renegades, two outlaws? No. What did she do to deserve her fate? She trusted Negroes.

He stopped, reread what he wrote, frowned, then ripped the paper out. After a moment's reflection, he inserted another paper, wiped his forehead, and started again.

Today, I cry because last night, my fiancée, Deborah Patterson, died. Not the quiet death you might expect of one who lived a giving life, but death at the hands of two despicable Negroes who had little to gain except the satisfaction of

Again he ripped the paper out, then leaned back in his chair, staring at the ceiling. The image of Debbie reappeared, and he knew he must honor her memory. He must write an editorial she'd approve of. Sweet Debbie, so loving, so caring, so trusting. He must not do anything that would cause her distress when she looked at him from Heaven. He could not violate the faith she placed in him. He swallowed hard, closed his eyes, shut off his mind, and followed his heart.

..*

At four o'clock, Eli walked out of the office of the *Dawson Times*, a box filled with newspapers under his arm. His face radiated sadness as he placed the container on a bench he had placed there earlier. A placard read, *FREE. TAKE ONE.*

He sat and picked up a paper. It was one page, four columns headed by a three-inch headline in bold black, *A NIGHT OF DEATH.* The first three articles chronicled the demise of Deborah

Patterson, Aunt Liddie, and Big Man. The fourth was an editorial. Eli read it again, looking for understanding, wondering what the future held.

Last night, the Angel of Death visited Dawson and reaped a terrible toll. We lost two citizens who gave so much to make this simple town the delightful place it is. The third to die was a parasite more despicable than the ticks sucking blood from your dog or the maggots burrowing through raw garbage. That third was Jeremiah Q Lincoln, who called himself Big Man. Big? Only in his own perverted world.

First, Aunt Liddie, a Negro woman who brought dignity to her race and kindness to every person she encountered. To have had the pleasure of knowing her is to be richer for the experience. It will be many years, perhaps never, before we meet another like her. I mourn her passing.

Second, Mrs. Deborah Patterson, Debbie to her friends, my fiancée, the woman I intended to spend the rest of my life with, the woman I searched the world for. The truth of what happened to her is best left undetailed. Suffice it to say, Big Man and his partner performed despicable acts as they mutilated her. I cannot imagine the terror she must have felt as she fought for her life. And yet, it is worse, far worse. For she defended herself against one she befriended, one she trusted, one she helped.

Our competent Chief of Police, Lowell Bowen, ended the life of Big Man, his blood mingling with Debbie's, which soaked his clothing. Lest there be any doubt about guilt or innocence, he had her wallet.

The second criminal, a young colored man who goes by the name of Scooter, is behind bars in the local jail. He will stand before a judge and a jury of his peers for her murder. At that time, he will receive the judgment of the court, be it freedom, incarceration, or death. I pray that justice prevails, and he be sentenced to die in the electric chair.

My initial reaction was to strike out at all Negroes, those who gave us Big Man and Scooter. Then I realized that Debbie would not want that. The Debbie I knew and loved would ask me to be fair and not judge all coloreds for the behavior of two mongrels. That was the kind of person she was—love in her heart for everyone.

At this time, I cannot rise to Debbie's expectations. I hope that someday I will view a colored without remembering what happened to Debbie. But for now, I can only feel the pain of her loss and know its cause. So, I shall still my pen lest I allow my true feelings to surface.

There will be those who seek advantage from this crime. Some will use it to spread hatred, while others will see it as an opportunity to denounce our town as racist. I beg the people of all colors to be calm and patient. There is nothing to be gained by speaking or acting rashly.

Let us not dwell on the evil of Big Man and Scooter. Let us cherish the goodness of Deborah Patterson and Aunt Liddie and mourn our losses.

Eli replaced the paper in the box and glanced around, a worried look on his face. "Cain't nothing good come from this. I sho hope folks think like Muster Flanagan. If they don't, ain't goin' be safe for no colored man on the street."

He heard footsteps and saw Pastor Turner coming toward him. "How do," he said, standing. "Good to see you."

"I come by to tell Mr. Flanagan how sorry I am and let him know the arrangements for Aint Liddie. I thought he might put them in the paper tomorrow."

Eli rubbed his jaw. "I don't know. He mighty upset right now, I mean, losin' his woman and all. Maybe you oughta jist giv'm to me, and I'll git'm ready."

"But I want to let him know how sad I am, and everybody in the church, 'bout what happened last night. What a terrible, terrible crime it was. I'm doin' a special service for Aint Liddie, and I want to include Miz Patterson. She was a mighty-fine friend of the colored folks here 'bouts."

Eli studied the pastor. "She was, that's for sure. Maybe he see you. But you oughta read this first. They's free today. Muster Flanagan say he gonna use it for an insert tomorrow." Eli handed him a paper, then motioned to the bench. "You can set down here."

Pastor Turner took the paper and sat. As he read, a frown appeared, deepened, then sadness took over. He looked at Eli. "Do you think we gonna be blamed for all this?"

Eli sighed. "I cain't see no other way. They's folks here on both sides what'll think the worst. They's white people be looking for somebody to hang, and they's colored ones what'll try to make out Big Man didn't do nothing."

After a moment of apparent concentration, Pastor Turner reached into his pocket and pulled out a lined pad. Tearing off the top page, he said, "Here's the information for Aint Liddie's funeral. I won't bother Mr. Flanagan now, but tell him I come by." He pointed at the editorial. "Hard to believe a man can write like that when he hurtin' so bad. You can feel the pain in his words. You tell him he welcome at the Holy Spirit Evangelical Church anytime. And I welcome him in my home. I'll include Miz Patterson in my prayers and sermons. I hope he'll attend."

He stood and and took a couple of steps, then turned back to Eli. "I fear you're right. This is a day we ain't ever goin' to forget. The South's just beginning to change, to recognize we ain't animals. Then something like this happens. Before it's over, a lot of folks gonna git hurt. Some of'm like Big Man deserve it. Others like Miz Patterson and Mr. Flanagan will be caught in the middle. Ain't right, but there ain't nothing we can do to stop it." He shuffled off, stoop-shouldered, his head down.

CHAPTER TWENTY-ONE

About the time Eli placed the special edition of the *Dawson Times* on the bench in front of the newspaper, Chief Bowen ushered Scooter into his office where Judge Jackson waited. "Scooter, I believe you know the Judge, don't you?"

"Oh, yas suh, I knows the Jedge. He be a fine man." He looked at the Judge's shoes. "Wisht I had my box. Looks like you need a shine."

"Things aren't like they used to be." Judge Jackson leaned forward, studying Scooter. "I've missed you. Too bad you quit on us."

Scooter refused to meet the Judge's eyes. "I made lotsa mistakes, ain't I? I oughta stayed with Aint Liddie."

"Things would have been different. We wish you had listened to her."

"The mistakes are what we need to talk about," Chief Bowen said. "Are you ready?"

"Yas suh. Whatever I can tell you, I will."

"Good," Chief Bowen said. "You sit right here." He pointed to a straight-backed chair.

As Scooter sat, he said, "I knows what got to happen."

"What do you mean?" Judge Jackson asked.

Scooter looked down as if staring between his knees. His voice grew quiet, somber. "I knows I got to die. That's the way it always been, and I don't 'spect nobody gonna change it for me."

"I don't understand," the Judge said. "Did you kill Mrs. Patterson?"

Scooter's head popped up, then returned to its down position. "Naw suh, I didn't touch Miz Patterson. I would never do that."

"Then why do you have to die?"

"Please, suh. Don't make me talk 'bout that. I wisht I never met Big Man." He looked at the Chief. "Did he git away?"

The Judge and the Chief exchanged glances.

"You haven't heard?" Chief Bowen said.

"Naw suh. I jist waked up a little bit ago. I musta been powerful tired."

A sigh escaped the Chief. "Big Man is dead. I had to shoot him."

Scooter stared at him. "That be good. He shoulda died. He was a bad person." He glanced around the room. "Since I went with him, I reckon I be bad, too. It be fittin' that I got to die."

The Judge and Chief Bowen exchanged quizzical looks. "Help me here, Scooter," Judge Jackson said. "I need to know why you think you have to die if you didn't hurt Mrs. Patterson."

"Oh, suh. I would never hurt that woman. She was my friend. She hepped me."

"Did you go to her house last night?" Chief Bowen asked.

"Yas suh. Me and Big Man went there."

"Why?"

Scooter fidgeted in his chair. "Do I have to talk 'bout that?"

The Judge pulled his chair closer to Scooter. "No, you don't have to tell us anything, but we'd like to help if we can." His eyes swept toward the Chief, then back. "You were there when Mrs. Patterson died, weren't you?"

"Yas suh."

"Who killed her?"

"Big Man, I think. He said she had money, and we could git away if she give it to us. But she run out the back door, and he run after her." He shuddered. "When I come out . . . That's when I seen her."

"I don't understand. What did you see?"

Scooter looked at the Judge, then at the Chief. "Please don't make me tell you. I knows I got to die, but I don't want to talk 'bout it. Aint Liddie said it was something a colored man oughta never talk 'bout."

Chief Bowen rubbed his forehead. "Judge, can I see you outside?"

The Judge nodded. "Scooter, you stay here. We'll be right back." He followed the Chief into the hallway.

In a whisper, Chief Bowen said, "I'm lost in there. Do you have any idea what he's talking about, I mean, this stuff about having to die?"

"Not sure. Perhaps there's some code among those down by the river that we don't know about. Want me to try to get it out of him?"

"I'd appreciate it." The Chief looked around. "I'll leave him with you, and clean up some paperwork." He scratched his head. "We'll have to move him to an interview room. I need my office."

"Think you can find him something to wear? That outfit is kind of rank."

"Sure. I'll get Oakley to change him into a jumpsuit. Meanwhile," he looked around, "Christopher, take the Judge to the interview room. Set him up with a pad, pencil, and anything else he needs. Stay and write down everything Scooter says." He started into his office, then turned back. "Let the Judge handle it. Scooter trusts him. Maybe we'll get the full story of last night."

"Can do," Christopher said. "Anything you need, Judge?"

"A couple of soft drinks might be nice," the Judge said. "No special kind."

"Soon's I get you settled," Officer Christopher said. "Follow me. Best hotel in Dawson."

..*

The Judge flicked his eyes toward Christopher sitting in the corner, his chair leaning against the wall, then examined Scooter across the small table. "I don't know if you're feeling any better, but you sure look better. How's your Coke?"

"Fine, suh. And I thank you for gittin' me some clothes. Miz Patterson's blood was all over them old ones."

"That's what we need to talk about." The Judge moved his chair closer to the table and picked up the pencil beside the tablet of paper laying there. "Tell me how you ended up at her house and what happened."

Scooter sighed, fidgeted, then said, "Big Man heard Rodney been arrested with the car loaded with bootleg." He looked at the Judge. "I told Big Man he was one worthless nigger what would git us in trouble, but he didn't listen. He oughta listened to me, but he was too hardheaded. He was the most hardheaded nigger I ever—"

"Scooter," the Judge said.

"Oh. Yas suh. You wants to know 'bout last night. The boy down the street . . ."

Thirty minutes later, Scooter had emptied his Coke bottle and told the story in detail up to when Big Man threw him against the tree, and he passed out. He stopped talking and looked at his hands resting on the table.

The Judge had filled two pages with notes as Scooter talked. He waited for him to resume his narration, his pen poised over the paper.

Scooter said nothing.

"What happened next?" he asked. "I know you woke up because you weren't there when I arrived."

"That's the part I druther not talk about. I knows I got to die."

Judge Jackson laid his pen alongside the pad and leaned back. "You said that when we were with the Chief. What do you mean?"

Tears squirmed from Scooter's eyes. "I seen Miz Patterson nekkid."

The Judge leaned forward. "When, and what does that have to do with dying?"

"Aint Liddie say any colored man what looks at a white woman when she nekkid, he gonna die—probably be hung from some ol' oak tree."

"I see," said the Judge, hating what he heard, but recognizing it as truth through Scooter's eyes. "Tell me about seeing her."

"Oh, I cain't do that. Ain't right to talk 'bout—"

"No, Scooter, I don't mean what you saw." The Judge hesitated, choosing his words with care. "I mean how you came to see her that way. Where she was, where you were—just that. Don't talk about what you saw. It's not right for a white man either."

"Really? I didn't know that. I thought . . . I mean, nobody—"

"What happened that caused you to see her?"

Scooter appeared to think. "At first, when I woke up, I couldn't 'member nothin'. Then I felt that knife in my hand and knowed somethin' was wrong." He looked at the Judge, his eyes beseeching. "I was scared, suh, real scared. I jumped up and started to run . . . then I tripped over somethin'." Scooter stopped and looked at the floor, his fingers working to a rhythm of their own.

"And," the Judge said.

Scooter mumbled, his head down. "They was blood everywhere. There won't much moon, but I could see her plenty good. She was white and red and . . . didn't have no clothes on. Last I 'membered, she had on that nice robe she wore sometimes. But laying on that ground like that, she was nekkid." He stared at the Judge. "Big Man musta gone crazy—all that blood."

"I see." The Judge rubbed his chin. "So you're saying she was dead when you tripped over her?"

"I think so. I mean, I didn't touch her or nothing. I just wanted to run away."

"What did you do?"

"I jumped up, but got my feet tangled in somethin' else. I seen it was her robe, so I covered her, then run as hard as I could."

"Where did you go?"

"Aint Liddie's. She cared 'bout me. I knew she'd hep me." His words ended, leaving a sadder look on his face.

"What happened then?"

Tears rained from Scooter's eyes. "She was layin' on the floor. I tried to wake her up, but it didn't do no good. I even built a fire so she wouldn't be cold. But nothin' hepped. She was dead." He stared at the Judge. "Why, Jedge? Why she have to die? She was the best person in town, and she died. It ain't fair. It just ain't fair."

"Sometimes, we don't know what God has in mind, Scooter. I think Pastor Turner would tell you it was her time to go to heaven to reap the rewards she earned here on earth. Don't you worry about her. She's in a far, far better place."

Scooter lowered his face into his hands, and cried, huge sobs shaking his body. "But I need her to hep me. I's scared. I don't know what to do."

"Yes, you do," the Judge said, leaning forward. "She taught you what was right and what was wrong. You went wrong, but now you're returning to the right side. It's up to you from now on. You have friends who will help you, but you have to pay for all you've done. Do you understand?"

"Yas suh. I got to die."

CHAPTER TWENTY-TWO

Alice Burnette stirred the pot of cabbage boiling on the stove. Her nose wrinkled against the familiar smell, reminding her of the odors in her mama's kitchen so many years ago. Memories flooded in of her and her sister, Shirley, working alongside their mother, learning the ways of womanhood.

"Now girls," her mother would say, "taking care of your man will be your most important job when you grow up. Make sure you pick the right one because he'll be your responsibility for the rest of your life." At this point, she'd pat each girl on the head. "The easiest way to make a man happy is keep his belly full of the food he likes. Your daddy likes his cabbage cooked down real good and flavored with the butt end of a country ham. Not like my mama cooked'm, but that's how I do it now." She'd pause and look out the window. "You just remember he's busy all day working hard to support you and your babies. When he comes home, he wants a good meal and an evening of peace and quiet. Then some nights . . . well, you'll find out for yourself." She would smile a self-satisfied smile and stir the pot.

Alice had discovered what her mother meant and often wished she could feel the same about *those nights*. They were wonderful during the first few months of her marriage to Charlie—until he began to change. He became more demanding and rougher, especially when he drank. At first, she assumed she was doing something wrong. She tried to please him, asked what she could do to make him happy, begged him to be gentle, and cried into her pillow, thinking she was inadequate.

She wanted to talk to Shirley about it, but couldn't bring herself to do so. Each time she tried, she froze. In her world, a wife did not talk about the relationship with her husband.

Later, she recognized the problem. Against her mother's best advice, she picked the wrong man. But it was too late. She'd said, "I do," in front of God. A woman stayed with and obeyed her husband.

Her ears perked up. Was that the creak of the front door?

"'Bout damn time you got here. Did you tell the others?" she heard Charlie say from the living room.

"Yeah, they'll be along directly. I tol'm seven o'clock, after it gits good and dark."

Marvin. What was he doing here? she wondered. And what were they talking about?

"Seven's good. Supper ought to be 'bout ready. You gonna stay and eat?"

"I smell cabbage," Marvin said. "Your Alice knows how to cook'm so tender they melt in my mouth. Yep, think I'll stay. I tol' the woman I pro'bly wouldn't be home for a while."

The kitchen door swung open. "How long 'til supper?" Charlie said. "Marvin's eatin' with us. Then you can go over to your sister's if you want to. We got a little business to take care of." He grinned at Marvin. "They gonna wish they listened to me."

"Farm business?" Alice asked. "If it is, I could—"

"Naw. And we won't need you here. This here is man talk. You just go on and visit your sister like I said. But first, me and Marvin is right hongry. You sure them cabbage ain't 'bout ready?"

"Ten minutes," Alice said. "I'll make the tea and set the table. By then, they ought to be tender enough to eat. Y'all just go on in the living room. I'll call you."

"C'mon, Marvin," Charlie said. "We can talk about how we gonna handle this nigger mess." As they walked from the kitchen, he added, "Ain't no way we can let them git away with murderin' a white woman. If they do, won't nobody be safe."

Alice spun from the stove. White woman? What was he talking about? She picked up the phone and dialed Shirley's number. Last night she said she was going to town today. Maybe she'd know what Charlie meant.

When Shirley answered, Alice asked if she'd heard anything about a colored man killing a white woman. Shirley's response about Deborah Patterson's rape, mutilation, and murder was all Alice needed to know. She had to stay home to find out what Charlie and the others planned to do.

..*

Charlie and Marvin were in good humor during supper, and Alice's hopes rose that the evening would be uneventful. That lasted until Charlie told her she could do the dishes tomorrow. She ought to get an early start visiting her sister.

"She won't be home tonight," Alice lied. "I called her before supper, and she said she has to go by the church to talk to the choir director. But don't worry 'bout me. You can go on with your meetin'. I'll just stay here in the kitchen. I got some sewing to do."

"That would be right convenient," Marvin said. "I mean, if it's goin' to be a long night, we could use a pot of coffee now and then."

Charlie cut him a look. "Ain't nobody said nothing 'bout a long night." His gaze returned to Alice. "I really wisht you'd go some place else. Don't you have someone you can visit?"

"Not really, and you know how this place'll stink if I don't clean up them cabbage dishes. Plus, I want to let the hem out on my skirt—the one you said was too short last Sunday."

Charlie gave her a long look. "Okay, honey, I reckon if you keep the door shut, things'll be okay."

Alice's heart sank. The only time he called her honey was when he had some shenanigan up his sleeve he wanted to keep secret from her.

"Go on and get your sewing before the boys get here. Make a fresh pot of coffee and leave it on the stove. If we need it, Marvin'll come get it. Don't you come into the living room unless I call you."

"I'll get what I need now, then start the coffee before I clean up the dishes." She rose and left the room.

..*

Alice sat, her head cradled in her hands. What she had heard from the living room frightened her to the core of her soul. She couldn't let Charlie and Marvin do what they talked about. It was too horrible to even consider.

There was a scraping of chairs. "Okay, boys," Charlie said.

"That's it. Everybody get your stuff. We'll meet on Main Street at ten o'clock. Don't be late."

Alice heard the front door open, the hinges squeaking. A moment later, it closed.

Charlie said, "Well, Marvin, that went 'bout as good as I coulda hoped. Think they'll be there?"

There's a couple I ain't sure about, but most of'm will come."

"You got your gun with you?"

"In the truck." There was a moment of silence. "Are you sure about this, Charlie?"

"As sure as I've ever been 'bout anything. Don't git weak-kneed on me. If we don't stop the niggers right here, we'll be workin' for'm soon."

"Yeah, but—"

"Save your buts for them cheap cigarettes you smoke. I don't want to hear them. We gotta job to do. We gotta lead this bunch of chickenshits to do the right thing. If we ain't strong, they'll run like scared dogs."

"Sounds good to me. I'm with you."

"Warm up your truck. I'll be right there."

Alice heard footsteps move toward their bedroom. That's where Charlie kept his guns—a high-powered rifle for deer and bear season and a shotgun for other game. There was also a pistol, but she didn't know much about it except it had a round cylinder where the bullets went.

A moment later, the kitchen door swung open and Charlie stuck his head in, a big smile on his face. "Honey, I'm going out with Marvin. Don't wait up."

The door closed, then the front door squeaked and slammed shut.

Alice listened. She heard Marvin's truck start, then Charlie's, and the strain of the engines as they pulled out of the yard. With heavy steps, she walked to the living room window. Two sets of taillights disappeared into the night.

She returned to the kitchen and sat at the table. For a moment, she did nothing, then picked up the dark blue skirt she'd been working on. She began to make tight, neat stitches around the hem.

Water spots appeared on the material as tears dripped from her eyes. What was she to do? On one hand, what Charlie planned wasn't right. But on the other, Mrs. Patterson died—raped and murdered. She heard Charlie tell the others the Negroes did unspeakable things to her. Alice's upbringing said a colored man who messed with a white woman had to die. If white folks didn't act, they would go crazy with lust. No white woman would be safe. Everybody knew colored men were animals when it came to sex—like dogs in heat. Yet she remembered the gentle colored man who shined shoes on Main Street. She couldn't picture him sex-crazed.

She rose and walked to the phone. "I'll call Shirley and tell her. She'll know what to do." She dialed the first number, then stopped. "No. This is my problem, not Shirley's." She set the phone down and leaned against the kitchen sink. *Oh, Mama, you taught me to honor my man, but I can't, I just can't let this happen.* She looked upward. *If I'm doing wrong, I hope You'll forgive me.*

She picked up the phone book, looked into it, and dialed a number. "Dawson Police, Officer Murphy," she heard.

"I . . . I need to tell you something," she whispered.

"Who is this, ma'am? I need to know for my paperwork."

"Please. Just listen," she said through sobs. "I can't tell you who I am. But you folks got to get ready. Be ready tonight."

"Ready for what, ma'am? I don't understand."

"Listen to me," she said in an agitated voice. "Get your people on the street. They're coming for him."

"Him? Ma'am, can you be more specific?"

"That colored man you have in jail. They're gonna hang him."

There was a moment of silence. "Ma'am, would you like to speak with the Chief? This is something he ought to hear. He's really a nice man."

"Uh . . . can't you do it?"

"No, ma'am. I just answer the phone. The Chief's the person you should talk to. He's the boss."

"Yes, please. Let me talk to him. Hurry."

She listened to a shuffling sound, then heard, "Chief. You need to pick up on this. A lady says we got trouble coming."

Another moment of background noise filled with mumbling, then, "This is Chief Bowen. How can I help you?"

She gathered her thoughts. "Do you know the Burnette

brothers?"

"Yes, ma'am—Charlie and Marvin. We talked a few times."

"They're gonna take that boy out of jail and kill him."

"I see. How do you know this?"

"I heard them talking. They . . ." She hesitated, wondering how much she could say. If Charlie found out what she'd done, he'd beat her with a tobacco stick. He had before, and she hadn't crossed him near as bad as tonight.

"Where did you hear them talking? the chief asked into her silence. "Can you tell me your name?"

"No. Not my name. I . . . I just know they're going to town tonight to get that boy. You better be ready." She hung up as sobs racked her body.

CHAPTER TWENTY-THREE

The gathering in the nave of the Holy Spirit Evangelical Church, called by Pastor Turner, included Joshua, Berta, and several other colored people who lived down by the river.

Pastor Turner opened the meeting. "I asked y'all to come tonight so we can put Aint Liddie away like she oughta be. She was a mighty-fine woman and deserves the best."

"Amen," said Joshua.

"Amen," echoed Berta, Joshua's wife.

The others in the room nodded and added their own amens.

"Preacher, I knows you gonna do it right," Joshua said. "Me and my woman and the whole fam'ly is ready to do whatever you asks. She was our friend for a long time."

"Yeah," Pastor Turner said. "It won't be no problem writing a eulogy for her. All I got to do is tell the truth. She was a good woman." He looked around the church. "I expect we'll have this place full and people listenin' in the yard."

Joshua glanced at his wife, then at Pastor Turner. "Do you reckons they let Scooter come to the funeral? Aint Liddie would shore like havin' him there. In her eyes, he was always the little boy she took in."

"I don't know. Chief might let him come—if he can. He had a lot of respect for her, just like us. And he always liked Scooter. Now, let's talk about the funeral. We better have a coupla extra pallbearers. She was a right hefty woman, and we don't want no mess-ups there. Joshua, can you take care of that? Get us eight strong men to carry her to her final restin' place."

"Yas suh. That won't be no problem at all." He grinned. "Well, it might be when it come to narrowin' it down. I spect 'bout everybody gonna want to lift her."

"I'm sure you can handle it," the Pastor said. "Now, Berta, I'd appreciate it if you take care of the flowers for the church. Aint Liddie loved bright colors. The church ain't got a lot of money, but do the best you can."

"Rev'nd, that shouldn't be no problem. Soon's I let the word out when we's havin' the service, flowers'll pour in here. Ev'rybody loved her." She hesitated. "I'll take care of the food, too. Gotta make sure we lay a feast. She shore 'preciated a good spread. I 'magine a bunch of the white folk in town will send wreaths and food, too. She worked in that drugstore a long time."

"I hope you're right," Pastor Turner said. "But the mess with Big Man, Scooter, and Miz Patterson might make some of'm back away."

"You don't really think Scooter hurt that woman, do you?" Joshua asked. "I knowed him his whole life. He wouldn't step on a ant at a picnic."

Pastor Turner studied the cracks in the old floor, then looked at Joshua. "We gotta accept that Big Man was bad for Scooter. I want to agree with you, but . . ." He sighed. "I never told nobody about them visitin' me a coupla weeks back. Scooter was a different boy from last year. He had a mean look, a hard edge on him. I hoped he was pretendin' so he look good in front of Big Man." He signed again. "But that don't change nothin'. We gotta do everythin' we can to help him."

"How 'bout the funeral?" Joshua asked. "It'd sure be nice if Scooter could be there."

"I tell you what. When we finish plannin' Aint Liddie's passin', I'll go to the police station and talk to Chief Bowen. Anybody that wants to come with me is welcome."

..*

"Hello, ma'am. Are you there?" Chief Bowen listened to the hum of the dead line, then replaced the handset. "Murphy, what do you think? Was that woman on the level?"

"I don't know. That's why I passed her off to you. There was something in her voice. I'd feel better if she had identified herself, but . . ."

"Yeah. *But* is the right word." The Chief paced the small

dispatcher area, rubbing the back of his neck. "I agree she sounded sincere." He took a few more steps. "Dammit, I can't take a chance. Get everybody in here. Tell'm we'll sort out the overtime later. I'm calling the Mayor." He walked out mumbling, "Probably wasting my time. He can't find his ass with both hands and a divining rod."

He entered his office, dropped into the chair behind his desk, and stared at the phone. He ran his fingers through his hair, then raked across his eyes with his left hand. "Quit stalling," he muttered.

Catching the Mayor at home, Chief Bowen explained his need.

"So," the Mayor said, "you want me to call the Sheriff and the state patrol, is that it?"

"That's my recommendation."

"You want to make us the laughing stock of not only Nolan County, but the whole damned state?"

"I don't quite see it that way, sir." The coldness in the Chief's voice resonated. "I have five officers plus a dispatcher. If a crowd gathers, what do you think I should do about it?"

"Start with doing the job you're paid for. Protect this town. If it's over your head, let me know, and I'll call a meeting of the Town Council. Perhaps a new chief could find a way to handle a couple of good ol' boys. I have better things to do than tell you your job. Don't call again unless you want me to come down and take charge."

"Ignorant sonnavabitch," Chief Bowen said staring at the dead instrument after he'd slammed it down. "He's just afraid somebody'll run against him in the next election." He sat a moment. "Maybe the Judge has some ideas." He dialed the phone.

"Dan," the Chief said. "I hate to bother you again, but I may have a problem building here." He explained the call he received, then added, "The Mayor thinks I'm running scared. Maybe I am, but you and I know how stupid those Burnettes can be. If they came marching down Main Street right now, I wouldn't be surprised a bit."

"So what can I do to help?"

"Maybe nothing. I guess I just wanted to talk to someone who wouldn't threaten my job."

"Suppose I come up there? Do you have enough manpower?"

"I'm bringing in everybody I got. Depends on what the Burnettes do." He was silent for a moment. "How well do you know the Sheriff? Think you could give him a call?"

"Sure. I helped him last election. He owes me."

The Chief sighed his relief. "Thanks. Let me know if he can send help, or at least have some deputies on stand-by. And if you'd come in for a while, I'd appreciate it."

"Give me time to explain things to Jane, and I'll be there."

..*

The Judge set the phone in its cradle and climbed the stairs, a frown marking his forehead. At Jane's bedroom door, he hesitated, then tapped, and walked in. "I have to go out for a while. Will you be okay?"

She looked up from the magazine she'd been reading. "Sure. Where are you going?"

He paused, knowing he risked a quarrel if he told her. But she was his wife, and he had never lied to her. No reason to start now. "The police station. Chief Bowen got a tip the Burnettes might try to take Scooter out of jail and lynch him."

With a sardonic grin, she said, "Good riddance to bad trash."

"Jane, I can't believe you really think that. Scooter is a harmless colored with less than average IQ. He—"

"Tell that to Debbie. No, can't do that, can you? Maybe Henry will believe you, but I doubt it." She threw the magazine across the room as she bounced to her feet. "When are you going to wake up? The whole damn town's laughing at you. Even your friends think you've lost it. You heard what Henry said when he all but threw us out. Have you talked to Flip? How about the Pastor?" She glared at him, her hands on her hips. "The only people that give a shit what you think are the niggers."

"I've asked you—"

"Who cares what you asked? I've been patient. I've waited, hoping you'd wake up, hoping you'd come to your senses, hoping there was a marriage to save. Now you come in and tell me you're going to rescue Scooter. Go, damn you, go. But when you get home, the house will be empty." She turned her back to him, crossing her arms.

"Jane, I—"

"Get out. I don't want to see you anymore tonight—maybe never again." Her hands flew to her face as sobs racked her body. "Get . . . out."

He wanted to touch her, to cuddle her, to wipe away her tears as he'd done in years past. He wanted his life the way it was before *Brown versus Board of Education*. But it was not to be. History was unchangeable. The only decision was which side of the fence you chose. He couldn't and wouldn't straddle it. That was for those without the strength of their convictions. While he disagreed with Jane, he admired that she stood behind what she believed. Her strength was what had attracted him to her, that and her intelligence. Once she had time to think it through, she'd change her mind. He knew she would. She'd see that things had to change—the Old South was finished.

..*

The Judge slipped into his topcoat, gloves, and hat and started toward the front door. He stopped, thought for a moment, then returned to the phone on the table in the hallway. "Almost forgot. I need to call the Sheriff."

"Herb," he said, when the phone was answered, "Sorry to bother you at home, but I need to call in a favor." He explained his conversation with the Chief regarding the Burnettes, then added, "If you're wondering why it's me instead of Lowell, the Mayor ordered him not to. I guess he's afraid of a backlash at the polls. Can you send a couple of patrols to help?"

There was a moment of silence before the Sheriff said, "Let me get this straight. Lowell has Scooter in jail for the murder of Deborah Patterson, right?"

"Yes, he may be involved."

"And Lowell received a tip the Burnettes might try to take him out of jail, right?"

"That's my understanding."

"And the Mayor is running scared at calling for support?"

"Yeah."

"So you want me to stick my neck out to protect a Negro who, if I heard right, raped, mutilated, and murdered a white woman?"

"Scooter says he had nothing to do with it. He was unconscious when the killing took place."

"You believe him? How many murderers have confessed to you? You don't have to answer. I know—zero, that's how many. Do you know how many votes I'll get in the fall if I do what you want? I'll tell you. Four. Mine, my wife's, yours, and the Chief's."

"Probably only three," the Judge said through a chuckle. "The Chief is a Republican."

"Great. Just great."

The Judge swallowed, then sighed. "This isn't about your re-election. This is about the oath you took to uphold the law, the ones you were elected to enforce."

"You know I respect you," the Sheriff said. "But you have to remember who voted for me. It wasn't the Negroes. Most of them don't go to the polls. It was the whites, and it was a white woman that died. All the rumblings I heard today side with the Burnettes."

"Are you ducking? If so, you can count me out of your corner from now on. I helped you because I thought you'd do the job. Now you're telling me you won't. Is that right?"

"Sorry. I like living in Nolan County."

The Judge hesitated, thinking fast. "How about a compromise? At least put some of your folks on alert in case Lowell needs help."

The Sheriff took a deep breath and let it out into the mouthpiece. "Okay, I can do that. I won't brief them, but I'll have a list to react if needed." He hesitated. "But make sure Lowell doesn't go off half-cocked. I like my job."

"You're all heart. I'll pass the word." The Judge hung up. "So much for his career. I'll have to take a hard look at the other candidates when they announce."

He stared at the phone. "Better let Henry know what's happening. Maybe the power of the press can have some influence." He dialed. When Henry answered, he said, "This is Dan. We may have a problem brewing at the jail. Thought you'd like to know."

"What kind of problem?"

"Could be a lynch mob." He ran through the conversation with Chief Bowen. "I'm going over to see if I can help. Want to join me? If it happens, we'll need every man we can get. Besides, it might finally give you a real front page."

CHAPTER TWENTY-FOUR

There was silence on the line, and the Judge wondered if Henry had hung up. No, he could hear him breathing.

"Why're you calling me?" Henry said. "My first impulse is to say I'll supply the rope."

The Judge took a deep breath, sensing the pain behind those words. "I can only guess at how bad you're hurting. But I know you're a fair man, and I know tomorrow or next week, you'll regret saying things like that. It's not you talking. It's your loss. You and I have discussed the law and justice many times. No matter what we think Scooter may have done, he does not deserve lynching. And, if it matters, he says he didn't have anything to do with her death. Big Man knocked him unconscious while Debbie was still alive." He paused. "No matter what occurred, he must receive a fair trial."

More silence filled the line before Henry said in a sad voice, "My brain says you're right, and my heart says Debbie agrees with you. But I don't think you know what you're asking. My feet won't put me in a position to defend Scooter. I fear what I might do in his presence. You speak of justice, but all I can think of is Debbie. You told me what you saw, and I'm hearing worse stories on the street. How can you possibly expect me to protect him?"

"Because I know that under all that anguish is the newspaperman I respect. Because I know that if you don't act, you will regret it for the rest of your life. You're too fine a man to allow a thirst for revenge to destroy you. Come with me, Henry. Recapture yourself."

More heavy breathing. "The most I can offer is I'll be in the area as a reporter, but not in the police station. I'll be as objective as I can be, but I make you no promises."

"Is that your last word? You won't join me?"

"No. You're in this without me. I wish you and Lowell luck if it comes to a showdown."

The Judge went silent, shocked at Henry's lack of support, remembering Jane's words. Was the whole town laughing at him? "I thought you'd want to know, if for no other reason, you run a newspaper. You're not sounding like an objective journalist."

"Objective? You think I care about objectivity today? Some sonnavabitch murdered the woman I love, and you expect me to care about journalistic standards? Think about Jane. Suppose it happened to her? Would you be so damned high and mighty?"

The Judge rubbed his face, finding Henry's responses hard to refute, struggling to find the right words. "Look, I'm sorry. I can't put myself in your shoes, but Scooter stands innocent until a jury says otherwise. And even if that happens, you know we can't allow vigilantes to take over."

"I've given you my best. I'll be in the area to report on whatever happens."

"Thank you," the Judge said. "I'm sorry I bothered you. In your mind-set, it's probably best if you don't come to the jail. I'll talk to you tomorrow." He laid the handset in its cradle.

Flip. I'll call Flip, he thought. He loves this town as much as I do. He'll give us a hand.

A few moments later, he hung up the phone even more disappointed, if possible. Not only had Flip refused to help, but he tried to talk the Judge out of joining the Chief, saying, "If Lowell wants to get himself killed defending a Negro, that's his business. But me, I'm not getting involved, and I advise you to do the same." Again, Jane's words echoed in his head.

What had happened to the town he grew up in, the town he loved, the town filled with friendly people? People were at one another's throats or in hiding. Was this a harbinger of the future? He hoped not, but for the first time had doubts.

The Judge left his house worried about how the night might end. But whatever happened, he had learned a lot about people he thought were his friends. Values differed. Priorities differed. He had no choice but to live with it.

..*

The Judge walked into the police station, acknowledged Murphy, then headed for the Chief's office. After telling him they could expect little to no help from the Sheriff, they sat, each nursing a cup of stale coffee. He had also told him Henry and Flip's reactions. He did not mention Jane.

"You know, Dan," Lowell said, "the Sheriff gives me something to think about. While I might disagree with his attitude, I understand it. And it helps me with the Mayor's position a bit more." He rested his face in his hands, appearing to be deep in thought. When he looked up, he said, "What about my guys? They're Nolan County, too. Should I give them a choice? Should I ask them if they can do what's necessary to protect a colored man against their neighbors?"

The Judge rubbed his hand over weary eyes. "I don't know. Perhaps you should, but before you do, accept that you might be standing alone against the Burnettes."

"Somehow, I don't think I'll be alone," Lowell said. "No way you'd desert me."

The Judge's look was vacant as he thought of his wife. "You're probably right. Jane says I have a Messiah complex—just have to save the world." He frowned. "I warn you though. I'm a lousy shot."

"If we start shooting, we've already lost. Glad you're sticking with me. I can use the company. Let's face the troops."

Chief Bowen called his six officers together. "Here's the deal. Murphy took a call tonight from a woman saying the Burnettes are going to bust Scooter out of jail and lynch him. I'm standing here saying it won't happen. I'll do whatever it takes to protect him. If that includes shooting a scatter gun into a mob, I'll do it." He took a deep breath. "It's not something I want to do, but I can't let the likes of the Burnettes make the law around here."

He paused. "You took an oath to uphold the law. However, after talking to the Judge, I realize it might be a bit too much to expect you to draw down on a neighbor. So if any of you want to resign right now, I'll accept with no hard feelings." His smile appeared forced. "Heck, I'll even give you a letter of recommendation. What do you say?"

There was a shuffling of feet and shifting of eyes from one to another. Oakley stepped forward and faced his fellow officers. "Guys, I was there when Big Man shot at the Chief. No way would I walk away from a man as cool as he was." He moved beside the Chief. "I'm here to stay."

Murphy said, "Oh, hell. Nobody else would hire me," and joined Oakley.

A moment later, everyone stood with the Chief except Clark and Cowan. The latter spoke. "I'm ashamed of myself, but I can't stay. My wife is first cousin to the Burnettes. Their mama is her aunt." He unpinned his badge. "I hope you understand and can forgive me."

"It's okay," the Chief said. "Each person has to make his own decision."

"One thing you can bet, sir. I'll never stand against you. I'm going home." Cowan laid the badge on the desk, turned, and walked out the back door of the building.

"Clark?" the Chief said.

Clark scratched the back of his neck. "You know, I've been on the force longer than anybody but Oakley. I'm still standing over here because I have a question." He looked toward the door. "Didn't want to ask it in front of Cowan 'cause I knowed the Burnettes was his relatives. For years, I've taken shit off Charlie Burnette and sometimes, that worthless brother of his. If they come after us tonight, can I park their asses in Hell?"

The Chief chuckled. "No. Well, only as a last resort. Let's say we'll match force with force. They might have more bodies, but we'll have superior firepower. Break out every weapon we have." He surveyed the group. "Anyone having extra in his car might want to get it. My eyes are blind tonight to unauthorized guns."

Lowell grinned at the Judge as the officers scattered, some toward the gun room and others toward the parking lot.

..*

Chief Bowen leaned against the front doorframe of the police station talking to the Judge. "I have Oakley stationed out on Route 125, Clark at the end of East Main, and Christopher on Washington. If anyone heads this way, one of them should see him. They'll give the alert, then trail them, giving us someone at their backs. Jones is on the roof. That leaves Murphy with us.

That's about as thin as I can stretch what I have."

"Sounds like a plan," the Judge said. "I don't suppose your informant gave you a time frame."

"You suppose right. She sounded terrified to even be talking to me. I suspect it was the wife of one of the troublemakers."

"Well, no need standing when we can sit. It may be a long night. What say we brew some fresh coffee? That stuff in the pot will strip wallpaper." The Judge walked into the station.

As they moved forward, the Chief heard a voice from the doorway. "Sir, can we talk to you a minute?"

Turning, he saw Pastor Turner entering the building. Joshua walked beside him, head down, hat in his hand.

"Of course. What can we do for you?" the Chief said.

The Pastor looked at Joshua, then said, "We'll be eulogizing Aint Liddie day after tomorrow, and we're wondering if you'd let Scooter attend."

Well, I don't know about that," the Chief said, "He—"

"Not so fast," the Judge said. "Let's jawbone this a bit. Aunt Liddie was a mighty important presence in this town. Everybody loved her. Jane and I will be there along with Flip and his family. Henry will probably cover it for the paper. In fact, I'm betting you attend, probably in uniform." He ignored the tinge of conscience reminding him of Jane's last words. "I'll be glad to take responsibility for Scooter if you want, and you can assign a couple of your men to make sure I don't turn him loose."

"I like dat idea," Joshua said from beside the preacher. "You knows you kin trus' the Jedge."

"It's not a matter of trust," Chief Bowen said. "C'mon, Judge, you know he's being held under suspicion of murder. I can't just let him go wandering all over town. The Mayor would—"

The Judge pulled Lowell to the side and whispered, "I know all that, and I certainly am not saying we should turn him loose. But a couple of hours for the funeral won't hurt anything. It might even help with things to come—if you get my drift. If the Burnettes ride in, we could end up in a war, and everybody in town, white and colored, loved Aunt Liddie. It could help smooth things over and show the Burnettes this town won't put up with their kind of hatred."

"But," Chief Bowen protested, "this is a murder case. I can't let him loose without a Judge—" He stared at his friend, then turned back to the visitors. "I think we can probably let Scooter attend the funeral. Of course, you know I can't let him out without proper authority. But if some Judge handed down an official ruling tomorrow that Scooter needs to attend, I'd have no recourse but to obey."

Joshua frowned and nudged Pastor Turner. "What he mean, no recourse?"

"I'll explain later," he answered, then looked at the Judge. "Would you do that? Put on your black robe and tell the Chief to let him go to the funeral?"

The Judge chuckled. "Looks like I talked myself into a corner, doesn't it?"

Murphy stuck his head out of the dispatcher area. "They're almost here. Christopher says they passed his area a moment ago. Eight pickup trucks filled with men dressed in white sheets like the KKK. He saw lots of guns."

"Okay," Chief Bowen said. "Call everybody in. Tell them to take positions behind whoever's in the vehicles."

"Yo, Chief."

"Hold it," the Chief said. "Tell them no shooting unless I give the order."

Murphy rolled his eyes. "Yes sir, I'll tell'm. But that's a hard order if things get out of hand."

"Just do it."

"Lordy, Muster Chief," Joshua said. "Did he say the KKK? I heered stories 'bout them when I was a chil'. Ain't been none here for a long time."

"And they won't be here now," the Judge said. "Chief Bowen's not about to let a bunch of hooligans hurrah this town. And don't you worry. You can spread the word. Scooter will be with me at Aunt Liddie's funeral." He turned to his friend. "Might be a good idea to ask the Pastor to get his people off the street until this is over. We can work out the details on Scooter tomorrow."

"Can't disagree with that advice," the Chief said. He spoke to the preacher. "Sir, I'd appreciate it if you'd—"

"Well, ain't this just cozy?" a man wearing Ku Klux Klan

headgear said. "Look'it this, friend," he motioned to a man beside him dressed in the same constume. "We done interrupted a meetin'. Evenin', Chief, Judge. I heered you talking 'bout that nigger going to a funeral. We's here to help you with that." He slapped his partner on the back and laughed. "In fact, he can be the guest of honor." He nodded toward Pastor Turner and Joshua. "If these other darkies want to come, they welcome to watch."

Chief Bowen stepped between the colored men and the Klansmen. "You need to check a mirror, Charlie. You too, Marvin. You ain't fooling nobody with those getups. Now, let me give you the best advice I can. Go home. Go before you get in trouble. There will be no vigilante action in my town. You have no chance of getting anywhere near Scooter."

"Oh, I wouldn't be so sure of that," Charlie said, a swagger in his voice. "I guess he don't know, do he, Marvin? He don't know we got a bunch of our kind out there, all looking to right the wrongs agin that poor white woman. And I bet he don't know we done rounded up a bunch of them darkies that was outside." He laughed a nasty laugh. "But he's gonna learn. He's gonna learn we ain't puttin' up with no niggers having their way and killin' white women, and we ain't puttin' up with none of that equal rights crap. The South was meant to be segregated, and that's how it's gonna stay."

Judge Jackson said, "Nice speech, Charlie. Good enough to put you in jail for a long time. The Chief gave you good advice. Go home to your wife before you dig your hole too deep. Marvin, you have a little one. Do you want him to grow up knowing his daddy's in jail? Go home while you can. The law will deal with Scooter. If he's guilty, a jury will convict him. But right now, in the eyes of the law, he's as innocent as a newborn baby."

Joshua moved beside the Judge. "It ain't that I know nothin' 'bout the law, but I knows good advice when I hears it. I done worked your tobac'a fields, Mr. Burnette, both of you. I knows you be hard men. But I ain't gonna believe you would hurt somebody like Scooter. Only thing wrong with him is he's a bit simple, and Big Man took advantage of him. I love that boy jist like he was one of mine. I know he didn't hurt Miz Patterson. Ain't a mean bone in his body."

Charlie slammed his open palm into Joshua's chest, sending him stumbling backward. "Git outta my face, you damn nigger. You ain't careful, we'll string you up with Scooter." He sneered toward the Chief and the Judge. "Jail? I don't think so. Ain't but one judge what'd fault us for what we doing. And ain't no way my lawyer gonna let you on the bench. The book say justice is blind, can't see neither side. You sure ain't blind. You done picked the nigger's side. I be surprised if you even git to stay a judge."

Judge Jackson grimaced, hearing the truth in Charlie's words. His participation could only be as a witness. He'd have to recuse himself. And there were judges across the state who would turn their heads on the lynching of one more colored man, especially one involved in the murder of a white woman.

Charlie laughed. "Gotcha thinking, don't I? Maybe you oughta step outside with me and Marvin. Then you'll see who controls this town."

Marvin opened the door and motioned them through.

CHAPTER TWENTY-FIVE

Henry sat in his office staring at a highball glass half-filled with Scotch. It was the first drink he'd poured since meeting Debbie. He wanted it, wanted it badly. However, each time he picked it up, the image of Bobby Joe popped into his head. Bobby Joe, his war buddy, who had come back from the dead to talk him off the booze. Bobby Joe who had promised there were happier days ahead if he straightened out his life. Even now, he couldn't be sure Bobby Joe had actually appeared. Maybe he was only a result of his drunken fantasies. But he did meet Debbie like Bobby Joe predicted, and she had brought him happiness beyond his most optimistic dreams.

And there was Debbie, who never once raised the subject of his past drinking problem. Could he betray her trust? It wouldn't be a betrayal. She'd understand.

He picked up the Scotch, wanting it, needing it. Maybe just a taste. If he couldn't have Debbie, he could at least hide from the pain in a bottle. Tilting the glass, he let the liquid caress his lips, smelling its slightly smoky aroma, and the taste of the liquor, its mellowness, and the smooth flavor of it.

He felt something along the back of the hand holding the drink, almost the feel of a caress. He stared at the spot then looked around, lowering the drink. No one. Nothing. He was alone. He withdrew the hand and lightly rubbed the tingling area. Imagination? His subconscious? Ghosts? A signal from Debbie? So much pain. So much loss. He wanted to drown it in alcohol. "Help me, Debbie. Make me strong." He felt the touch again and grabbed at his hand, hoping to capture Debbie's spirit. Nothing physical there, but he knew it was Debbie. His Debbie who now stood beside him to protect him from making the mistakes of his past. He pushed the glass away and left his office, walking toward the front of the building, lost in a world of despair.

Yelling from the outside penetrated the fog of his self-pity. The noise sounded like many people talking at once, and it wasn't a friendly conversation. Could this be the beginning of what the Judge called about? He picked up a steno pad and several pencils, then moved into the street.

Looking toward the police station, he saw people milling about. He walked in that direction, seeing that some wore all white and carried rifles and shotguns. They appeared to surround a rebellious gathering of colored people—men, women, and children. Angry words laced the air. Pictures from the past flashed into his mind—Ku Klux Klan.

Henry started toward the crowd, but stopped along the edge when he saw the front door to the police station open. A file of people came out. Leading the parade was Pastor Turner, then another colored man who looked familiar, Chief Bowen, and Judge Jackson. Two men in KKK robes, carrying rifles, brought up the rear. Heads came up and shushing sounds filled the air. The crowd quieted.

Henry pushed through to the front of the group. His reporter's sense told him this was an occasion demanding documentation. His pencil hovered over the pad he carried.

Chief Bowen said, "Charlie, tell your people to put their guns down and go home. If they don't, I'll put every one of them under arrest."

The man in the hood said, "You're a funny man, Chief. Looks to me like we got the upper hand here. Now you drag that nigger what killed Miz Patterson out here. After that, we'll let you go home. You won't be needed no more." He laughed, the sound venomous.

The realization slammed into Henry that this situation was real. It was no movie. The leader was Charlie Burnette, and he and the rest of the idiots in their KKK regalia were serious, not just dressed like circus clowns. He'd fought their kind in Europe—now he had to do it again. "Chief," he called. He had to let Lowell and Dan know his position, know he was with them. He couldn't allow the

Charlie Burnettes of the world to gain power.

Chief Bowen said, "Won't happen, Charlie. I have officers covering you from all around with high-powered weapons. Put your guns down."

A young colored woman, holding her dress together at the shoulder, stumbled to the front of the group, sobbing. "Pastor, what we gonna do? I's scared."

"Shut your black mouth," Charlie said, shoving her in the chest, knocking her to the ground. He straddled her. "You don't behave yourself, I might just let you go out back with me. Give you a taste of something white." He reached for her arm.

"Leave my woman alone." A Negro leapt at Charlie, knocking his hood off as they tumbled to the ground.

"Kill'm all," someone shouted, followed by screams, the sounds of scuffling, panic, and fists hitting flesh as a full-fledged brawl erupted.

Henry ducked to the side, aghast at what he saw around him. How could the friendly people of Nolan County be tearing at one another like a pack of wild animals? He watched in horror as the free-for-all intensified—people he exchanged pleasantries with on the street every day swinging and punching one another.

Henry went down with a thud, a large Negro riding his back. He pushed the body off, then rolled away. "Wha . . . who . . ."

"I's sorry, Muster Flan'gin. I didn't know it was you." The man jumped up and ran into the fray, leaving Henry staring wide-eyed at the fighting in front of him.

He scrambled to his feet and retreated, far enough away for safety, but close enough to watch the brawlers. One side of his mind screamed he should take action, do something to stop the fighting. No matter the rights or wrongs of their grievances, fists and feet wouldn't settle it. It had to be stopped—and stopped now. But his journalist training demanded he remain above it and record everything in an objective manner. He was witnessing history. Capturing it for his readers and the generations to follow was the most important contribution he could make.

EPILOGUE

THIRTY-FIVE YEARS LATER — 1991

Henry folded the *News and Observer* and lay it across his lap, a sad look on his face and a sigh on his lips. Amid the articles on the Persian Gulf War was an item about a local death. It was unusual in its placement, but the event demanded it. Henry rubbed his hands over his eyes as memories flooded in. "Honey, would you bring me the scissors, please?"

"You clipping something else?" Evelyn, his wife of fifteen years, walked into the room. "I swear those files of yours are the biggest fire hazard in Raleigh. One of these days—" She stared at him. "What is it, Hank? What's in the paper?"

"Dan Jackson died. Says here he had a heart attack yesterday. Died instantly. You remember him, don't you?"

"Oh, yes. You've told me so many times. You were good friends when you owned the *Dawson Times*." She sat beside him and lay her hand on his. "He introduced you to the woman who taught you how to love. While I've always been a little jealous of her, I'm glad it happened."

"That's the one. And you never had a rival. You've been number one since I interviewed you for my *Woman on the Street* column during the feminist seventies." He patted the sofa beside him. "Sit and let's cuddle."

She kissed the top of his baldhead, then settled onto the cushion. "Too old, dear. But I will sit with you for a while. The dishes can wait." She scooted toward him so their hips touched. "Tell me about your friend again. I never tire of your stories."

Henry slipped his arm around his wife's shoulders and pulled her to him. "Dan Jackson was the most honest man I ever knew. And according to some, the most bullheaded." He grinned. "Before I retired, you said you played second-fiddle to the newspaper. Of course, that was wrong." He rubbed her upper arm. "But with Dan, everything took a backseat to the law. Not just loving it, but living it. It cost him his wife, and he never remarried. When Jane filed for divorce, he told her lawyer to draw up the agreement. He loved her that much, but, when she wouldn't support his beliefs, he let her walk away." He sighed. "Damn shame. They were a fine couple."

"Like us?"

"Exactly like us, except you support everything I believe."

"Not a chance," she said, chuckling. "But my momma taught me how to *live* with a man. Let him think he's the boss while he does what you want."

"Hush that kind of talk. I'm telling you about Dan." He reflected for a moment. "Get my clippings from the *Dawson Times*, the ones about when everything changed. I'd do it, but this old knee is hurting again." He dramatically straightened his leg.

She slapped him on the thigh. "Yeah, I notice it bothers you anytime you don't want to do something, but you can play eighteen holes of golf." She got up and went into his office.

He heard her rummaging through the file cabinet, then he picked up the *News and Observer*, opening it to the front page. The headline read *Chief Justice Jackson Found Dead*. He scanned the article again. An Associate Judge found Dan slumped over his desk. He called 9-1-1, and paramedics rushed him to the hospital. The emergency room doctor pronounced him dead from a massive coronary. The article continued on an inner page, more in the form of an obituary. After noting the lack of kin, it detailed the Judge's career, emphasizing his ascendancy through the state's judicial system—Recorder's Court, Superior Court, Associate Justice of the State Supreme Court, and for the last five years, Chief Justice. It noted cases he ruled on dealing with his first love, civil rights, and ended with the statement, *Without Judge Daniel J. Jackson, North Carolina would still be locked in the Jim Crow days.*

Evelyn walked into the room holding a box in her arms. "Thought I could save a couple of trips if I brought everything from those days. What do you want to start with?"

He laughed. "Is this an example of you getting what you want by making me think it's what I want?"

"Could be. But Mama also taught me to keep a man guessing." She sat the container on the coffee table and stood in front of him, hands on hips. "Well?"

"The one I put out after the fight. That's when the world changed."

"And chased you into my clutches. Ever think about that? If you hadn't sold the *Dawson Times* and taken the job with the *News and Observer*, we'd have never met."

"And I might not have sold if there'd been no brawl. So, I reckon I owe the Burnette brothers."

They laughed, the laughter of two people who'd shared life and the same jokes many times.

"Read the article," she said. "I love the way you wrote before the editors at the N&O got ahold of you."

"You know there were two of them—the news article and the editorial. Can you take both?"

She dropped onto the couch and leaned back in a sexy pose. "Seduce me with your dulcet tones."

He grinned. "Better be careful, woman. I might not be as old as you think."

"I'm hoping. Now read."

Henry fumbled in the box, then brought out a copy of the *Dawson Times*. "First, the news column."

On Tuesday evening, Dawson may have seen the first stage of Armageddon. Whites and Negroes battled in the street, driven by generations of distrust and hatred. The immediate cause was a group in Ku Klux Klan garb who stormed the jail demanding the release of Scooter, the young Negro arrested in connection with the death of Deborah Patterson. Only the quick actions of Chief Lowell Bowen and his officers, assisted by Sheriff's deputies, thwarted the attempted abduction.

At night's end, Charlie Burnette, one of the leaders of the group lay dead in the street. Chief Bowen said the body had been trampled so badly, the cause of death was not obvious. An autopsy will be performed.

Charlie's brother, Marvin, the co-leader, was in jail. Several other local white men were booked and released on their own recognizance. Chief Bowen said, "I'd have locked the whole bunch up, but I don't have enough cells."

Chief Bowen further reported he moved Scooter to an undisclosed location where he will stay until his trial.

Other than Charlie Burnette, there were no serious injuries, although there are most likely many bruises today among the participants. Even Judge Daniel Jackson sports a black eye. He would only state that it was self-inflicted.

"What really happened to the Judge?" Evelyn said. "You never told me."

Henry smiled. "He swore me to absolute secrecy before he'd tell me." A sad look replaced his smile. "Now that he's gone, I don't think he'd mind that I share the story with you. When the first shot sounded, Dan rushed into the police station to call the Sheriff. He grabbed the phone and managed to clunk himself with the handset." He slapped his leg, laughing. "Till the day I left Dawson, I never let him live it down."

His mirth turned to sadness. "Dan never got over that horrible time. Of course, he immediately recused himself as a possible judge in Scooter's trial. Then he threw himself into the defense with his whole being. He couldn't be the attorney of record, but he counseled and helped the young lawyer who defended Scooter. No experienced defense counsel would take the case. Although they worked as hard as any men could, an all-white male jury convicted Scooter of first-degree murder and sentenced him to death. That's when I put the paper up for sale. I just couldn't live there anymore. I shall never believe that Scooter took an active part in Debbie's murder. He didn't have it in him." Another reflective look crossed his face. "He was quiet—a mellow young man whose biggest pleasure was pleasing someone. Debbie believed in him."

He fell silent, and Evelyn didn't move as the grandfather clock in the den ticked several minutes away.

"What about that rascal, Burnette?" Evelyn asked. "What was his cause of death."

"Knife wound. It went straight into his heart. In that bedlam, there was no way to know who did it."

After another moment of silence, Evelyn said, "Read me the

editorial. I've always thought it's the best thing you ever wrote."

Henry started, jerking himself out of his recollections of those sad times. He forced a smile. "You're just setting me up to take you out to dinner tonight. Your womanly wiles don't fool me anymore."

"Whatever you say, my dear," she said, batting her eyelashes in an exaggerated Hollywood way. "You're the master."

He grinned at her, then opened the *Dawson Times* to the editorial page.

Last night, I witnessed a situation that I fear was a glimpse of the future. On one side, I saw the ignorance and hatred of whites who cannot accept the equality of all mankind. On the other, there was defensiveness, as there well should have been. In the middle were responsible law enforcement officers attempting to establish peace between the two groups. The fact the Negroes fought back is a symbol of the change in our society. I feel confident the Burnettes and their thuggish friends were shocked. Yet that strength of unity among coloreds is occurring all over the South.

But is this what we want? Do we want confrontation between the races? I think not.

We must recognize the equality and equal rights that our Declaration of Independence guarantees. The founders of our country wrote, "We hold these truths to be self-evident, that all men are created equal, that they are endowed by their Creator with certain unalienable Rights, that among these are Life, Liberty and the pursuit of Happiness." Can we now scoff at those words and say they don't include those of color? I say, no.

The Preamble to our Constitution says, "We the people of the United States, in order to . . . promote the general welfare, and secure the blessings of liberty to ourselves and our posterity, do ordain and establish this Constitution for the United States of America." Can there be any doubt about what was meant by "promote the general welfare"? Can there be disagreement about the phrase "secure the blessings of liberty to ourselves and our posterity"? I say no.

And last are the words of the U.S. Supreme Court in Brown versus Board of Education. Not quite two years ago, Chief Justice Earl Warren wrote, ". . . We conclude that in the field of public education the doctrine of 'separate but equal' has no place . . ." The ruling addressed education facilities, but can there be any doubt it says the same as our Constitution and Declaration of Independence? I say no.

Thus, in this year of 1956, we must view everyone through the prism of equal rights. It is time for all people to accept the responsibility of acting to benefit mankind.

We can choose between a future filled with divisiveness, or a future where citizens of all races, creeds, and religions achieve equality and accept the responsibility carried with it. Only then will we truly be free. Your humble editor hopes to live to see it.

THE END

www.ingramcontent.com/pod-product-compliance
Lightning Source LLC
Chambersburg PA
CBHW030031180626
46810CB00001B/314

9780989990400